We live in a world that can be viole[...]
With all the brutality that war enta[...]
most regrettable result of war, is th[...]
done to its most innocent victims—c[...]

Children who have experienced war firsthand are inevitably affected by it, and bear its impressions upon their hearts, minds and—too often—bodies.

In 1993 two individuals in Britain were so shocked by the news reports coming out of Bosnia and the former Yugoslavia that they pooled resources to send material aid to help those in the region, with a focus on the most unfortunate victims, the children. Thus, War Child was born.

From that beginning in the U.K., War Child organizations emerged in the Netherlands, France, Canada, Australia and the U.S.A. All are united in the mission of assisting children affected by conflict.

War Child has been known for its emergency bakeries that could be set up rapidly and feed thousands, and its innovative psychosocial programs to defuse the stress of war in its young victims. We still do that, but while we deal with the immediate needs in war-torn areas, we are also committing to long-term educational programs that train teachers in these war-ravaged areas. Without education, children are destined to become adults that are disenfranchised from ever participating in their country's rebuilding. Ignorance is what sustains conflict. These teachers can pass on the promise of real hope to children for their future.

War Child USA offers this story collection in your hands, which continues the tradition started in the U.K. with the publication of *Girls' Night In* (U.K.), *Girls' Night Out/Boys' Night In* and *Big Night Out*. These collections of entertaining stories allocated £1 of the sale price to War Child UK for every book sold. A portion of the profits from this book will benefit War Child USA to help further the work it does.

Children everywhere are our future. Thank you for your contribution to improving that future by purchasing this book. And enjoy your reading.

Ron Witzke, Executive Director, War Child USA
Greg Spitzfaden, Chairman, Board of Trustees, War Child USA

War Child is an international relief and development agency, dedicated to providing immediate, effective and sustainable aid to some of the most vulnerable children caught up in conflict around the world.

War Child exists because caring and compassionate people have come together to give of their time and resources to better the lives of children affected by war.

Without the support of people like you,
War Child could not exist.

If you would like to make a donation directly to War Child USA please visit www.warchildusa.org

Or you can send a check to:
War Child, P.O. Box 212, Peterborough, NH 03458

You can contact us at War Child by e-mail at info@warchildusa.org or by phone: 603-924-4318.

Your contribution to War Child will help children in a profound way and is greatly appreciated.

girls' night in

edited by Lauren Henderson, Chris Manby and Sarah Mlynowski

RED
DRESS
INK
™

First Edition September 2004

GIRLS' NIGHT IN

A Red Dress Ink novel

ISBN 0-373-89539-9

© 2004 by Harlequin Books S.A.

Author Photo credits listed as follows:

Jenny Colgan © Graham Jephson
Sophie Kinsella © John Foley/Opale
Adèle Lang © Tim France
Jennifer Weiner © Jerry Bauer
Anna Maxted © Jake Gavin
Lynda Curnyn © Julie Ann Coney
Louise Bagshawe © Andrew Entwhistle
Chris Manby © Michael Pilkington
Marian Keyes © Mark McCall
Jill A. Davis © Joyce Ravid
Meg Cabot © Studio 16
Megan McCafferty © Sonya Sones

www.RedDressInk.com

Printed in U.S.A.

Dear *Girls' Night In* Reader,

Despite its title, *Girls' Night In* is a book that owes its existence to three big nights out! The first, way back in May 1999, when Jessica Adams, Fiona Walker and I had an "aha" moment over the traditional chick-lit Chardonnay in London's Groucho Club. We pooled our address books and persuaded every girl writer we knew to submit a story for nothing to raise money for War Child, a humanitarian organization which, as the name suggests, directs aid and assistance to children affected by war. The first book in what was to become a *Girls' Night In* series was published in Britain in the year 2000, selling more than 300,000 copies and raising almost half a million dollars for War Child in the process.

Two sequels later, we'd raised a million dollars, been translated into dozens of languages and topped book charts in the United Kingdom, Europe and Australasia. Meanwhile, War Child had taken that money and made a real difference to children all over the war-torn world. I was lucky enough to travel to Kosovo in October 2001 and see the opening of the first *Girls' Night In*/War Child "safe play area"—essential in a country where many of the traditional childhood haunts were still riddled with land mines and unexploded munitions. Further funds helped support a girls' school in Rwanda and provided radios so that children in remote parts of Africa might have access to broadcast educational programs. We bought an ambulance for use in East Timor and were proud to know that money raised by *Girls' Night In* helped War Child be one of the first nongovernmental organizations to take aid to the children of Afghanistan.

It was around this time that I went on a second big night out that would have a far bigger impact than a hangover. Sarah Mlynowski ambushed me over a martini at Red Dress Ink's first birthday party in a swanky Manhattan bar. She had read the *Girls' Night In* books and wanted to know why they had never been published in the U.S. I responded, "Because no one's asked."

Sarah said, "I'm asking."

And that's when the idea for an American edition was born.

A few weeks later, at a launch party for Jenny Colgan back in the U.K., I ran into Lauren Henderson, author and editor of the Tart Noir crime anthology. After many refills of champagne, Lauren foolishly slurred her agreement to don her editing hat once more for *GNI* USA.

We then began begging our favorite female authors on both sides of the Atlantic to give us more stories for nothing so we could raise even more money for War Child.

Amazingly, they did. And here's the result!

We hope you have as much fun reading it as we did creating it.

Chris Manby
www.girlsnightin.info

ACKNOWLEDGMENTS

We want to thank:

the fantastic authors who've generously contributed the wonderful stories that make up this book;

the editors of past editions, especially Jessica Adams and Nick Earls;

Deborah Schneider for her excellent negotiations and Cathy Gleason for answering our seven thousand questions;

our agents, Laura Dail and Tony Gardner, for their eagle eyes and support;

the Red Dress Ink team for making it happen:
Margaret Marbury, Farrin Jacobs, Laura Morris, Tania Charzewski, Stephanie Campbell, Margie Miller and Tara Kelly;

the team at War Child for being such an inspiration;

each other, for being so easy to work with—not a cross word or catfight this entire time!

And, above all, you, whoever you are, for buying this book and helping to make a difference.

—Lauren Henderson, Chris Manby and Sarah Mlynowski

CONTENTS

Meg Cabot is the author of many bestselling, critically acclaimed books for teens, including *The Princess Diaries* series, *All-American Girl*, *Teen Idol*, as well as the *Mediator* and *1-800-Where-R-U* series. When she is not reliving the horror that was her high-school experience, Meg also writes books for adults, including *Boy Next Door*, *Boy Meets Girl*, and the forthcoming *Every Boy's Got One*. You can read more about her upcoming books at www.megcabot.com. She lives in New York City with her husband and a one-eyed cat named Henrietta.

Party Planner
by Meg Cabot

To: All Employees of the *New York Journal*
Fr: Charity Webber <charity.webber@thenyjournal.com>
Re: Company Holiday Party
Just a reminder that all departments will close at 4:30 p.m. today so that employees can get an early start on their holiday merrymaking. We hope to see all of you at Les Hautes Manger (57th and Madison) for cocktails and hors d'oeuvres (not to mention entertainment by the nationally acclaimed Magical Madrigals) from 4:30 to 8:00 p.m. All you need to bring is your holiday cheer!
Charity Webber
New York Journal Events Coordinator

To: Charity Webber <charity.webber@thenyjournal.com>
Fr: Natasha Roberts <natasha.roberts@thenyjournal.com>
Re: Holiday Party

Char—

How in the hell did you get old "Pinchpenny" Peter Hargrave to shell out the bucks for a swank shindig at a top restaurant like Les Hautes Manger? Last year's Christmas party was in the Senior Staff Dining Room, where the refreshments consisted of nonalcoholic eggnog and pigs-in-a-blanket. Now suddenly we're having cosmos and salmon tartare someplace where ties and jackets are required? What gives?

Did you talk the guys in tech support into diverting funds from office supplies into the events budget again? Char, don't you remember what happened last time you did that? You ended up spending five Saturday nights in a row watching *Robot Wars* with the likes of Danny "When's the last time you updated your software" Carmichael. Do I need to remind you that Danny volunteered to *marry* you when you had too many rum and Diet Cokes and were bewailing the fact that there are no good men left out there? I believe he said that the two of you could live in his mother's basement in Long Island until he'd saved up enough to get his own place....

Didn't you swear to me then that you would never again exceed your departmental budget? *Didn't you?*

Just wondering,

Nat

To: Natasha Roberts <natasha.roberts@thenyjournal.com>
Fr: Charity Webber <charity.webber@thenyjournal.com>
Re: Holiday Party

Shut up! I told you never to mention the *Robot Wars* incident to me again. That was *years* ago.

Well, okay, two years ago. Still, don't you think I've learned my lesson?

Besides, sometimes I think I did the wrong thing, turning Danny down. He would have made an excellent husband. I mean, at least if I ever needed my hard drive defragmented, I'd know who to ask.

And I hear his mother is a great cook.

In any case, it wasn't "Pinchpenny" Peter Hargrave's idea to have the party at Les Hautes Manger. It was his nephew Andrew's idea. You know Andrew's taken over day-to-day operations since his uncle's bypass surgery. Everybody's saying Mr. H is going to announce his retirement after New Year's, and that Andrew will be taking over as the new chief exec.

I just hope nothing goes wrong tonight. It'd be just my luck to screw up my first party under the new chief exec. I really want to make a good first impression on the new boss....

Although I don't see what was so bad with last year's party. I happen to like pigs-in-a-blanket.

Oh my gosh! An e-mail from the soon-to-be new CEO himself! Gotta go—
Char

To: Charity Webber <charity.webber@thenyjournal.com>
Fr: Andrew Hargrave <andrew.hargrave@thenyjournal.com>
Re: Tonight
Just a quick note to let you know how much I appreciate the great job you've done planning this year's holiday party. I know it must have been a lot more difficult for you to set up than in previous years when the event was held in the Senior Staff Dining Room.

But I think having the party off-site will be a real morale booster for the staff, who certainly deserve it after all the hard work they've put in this year, outselling the *Chronicle* for the first time in the *Journal*'s history. Les Hautes Manger is one of the best restaurants in New York and I'm hoping the staff will appreciate it, as well.

I look forward to meeting you tonight. I've heard nothing but great things about you from my uncle, and am glad I can count on you to provide a memorable and smooth-running event for our hardworking staff.

Andrew Hargrave

To: Natasha Roberts <natasha.roberts@thenyjournal.com>
Fr: Charity Webber <charity.webber@thenyjournal.com>
Re: Holiday Party

AAAAAAAAAAAAAAHHHHHHHHHHH! He's counting on me to provide a memorable and smooth-running event for our hardworking staff! He's looking forward to meeting me! What if I screw it up??? What if I make a bad first impression?

Oh, God, why me????

C

To: Charity Webber <charity.webber@thenyjournal.com>
Fr: Natasha Roberts <natasha.roberts@thenyjournal.com>
Re: Holiday Party

What could go wrong, you schmo? You've only done a million of these things since you started working in this god-forsaken hellhole. So what's the problem?

And how could you make a bad first impression? You know perfectly well everybody loves you. They can't help it, you're one of those types. You know, all bubbly. What are you worried about?

Oh, wait a minute…. This doesn't have anything to do with the fact that you and Andrew Hargrave have already MET, does it? Didn't you run into him once last month, down at the newsstand? Oh my God, I remember now: You were buying Skittles, and so was he, and the two of you laughed about it, but you were too nervous to introduce yourself because he was so tall and cute and single and had a really nice butt, or something, so you ran away?

Is THAT where all this worry about making a good impression is coming from? Because you're warm for his form?
Nat

To: Natasha Roberts <natasha.roberts@thenyjournal.com>
Fr: Charity Webber <charity.webber@thenyjournal.com>
Re: SHUT UP
SHUT UP SHUT UP SHUT UP

This has nothing to do with that. Well, not the butt part. He's just REALLY cute. And nice. And he likes Skittles! Who else do you know who likes Skittles? I mean, besides me? No one!

Oh, God, this party just HAS to go well….

I have to write him back and I want my response to sound witty and professional yet breezy and casual. But now all I can think about is his butt. Thanks a lot.
C

To: Charity Webber <charity.webber@thenyjournal.com>
Fr: Natasha Roberts <natasha.roberts@thenyjournal.com>
Re: No, YOU shut up
Hee hee.
Nat

To: Andrew Hargrave <andrew.hargrave@thenyjour-nal.com>
Fr: Charity Webber <charity.webber@thenyjournal.com>
Re: Tonight
Dear Mr. Hargrave,
     Thank you so much for your note. Please don't worry at all about the party tonight. I'm sure it's going to go well. The staff at Les Hautes Manger seem eminently profes-sional, and almost everyone here at the paper is delighted that we won't be having pigs-in-a-blanket again this year.
     Looking forward to meeting you as well,
Charity Webber
Events Coordinator

To: Charity Webber <charity.webber@thenyjournal.com>
Fr: Andrew Hargrave <andrew.hargrave@thenyjournal.com>
Re: Tonight
Glad to hear it! And please, call me Andrew. See you tonight!
A

To: Natasha Roberts <natasha.roberts@thenyjournal.com>
Fr: Charity Webber <charity.webber@thenyjournal.com>
Re: No, YOU shut up
ANDREW!!!! HE SAID FOR ME TO CALL HIM ANDREW!!!!!!!
     Oh my God, maybe this evening is going to turn out fine after all…. Maybe Andrew and I will meet at the party

and our hands will touch as we both reach for the same cosmo, and he'll gaze into my eyes and realize I'm the Skittles girl from the newsstand downstairs, and it will be like we can see into each other's souls!!! And he'll ask me to go on a carriage ride with him in Central Park and afterward we'll go back to his penthouse and make sweet tender love and then he'll ask me to marry him and we'll move to Westchester and have three kids and have big bowls of Skittles in EVERY ROOM....

To: Charity Webber <charity.webber@thenyjournal.com>
Fr: Natasha Roberts <natasha.roberts@thenyjournal.com>
Re: No, YOU shut up
You do realize that the scenario you just described is this bizarre mixture of *Maid in Manhattan* and *Willy Wonka and the Chocolate Factory*, don't you? But far be it from me to rain on your parade.
Nat

To: Natasha Roberts <natasha.roberts@thenyjournal.com>
Fr: Charity Webber <charity.webber@thenyjournal.com>
Re: No, YOU shut up
A girl can dream, can't she???
   Oh, God, things just HAVE to go well tonight!!!!!!!

To: Charity Webber <charity.webber@thenyjournal.com>
Fr: Frank Leonard <frank.leonard@thenyjournal.com>
Re: Holiday Party
Ms. Webber,
   The guys down here in Shipping and Receiving want to

know if they have to dress up for this thing tonight or not. Are they gonna get thrown out of this place if they don't have ties on? 'Cause I looked it up in *Zagat* and it's one of those capital-letter places. And I know they usually like you to wear ties at those capital-letter places. So maybe I should run out and buy a bunch of ties? Can I expense that, do you think? Let me know.

Frank Leonard
Scheduling Manager

To: Frank Leonard <frank.leonard@thenyjournal.com>
Fr: Charity Webber <charity.webber@thenyjournal.com>
Re: Holiday Party
Don't worry about buying ties for your guys, Frank. We are renting the entire restaurant for the evening, so there shouldn't be any complaints about the dress code. Tell your guys to come as they are. All they need to bring is their jingle balls!

Charity Webber
Events Coordinator

To: Frank Leonard <frank.leonard@thenyjournal.com>
Fr: Charity Webber <charity.webber@thenyjournal.com>
Re: Holiday Party
Obviously, I meant jingle bells, not balls. Please ask your staff to stop faxing me their interpretations of what jingle balls might look like. Although they are amusing, they have offended some members of my staff.

Charity

To: Charity Webber <charity.webber@thenyjournal.com>
Fr: Antoine Dessange <adessange@leshautes.com>
Re: Event Tonight
Cher Mademoiselle,

  I don't know what you may have been told by our events hostess Chantelle, but there is no possible way I can provide salmon tartare for three hundred. There is a nationwide salmon shortage due to a recent act of sabotage by the People for the Ethical Treatment of Aquatic Life. They broke into the salmon farm from which our restaurant receives its supply, and released all of the fish there back into the wild! Attempts to recapture the escaped salmon have been in vain, and it will be weeks before the farm can hope to replenish its stock.

  In the meantime, there will be no salmon on our menu. We could, if you wish, substitute crab-stuffed mushroom caps for the tartare. However, this will significantly increase the cost of tonight's event.

  Please let me know as soon as possible what you would like us to do.

I remain, as always, yours faithfully,
Antoine Dessange
Manager, Les Hautes Manger

To: Charity Webber <charity.webber@thenyjournal.com>
Fr: Cara Powalski <cara.powalski@thenyjournal.com>
Re: Party Tonight
Dear Ms. Webber,

  Hello, it's Cara from the lobby reception desk. I know you are probably busy planning the big party and all, but I was wondering if you could tell me whether or not Bobby Hancock down in Shipping and Receiving had RSVP'd. Because if he RSVP'd yes, I just want you to know that I have a restraining order against him and he's not allowed to come within five hundred feet of me. So unless this restaurant is big enough that he can stay five hundred feet from me I want you to know that I will be obliged to call the police if he shows up. Please call me if this is a problem.

Sincerely,

Cara

To: Charity Webber <charity.webber@thenyjournal.com>
Fr: Bobby Hancock <robert.hancock@thenyjournal.com>
Re: Cara Powalski

Dear Ms. Webber,

Cara told me she e-mailed you about us and I just want to make sure you know that whatever she told you is lies. She doesn't have a restraining order against me—her ex-husband does. I'm not allowed to go within five hundred feet of the guy because of an unfortunate incident involving his eye, which got in the way of my fist last month.

But the judge didn't say anything about me hanging around Cara.

So I'll be at the party tonight, wearing my jingle balls, just like you said to.

Bobby

To: Natasha Roberts <natasha.roberts@thenyjournal.com>
Fr: Charity Webber <charity.webber@thenyjournal.com>
Re: Where ARE you????

I hate everyone. Why aren't you picking up?

To: Charity Webber <charity.webber@thenyjournal.com>
Fr: Bernice Walters <bernice.walters@thenyjournal.com>
Re: Tonight's Party
Dear Ms. Webber,

   Hello, I don't think we've actually met, but my name is Bernice and I work in ad circulation. I just wanted to let you know that I have a severe shellfish allergy. If I so much as smell crab, lobster or shrimp meat, I go into anaphylactic shock. I do hope you aren't planning on serving anything at tonight's event that contains shellfish. I've noticed that it tends to spoil the holiday mood when I go into convulsions.

   Although I do carry an epi stick with me just in case. If you should happen to see me grab my throat and collapse, would you kindly remove it from my purse and stab me in the thigh with it?
Many thanks,
Bernice Walters
Ad Circ

To: Charity Webber <charity.webber@thenyjournal.com>
Fr: Sol Harper <s.harper@madrigalmagic.com>
Re: Tonight
Just a quick note to let you know that the singers you requested for this evening's event are running a little late due to the traffic in and around the Holland Tunnel. Apparently everybody and his brother decided to drive into the city today to see the tree at Rockefeller Center.

   But never fear, they'll be there on time, gridlock alert

or not. Nothing can keep OUR knights and fair ladies from
"wassail"ing the house!
Sol
Manager, Madrigal Magic
****Don't hire a DJ for your next party. Let our medieval
   madrigals "wassail" you with traditional song in traditional medieval costume! "Simply the best madrigals this
side of the Rocky Mountains!"—*New York Chronicle*****

To: Natasha Roberts <natasha.roberts@thenyjournal.com>
Fr: Charity Webber <charity.webber@thenyjournal.com>
Re: Killing self now
Not that you care, obviously, or you'd have e'd me back
by now.

To: Charity Webber <charity.webber@thenyjournal.com>
Fr: Daniel Carmichael <daniel.carmichael@thenyjour-
nal.com>
Re: Party Tonight
Hey, Char! Just wanted to let you know me and the guys
up here in tech support are really excited about the party
tonight. We hear it's at a real happening place. I think it's
a real good choice for a company holiday party. According to *Zagat*, it's the kind of place where a lot of marriage
proposals take place because it's so romantic. I just hope
I don't get too carried away by the romance in the air and
propose to anyone! Especially since my grandma left me
her two-carat diamond cocktail ring and I just happen to
have it in my pocket *right now*.
   See you at the party.
Danny

To: Charity Webber <charity.webber@thenyjournal.com>
Fr: Antoine Dessange <adessange@leshautes.com>
Re: Event Tonight
Cher Mademoiselle,

It pains me to have to inform you that despite the un-
usually warm weather, the back garden will not be open
for use by your guests, due to the fact that at lunch today
the fountain there was vandalized by members of the Yardley Middle School French Club, who poured a box of Mr.
Bubble into it when their teacher wasn't looking.

As the garden area is the only place in the restaurant
where diners may legally smoke under New York City law,
any members of your party who wish to indulge will now
have to do so in front of the restaurant. I hope this will not
be an inconvenience.

I remain, as always, yours faithfully,
Antoine Dessange
Manager, Les Hautes Manger

To: Natasha Roberts <natasha.roberts@thenyjournal.com>
Fr: Charity Webber <charity.webber@thenyjournal.com>
Re: Still killing self

I don't know where you are, but I just thought I'd let you
know that I'm leaving for the restaurant now. If you want
to hook up later—you know, like after the party—you'll be
able to find me floating in the Hudson…if the concrete
block I plan on tying to my ankle fails to do its job, I mean.

This party is going to be a complete disaster. Andrew
Hargrave's first official act as CEO is undoubtedly going
to be to fire me for organizing such a completely

screwed-up event. There's zero chance now that we'll ever get married and move to Westchester to raise little bitty Skittles-lovers. I should have known it was all just a pipe dream.

Goodbye, cruel world.

Char

To: Charity Webber <charity.webber@thenyjournal.com>
Fr: Natasha Roberts <natasha.roberts@thenyjournal.com>
Re: I'm so sorry!!!!!

I was in an art meeting. They just let me out. Have you left yet? I tried to call and just got your voice mail. I hope you check your Blackberry.

I'll be there in ten minutes. Don't start drinking! Remember how you nearly became Mrs. Danny Carmichael after all those rum and Diet Cokes? We don't want a repeat performance of that, now, do we? Especially if you're saving yourself for Andrew Hargrave, aka Mr. Skittles.

See you soon.

Nat

To: Andrew Hargrave <andrew.hargrave@thenyjournal.com>
Fr: Peter Hargrave <peter.hargrave@thenyjournal.com>
Re: Holiday Party

What's this I hear about your having the annual holiday party at some restaurant? What's wrong with the Senior Staff Dining Room? We always had a good time there. The staff really seemed to like the pigs-in-a-blanket.

I hope you know what you're doing. Those boys down

in Shipping and Receiving have a tendency to go a little nuts when there's an open bar.
Peter

To: Peter Hargrave <peter.hargrave@thenyjournal.com>
Fr: Andrew Hargrave <andrew.hargrave@thenyjournal.com>
Re: Holiday Party
Don't worry, Uncle Pete. Charity Webber has it all under control. That girl's a real firecracker, just like you said. Well, not that I've gotten a chance to meet her, yet. But I'm leaving for the party now. And don't worry about the boys in Shipping and Receiving. With Charity in charge, I can't imagine anything could possibly go wrong.
Andrew

New York Journal Employee Incident Report

Name/Title of Reporter: Carl Hopkins, Security Officer

Date/Time of Incident: Thursday, 5:30 p.m.

Place of Incident: Company Holiday Party
　　　　　　　　　 Les Hautes Manger Restaurant
　　　　　　　　　 57th and Madison

Persons Involved in Incident:

Robert Hancock, Shipping and Receiving, aged 29

Cara Powalski, Reception, aged 26

Fred Powalski, Security Officer, aged 29

Nature of Incident:

Security Officer F. Powalski, on door duty at company holiday party per the request of C. Webber, Event Organizer, asked R. Hancock what he was doing at company holiday party.

R. Hancock said he was enjoying the company holiday party, as was his right as an employee.

S.O. Powalski stated that R. Hancock had no right to be at company holiday party, as S.O. Powalski has restraining order against him.

R. Hancock said if S.O. Powalski doesn't like it, why doesn't *he* leave?

S.O. Powalski replied because he was on duty and could not leave, but R. Hancock under no such obligation.

R. Hancock refused to leave.

S.O. Powalski attempted to physically remove R. Hancock from the party.

R. Hancock punched S.O. Powalski in the face.

C. Powalski begged them to stop fighting and not to embarrass her in front of her co-workers.

S.O. Powalski threw R. Hancock through plate-glass window.

Follow-up: New York Police Department alerted, arrived, arrested R. Hancock, S.O. Powalski.

To: Charity Webber <charity.webber@thenyjournal.com>
Fr: Sol Harper <s.harper@madrigalmagic.com>
Re: Last Night
Dear Ms. Webber,

   The Magical Madrigals are a group of musical profes-
sionals who are not in the habit of being groped, but that's
what they tell me happened at your party last evening.
Suggestive comments were made to both the flutist and
harpist, and one of my singers says she was frequently im-
plored to "take it all off," apparently in reference to her
kirtle, which some guests appeared to mistake for a chas-
tity belt.

   I'm afraid I will be unable to offer the services of the
Magical Madrigals at any future events at your company.
You should be aware that my lute player is considering fil-
ing a sexual harassment suit against your firm.
Sol
Manager, Madrigal Magic
 ****Don't hire a DJ for your next party. Let our medieval
   madrigals "wassail" you with traditional song in tradi-
tional medieval costume! "Simply the best madrigals this
 side of the Rocky Mountains!"—*New York Chronicle*****

To: Charity Webber <charity.webber@thenyjournal.com>
Fr: Antoine Dessange <adessange@leshautes.com>
Re: Event Last Night
Cher Mademoiselle,

   Please note that, in addition to the cost of food and
beverage, I must add a damage fee of $1,560.47 for re-

pair and replacement of the plate-glass window, $532.67 for replacement of one of our art deco wall sconces and $267.53 for regrouting the tiles in the back-garden fountain, which were loosened when a number of your guests felt compelled to leap into the water.

Additionally, I would like to mention that Les Hautes Manger will no longer be available for private parties of any size. Please remove our card from your Rolodex.

I remain, as always, faithfully yours,

Antoine Dessange

Manager, Les Hautes Manger

To: Charity Webber <charity.webber@thenyjournal.com>
Fr: Bernice Walters <bernice.walters@thenyjournal.com>
Re: Many Thanks

I just wanted to say thanks one last time for giving me that shot last night. I had no idea that was crab meat inside those mushroom caps! They were delicious. It was almost worth going into shock for. That is one good restaurant. Thanks again.

Much love,

Bernice

To: Charity Webber <charity.webber@thenyjournal.com>
Fr: Daniel Carmichael <daniel.carmichael@thenyjournal.com>
Re: Last Night

Listen, I know after the fight and the arrest and that fat lady going into shock and all, you had a few drinks, and maybe weren't quite feeling like your normal self last night. So I just thought I'd ask one more time:

Are you SURE you don't want to marry me? Because the offer still stands. My mom even promised to move her circular-saw collection out of the basement if we do decide to tie the old knot.

What was that you kept saying about Skittles, anyway?
Danny

To: Charity Webber <charity.webber@thenyjournal.com>
Fr: Frank Leonard <frank.leonard@thenyjournal.com>
Re: Holiday Party
Just wanted to say thanks from me and all the boys for inviting us to such a swell soiree last night. We took a vote, and we all agree—it was the best office holiday party any of us has ever been to!

And I'm sure you'll be interested to know—in the drinking contest between us and Budget, well, we won! Bet they can't wait for a rematch next year!

By the way, we all think you look real good wet.

Well, thanks again!
Frank
and all the guys in Shipping and Receiving
Ringing their Jingle Balls

To: Charity Webber <charity.webber@thenyjournal.com>
Fr: Cara Powalski <cara.powalski@thenyjournal.com>
Re: Last Night
Dear Ms. Webber,

I hope you know that you've ruined my life. My Bobby's

in jail, and it's all YOUR fault! Why didn't you look at the last names of the officers Security sent down to guard the doors at the party? Couldn't you have guessed that Fred Powalski is my ex?

Thanks for nothing,
Cara

To: Andrew Hargrave
<andrew.hargrave@thenyjournal.com>
Fr: Peter Hargrave <peter.hargrave@thenyjournal.com>
Re: Holiday Party
What's this I hear about a brawl at the party last night? And an arrest? And people making lewd suggestions to Christmas carolers? And someone stripping naked and jumping into a fountain? Is this really the kind of behavior we want to encourage at our company holiday parties?

I sincerely hope you plan on doing something about all of this, Andrew.
Peter

To: Peter Hargrave <peter.hargrave@thenyjournal.com>
Fr: Andrew Hargrave
<andrew.hargrave@thenyjournal.com>
Re: Holiday Party
Don't worry, Uncle Pete. I'm on it.
Andrew

To: Charity Webber <charity.webber@thenyjournal.com>
Fr: Natasha Roberts <natasha.roberts@thenyjournal.com>
Re: Last Night

Oh my God, are you all right? You look TERRIBLE. How many drinks did you have, anyway? I TOLD you to stay away from that bar.

Although I can't really say I blame you. If that had been MY party, I'd have had a few, too. Could you BELIEVE all that?

Though the topper, if you ask me, was you jumping into that fountain.

Nat

To: Natasha Roberts <natasha.roberts@thenyjournal.com>
Fr: Charity Webber <charity.webber@thenyjournal.com>
Re: Last Night

WHY ARE YOU TRYING TO TORTURE ME???? My head is POUNDING. I could hardly WALK this morning. And you're teasing me about jumping into some fountain?

Nat, my CAREER is probably over. I'm probably going to be FIRED today. Someone at my party got THROWN THROUGH A PLATE-GLASS WINDOW, and then arrested. Somebody else went into anaphylactic shock. One of the Magical Madrigals smacked a wall sconce with her pointy cone hat trying to get away from some pervert in Accounting, and now the company has to pay to replace it—not to mention the sexual harassment suit, if she sues us.

And who knew so many of our fellow employees were alcoholics! The Budget department alone drank, if my estimates are correct, a thousand dollars' worth of call liquor.

And to top it all off, apparently I only just avoided becoming Mrs. Danny Carmichael again.

PLEASE, do not torture me about some nonexistent dip in Les Hautes Manger's back-garden fountain. You don't have to. My reality is quite bad enough.
Char

To: Charity Webber <charity.webber@thenyjournal.com>
Fr: Natasha Roberts <natasha.roberts@thenyjournal.com>
Re: Last Night
Char, I'm not trying to torture you, I swear. Last night, you DID jump into the fountain. And a number of our colleagues immediately followed suit, particularly the guys from Shipping and Receiving.

I can't believe you don't remember. I TRIED to get you out, I swear. But Char, that's not even the worst part:

When I tried to reason with you, telling you it was too cold to go swimming, and that you were getting your clothes all wet, you said, "Well, I'll just take them off, then," and started unbuttoning your blouse...

...right as Andrew Hargrave came outside to introduce himself.

Please, please don't shoot the messenger.
Nat

To: Natasha Roberts <natasha.roberts@thenyjournal.com>
Fr: Charity Webber <charity.webber@thenyjournal.com>
Re: Last Night
I DID NOT!!!! YOU ARE LYING!!!! I DID NOT DO ANY OF THOSE THINGS!!! I DID NOT JUMP INTO THE FOUNTAIN! I DID NOT TAKE OFF MY TOP!!!

AND ANDREW HARGRAVE DID NOT WALK OUT JUST AS I WAS DOING SO!!!!!

Please tell me you're making this up. Please. I'm begging you.

To: Charity Webber <charity.webber@thenyjournal.com>
Fr: Natasha Roberts <natasha.roberts@thenyjournal.com>
Re: Last Night

Sorry, Char. But it's the truth. Thank God you were wearing a bra.

If it's any comfort to you, it looks as if those spin classes you've been taking at the Y have really been paying off.

Nat

To: Natasha Roberts <natasha.roberts@thenyjournal.com>
Fr: Charity Webber <charity.webber@thenyjournal.com>
Re: Last Night

NOOOOOOOOOOOOOOOOOOOOO!!!!!!!!!!!!!

Oh my God. It's all coming back to me now. After Bobby Hancock went through that window, I grabbed a drink off the first tray that passed by me—a cosmo, I think. I must have had six or seven more as the evening went on…. Those bubbles. They just looked so inviting….

WHAT DO I DO NOW???? He's going to fire me!!! What choice does he have? Oh, God, Nat!!! WHAT SHOULD I DO????

To: Charity Webber <charity.webber@thenyjournal.com>
Fr: Natasha Roberts <natasha.roberts@thenyjournal.com>
Re: Last Night
Might I suggest groveling?

To: Andrew Hargrave
<andrew.hargrave@thenyjournal.com>
Fr: Charity Webber <charity.webber@thenyjournal.com>
Re: Last Night
Dear Mr. Hargrave,

   I just want to apologize for the appalling way that I behaved last night. I want to assure you that I am normally much more levelheaded than my actions last night might have led you to believe. I will admit to having been slightly unnerved by a few things that occurred during the course of the party last evening, and for that reason may have imbibed more than I'm used to. I just want to make it clear that what happened last night in the fountain behind the restaurant was a complete anomaly, and will never happen again.

   And I would also like to say, on behalf of my fellow staff members, whose behavior last night you might also have found somewhat uncircumspect, that we've all been under a lot of stress this year, and I think they really, really appreciated the effort and expense you exerted on their behalf, and were only letting off a little steam.

   I will perfectly understand, however, if under the circumstances, you feel you cannot keep me in your employ, and will tender my resignation at once.

Very sincerely yours,

Charity Webber

Events Organizer

To: Charity Webber <charity.webber@thenyjournal.com>
Fr: Andrew Hargrave
<andrew.hargrave@thenyjournal.com>
Re: Last Night

Dear Charity,

You're kidding me, right? That was one of the best parties I've ever been to! And exactly the kind of shot in the arm this company needed. And I'm not the only one who thinks so. People around here can't seem to stop talking about what a great time they had. That fight breaking out—not to mention you saving that lady, the one who went into convulsions—were definite highlights.

But your jumping into that fountain was a stroke of genius. Who knew cavorting in foam could be such a bonding experience? Departments that were barely civil to each other all year were actually having fun together—exactly what I've been trying to achieve since I started working here! After all the money my uncle spent on expensive corporate retreats and management seminars, you proved that all we needed to come together as a company was a fountain and a box of Mr. Bubble.

By the way, I realized last night that—though you probably don't remember it—we've actually met once before.

I ran into you some time ago down at the newsstand. We were both buying, of all things, bags of Skittles. I tried to get your name then, but you disappeared, and I thought I'd never see you again. Although admittedly you were wearing considerably more clothing then than you were last night, I recognized you right away: I never forget the face of a fellow Skittles fan. We're a dying breed.

If you have time next week, maybe we could have lunch? I believe there's a party or two in my future that I'm going to need your help planning.

Andrew

Carole Matthews is the internationally bestselling author of eight outstandingly successful novels. Her unique sense of humor has won her legions of fans and critical acclaim all over the world.

In the U.S.A. her books include *For Better, For Worse, Bare Necessity, A Minor Indiscretion, The Sweetest Taboo* and *Let's Meet on Platform 8.*

The film rights for both *For Better, For Worse* and *A Minor Indiscretion* have been sold to Hollywood. *For Better, For Worse* was selected by Kelly Ripa as her "Reading with Ripa" book of the month on *LIVE with Regis and Kelly,* sending it straight on to the *USA Today* bestseller list. Carole has presented on television and radio and when she's not writing novels and film scripts, she manages to find time to trek in the Himalayas, in-line skate in Central Park, take tea in China and snooze in her garden shed in her native England....

To find out more about Carole and her books go to www.carolematthews.com.

Traveling Light
by Carole Matthews

The myth is that Americans don't like to travel. Yet wherever I've been in the world they seem to get there—in droves, usually. Though I hadn't quite expected to see one here for some reason.

"Hi," he says, looking up from his unpacking.

I just love how casual Americans are. We Brits are so much more self-conscious, reserved, uncomfortable with etiquette. Our brothers across the pond wade in affably without preamble. "Hello."

"How are ya?"

"Fine, thank you." I edge into the small compartment from the corridor of the carriage. Our train is traveling overnight from Gaungzhou to Guilin and I've booked "soft" class, which means that I get a lovely comfy bunk bed, a little bathroom shared between fifty of us at the end of the carriage and a pair of complimentary fluffy blue slippers from the railway company, whose name is spelled out in Chinese characters, so I can't tell you what it is. It does mean, however, that I get to share my compartment with a complete stranger and it looks like this is him. I'd sort of expected to be sharing with another woman, but then I might have learned by this stage of my travels that I should always expect the unexpected. My roommate is already wearing his complimentary slippers and his are pink and fluffy. As they're intended for tiny Chinese feet, he's cut the toes out of them and is wearing them flip-flop style. I can't help but smile at them.

"Cool, right?" He holds up his peep-toes for my inspection.

"Very."

Discordant Chinese Musak plays, plinky-plonking over the intercom system, and there's no way of turning it off.

"Do you want to be on top or on the bottom?" If only the other men in my life had been so direct! "I'm easy," he says.

"I'll take the top bunk, if that's okay." I reason that if he's planning to murder me during the night, then at least I have a chance of hearing him clambering up to my aerie. If I keep one of my boots handy I could whack him on the head before he has the chance to do his dastardly deeds. These are the considerations of a lone female traveler in today's society.

"I'm Kane," he says. "Kane Freeman." I have to say that he doesn't look much like a murderer. He looks more like one of those surf-dudes—if that's the correct term. We don't have many surf-dudes in England, so I'm having to rely on

Hollywood teen movies for my terminology. Anyway, he's wearing surf's-up-type clothes, he's got spiky blond hair that bears some witness to sun damage, a ridiculously golden tan (ditto the sun damage), a freckly but otherwise perfect nose and clear blue eyes that if I were up for being mesmerized would be truly mesmerizing.

"Alice." I shake his hand formally because that's what Brits do.

He grins at me. "Alice."

I should point out that I don't feel like an Alice. This was my mother's idea of a sober name for a well-behaved, studious child. She thought that by calling me Alice, I wouldn't climb trees or fall off my bicycle, tie fireworks to my brother's head or try to torture frogs. And, for a while, she was probably right. I have gone through life with a name that I don't feel suits me.

"Well, Ali…"

I'm taken aback at the familiarization of my name. No one calls me Ali. And I suddenly wonder why not.

"…shall we crack open a beer? It's going to be a hell of a long night."

I don't normally drink. Stephen, my fiancé, doesn't like women who drink—or smoke, or wear revealing clothes, or say "fuck" in public.

Kane wiggles a bottle of beer in my direction.

"Yes, please." My feet are killing me and my shoulders are aching from the weight of my backpack. I need something to help. "Beer would be nice."

My companion snaps off the cap and offers it to me. "I

also have a French baguette and cheese." His eyes flash with unspoken wickedness.

I barely stop myself from gasping. In mainland China, the rarity of these jewels shouldn't be underestimated. I have been traveling across the country here for three weeks now and have lived on nothing but noodles—prawn noodles, chicken noodles, occasionally beef noodles. Noodles, noodles, noodles and more bloody noodles. Dairy products and bread are as scarce as blue diamonds. He could ask me to perform any dastardly deed he jolly well liked for a quick bite of his baguette.

"Oh, my word."

He gives a smug smile, knowing that he has me in his grasp. Kane starts to prepare our impromptu picnic while I heave my rucksack onto the top bunk and fuss with settling in for the journey. The small compartment is spick-and-span. We have a lacy tablecloth on a little shelf by the window that bears a plastic rose in a silver-colored vase. There are lacy curtains at the window, obscuring the view of the seething mass of humanity at Gaungzhou station. I have never seen anywhere as crowded in my entire life. I inspect the bedding, which is spotless, starched within an inch of its life and embroidered with the same characters as our complimentary footwear.

I put on my slippers, position my boots in case I need them as a weapon and slide down to sit next to Kane on his bed. It feels terribly intimate to be in this situation with someone I've barely been introduced to. Stephen would pass out if he could see me now.

Kane carefully slices the cheese onto the bread. I can feel

myself salivating and sink my teeth in gratefully, the minute he hands it over. I can't help it, but I groan with ecstasy. Unless you've been there, you will never imagine how good this tastes.

Kane shows off his set of perfect pearly whites. "Good, huh?"

"Mmm. Marvelous."

The train whistle blows and we rattle out of the station, out of the town, leaving the squash of people behind, and head into the countryside.

"So?" he mutters through his bread. "You're traveling alone?"

I like men who are keen-eyed and sharp-witted. "Yes." It pains me to have to pause in my eating. "I'm getting married in a few weeks." I want him to be absolutely clear from the beginning that I'm not available. I would flash my gorgeous engagement ring—which is a whopper—but I've left it at home in case I got mugged. "This is my last chance to travel alone."

Kane frowns. "Should you want to travel alone if you're getting hitched?"

He isn't the first person to voice this concern. My parents were particularly vocal. As was Stephen.

"I just needed to get away," I say. "It was all getting too much. I had to escape. You know how it is."

"No," he says. "I've never even gotten close."

"Oh." I give a dismissive wave of my hands. "There are so many things to organize. It's hell."

"So why are you doing it?"

My French bread nearly falls out of my mouth. Why *am* I doing it? "My fiancé. Stephen. We've been together for years. Many *happy* years. He felt it was time we settled down."

"So you're here on a Chinese train with a stranger and he's at home ordering bridal corsages?"

I give a carefree laugh. "You make it sound a lot worse than it is."

Kane contemplates that while he chews. "He must be an understanding man."

"He's very…understanding." Actually, I'm not sure that Stephen understands me at all.

Kane says nothing. We eat in silence. Try as I might, I can't recapture the joy of my cheese again.

"What about you?"

Kane shrugs. "I've always been a drifter. I like to see the world. I have no ties, no commitments, no permanent base. I go wherever the wind blows me."

I can't even begin to imagine what that must feel like. My life is layer upon layer of commitment, confinement, duty. I live by timetables, schedules, appointments, mortgage payments. Doesn't everyone?

We finish our meal and the grinning guard comes and checks our tickets and gives us a thermos of hot water for tea. I reciprocate for the bread and cheese by supplying tea bags. We Brits may like to travel the four corners of the globe, but we also like to do it with "proper" tea.

"Do you work?" Kane asks as he examines his brew suspiciously. Quite frankly, most Americans just don't understand the concept of decent tea, so I don't wait for his approval.

"I did. As a radio producer." I had to resign from my job to take this trip as my employers at Let the Good Times Roll Radio also failed to "understand" my need to fly—particularly when I've already got two weeks in the Bahamas booked as a honeymoon. Who could possibly want more than that? And yet I do. Is that greedy? Does it make me a bad person? "I'm taking some time out." Not necessarily voluntarily. "I'll look for something else when all the fuss from the wedding has died down."

"You're using a lot of negative images with reference to your forthcoming nuptials," Kane observes.

"That sounds terribly Californian, if you don't mind me saying," I observe back.

He smiles. "I *am* from California. I'm allowed."

At ten o'clock it's lights out on Chinese trains, which reminds me of my time at boarding school. The sudden plunge into darkness curtails our conversation and we scrabble to our bunks, clicking on the faint night-lights above our heads. I decide to stay clothed for modesty's sake, but Kane has no such inhibitions. He's wearing battered, baggy shorts and a sleeveless T-shirt that bears the faded remains of a logo, now too pale to discern. I'm used to a man who favors pressed chinos and striped shirts and who goes into the bathroom to change. In a moment, Kane is stripped down to his boxer shorts. He's clearly comfortable with his body and, I suspect if I had a body like that, I would be, too. I know that I should look away, but I'm afraid to say, I can't.

I just can't. He has a tattoo of a dragon high on the broad sweep of his shoulder. I wonder where he had it done and if it hurt him, and I find myself thinking that I'd like to trace the outline with my finger.

He turns and smiles up at me. I do hope he's not a mind reader. "Sleep tight," he says, and hops into the bunk below me.

I do no such thing. I lie awake looking at the air vent in the ceiling, occasionally peeping out of the lace curtain to the blackness of the paddy fields beyond and watching as, even through the dark hours, we stop at brightly lit stations to let passengers come and go.

The train runs minute perfect. Stephen would like that part of it. Stephen likes things to be regular. His habits, his meals, his bowels. Sorry, that's not nice of me. You don't need to know that. Even though it's true.

Stephen, on the other hand, wouldn't like the crowds, the smells, the squatty loos—apologies, back to toilet preferences again—the food, the heat, the pollution, the whole damn foreignness of the place. We'll be taking our holidays in the Caribbean from now on, with maybe the odd deviation to the Côte d'Azur. We'll stay in five-star hotels, with fluffy towels and spa facilities—someplace where we don't have to mix too closely with the locals. We won't even have to trouble ourselves to go to the bar for a drink—it will be brought to us on a tray at our sun-loungers by a smiling waiter. Is this what I want?

I close my eyes and try not to think of anything connected with the wedding. Have you ever felt like everything was crowding in on you? My whole world was becoming smaller and smaller, until I felt like my namesake Alice in Wonderland after she'd drunk the potion and had shrunk to barely ten inches high. I felt I just didn't matter anymore, that I had become too tiny to be of consequence. My days were taken up with invitations and flowers and bell-ringers and wedding cars and who the hell was I going to sit next to who? Everyone gets prewedding nerves, I was told—time after time. Is that all it is, this nagging feeling? I screw my eyes more tightly shut but still sleep eludes me. The stations, towns, miles flash by. I hear the sound of my neighbor's soft snoring from the bunk below. Kane doesn't look like the sort of man who worries if he misses a poo.

Bang on time, the train pulls into Guilin station just after dawn. Kane and I haven't said much to each other this morning. Kane, because he's only just woken up after sleeping like a bear—his words not mine. Me, because I'm not sure what I want to say.

We pack our rucksacks, bumping into each other in the tiny space as we prepare to leave the train. The doors open and the slow shuffle toward the exit starts. Kane and I make to join it.

"Thanks for the bread and cheese," I say. "It's been nice…"

"Where are you heading?" Kane asks.

"Yangshuo."

"I've been there before," he informs me. "It's a blast. I know a great hotel. Want to hang out together?"

I nod, mainly because my brain is urging my mouth to say no.

★ ★ ★

The Fawlty Towers hotel in Yangshuo is, indeed, a great place. It has showers complete with hot water and clean sheets. And "hanging out together" also seems to involve sharing a room. Single beds—I'm not that reckless. After spending a night together it seemed churlish to refuse. And it will help keep down the costs. I don't think I'll mention it to Stephen though. It's another thing he wouldn't understand.

Kane rents bicycles with dodgy brakes and we head out into the countryside weaving our way through narrow valleys and straggly villages whose houses are still pasted with red and gold New Year banners to bring good luck to those inside. Weather-worn mountains molded by the rain into sugarloaf shapes tower over us. I can't remember last when I was on a bike and I'd forgotten how great the wind in your hair feels as it lifts the strands away from your neck to kiss the humid dampness away. We climb Moon Hill, Kane tugging me up the steep slope by the hand, until we look over the landscape that spawned a thousand paintings—soft, misty mountains, meandering rivers, the pink blush of cherry blossom trees. I return to Yangshuo feeling achy and strangely liberated—like a dog who's dared to stick its head out of a car window for the first time.

In the Hard Luck Internet Café, I pick up an e-mail from Stephen. "Hello Alice—the caterers have suggested these canapés." There is a list of a dozen nibbly-bits, all of which sound perfectly acceptable. "Shall I give them the go-ahead? Stephen."

I stare at the picture of Bruce Lee on the wall and wonder if you should be addressing your future wife "Hello Alice"—particularly when she's been away for nearly three weeks. Shouldn't the word *love* appear in there somewhere? Perhaps Stephen is beginning to wonder why his future wife has been away for nearly three weeks. There has been a distinct lack of "I'm missing you" type e-mails. But then Stephen is very reserved with his emotions. It's one of the things I love about him. Really, it is. I've never been one for gushy stuff.

I type: "Dear Stephen. Canapés sound fine." And then in a rush of guilt or something, "Missing you. Love Alice."

As I head back to the hotel, I see Kane sitting outside the Planet China restaurant drinking green tea and Yanjing beer with his feet up on a chair. I've never seen anyone look so laid-back. My stomach lurches when I approach him and it might not be due to the fact I'm back on the noodle diet. How old is Kane? I wonder. The same as me? Not quite thirty. He is so loose and carefree with his life that it makes me feel older than time itself. I plonk myself down next to him and hear myself sigh wearily.

"You look stressed."

"I am."

"Wedding arrangements not going to plan?" Kane grins. I'm sure he doesn't believe that this wedding is ever going to go ahead.

"I've just agreed to the canapés," I say crisply. "They're going to be wonderful."

"Try this." He hands me a cigarette.

"I didn't know you smoked." But then there's a lot I don't

know about Kane, even though I'm sharing a hotel room with him. I have no idea why I'm taking this, as I don't smoke either. Stephen doesn't like women who... Oh, you get the gist.

"It's herbal," he says. "It will relax you."

I drag deeply on the cigarette and then the smell hits me. "Oh good grief," I say. "Do you know what this is?"

Kane grins at me.

"Of course you do." I take another tentative puff. I'm not a natural lawbreaker. "Is this legal here?" I suspect not. It's making me even less relaxed than I was. I can't do drugs, not even soft ones. Quickly, I hand it back. "I could end up in prison for twenty-five years."

Kane fixes me with a wily stare. "Isn't that where you're headed anyway?"

"I need a drink." In what sounds to me like passable Mandarin, Kane orders me a steaming glass of jasmine tea and some rough Chinese vodka. I pick my way through the beautiful white blooms, inhaling the fragrance as I sip the tea, spoiling it with the raw cut of the alcohol as I chase it with swigs of vodka. I was going to have jasmine in my wedding bouquet, but now it will always remind me of Kane. And that might not be a good thing.

From Yangshuo we take a plane to Chengdu to see the giant pandas and, I don't want you to read too much into this, but we're already acting like an old married couple. I can't believe how easily I've fallen into step with this man. At the airport Kane looks after the passports while I go and top up on "western" snacks—potato chips and boiled sweets rather than scorpions on sticks.

The next morning, we join the old grannies in the park doing tai chi, causing great hilarity as we heave our bulky frames alongside the delicate, birdlike movements of the elderly Chinese ladies. Kane causes a particular stir. He laughs as they cluck round him like mother hens and come to touch his spiky blond hair and his bulging biceps, which makes me flush as it's something I've considered doing myself. The old men, some in aging Maoist uniforms, promenade proudly with their songbirds in cages, and a feeling of sadness and oppression settles over me. Without speaking, Kane takes my hand and squeezes. I can feel the edge of my engagement ring cutting into my finger even though I'm not wearing it, but I don't try to pull away.

Kane keeps holding my hand while we travel farther into the country to visit the Terracotta Army at Xian. Beautiful, untouchable soldiers, frozen in time, unable to move forward. I cry at the sheer spectacle of it and at other things that I can't even begin to voice. He's still holding it a week later when we hike up to the mist-shrouded peak of Emei Shan and book a simple room in the extraordinary peace of a Buddhist monastery that looks like something off a film set.

We have dinner in a local café with no windows and a tarpaulin roof, lit only by smoky kerosene lamps, the sound of monkeys chattering in the trees high above us. A group of local men play mah-jongg boisterously in the corner, each tile slapped down with a challenge and hotly contested. A scraggy cat sits hopefully at my feet. We're the only diners and the waiflike Chinese owner brings us dish after dish of succulent, stir-fried vegetables—aubergine, spring greens, bean sprouts, water chestnuts.

Kane has been on the Internet at the monastery. It makes you realize that there's nowhere in the world that can truly be classed as remote anymore. It also makes me realize that our time together is coming to an end. He's planning another leg of this trip, which will eventually take him round the world. I had always dreamed of traveling the world and I feel a pang of envy that he'll be continuing the rest of his journey without me. He says the surf is good in Australia right now and that he'll probably head out that way. See? I knew my assessment of him was right all along. Do surfers attract groupies? I think they do. And I wonder, will he hook up with someone else as easy? Someone less tied, less uptight, less duty-bound.

Kane is adept with his chopsticks while I still handle them like knitting needles. Give me a plate of chow mein and I could run you up a sweater, no problem. We finish our meal and bask in the warm night air with cups of jasmine tea. He plucks at the plaited friendship bracelet on his wrist and, not for the first time, I contemplate when and how he acquired it. We both look so terribly mellow in this half-light and I wish I could capture this moment forever. Me and Kane cocooned in our own microcosm.

His fingers wander across the table and find mine. "Just in case you were wondering," he says gently. "This brother-sister thing we're doing is taking its toll on me."

I don't know what to say, so I say nothing.

Kane sighs, his eyes searching mine. "What I really want is to make love to you."

"Oh," I say. "Okay."

He looks at me for confirmation, and I nod. "Let's go."

Kane wraps his arms around me and holds me tightly as we pay the bill and hurry back to the shelter of the monastery. Is it a sin to make love in a monastery? I don't know. I don't want to know. I'm too Catholic by half. I might burn in hell for this at some later stage, but I think it will be worth it. Can something so beautiful be punishable by fire and brimstone? I hope the monks don't mind. I wouldn't like to offend anyone. As I hold on to Kane in the dark, I don't consider that it might be a sin against Stephen. I don't consider anything but the curve of his spine, the strength of his arms and the look of love on his face. And it takes me by surprise, as no one has looked at me with such passion for a long, long time.

We take another overnight train to Beijing, to the Forbidden City. How appropriate. This time we squeeze together in one bunk, making love to the rhythm of the rattling rails, falling asleep in each other's arms.

The pollution in Beijing is worse in the spring, when the sands from the Gobi Desert blend with the exhaust fumes of a million, ozone-unfriendly cars. The mixture stings your eyes, strips your throat and makes it hard to see too far ahead. A grey veil blocks out the sun, which tries hard to break through, but is generally thwarted.

When in China you must do as the Chinese do and we hire sit-up-and-beg bikes again to cycle through the jammed streets to the vast expanse of Tiananmen Square—the symbol of freedom to an oppressed world. We join the throng of Chinese tourists flying kites and are royally ripped off as we buy flimsy paper butterflies from a canny, bowlegged vendor. He could feed his family for a week on what we pay him for a moment's fleeting pleasure, but I begrudge him nothing, as our lives are so easy compared to his. It makes me appreciate that I have very little to complain about.

We laugh as we run through the square, trailing our kites behind us, watching them as they duck and dive, playing with the erratic wind. But even then, I notice that my kite is not as exuberant in its swoops and soars as Kane's. It's more hesitant, fearful, and it's tearing easily. I trail after him while he takes the lead, clearing a route through the crowd, leaving me to follow behind. And then he holds me close and I forget everything. I forget to hold tightly to my kite and it floats away, bobbing, bobbing on the air, reaching for the hidden sun until it's quite out of sight. Free.

"I love you," Kane says. But I watch my kite fly away from me.

E-mail from Stephen. "Hello Alice—have ordered cars. Think you'll like them. Dr. and Mrs. Smythe have said no. Shame. Missing you too. Stephen." Is it a shame that two people who I don't even know aren't coming to my wedding? Do I really care what car will take me there? I stare at the screen, but can't make my fingers type a reply. Now what do I do?

That night we lie on the bed in our horrible Western-style hotel, which has matching bedspreads and curtains and shower gel and shampoo in tiny identical bottles. Already I can feel my other life calling me.

"Have you told him?" Kane asks.

"No," I say.

"You can't go back," my lover states. "You know you can't."

But I can. And I will. I can't explain this to Kane, but I love Stephen because he's anchored in reality. He understands about pensions, for heaven's sake. He polishes his shoes. He has chosen the wedding limousines. He may not make love to me as if it is the last thing he will ever do in this life. He may not chase life with an insatiable, unquenchable thirst. But Stephen is safe and solid and secure. We'll grow old together. We'll have a joint bank account. I will never feel the same about anyone in my entire life as I do about Kane—never. Not even Stephen. Kane is the sun, the moon and the stars. He is all the things I'm not, but that I would want to be. In a different life. I have never loved anyone more or as hopelessly. But Kane is as flighty as the paper butterfly kites, answering every tug of the breeze. How can you base a future, a whole lifetime, on something as unreliable as that? What would we do? Spend our lives wandering the earth, hand in hand, rucksack slung on back. Or would there come a time when I'd want to settle down, to pin the butterfly to the earth, stamp on it, crush it flat? Would I eventually become Kane's Stephen?

We make love and, this time, I feel that it *is* the last thing that I will ever do in my life. Every nerve, fiber, tissue, cell of my body zings with the prospect of life. Beneath him I lose myself, my reason, my mind. I'm part of Kane, and he'll always be a part of me. But this excitement would die, wouldn't it? Could we always maintain this intensity, this intimacy? Isn't it better to have loved so hard and so briefly than to watch it sink and vanish from view like the setting sun?

I wake up and reach for Kane, but he's gone. The bed beside me is empty. There's nothing left of my lover but a crumpled imprint in the sheets. I pad to the bathroom and take a shower, concentrating on the chipped tiles so that I won't feel that my heart is having to force itself to keep beating. You can taste devastation—did you know that? I didn't until now. It coats your teeth, tongue and throat and no amount of spearmint mouthwash will get rid of it.

I decide to check out of the hotel, even though my homeward flight isn't until tomorrow. I can't stay here alone. Not now. Slowly, methodically, I pack up my things and take the lift down to reception where I queue for an interminable amount of time behind a party of jocular Americans to pay my bill. I told you. Americans get everywhere. Inside your undies, inside your heart, inside your soul. Eventually, I reach the desk and hand over my credit card and my key. In return I get a receipt and a business card. The receptionist taps it.

"It was left for you," he says.

I flip it over and my broken heart flips, too. Somehow its jagged edges mesh back together. There's a caricature of a scruffy surfer and in big, bold type—BARNEY'S SURF SHACK, BONDI BEACH. Kane has scribbled, "I'll wait there every day for two weeks."

But I don't think he'll need to. I know now that there'll be no wedding. No hymns. No white dress. No bridesmaids. Not now. And maybe not ever. But I know that it's the right thing to do. I only hope that Stephen will understand. He deserves more. I shouldn't spend my life with someone I can live with. I should be with someone I can't live without. Wherever that may take me. My pension fund will just have to wait.

I hail a taxi and jump inside. I might just make it.

"Beijing Airport!" I say. "As quick as you can!" My word, I've always wanted to say that! It doesn't matter that the driver can't even speak English. He must sense my haste as he careens out into the six lanes of traffic, horn blaring. I feel as if I'm swimming in champagne, bubbles rising inside of me.

We pull up outside the terminal building and I race inside. There, standing by the check-in desk, is an unmistakable figure. His rucksack is over his shoulder.

He's head and shoulders above everyone else. One blond mop above a sea of black.

I run toward him as fast as I can. "Kane!"

He turns. And when he sees me he smiles.

Alisa Valdes-Rodriguez is the *New York Times* best-selling author of the novel *The Dirty Girls Social Club*, which has been optioned by Columbia Pictures with Jennifer Lopez attached. Her second novel, *Playing with Boys,* will be published in October 2004. An award-winning print and broadcast journalist, Alisa was on staff at the *Boston Globe* and *Los Angeles Times* and holds a master's in journalism from Columbia University. Alisa is also a jazz saxophonist and is at work on her debut album, due out sometime in 2005. She lives in New Mexico.

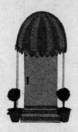

Cat Lady
by Alisa Valdes-Rodriguez

Teresa looked at her watch again, just to be sure. Gucci, good watch, time and date. Diamonds. January fifteenth. Birthday. Thirty-five, an age not even diamonds could help.

There was a time, twelve years ago, when Teresa believed a Gucci watch and the cool job that allowed a girl to buy it for herself would naturally facilitate a lifestyle that would naturally facilitate the meeting of great guys. Or at least *one* great guy. The kind who read books and might look good helping a child learn to ride a bike. That's all she asked for. But now it looked as if Teresa's mother—absolutely never to be confused with Mother Teresa—had been right all along.

"No mens want a girl so smart, so independent as you, with your expensive car that makes him feel so small," she had said the last time they met, at Versailles, for some post-Christmas *buñuelos* and *café con leche*. "A man wants to be needed, *y tú,* you don't need nobody."

Teresa's mother had been in Miami since 1960, and still the double-negative thing vexed her, as did the notion of her only daughter, the youngest and unmarried, living on her own, rather than living at home where she could be useful in helping serve her father.

Teresa popped open the white plastic file box beneath her glass-top home-office desk and took out the letter she had written to herself. She often typed such letters on her word processing program, printing them in soothing dark blue ink before folding them into neat squares, tucking them into greeting cards, and sealing them until whatever doomsday she wrote in clean, clear script on the front.

This envelope was marked "thirty-fifth birthday" and the message inside was simple:

Dear Self:
    If you are still single and haven't had one good date in the preceding two years, you must admit the search is over. Get rid of the belly shirts. Toss the miniskirts. Save yourself a future of humiliation and too much makeup and realize one important truth: You are now a cat lady.
With love,
Teresita

When Teresa wrote this to herself, she was only twenty-two, and had never owned a cat. She did not own a cat now, and had never owned a cat in her life. Her mother was from Cuba. And in Cuba, according to her mother, no one in her right mind had cats for pets.

"To kill the mouse, she is fine," griped Mami. "To kill the cock-a-roach, is good. As pet?" Ugly face. "Filthy. Disgusting. Only an American would have a cat pet."

Teresa folded the letter and replaced it in the card and envelope. She owned no belly shirts and no miniskirts. She had not owned these even as she wrote the letter to her future self. At her dressiest, she was a Liz Claiborne kind of girl. Otherwise, khakis and oversize shirts were fine. As it so happened, this was precisely the outfit she had on at the moment. Beige pants, black T-shirt, black button-down hanging open on top of that. But makeup? That was another matter. She wore a lot of the stuff, more out of ritual and habit than anything else. She walked up her condo stairs to the master bedroom, through to the bathroom, and began dumping her cosmetics one by one into the wastebasket, leaving only a tube of foundation, a blusher and a mascara. A cat lady did not need more than that.

Finished with her task, Teresa observed herself in the mirror. She would have to stop coloring the gray. And no more round-brushing with the blow-dryer to get it straight, no more slicking balm. Cat ladies ought to have bushy hair, she thought. Witch hair. She bent over and shook her head, tugging on it, plumping it with her hands. Upright once more, she looked wilder than she remembered looking in a long while, red in the cheeks and uncontrolled.

"Okay then," she said to her reflection. "Let's go get a goddamn cat."

As Teresa steered her white Volvo sedan through the traffic on Biscayne Boulevard, she thought about how different the words *lady* and *woman* were when paired with the word *cat*.

Cat Lady—crumbs on shirt, hair grease, newspaper stacked in towers inside the house, the same paisley dress for years on end, said dress worn with flat black Easy Spirit shoes.

Cat Woman—slinky, black leather, sex goddess. She felt heat spread in her lower belly and willed it away. She wasn't supposed to feel this anymore, was she?

Teresa eyed herself in the rearview mirror. She did Pilates and ate organic produce, just the sort of activities that invited scorn and ridicule from Mami, who preferred her milk "normal" and full of damaging hormones. Teresa took good care of herself. She didn't look a day older than twenty-nine. Or was it thirty?

"I'm not ready to be a cat lady," she whispered to her face. The man driving the car behind her laid on his horn. The light had turned green, and Teresa sat staring at her aging face. "Sorry," she said, though he couldn't hear her. Nervously, she drove on, toward the pet store.

A bell on the door jangled as Teresa opened it and stepped into the shop. The sound of the bell signaled a cageful of parrots to screech and gargle. Teresa looked around, but saw no one.

"Hello?" she called out.

A worker sulked out of a back room and bucked his head in her direction, some sort of pet store–employee greeting. He looked like Harpo Marx, with a big blond Afro. Justin Timberlake, Teresa's mind corrected her. That would be the modern comparison. Harpo Marx? That wasn't even her generation. Not only was she getting old, but her references were older than she was. Pathetic.

"Do you sell cats?" she asked. She tugged her outer shirt closed, wishing for a large paisley dress to hide in. The worker led her to the back, to a glass wall with rows of cages like drawers of a mausoleum on the other side. Inside each cage was at least one cat, usually two or three. Some were full-grown, most were kittens. All seemed to have cat poop in their fur and sad, scared eyes. They all stared at her, and looked half-dead. Except for one.

A small white cat stared at the lock, intelligent, focused. It swatted at the lock mechanism, squinted its eyes at its failure, and tried again. Failing once more, it stood up and circled its pen. It had no tail. Then, it sat again, and swatted from a new angle, ever hopeful. A patient cat. A cat that wanted freedom more than it wanted a human. Teresa identified with it instantly.

"That one," she said.

"Japanese bobtail," said the clerk. "Good choice."

Mami came for dinner with a birthday cake, and screeched like a parrot at the sight of the cat sitting patiently in Teresa's entryway, staring at the front door.

"What is that *rat* doing here?"

Teresa took her mother's fur wrap—it did not get cold in Miami, ever, but Mami still had to dress for winter—and hung it in the closet. It felt like the cat's fur. The cat stared coldly at them both, incriminating, and padded away toward the litter box in the guest bathroom.

"I'm a cat lady," Teresa announced. "Congratulate me."

"You should have kept Richard," said Mami, lighting a cigarette. Teresa had asked many times that Mami not smoke here, and many times Mami had completely ignored her.

"Richard?" Teresa asked, feeling dizzy. She sat on the sofa across the living room from her mother and gagged on the smoke and memories. Richard. The asshole. The womanizer. The cheat. The liar.

"Richard." Mami made a face to indicate she found her daughter retarded.

"I like being a cat lady," said Teresa. "Next subject please."

"He was a good man."

"I named her Eli, after Grandma," said Teresa, pointing to the cat who had returned to her post at the front door. Eli stood on her hind legs and with one paw fiddled with the doorknob. Mami blew smoke from her widened nostrils, like the devil, and narrowed her eyes.

"There is a hot place in hell for you," she hissed.

As if she'd understood, Eli pivoted her head on her neck and stared at Mami. Never had anyone been able to outstare Teresa's mother. But this cat did it. For ten full minutes they glared and glowered, until, at last, Mami broke.

"Filthy creature," she said, standing to fetch her stole. "I go now. From now on, we visit on my house, not here on the rat nest."

In, on. Since 1959 the words had confounded Mami. In Spanish, there was only one: *En.* Life was so much simpler for Mami.

Since bonding over their discomfort with Mami, Eli and Teresa had become friends. Eli slept on Teresa's feet, and in exchange for the physical affection, Teresa scratched behind Eli's ears and fed her something in a fancy pink can that once opened smelled noxious and fish-guts. Why, Teresa wondered, did pet food manufacturers lie like Richard? Eli obviously liked the food, which smelled nothing like the pâté it purported to be, and everything like the mouse-ass and sparrow-trachea it actually was. They lied to appeal to the ones with the money and the power, Teresa realized, sort of like porn directors who told men women enjoyed choking on their snotty fluids.

Teresa began rushing home to see Eli after work. She had never known what it felt like to look forward to a creature with a beating heart cuddling up with her after a long day of crunching numbers and making insincere phone calls. It was heavenly. To thank Eli for her love, Teresa did something the vet begged her not to, and started to let the animal roam free outside. Teresa lived in a quiet part of Coconut Grove, with lots of trees for a cat to climb and few cars to run over her. Eli, ever wishful of freedom, had run far and fast the first day out, unsure whether she would come back. But memories of the mouse-ass food and the ear-scratching overcame her, and ten hours later, she was there, at Teresa's back door, mewing sweetly. After several weeks of this, Eli thought her keeper deserved a thank-you, and so dragged home a half-dead bird for Teresa to kill.

Teresa opened the door with her hair wild and graying, and screamed at the flopping feathered mess on the door-mat. She gripped the front of her paisley dress. "Oh, Eli, what did you do?"

"Meow," said Eli. The cat tilted its head and Teresa understood. It was an offering, a token of affection. A Gucci watch, from a cat.

"Eli," Teresa purred, scooping the cat into her arms and leaving the bird outside to its fate. She shut the door and carried the cat to the pantry for another can of mouse-ass. Teresa shed a tear as she pulled the pop-top. In her life, she'd had exactly three boyfriends. And none had ever been as thoughtful as this cat.

Teresa ate a wedge of cheese for breakfast with artificial-orange drink, because this was the sort of thing cat ladies ate. She tried to read the paper through Eli, who flipped and flopped across the broadsheet like a showgirl. Normally, Teresa cared less about what was in any section of the paper other than business, which pertained to her job. But today, the metro section wrote of a cat lady who'd died and left 341 cats homeless. The city was going to exterminate them all if people didn't rescue them. Three hundred cats! Teresa chewed her cheese and observed Eli.

"You know what your problem is?" she asked the cat. "You're a loner. You need friends."

Teresa had never been to an animal shelter before, and the sight and smell of the place made her want to cry. Hundreds of wet eyes stared at her, begging. Take me. She approached the counter and informed the volunteer that she could take home two of the cats left behind by the cat lady. The volunteer eyed Teresa's paisley dress with suspicion.

"Sorry, ma'am," she said. "Another…lady beat you to it. They're all gone."

Teresa felt tears of envy sting her eyes. "But I only wanted another cat." One of *her* cats, thought Teresa. The cat lady's cats.

"We have plenty of cats," said the volunteer. "But if you want *free* cats, you should go to the beach. The city's rounding up all the strays under the boardwalks, to kill them." She leaned forward. "I can tell you love cats," said the volunteer. "Save them."

Because Teresa expected to crawl beneath the boardwalk with the cat trap the volunteer at the shelter had loaned her, she did not wear the paisley dress to the beach. She wore a flirty pink velour J.Lo jogging suit she had promised herself she'd get rid of now that she was the same age as the singer/actress. It was the only exercise outfit she had left, and she wore it with white sneakers stained with pink mouse-ass splatters.

Teresa followed the volunteer's instructions and waited beneath the boardwalk, in the sand, listening to the people walking up above. They had no idea there was a society of felines down below, hundreds of them, going about their lives. The strays were skinny and wiry and wanted nothing to do with Teresa, no matter how many times she clicked her tongue gently at them. *It's like when the old Cuban men do that to me,* she thought. *I don't look at them.*

Teresa decided to stop trying to degrade the animals, and simply sat in silence. That is when she realized she was not alone among cats. Not twenty feet away, partially obscured by a wooden support beam, sat a man. She saw his toes first, then his knees, then his beer bottle. He was balding, but no less cute for it. At first she thought he might be homeless, and her blood ran cold. But then she saw the Old Navy T-shirt and trendy carpenter jeans in a dark blue color that indicated they were new. He also wore fashionable eyeglasses, and bracelets. No ring. Why was she still checking for that, especially here, under a bridge? His beer bottle dripped condensation, indicating it was cold, and had likely come from the ice chest he sat on. Seeing her, he smiled and tilted the beer bottle her way. Cats swirled around him, unafraid. They knew him, and liked him. He talked to the cats, touched them gently. He applied some sort of salve to the cut ear of one of the creatures, and forced pink liquid Teresa now recognized as cat antibiotic into another's mouth. He cleared his throat. And waved. Friendly. He looked comfortable here, as if he were sitting at a café table.

"Javier," he said. "Nice to meet you."

He had a beautiful smile.

"I'm Teresa, the cat lady," she said sullenly. Javier stood and opened the chest. He took out another beer and offered it to Teresa, laughing. He looked her up and down as she politely took the bottle.

"More like cat woman," he said.

Teresa blushed. "I'm thirty-five," she said, as if this explained something.

"I'm forty," he said.

"Oh," she said, surprised. "You don't look, I mean, the jeans and all."

He continued to smile. "It's too bad the city wants to kill them," he said.

"Horrible," she agreed. She watched the cats rub against his new jeans. "They seem to like you," she said.

"I'm a vet," he said.

"What war?" she asked. If he was forty, it would have to be, what? The Gulf War or something.

He laughed, but she hadn't meant it as a joke. Then she got it. He was a *vet*. As in *veterinarian*.

"I've always loved animals," he said.

"Me too," she lied. Then she decided that cat ladies didn't need to lie to impress men, because cat ladies no longer concerned themselves with men.

"No," she said. "That's not true. I've never had a pet until this year. I wasn't allowed."

"Wasn't allowed?" he asked.

"My mom," Teresa said with a sigh. "There were lots of things. No sneakers, no bike riding. No pop music."

"She sounds like my mom," he said.

"Really?" Teresa's heart fluttered again, against her will. He nodded kindly and she continued to speak. "I'm collecting cats because I swore to myself I would if I got this old and was still single."

He looked into her eyes for a brief moment, and looked away, blushing a little and smiling to himself. "Thus, the 'cat lady' thing," he said.

"Right," she said.

He chuckled to himself, and felt for lumps or something beneath the chin of one of the cats. "You don't dress like a cat lady," he said. "I know lots of cat ladies, trust me. Bread and butter of my business."

"No, I *do!*" she cried. "I usually do. I have this paisley dress I got at a thrift store. It's quite stained, with a frayed hem. It's perfect. Just today I didn't."

"You look nice today," he said. "You shouldn't dress like a cat lady."

"But I'm getting old," she said. "Cats love you no matter what you wear, unconditionally."

"That shows how little you know about cats," he said. "A real cat lady would never say something so misguided. Cats prefer cashmere."

Misguided. He was literate. Her heart beat faster yet. Did he say *cashmere?*

"So," he said to Teresa without looking at her. "How many cats do you have now?"

"One," she said.

He laughed, then apologized. "One? That's nothing. You have to have at least a hundred to qualify as a bona fide cat lady," he said.

"Why do you think I'm *here?*"

"These guys are feral," he said. "They'll never be happy as housecats, unless you take the kittens. That's what I'd suggest. The older ones are wild as raccoons."

Teresa watched the cats roll and play. "They seem tame around *you,*" she said.

He grinned, winked and raised one eyebrow. "I'm the cat whisperer," he said.

Cat whisperer? *Super* literate.

"What do you whisper to them?" she asked.

"Ancient Cuban secret," he said with an exaggerated Cuban-Spanish accent. He was Cuban? There *was* a God.

"You seem cheerful for a guy who knows his little friends are going to die," she said.

"It's called denial," he said simply.

Denial? Super literate, cute, smart—and up to date on psychobabble? Amazing.

Before she knew it, Teresa had blurted her thought into the air: "Why aren't you *married?*"

"Who says I'm not married?" He looked surprised.

"You don't wear a ring." He must be gay, she thought.

He looked at his hand. "No, I don't wear a ring."

"Gay?" she asked. He threw his head back and laughed loud enough to scare a few cats away.

"Not quite," he said. "I *was* married. She…was killed."

"Yikes. Sorry."

For a moment, Teresa wondered if *he* had killed his wife, and whether to scream now, run later, or run now, scream later.

He shrugged. "It was five years ago. Drunk driver."

He looked at her again, and smiled. He didn't look dangerous. He looked nice. Huggable. She didn't know if he meant the wife had been a drunk driver, or that a drunk driver had killed her; now was not the right time to ask, she decided. She noticed a book next to the cooler, a popular nonfiction hardcover about a political subject she agreed with.

"I'm sorry," she said again. *For thinking you were a murderer.* "About your wife."

"Don't be. It wasn't your fault."

"Good book," she said, changing the subject. She wondered if he had ever taught a child to ride a bike, and decided a cat woman would simply ask. She did.

He laughed again, a laugh like bells ringing. "I have a son. He's ten. I helped him learn to ride a bike, yes. You ask a lot of probing personal questions for a dried-up spinster," he added.

"Cat lady," she corrected him.

He shook his head. "Nah," he said. "Far as I'm concerned, you're ninety-nine cats short."

Teresa thought of Eli, and wondered how she'd adjust to a sibling. Not well, she imagined.

Javier cleared his throat again, and Teresa saw him blush.

"Listen," he said. "I don't usually meet girls here, but— you want to go get a bite to eat or something?"

Teresa nodded, almost too quickly. She felt the heat in her lower belly again and wondered if it was possible for a woman of thirty-five to go into heat.

Mami had always wanted Teresa to marry a doctor. A real doctor, not a cat doctor. But given her age and disposition, Javier would have to do. He wasn't even from a real Cuban-exile family, either. He was a Marielito, and *prieto.* But that's how it was with Teresa. You told her one thing, and she did the opposite, just to spite you.

Mami pulled her legs closer to her, scrunched up in her seat. Dogs everywhere! And cats. And birds. Whoever heard of a wedding open to animals? Teresa had lost her mind. And the wedding announcement in the *Herald?* It had Teresa's picture, but not her name. Instead of her name, it said "Cat Lady," and instead of Javier's name, it said "Pet Savior." They were crazy. They thought it was the funniest thing in the world. How crazy? So crazy that between them they now had nine cats, six dogs and God only knew how many hamsters, fish and birds. And something called a pig that didn't look like a pig. It looked like a rat.

"What is that thing they have in the cage?" she asked Papi.

"What?" Papi was distracted with shooing off a dog that insisted on sniffing his crotch.

"That thing, the furry thing they call a pig."

"Guinea pig," he said.

"Why would they want such a thing?" Mami wailed, dabbing her eyes with a tissue. A few of her daughter's new friends looked over from across the church and smiled, thinking Mami was crying in happiness for her daughter. She was in truth crying because her daughter was insane.

"Thank God they're too old to have children," Mami whispered to Papi.

He did not answer, but rather stared at a woman with a snake slithering across her breasts. Who were these people?

"Did you hear me?" she chided, slapping his arm.

"I heard you," said Papi. "She's going to have children. She's not too old yet. Now be quiet. Your daughter's wedding is about to start."

Sophie Kinsella is the author of *Can You Keep a Secret?*, *Confessions of a Shopaholic, Shopaholic Takes Manhattan* and *Shopaholic Ties the Knot*. She lives in London with her family and may also be spotted in shopping meccas around the world, credit card in hand. (Purely for research, of course....)

Changing People
by Sophie Kinsella

So we're sitting on the couch watching *Changing Rooms*, eating pizza, and Fizz, my flatmate, is deciding what she might do with her life. Fizz is what you would describe as "between jobs," if she'd ever had one. She's got a sheet of paper and list of "possibles," which so far consists of "corporate troubleshooter" and "taste-tester for Cadbury," both crossed out.

"Okay, what about...aromatherapist?" she exclaims. "I love all that kind of stuff. Massage, facials..."

"That would be good," I say. "You'd have to train, though. And buy all the oils."

"Really?" She pulls a face. "How much are they?"

"About...three quid each? Four, maybe?"

I'm not really concentrating on her—I'm looking at some people from Sevenoaks whose living room has just been transformed from chintzy blue into sleek, pale minimalism.

Their faces remind me of my parents when they came to meet me at the airport, after it had happened. They had the same wary eyes; the same mixture of anxiety and relief; the same initial shock, which they tried to mask beneath welcoming smiles. They gazed at me, searching for signs of the old Sarah—as these owners are peering disorientedly around their room, wondering where their curtains have gone.

"I can't believe the transformation!" someone is exclaiming. "In such a short time!"

I was away for ten months in all. Plus the two months in hospital. A year to change a person. Linda Barker would do it quicker.

I open my mouth to say something about this to Fizz. Something about change, about growing up. But she's gesticulating wildly, her mouth full of pizza. She often does this, Fizz. Monopolizes airtime. *I'm thinking—therefore no one else may speak.*

"I've got it!" she says at last. "I'll be an interior designer!"

"An interior designer!" I echo, trying to hit the right note of support. "Do you know anything about interior design?"

"You don't have to know anything!" She gestures to the screen. "Look at that. It's easy!"

"I wouldn't say 'easy,' exactly…"

"All you need is loads of lilac paint and some MDF…"

"Oh really?" I raise my eyebrows. "So what does MDF stand for, then?" Fizz shoots me a cross look.

"It stands for…micro…dynamic…federal… Anyway, that's not the point. I won't be bloody Handy Andy, will I? I'll be the person with creative vision and flair."

I roll my eyes and take a swig of wine. I know I should be more supportive. But the thing is, I *have* been more supportive. I was supportive all through the writing-a-film-script phase, the opening-a-dancing-school phase and "Dial-A-Dessert—we'll deliver a freshly made pudding to your door!" That last one might actually have been a winner if we hadn't ended up buying ingredients worth about two hundred pounds in order to deliver one small trifle to West Norwood.

I say *we,* by the way, because somehow I always end up getting dragged into Fizz's little schemes.

"Fizz—listen—why does it always have to be some great entrepreneurial plan? Why don't you get a job?"

"Get a job?" she says, as though I'm mad. "Everyone knows it's impossible to get jobs these days."

"It's not impossible. You get a paper, look through the adverts—"

"Oh, right. Easy. So I'll just apply for…" she grabs the *Evening Standard.* "For…Product Unit Manager (retail), shall I? Look, I get a company car, and a pension. Ooh, goody."

"Not that sort of job…"

"It's all right for you! You're still a student!"

"Yes," I say patiently, "and when I finish my thesis, I'll get a job."

"Yeah well…" She sighs. "God, it's all such bloody hard work, isn't it? I mean look at her." She gestures at Mrs. Sevenoaks. "I wish I could just get married and do nothing." She takes a thoughtful bite of pizza. "Hey, Sarah, when you were engaged, were you going to give up work?"

"No," I say after a pause. "No I wasn't." And before she can ask anything else, I change the subject.

There's a lot of things I don't talk about to Fizz. In fact, there's a lot of things I don't talk about to anyone. Part of me is afraid that if I once started talking, I'd never stop.

I was twenty-two and thought I owned the world. The first time he asked me to marry him, I laughed in his face. The second time I shrugged, the third time I agreed. We bought a ring; he talked to my parents. But I couldn't take it seriously. Even when he was telling me he loved me, I barely listened. I used to act like a spoilt kid around him. It was like the time my parents gave me a watch for my seventh birthday. They wrapped it up in layers and layers of papers, and I got so impatient, ripping it all off, I cried, "There's nothing in here, is there?" and threw the whole lot in the bin.

My parents should have just left it there. If my father hadn't screwed up his sleeve and reached, grimacing, into the mess of tea leaves and eggshells, maybe I would have learned a lesson. That sometimes you throw things away and no one, not even your dad, can get them back for you.

When Fizz tells me three weeks later that she's got her first appointment with a client, I nearly drop down dead with astonishment.

"It's an Arabella Lennox, in Kensington. She saw my insert in *Homes & Gardens*!"

"You put an insert in *Homes & Gardens*? My God, Fizz, how much does that cost?"

"I didn't pay, you moron. I went to Smiths on the King's Road and when they weren't looking, I slipped a load of leaflets into all the posh magazines. Felicity Silton, Interior Consultant. Our appointment's at two."

"*Our* appointment?" I echo suspiciously.

"You're my assistant." She looks up and sees my face. "Oh, go on, Sarah, I need an assistant, otherwise they'll think I'm crap."

"I don't want to be your crummy assistant! I'll be your partner."

"You can't be my partner. It's not a partnership."

"All right then…your creative design consultant."

There's a pause while Fizz thinks about this.

"Okay," she says grudgingly. "You can be my creative design consultant. But don't say anything."

"What if I have some really good ideas?"

"I don't need ideas. I already know what I'm going to do. Designer's Guild wallpaper and huge candles everywhere. I've found a rather wonderful local source for those, actually," she adds smugly.

"Where?" I ask, intrigued in spite of myself.

"The pound shop! And we can charge her a tenner for each one."

Arabella Lennox has short blond hair and widely mascared eyes, and sits on an old piano stool while Fizz and I sit side by side on the sofa.

"As you can see," she says, gesturing around, "the whole place needs an overhaul."

I look around at the fading paintwork, the wooden shutters, the battered leather chair by the fireplace. There's a bookshelf by the fire and I run my eyes over the spines of the books. I've read most of them. Or I'm intending to.

"It's not my style at all," she adds, adjusting her pearls on her cashmere cardigan.

No, really?

"My…" I see her weighing up a choice of words. "My…chap has handed over the job to me to do. Or rather, I insisted!" Arabella gives a little tinkly laugh. "I mean, if I'm going to live here one day… It's hardly the lap of luxury, is it? And all these awful old books everywhere."

"So you're moving in here?" says Fizz. She's writing on her notepad and doesn't see Arabella's face tighten.

"Well. I mean, it's the next obvious step, isn't it? And when he sees what a fabulous job I've done with the place…I'm sure he'll come round." She leans forward earnestly. "I want to transform it. Bring in bright colors, and some lovely gilt mirrors, and lots of chandeliers… My favorite color is pink, by the way."

"Pink…chandeliers," says Fizz, scribbling on her notepad with a serious expression. I look over, see that she's written *Barbie's Fairy Palace,* and try to conceal a giggle. "I really must say, you've got some fantastic ideas there, Arabella."

"Thank you!" she dimples. "So—did you have any initial ideas for this room?"

"I was thinking…" Fizz pauses consideringly. "Off the

top of my head…Designer's Guild wallpaper—in pink, of course—and candles. Candles everywhere."

"Ooh, I love candles!" trills Arabella. "They're so romantic."

"Good!" says Fizz, scribbling again. "I'm afraid they *are* rather expensive…"

"That's okay." Arabella gives a coy smile. "Dee-Dee has given me a very generous budget."

"Your boyfriend is called Dee-Dee?" I say disbelievingly.

"It's what I call him," says Arabella. "I love pet-names. Don't you?"

"Well," I say. "For a pet, perhaps."

Arabella stares at me, eyes narrowed.

"What's your role, exactly?" she says.

"I'm the creative design consultant," I reply pleasantly. "Plus, I'm a qualified specialist in mantelpiece adornment."

Arabella gives me a puzzled look.

"So you advise on…?"

"Which *objet* to place where," I say, nodding. "It's a very underrated skill."

We all turn our heads to look at the mantelpiece in this room, which is bare apart from a box of matches.

"If you like," I say generously, "I'll throw in a mantelpiece consultation for free."

"Really?" Arabella's eyes widen. "That would be great!" She peers more closely at me. "You don't mind me mentioning it—but is there something wrong with your face? Under your chin. Is it psoriasis? Because my beautician says—"

"No," I say, cutting her off. "It's not psoriasis." I smile at her. "But thank you for drawing my attention to it."

"Let's look at the rest of the flat," says Fizz firmly. "Okay?" And as she gets up she gives my hand a sympathetic squeeze.

We walk through the spacious hall, and I can hear Fizz blathering on quite impressively about proportions and color palettes. Then we turn down a little corridor towards the bedroom. There's an abstract painting hanging up above the door, which sends an unpleasant little twinge to my chest as I glance at it. Because it looks very like...

It looks almost exactly like...

As I get near, my heart starts to thump. I run my eyes quickly over the canvas, looking for discrepancies. It can't be the same. It can't. But it is. I know every square inch; every brush stroke of this painting. Of course I know it. I helped to choose it.

I stare up at it, transfixed; unable to breathe.

"Oh, the painting," says Arabella, turning back. "Yes, it's quite nice, isn't it? Not really my thing, but apparently the painter is quite up-and-coming. He's—"

"Spanish," I hear myself saying.

"Yes!" she says, and eyes me in surprise. "Goodness, you do know your stuff, don't you?"

"Where did you get it?" My voice is too urgent; too clumsy.

"It's not mine," she says. "It belongs to my chap. So this is the bedroom..."

I follow her numbly into the room. And now, of course, I'm seeing the signs everywhere, like fingerprints appearing under dust. The old leather trunk. The books in the living room.

I glance at myself in the mirror—and my face has drained of color.

"Ooh, look!" says Fizz, spying a photograph by the bed. "Is that him? Is that your chap?"

"Yes, that's him!" beams Arabella. "That's Dee-Dee. Of course, his real name is David—"

I saw it coming; I had the four-minute warning. But hearing his name again is like being hammered in the stomach.

"Excuse me," I say. "I…I don't feel well. I think I'll go and wait outside."

"Are you okay, Sarah?" says Fizz, and puts a hand on my arm.

"I'll be fine," I manage. "Really. I just need to sit in the fresh air for a bit."

As I walk blindly back down the corridor, towards the front door, I can hear Fizz explaining: "She was in this car crash in Peru a couple of years ago…"

We used to tease each other about sleeping with other people. I used to pretend I fancied his friend, Jon. I used to flirt outrageously. It was all a big joke. Even when I found myself letting Jon slip his hand inside my shirt; even when I agreed to meet him for secret lunches, it was still supposed to be a joke. A kind of a game. Look, your friend fancies me! Look, I've been to bed with him! I still prefer you, though. Of course I do. I was just playing around, silly! When he found out, I felt a thud of fear—but still I thought I was invincible. I thought he would forgive everything, if I explained properly. I practiced my kittenish phrases; put on my most charming smile.

Somehow it didn't work. I couldn't make him understand; couldn't get past the betrayal in his face. When I tried to touch him, he flinched. When I tried to laugh, it was a shrill, grating noise, like nails on a blackboard. He called me very young and said that I would grow up. That was the worst bit of all. The disappointment in his voice as he said it.

Can you believe, Arabella fell for Fizz's spiel? And to my amazement, Fizz seems to be doing a pretty good job of it. She's found a friendly local decorator named Danny, and she seems to spend most days over there, drinking coffee with Arabella and flicking through magazines and wallpaper books. They go out for lunch, too—which Fizz can afford, because of the enormous down payment she's managed to extract from Arabella, her New Best Friend.

To be fair, she's invited me along a few times, but I've always managed to invent excuses. Not that I don't listen to all the details of Arabella's life with a kind of masochistic fascination.

"What's 'the chap' like?" I ask casually one day. I cannot bring myself to say "Dee-Dee."

"Dunno," says Fizz vaguely. "He's abroad all the time." She starts giggling. "God knows what he's going to think of his flat when he gets back. You know Arabella's latest idea?"

"What?"

"Gold tassels on all the light switches. For that luxury touch."

"As creative design consultant," I say, "I'm afraid I veto that."

"Too late, I've bought them! Six quid each, I'm charging her."

"Where from?"

"The pound shop."

Then, overnight, the New Best Friendship disintegrates. Fizz has a huge row with Arabella over the placement of a curtain tie-back (something like that, anyway), and Arabella threatens to sack her. She complains that Fizz's taking far too long and she wants the sitting room finished now.

"Stupid cow," says Fizz, when she's finished telling me. "Stupid stuck-up cow! We're supposed to be friends." She takes a swig of wine and eyes me wildly. "Listen, Sarah, you have to help me."

"What?" I say apprehensively. "What do you mean, help you?"

"I told her I'd get the sitting room finished by tomorrow. Danny's buggered off, leaving one wall unpapered."

"Why did he bugger off?" I say suspiciously.

"He always wants cash up-front. And I've kind of…" She bites her lip. "Run out of money."

"Oh, Fizz!"

"Look, Sarah, you know how to paper walls. I've seen you."

Unfortunately, this is true.

"Please, Sarah," she wheedles. "Just this once. I'll owe you forever. Otherwise, Arabella's going to sue me!"

Oh God, I always fall for her blarney.

"Will anyone be there?"

"No!" says Fizz confidently. "It'll be completely empty."

We arrive at the flat just as dusk is falling. As Fizz lets us in, I can't help gasping. The place is transformed from when I saw it last—all pastel paint colors and stencils of grapes.

"Where's that abstract painting gone?" I ask as we walk down the corridor. "It was up there."

"Dunno," says Fizz vaguely. "Arabella never liked it, apparently. And it doesn't go with the stencilling, so…okay." She opens the door of the sitting room. "Here's your paper…and here's your ladder."

"What do you mean, *my* ladder?"

"Oh, I can't stay," says Fizz in surprise. "I've got a meeting with another client."

"What?" I exclaim. "What other bloody client? You're expecting me to do this alone?"

"I'll be back as soon as I can, I promise," she says, blowing me a kiss. "Look, there's hardly anything left to do. Take you five minutes."

She disappears out of the room and I hear the front door slam. I know I should feel furious with her. I should walk out and leave her in her own mess. But I'm feeling too confused to move, or even feel angry. I'm in David's flat, alone.

I look slowly around, trying to see some clues of his life amid the pinkness. It's been three years since I saw him. What's happened in that time? What kind of person is he now?

I sidle over to a side table and am cautiously opening a drawer, when there's a sound at the door. Quickly, I close the drawer and hurry back to the ladder.

"Hello!" says Arabella from the doorway. "Just popped back for my umbrella. Fizz told me you were coming. Doesn't it look good?"

"Lovely," I say politely. "It's very smart. Except…"

"Except what?"

I rub my face, not sure how to say it.

"Arabella, are you sure your…chap is going to like it?"

"Of course he is!" she says. "It was a horrible hotchpotch before. This is a finished look."

"But don't you think…wouldn't he prefer…"

"I think I know my own boyfriend," snaps Arabella defensively. "He's going to love it."

"But—"

"Do you have a boyfriend, Sarah?"

"No," I say after a pause. "No, I don't."

Arabella's eyes run dismissively over my face and I can see the words *no wonder* forming above her head in a thought-bubble. Then she taps out of the room—and a moment later I hear the front door closing.

I stare at the empty wall in front of me. Clean and prepared, ready to be papered. The wallpaper is ready, all cut into lengths. Fizz is right—it'll take no time.

But something is building up inside me; something hot and heavy, like a scream.

Before I can stop myself, I'm reaching for a paintbrush and a pot. I'm opening the pot and dipping the brush in, and writing on the blank, empty wall.

Things you don't know about David.

1. He hates pink.

I breathe out, feeling a small satisfaction. And then, almost at once, I'm dipping the brush in again, and scrawling some more.

2. If he says he likes being called Dee-Dee, he's lying.

3. He used to kiss my hair goodnight.

I write and write, feverishly dragging the ladder to the wall, using up nearly a whole pot of paint. Soon I'm not just writing about David, I'm writing about me—about all the mistakes I made, all the regrets I've had.

About my months abroad, about South America, about the crash. The way the plastic surgeons skillfully rebuilt my face afterwards. How although I recognized myself, it was a different me.

Like a junkie, I just can't stop. Words and words; everything I've wanted to say for years and never have.

When I've finished, the whole wall is covered in writing and I'm exhausted. I lie on the floor for a long while, staring up at the ceiling rose. At last, calmly, I get up. I have a drink of water, and take a deep breath. Then I mix my paste, climb up the ladder again and begin to paste length after length of fuchsia pink paper to the wall.

Just as I'm on the last length I hear a key in the lock of the front door.

"If you're here to help, you're too late," I call out cheerfully. I'm feeling happier than I have for months. It's an effort, putting up wallpaper by yourself, and I know my bad leg will throb tomorrow. But even so, I feel as though months of tension have drained away, leaving me light and optimistic. As I turn to greet Fizz, I'm actually smiling.

Except it's not Fizz.

We stare at each other in a shocked silence. The air seems to be prickling at my face.

"Hi," I say at last in a strangled voice.

"Hi." David puts his hand to his head. "What—what are you—"

"I'm helping out. It's a...it's a long story..." My voice doesn't seem to be working properly. Suddenly I remember I haven't pasted down the last length of paper. I turn back to the wall and quickly smooth it flat. When I look back, he's watching me with that look.

"Are you all right? You look...different. Your face..."

I duck my head down and lift my hands defensively to my chin, feeling the familiar scar line; the rough scar tissue which will never go away.

"I'm fine," I say, running my eyes over the papered wall, searching for bubbles. But it's perfect. A flawless finish. "I...I have to go. It should dry all right if you just leave it."

As I gather my things, my hands are trembling. I look up, and see that he's finally noticed the wallpaper.

"I didn't choose it," I mutter as I pass him. "Don't blame me."

* * *

A few weeks go by, and Fizz has somehow snaffled two new clients, who occupy all her waking thoughts. I don't hear an awful lot more about David or Arabella—until Fizz tells me I've been invited to the "new-look flat christening party." Fizz is determined to use it as a promotional event and equally determined I should come, too. She dismisses all my excuses and keeps demanding, "Why not?" And after a while I start to think, "Why not?" myself. I'm strong enough to face him. I can do it.

Besides which I have a secret desire to see him being called "Dee-Dee" in public.

When we arrive, people are milling around in the hall, gazing at all the stencils and gold tassels and pound-shop candles with shell-shocked expressions on their faces.

"What do you think?" says Fizz to me. "It's frightful, isn't it?" She giggles. "But it's what Arabella wanted. She thought it was fabulous." She takes a sip of wine. "Quite ironic they split up, really."

I freeze, glass halfway to my lips.

"Split up? What do you mean, split up?"

"Didn't I tell you? They had some huge row. About the wallpaper, apparently! I did recommend something more subtle, but she just wouldn't listen…"

I take a sip of wine, trying to stay calm.

"Fizz, you know, I think I might leave."

"You can't go! We've only just—David! Hello!"

"Fizz," I hear him saying behind me. "You made it."

"Absolutely! And this is Sarah, my creative design consultant." She pulls at my shoulder and I find myself forced to turn round.

I've prepared a formal, polite expression—but at the sight of his warm, brown gaze, I feel it starting to slip.

"We've met," says David. "Haven't we, Sarah?"

"So!" says Fizz, swigging back her wine and pouring another one. "Doesn't it all look fab? Let's go and look at the sitting room! The *pièce de résistance*!"

"Yes," says David, and shoots me a swift glance. "I think you might be quite interested to see that."

"So sorry to hear about you and Arabella," I can hear Fizz saying as we walk across the hall. "Was it really the wallpaper?"

"Not the wallpaper, exactly—" he replies, and opens the door to the sitting room with a flourish.

And my heart stops still.

The facing wall is completely blank. All that fuchsia-pink paper I put up has gone—and it's been repainted in a light, spring-like color.

"Hang on!" says Fizz, peering puzzledly ahead. "What's happened to the wallpaper? Who pulled it off?"

"I did," says David.

"But why?"

"Good question," says David. "I had a hunch I might like to see it uncovered." He shoots me a deadpan look. "And I'm pleased I did. It was very…illuminating."

My heart's thudding. I can't meet his eye. All those things I wrote. Things about him, about me, about Arabella. In huge painted letters, from ceiling to floor.

"But what did Arabella say?" Fizz's demanding. "Wasn't she furious?"

"Arabella?" He pauses thoughtfully. "I have to admit—she wasn't too pleased. Especially when she saw the evidence."

"Well, I'm not surprised!" says Fizz. "I mean, that wallpaper wasn't cheap! Designer's Guild, twenty-eight quid a roll. I mean…thirty-eight quid," she hastily amends, "including unavoidable surcharges. It's all perfectly clear on the invoice…"

"What do you think, Sarah?" says David lightly. "Do you think I made the right choice? Or should I have left it as it was?"

I can feel the blood pulsing in my ears. My fingers are slippery around my glass.

"I think you made the right choice." I say at last. "Because now at least you know."

He's staring straight at me, and very slowly, I tilt my face upwards. I see his eyes running over the scar line along my chin. The place where they made a new me.

"So listen, David," says Fizz, leaning forward confidentially. "Tell me honestly, I won't be hurt. Do you *like* this decor?"

"Truthfully?" He takes a swig of wine. "I loathe it."

"Me, too!" says Fizz. "Isn't it awful? But it's what Arabella wanted. A Barbie palace. Barbie and Dee-Dee."

"I miss what I used to have," says David, and his brown eyes meet mine with a sudden affection. "Whether it's ever possible to go back… What do you think, Sarah?"

There's a long silence.

"Not go back, exactly," I say. "But maybe…start over?"

"Well!" Fizz's voice rings out triumphantly. "You're in luck, because my new venture offers exactly that service. 'Restore-a-room. Has a designer wrecked your house? We'll put things back the way you always liked them—but better!' Honestly, this one is going to be a complete winner..."

Jill A. Davis is the author of *Girls' Poker Night*. She was a writer for *Late Show with David Letterman* where she received five Emmy nominations. She has also written several network pilots, screenplays and short stories. She lives in New York with her husband and daughter.

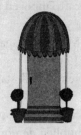

New York
by Jill A. Davis

Monday

My boss is a nightmare. She resembles every gym teacher I've ever had.

Anyway, this is my first day on the job—my very first day on the job. She calls me into her office. It's time for the traditional welcome-aboard speech. The if-you-need-anything-just-ask speech. I know that my assigned response is to reiterate how excited I am to be here at *IT* magazine. *IT*'s such an honor to make so little yet work so hard.

Instead, the boss had a warning for me: "Anne, you need to spiff it up," she says.

"Excuse me?" I say.

"Your blazer. It's not pressed," she says.

Okay, admittedly, not the welcome I was expecting.

She takes a deep breath, annoyed that I haven't coughed up an excuse or apology.

"You represent us. Me. This magazine," she says.

"In my cubicle…" I say.

"And in your cubicle you'll stay—dressed like that," says Carly.

It's a fine cubicle. I've got no complaints about the cubicle. But I think the implied demotion is what's troubling me. All based on a slightly creased jacket?

"What if we need to send you to interview someone? We simply couldn't. Not dressed like that," she says.

I didn't sleep in it, for fuck's sake.

"Point taken," I say. "Thank you for bringing it to my attention."

I dart for the door in complete humiliation. Her voice grabs me before I reach it.

"There's more," she says. This is followed by a very long pause, which gives me time to slowly turn around and face my tormentor.

"The hair…" she says.

"The hair," I repeat. I use a knowing tone, indicating I know exactly what she is talking about. We are conspirators in this recognition of disgrace. Except—I do not know what "the hair" means.

Is there hair on my blazer? Are we discussing leg hair? Is "the hair" possibly a nickname for one of our co-workers who I've yet to meet? The hair on my head? Could we be talking about the hair on my head? I've never discussed hair of any kind with any boss—so I know not of what hair she speaks. Besides, and this is the chilling part: Today is a very good hair day for me—not that I've ever been the type to borrow pop moronic phrases like "good hair day" but in this situation I think it applies.

"Who does your hair?" she says in a voice that suggests she might be considering filing a restraining order against him so he can do no more harm.

"Who does *your* hair?" I ask.

Carly scribbles the name Fabian on a piece of paper along with a phone number. At lunchtime, I trot off and spend a hundred and fifty dollars on a haircut I can't afford. And now...I look like a gym teacher, too.

New York is harder than I thought it would be. And New York is easier than I thought it would be.

After lunch I go to the ladies' room to check out the new haircut for the, well, let's be conservative and call it the fifth time. The other women from the lifestyle department pack into the bathroom waiting patiently to puke up their lunch. This is the female version of the shoeshine line. They just shoot the breeze, read newspapers and file their nails until it's their turn to heave.

They all dress the same. Wear the same perfume. And they're all named something deriving from the name Elizabeth: Liz, Lisbeth, Beth, Betsy, Lizzie, Liza, Eliza, Bizzy.

They drop to their knees at the altar of thinness and heave up their lattes and salads. If you're going to heave it up— why not go to town and have spaghetti with meatballs?

You can never overestimate the importance of being thin in New York City. And the Elizabeths are no slackers. When it comes to blowing lunch, these women rule.

When I'm at my desk, I can hear the sounds. The disgusting puking sounds. But by midafternoon, it's white noise. The noise of my new landscape. There is a rhythm to it.

If the Elizabeths harnessed all of the energy they spend in pursuit of inexpensive frozen margaritas and "cute boys," they would own the magazine. And in a way, they already own the world. This shiny corner of it. I guess I should be grateful that they haven't confused pretty with capable, though I think they could get away with it.

Tuesday

I've spent the better part of today doing exactly what I did on day one: writing lame blurbs under photographs of glamorous parties.

I use words like *pensive, sultry, myopic.*... The Elizabeths describe dresses as fun, and sassy, and "this season's must have" clogs...clutch...jumpsuit.

I've decided I may begin smoking out of sheer boredom. If you're a smoker, you get a break every few hours and you get to go stand out on Fifth Avenue and inhale carcinogens with other disgusting people who smoke. *Any* club is better than no club, right?

Someone said they saw Andy Rooney almost get hit by a car today. I'll never see stuff like that sitting all the way up here.

The good news is that earlier I looked through the Yellow Pages and I found three hypnotists. Would they be willing to hypnotize me and use the power of suggestion to get me to start smoking? Two said no. One said, "Yes, for forty dollars."

Did I mention that since getting my new haircut, I'm the

darling of *IT* magazine? I find popularity unsettling and hope it will soon pass. And then I will get to long for it and crave it.

The gym teacher could not be nicer to me. But maybe that's all part of her diabolical plan.

It's after lunch—congratulate me. Thanks to the wonderful world of hypnosis, I'm now a smoker. After all of the hocus-pocus I immediately walked over to Nat Sherman's and bought some mint cigarettes and the most adorablicious (actual word invented by one of the Elizabeths to describe a dress that wasn't just adorable, and not just delicious but a happy marriage of the two) sterling-silver pocket ashtray. If I'd known about the cute little ashtrays I'd have started smoking years ago. I feel like a coma victim, waking up to discover she'd squandered the most precious years of her life.

Anyway, I started smoking my mint cigarettes on the way back to the office and the cutest boy in the cutest starter suit said: You know each one of those cancer sticks will take seven minutes off of your life. So cute, but sooo stupid!

The seven minutes is a reference to the amount of time it takes to smoke a cigarette, bonehead.

"Let's talk about it over dinner," he says.

"As long as there's a smoking section," I say.

I know what you're thinking. What? She's meeting men on the street now? Forgive me, a smoker who looks like a gym teacher hasn't the luxury of playing hard to get.

After smoking all those cigarettes I threw up. Apparently smoking is like exercising. You need to approach it sensibly. I never should have smoked an entire pack. But they really are like yummy chocolates. Have just one? How can you! My heaving put me in good favor with the Elizabeths. They believe I am a convert to their eating disorder.

Wednesday

I've got some great news! Or, in Elizabeth-speak, fun-tabulous news! Carly aka the cow liked the piece I wrote about being hypnotized to smoke. Thought it was clever. She said to make some small changes and then it's a go.

I called home and my father said it was terrific news. And says the ashtray and the hypnotist are both tax deductible. If that's how it works, perhaps my next project will be a gals' guide to top-shelf liquors.

When the issue hits the stands my father says he plans to buy up every copy. They don't sell *IT* magazine back home. But it was nice of him to say. I am picturing my byline. Anne S. Wheeland (the woman who has no one to share her joy with but her parents).

You know how everyone says New Yorkers are nuts? Well, at dinner Henry didn't seem so nuts. Then he let it slip that he was born in Hoboken.

He took me to his "club" because it's the only place left in New York to smoke, he says. I told him we didn't really have to go somewhere that allowed smoking. He insisted. He said it was the polite thing to do.

Back home the men are polite, too. But they're different. They could be falling in love with another woman and still tell you that they love you. They're dangerous men. And I always did fall for the dangerous ones.

I keep remembering when I left last Saturday. Her voice. I hear it perfectly.

"No stunts," she said. "Problems are patient, they'll be waiting for you when you come home." The screen door slammed behind me. I threw my suitcase into the back of the taxi. I looked up at the house for a moment. I memorized my mother's silhouette in the doorway. My father glanced up from his drink, and the TV, and waved.

"I love you," I said. And then I promised myself I'd never go back. Not to them, and not to him.

No stunts, mother said. No stunts. I cannot travel far enough away from that voice. I want to cry when I think of her saying that to me. One bad decision and I am a person who pulls "stunts."

Thursday

Today the piece was typeset. Fourteen column inches! Now I am absolutely certain I will die before the next issue hits the newsstands.

I've been alive a little more than two decades and I have done nothing. I would like to have my obituary set in 78-point type, to take up a lot of room and make it look as if I actually *did* something while I was here. Except, there's no one in my life who likes me enough to get that creative on my behalf. How sad.

Everyone pads obituaries. It's a well-known fact. It's done every day. So and so was a lifelong member of the Kiwanis Club... Yeah, yeah. Sure. Sure. Who's going to check?

★ ★ ★

I have lunch with Carly and the publisher, Samuel Manley. Hell of a name for any man to have to live up to each and every day. But I can't focus on that because I'm obsessed with what seems like must have been a mix-up, in that I was invited to this lunch at all. But I didn't mention it, and neither did they. We were all in cahoots and too embarrassed to bring the mistake to center stage.

"Most new employees are too intimidated to touch the computer the entire first week they start working here," Mr. Manley says. "And you, Anne, on your second day write a column that we will feature in our next issue. That, my dear— sorry, that, Anne, is why we are having this celebratory lunch."

Good cover-up, I'm thinking.

"Wait," I say. "You mean I could have done *nothing*—for a few *weeks*?"

He laughs. I used to be able to make Nick laugh, too.

"Carly says great things about you," he says.

"Thank you, Mr. Manley. I could not be more grateful to you, Carly and *IT* magazine," I say. "Truly, I mean this. As you are aware, it has long been a dream of mine to work for your magazine. When I say 'long' I mean since September 1997 when your fine example of gloss was launched."

They laugh. I'm not exactly sure why. And it's all sort of true. When the magazine was first published I had a subscription. And I read it not for its content, but for its massive number of typos, which was really something of a marvel.

Anyway, the Elizabeths—they all hate me now. I didn't even have a chance to hate them. They seemed okay to me.

I mean, okay enough to have coffee with now and then. Okay enough to see a movie with.

When I got to work this morning there was a package waiting for me. Inside was a gold pen from my father. "Dear Anne, The keeper of words wise and sweet, be true in verse and heart. Love, Dad." It was so warm and melodic and it reminded me that he is one of those dangerous men. Sometimes I'm just sure you never really know anyone.

Friday

The entire city smells of trash. Carly assures me it's only this smelly in the summer. I feel like my lungs are being coated with toxic dust. Like my organs need to be vacuumed. I imagine my blood is thick and sticky with bugs and germs just stagnating in it. And when I blow my nose, black soot comes out.

I got my first paycheck today. Depressing! I'll never be able to afford rent and cigarettes. I still have some money left from my work at the newspaper. But I didn't want to spend that money just yet. That's my run-away-from-the-world, don't-ever-call-home money.

On my lunch break I sat on the steps of the public library with the concrete lions. Every other man who walked by looked like Nick. And it made me want to go home. Not home actually, but to be someplace familiar. To be in a car and know where I am going. To drive by and see Mrs. Hathaway's white house, and see her balancing on tiptoe, hoisting a watering can over her head and drenching the hanging geraniums on her porch.

Good news. Carly just called me into her office. She promoted me to general assignment writer. Gave me a raise. I'm happy to report that my allegiance to smoking has been renewed.

"Don't let them bother you," she says. "They're just parking here until they get married. They're too worried about breaking away from the pack."

I wanted to tell her I am just like them. I'm terrified of not being liked—but if I tell her, maybe she won't like me.

The next thing I know, Carly and Manley and I are sitting, eating thirty-dollar hamburgers at the 21 Club. And then, a fourth person joins us. Carly's husband, James. Apparently she doesn't wear a ring for fear the street goons will cut her fingers off or something.

"Isn't it more about not letting people know you aren't really married to your job?" I say.

That silences the table. What's wrong with me?

"So, Anne, I hear you're on some kind of meteoric rise at the magazine," James says. "How is it that you came to New York?"

"James," I say, "it's no big secret. There are these tin things nowadays called buses."

There is no polite way to tell this kind man, or anyone else, the truth. My unfaithful husband. The mental hospital. The hair-dryer incident. The good thing about the bin, I could have explained, was not having to decide what to wear every day. But it never got that far. I should have stayed long enough to acquire a charming story or two.

Mr. Manley…it's so depressing that I think of him as Mr. Manley and that I come from a backward place where women call men mister…even if he's only ten years (a guess) older.

He stared at me. Those big brown eyes. They were just focused right on me throughout the whole meal. Perhaps he instinctively knew he was dining with an outpatient and was being careful not to let the knives out of his sight. To use a ninth-grade description, it felt as though he was eavesdropping on my soul.

"Knock it off," I say.

He smiles.

Carly blushes. James blushes. And of course, I just about die.

Saturday

I didn't get up until noon. Went shopping for a nice big heavy ashtray for my new office...newest office.

I bought blinds for the windows in my apartment. The poor guy across the street will have to buy a TV or something now. The phone rang six different times. I was happy not to answer it. It allowed me to imagine who it could have been.

Sunday

I can't help but think about Nick. Uninvited, he has a way of creeping across my thoughts. Then I looked at the date on the newspaper. Today is our first wedding anniversary. And there is something sad about Sundays anyway.

There's someone out there for everyone. But what if there is only *one* someone for everyone? What if I was meant to live in my hometown with a dishonest man?

There are things to run away from. And there are things to confront. Nick was someone to run from, and for a day or two maybe I thought I was going crazy. And I did attempt to check myself into the state hospital, but when they tried to take my hair dryer away, I snapped out of it. It turns out, that in many cases, mental hospitals are for people who can't afford a few days at Canyon Ranch.

I was staring at the hair dryer. Contemplating.

"Why would you take this away?" I asked the intake nurse.

"You might try to injure yourself with it," she said.

"It's a hair dryer..." I said.

"You could hang yourself. Scald yourself. Electrocute yourself," the nurse said, bored, and then she continued in greater detail.

"I could have done those things at home with any number of objects," I said. "Besides, I'm no engineer. I couldn't figure out half of the things you just described."

"Maybe you need a drink, not a hospital," she said.

We went and had a beer during her break. That's when I decided to move to New York. I was always afraid to move to New York. Now I had nothing to fear. I'd already made the biggest mistake of my life.

The day before I left for Manhattan, Nick called. My mother handed me the phone. She wore a hopeful look. Her happiness makes me want to do things that don't insure my happiness. Perhaps reconciliation was not out of the question, her eyes said. Maybe New York City *was* out of the question.

"Hello, Nick," I said.

"I don't know what to say," he said.

Sure, sure. Turn my life ass-over-teakettle and then call me and try to get me to do all the talking and make you feel okay.

"You deserved better," he said. It sounded like a question. You deserved better…I'm not even sure I did. After all, I married a man who had a tattoo of Sylvester the Cat on his thigh. A permanent child. I run toward red flags.

Of course, it's not Nick who I can't forgive. And it's not Nick I need to prove something to.

Henry calls. Just in time. Yes, I'm free, I tell him. Dinner at Da Silvano? Yes, sounds great.

Replacing one drug with another is no way to live one's life. I know that. But he's cute, and today is my first wedding anniversary. The menu will count as paper.

Emily Barr is the author of *Backpack*, *Baggage* and *Cuba*. She started out as a journalist, but changed direction when a year traveling led to her first novel, *Backpack*. She met her husband on the road, and they now live in the south of France with their two young sons. Her new novel, *Solo*, will be published in the U.S. in 2004.

Revenge
by Emily Barr

As I hold the binoculars to my eyes, the wind whips
through my hair, and I see the thing I have been waiting
for, and dreading. On the mainland, heading in my direction, is a white car. I follow its progress for a few seconds.
In a couple of minutes, it will cross the causeway and stop
while the passenger gets out and opens the gate. It will move
forward a couple of meters, and wait for the passenger to
close it again.

I know the men who are inside. I met them both in the
pub last week. In fact I knew the younger one years ago,
when I used to come to the island as a child. Then he was
skinny, with permanently scabby knees. Now, he's quite
handsome. They were both friendly to me last week, but
they won't be friendly now. Usually I like having visitors.
It's a rare event, and it breaks the solitude. It stops me thinking about what I've done. I do not, however, plan to wel-

come these guests. They are the police, and they have come to arrest me.

I knew it would happen sooner or later. In a way, I am almost relieved. I have no chance of getting away, but my instincts still urge me to try. I've got this far. I have hung onto my freedom, and I won't give it up without a struggle. I'll be in trouble for the rest of my life. I rush inside and wrap myself up in coats and scarves.

I give myself a quick glance in the hall mirror, as if anyone here cares what I look like. I never wear makeup now, but I seem to look better without it than I did when I was dolled up for work in London. I examine my messy hair and pasty face. I look young, and innocent. I am neither.

"Floppy!" I call, as I run down the stone steps, two at a time. "Skip!" I add, just in case.

Normally my dog comes running as soon as he hears either of his names. I don't know where he's gone. I shout a few more times, and then set off on my own, half running to get away in time. I rush downhill to the edge of the island, staying where I can't be seen from the road. I am aware, all the time, that my flight is futile. I can't get the image of what I did out of my head. She looks at me. She is horrific. I never saw her, but I can imagine it.

I make myself concentrate on my surroundings. This island is spectacular. The grass is mossy and green. The sky is invariably cloudy, and the soft light heightens everything. I breathe the cold, fresh air and appreciate it. I might not be breathing it for long. Dry stone walls crisscross the fields. The sheep get up and walk away, with dignity, whenever I lurch in their direction. Flop, wherever he is, is always kind to the sheep. I wonder whether a London dog, abruptly re-located, thinks he's died and gone to heaven. There are no scrawny poodles rushing up to smell his bottom, and he has the run of the entire island. Sometimes I watch him leaping around on the hillside, going crazy. Once he tried to swim in the loch, but it was too cold for him. It will, however, be spring next month.

It will be spring on the island, but that will make no difference to me. I notice I am shaking. By spring I'll be in Holloway Prison, and Flop will presumably be back with Stuart and Alison. I wince as her name comes into my head. I can hear the car driving faster than advisable over the stones. I should have got a boat for when this happened. I wonder idly where the dog is. As I scramble down to sit at the water's edge, I realize that it was probably Skipper's new name that led to my downfall.

When Stuart dumped me, we both wanted the dog. We each thought we had a claim. I'd adopted him from the shelter, but Stuart had housed him. I'd walked him, but Stu had paid for his food. I kidnapped him from Stuart's house, without leaving a note. Stuart and Ally turned up on my doorstep the following weekend, and demanded him back. They came together just to taunt me. She was looking rangy and elegant. If I'd known she was coming, I'd have brushed my hair, but I knew I couldn't compete. I hated her. I couldn't believe she had the nerve to come to my flat.

We all stood awkwardly in the kitchen, and I showed them the way the dog answered to his new name. Stuart looked at me with something like pity, and said "My God! You're a psycho!" They both laughed, shook their heads, and left. I suppose I'd shown them my true colors. I'd been the doormat for years. If I'd kept it up a little bit longer, I might not, now, be running away from the law. I should have sacrificed the dog.

My stomach is scrunched into a ball. I didn't mean to do it. This has been my mantra for the past ten days. I don't know whether that makes it better or worse. I didn't mean to do it; but I meant to do something. I wanted revenge, and I suppose I have got it. A life is ruined, and I should be glad.

I don't know how my relationship with Stuart led to this. I used to think our biggest problem was the fact that we worked together. Our colleagues loved him and hated me, but we didn't care. We loved each other. We had happy Sunday mornings, reading the papers and eating toast in bed, while Skipper (Floppy) lay across our legs. Stuart could talk for hours about Crystal Palace's hopes of promotion (lack thereof) or about rare plants. He was a horticulturist, by training. A horticulturist stuck in an office job. We would stand by his front window and look at his hedge. It was his pride and joy. He adored his rare shrubbery. He would talk, and I would listen, because that's the kind of woman I am. I am quiet. I'm a good listener.

I'm boring. That's what they used to say in the office, because I could never be bothered to talk to them. They'd sneer at me, and talk about me, and because I was so quiet, they'd forget they were within earshot. I've always held myself back. People have overlooked me since my first day at nursery school. The mistake people make is to assume that just because someone's quiet, they are necessarily good. The world at large sends quiet people to the bottom of the heap, assuming that they are lacking in confidence, that they are shy, that they want to be liked, that they are eager to please and therefore easily dismissed with contempt. No one would think to feel threatened by me.

I sit beside a rock. It's a big rock and I hope it might screen me. The air is bitterly cold, and I huddle into myself. By now they will be inside the house. I never lock the door. No one does. The police are in my house, looking for me. They are ready to arrest me. If the dog comes home, they'll ask him where I am. He might help them look for me. He'll be able to smell me. He'll help them find me. I throw a stone into the water. Treacherous Mr. Floppy.

I disliked Ally from her first day at work, but it took me a while to notice that she was stealing my boyfriend. I knew she was taller, slimmer and prettier than me, but I despised her because she was self-consciously bubbly. I could see through her, so I imagined Stuart could, too. She was desperate to be liked. I could see how insincere she was.

"I'm going to the canteen," she simpered to Stuart, in her second week. "I need a chocolate boost. Not to mention a packet of fags. Can I get you anything?"

"Oh, no, cheers," he said. "I'm not a chocolate fan. I prefer savory things myself. And I definitely don't smoke."

"Oh, me neither," she said, performing an inept U-turn. "At least, I'm quitting."

And off she skipped. When she came back, she'd bought them each a packet of salt and vinegar crisps.

Then Stuart started dropping her name into the conversation, on almost any pretext.

"Shall we go to France at Easter?" I asked him about a month ago.

"Okay. You know, Ally was saying she grew up in France. She speaks perfect French. I got her to say something for me, and she really did sound like a French person."

"Well you don't speak French, so it's easy for her to impress you."

"No, she went to school there and everything. She even has that weird curly handwriting they have abroad. Really, you should ask her to say something. Being bilingual is such a blessing. I'd love my children to be bilingual." He hastily corrected himself. "Our children."

I told myself that he was just infatuated, that she probably had a boyfriend, that it didn't mean anything. I knew I was wrong on all counts. He fancied her, and she fancied him. It was staring me in the face. I noticed it and everyone else noticed it, too. They loved it. It had all the ingredients of the perfect office scandal: boyfriend of unpopular girl goes off with gorgeous, lithe, friendly girl. Unpopular girl is humiliated. Friendly girl is triumphant. Office is bitchily happy.

I became tense. I didn't want to be dumped. I started asking him about her, pestering him, demanding answers.

"Of course I fancy her," he admitted, warily. "Everyone does. She's gorgeous. That doesn't mean I don't love you. Everybody looks at other women. It doesn't mean anything."

"Well, what would you do if she came on to you?"

"I'd never cheat on you, if that's what you mean."

"What if she was persistent?"

His eyes lit up. "I suppose I'd just be flattered and walk away."

He was lying. I knew he was lying. He knew that I knew he was lying.

I throw another stone into the water, and stare out to sea. There is no way I can escape now. When it happened, it came in an irresistible whirlwind. It was almost comically predictable. I came to Scotland to visit my parents one weekend. It's not something I particularly enjoy, but it has to be done from time to time. Leaving Stuart for two days felt wrong, but I knew I couldn't stay by his side forever, just to ensure his fidelity.

As I left the office on Friday afternoon, I watched Stuart and Ally flirting. I'd brought my weekend bag with me, and by the looks of things, one of them should have done the same. He was standing by her desk, talking to her, leaning forward, being overly attentive. She was looking into his eyes and giggling. They both looked as though their next logical step was to rip each other's clothes off. I seethed, and didn't say goodbye.

Sometime during the weekend, he'd pushed a note through my door. I had expected to be asked out for a drink or something else ominous. I hadn't expected to be given my marching orders on a scrappy piece of paper torn from his filofax. He didn't mention her name, either out of a misguided attempt to avoid hurting me, or, more likely, through cowardice. It was not a friendly letter. Three years, and that was all I got.

It still pains me, although I know I've cancelled my entitlement to feel wronged. At the time, I was in agony. I'd been half expecting it for weeks, but I still wasn't prepared for losing Stuart.

I sat down in my kitchen, and crumpled the note. I poured myself half a pint of whisky. I straightened the note out again, and smoothed it down. I read it. It hadn't changed. I knocked back the whisky. I hated him. I hated her. I realized I had to be at work in twelve hours, and that they would both be there. Everyone would know. I decided to resign.

So I went to the office, just to check that the obvious was, indeed, the case. I put on my best, red suit, and more makeup than usual. I kept my chin up, and applied a fixed grin to my face. When I walked over to my corner, everyone went quiet. They looked at me and I caught a few sniggers. They were so predictable. I looked around. Stuart was at his desk, head down. He knew I was there, but he wasn't making eye contact. Ally was there too—of course she was; they must have come in together. She caught my eye, and looked away quickly with a small smile.

"Good morning, Alison," I said loudly. She mumbled something.

"Morning, Stuart," I added. "Thanks for your scrap of paper. Very gentlemanly. I'll have the dog."

I got a laugh, and for a few seconds I was triumphant. Then I was wretched. I didn't want him back, but I was humiliated.

I left work at lunchtime, and I never went back. I knew they weren't going to bother to take me to court. I wasn't important enough. I stayed at home for a while, fuming. I wondered why he had said he loved me, if he didn't mean it. I wondered why I'd let myself get so involved. I'd never done it before. I might not do it again.

As the days went by, I disgusted myself by acting like a parody of a woman scorned. I sat around in my pajamas, writing him furious letters and throwing them into the bin, while Richard and Judy murmured platitudes in the background. I went to his house while he was at work, and took the dog. Some piece of faulty wiring in my brain made me decide that if I renamed Skip, everything would be all right. Mr. Floppy kept me company, but he didn't make me feel any better. I came to realize that I would only be able to overcome my rage by unleashing it. The more I thought about it, the more logical it seemed. All I needed was to exact some fleeting revenge on them. They wouldn't know it was me, but I'd know that I'd caused them anguish of some sort, and that would be enough. Then I'd be able to get on with my life, such as it is. My jobless, friendless life. That was when I decided to come to Scotland. I'd cause Stuart some misery, and immediately afterwards, I'd drive north. I ascertained that my great-aunt's cottage was available, and that the key was under the stone.

I made a plan. I would set Stuart's precious hedge ablaze while he was in his house with Alison. They'd be scared, they'd call the fire brigade, they'd be fine, and the rare and wonderful hedge would be ruined, by which time I'd be miles away.

I drove out of town, so no one would remember me, and bought a small container of petrol. At ten-thirty one night, I poured it generously over the leaves. They were drenched. I was excited. I had a box of matches in my pocket, but the house was empty. I knew Ally lived in a shared house, so I was banking on them staying at Stuart's. They'd come home soon—they'd have to—and then all I had to do was walk past, toss a lighted match over, and move swiftly away. I knew that I could cut through the alleyway two houses along, and be on the main road within seconds. Normally I would have avoided the passage, in case I met anyone dodgy, but in this instance I was the evil one, and I calculated that the chances of there being two of us about were remote. I was hugging myself in anticipation. I wanted to bring Floppy with me, but I feared he'd give me away, so I made him wait in the car, with all my possessions.

Soon, I saw them coming down the street. He was holding her hand. This sent a hot wave through me. He never, ever used to hold my hand in public. He just didn't want to.

"Hey, don't think it's because of you," he once told me, when I complained.

"Why is it, then?"

"Public displays of affection just aren't my thing. That's all. Never have been. Nothing personal." He rumpled my hair. And now here he was, with Ally's skinny hand in his. She was tottering along on high heels. I caught a good glimpse of her pretty face in the light of a street lamp. I knew she smoked, but I never gave it a moment's thought. I knew that Stuart was bitterly opposed to anyone smoking in his house. I should have realized what might happen. It came as a complete shock. I was hidden in the shadows across the road, wearing black. I was waiting for them to go in so I could make a pretty conflagration, and get into my car, which I'd parked at the top of the alley.

It happened quickly. She said something to him, and stopped. He walked on, and put his key in the door. She took out a packet of fags, and leaned into the hedge to get out of the wind. A second later, she went up in flames.

I ran.

I woke up in a nondescript hotel at some motorway services near Leicester, with Floppy curled up in a corner, and I turned on the radio. I hoped it would be a dramatic enough story to make the national news, and it was. She was alive, but she'd lost her lovely face. She was covered in burns. She was in intensive care. I got in my car, and drove as fast as I could towards my new life, as she began to come to terms with hers. I reflected that this would test their great so-called love, and then I remembered that they'd never claimed to be in love at all. I tried to tell myself she deserved it for stealing my boyfriend, but I knew she didn't. I tried to banish the knowledge that it was entirely my fault. I thought I might get away with it. My trump card was the fact that I was so meek. No one would even remember that I used to go out with him.

I cannot feel triumphant, however hard I try. When I close my eyes, I see her lovely face, lost forever. I try to picture it covered in burns. I cannot believe I did that to someone. It's funny how fine is the line between good and evil. You go through life with yourself firmly marked down as good and law abiding and sinned against. With one easy act, you shift yourself straight into the other column. You become a criminal. I am an accidental perpetrator of grievous bodily harm.

I've known all along that the police would come for me. I have been dwelling on the miracles of forensic science. It's not easy to get away with things. They know someone poured petrol on the hedge. The consensus seemed to be that it was random vandalism, but I can't assume it's going to stay that way. There must be ways that I've never even thought of for them to identify me. You always leave a trace. Apart from anything else, I had a motive.

It could be the fact that I changed the dog's name. Where is that bloody dog? It could be that I left a hair at the scene. It could be that someone saw a short woman in black running down the alleyway and leaping into a car. It could be anything. The chances are, however, that they don't actually *know* it was me. I'm going to have to be clever with my answers. They'll make me go to London. I'll be back in the city, breathing the foul air. I'll go to prison. People will only want to talk to me in the same way they want to talk to Myra Hindley, so that they can tell people they met me. No one will want to be my friend, except the sick people who fall in love with people in prison, and that only works when it's the man who's incarcerated. Men are too practical to kid themselves that they're in love with an evil witch like me.

I am crouched at the water's edge, in a futile attempt to be invisible. I hear their footsteps, and I know I'm doomed.

"There you are!" says the younger policeman, Robbie. He seems to be smiling. I wonder how he'll tell the story of the day he discovered the village had a psychopath on its outskirts.

"Hi," I tell him, weakly.

The older one speaks.

"We've looked all over for you," he says. "I'm afraid we've got some bad news."

I force myself to look at him. "What?"

"It's your wee doggie. He's been run down."

"It was an accident," adds Robbie. "The postman's terribly sorry."

"My wee doggie? Mr. Floppy?" Poor Floppy. He'd never deserved that name, and now he's dead. "Is that why you came?"

I live in a village where the police solemnly inform you that your dog is dead. In London he'd have been scraped off the tarmac by unscrupulous restaurateurs by now.

"That's terrible news," I add. Mr. Floppy has been sacrificed so that I may walk free. I am not going to prison. Not yet, at least. I can't take it in.

I look at the police, trying to remove all traces of guilt from my features. Robbie smiles sympathetically. I realize that he's not exactly spoilt for choice round here when it comes to the ladies. I think I've known all along that the best revenge I could ever exact on Stuart would be to have a happy life without him. Perhaps I am beyond revenge now, but I might try to do it anyway. It might ensure my continued freedom.

"I'm going to have to pour myself a drink," I say loudly, startling myself. "Will either of you join me? And, um, do you have the…body?"

Two hours later, a slightly drunk young policeman is digging a grave outside my cottage. Floppy has gone, and now I have Robbie. He's grown up well, since he was a scabby-kneed boy. He's going to get me a puppy. He and I seem to get on well. I vow to give it my best attempt.

If any other woman looks at him, I think I'll be able to sort her out.

Jessica Adams is an astrologer and professional psychic, whose worldwide clients include *Vogue*, *Cosmopolitan* and Bloomingdale's. She has been on the editorial team of four fund-raising anthologies for War Child in Australia and the UK, including the original *Girls' Night In,* helping to raise $1.5 million for children in war zones including Iraq and Afghanistan. Her own novels include *Tom, Dick, and Debbie Harry* and *I'm a Believer,* published by Thomas Dunne. For more information, please visit www.jessicaadams.com.

Here Comes Harry
by Jessica Adams

New York, April 1994

Kurt Cobain has just shot himself. He is grunge. I am not grunge. I am English, aged twenty-one, in a white Ralph Lauren shirt, working in my new job at the Ralph Lauren flagship store in New York. I listen to Seal. I don't listen to Nirvana. At least, not on purpose.

Nevertheless, when Harry wanders into the store at lunchtime and tells me that Kurt is dead, I find myself starting to cry at the cash register, and have to excuse myself to go to the loo. Except nobody knows what a loo is in this place. They are all mad for Hugh Grant, *Four Weddings and a Funeral* and Twinings English tea bags in this shop, but still, they can't translate the word *loo*.

"The toilet," I stammer to my supervisor. "Where is it?

The john. Oh God. What is it? What do you call a loo again? The ladies' room? The women's room? The rest room?" The shock of hearing that Kurt is dead has made me forget my new adopted language, along with the location of the Lauren staff lavatory.

"It's over there." My supervisor points and smiles. He is a man, but he secretly wears women's perfume. And it's not Ralph Lauren, either. It's Dune.

Harry waits for me while I cry for Kurt in my little cubicle.

"It's not as bad as the day River Phoenix died," he tells me when I finally emerge.

"No, it's worse," I tell him as the supervisor gives me a discreet nod, and I walk out into the street, rubbing at my mascara while Harry holds my arm.

"I didn't pick you for a Nirvana fan," he says as we cross a red light. "You don't like Beavis and Butthead. You don't even like me wearing sneakers."

"It's not that," I say. "It's not about Nirvana."

"What is it then?" he asks as he steers me toward our usual lunchtime deli.

"Kurt's little girl. That dear little girl with great big eyes. And now he's shot himself through the head. Poor Courtney Love. Poor her. Oh God." I start crying again and we have to find another loo—I refuse to call it a rest room—in the deli.

We have small bowls of potpourri in the cubicles at Lauren, but there is no potpourri here, just bad smells and weird sounds on both sides. Next door to me, a woman is groaning. Not because of Kurt, I think, probably because of constipation. Or maybe she's recently had an abortion. I recently had an abortion—it cost me several weeks' salary—and there were women moaning and grunting all over the place.

When I return to find Harry, I see that he has bought coffee for both of us, and picked out lots of salads for me, and an orange for dessert. He couldn't come with me to the abortion place, so just lately he has been compensating in other ways, by buying me healthy lunches, and giving me little shoulder massages, and walking to Ralph Lauren to pick me up after work, even though he says he hates Ralph Lauren.

This morning, a friend in London sent me a copy of *Harpers & Queen*—I've never managed to find it here—and there was an article about a woman in England who has started a business where she makes casts of babies' hands in plaster of paris, and then puts them in frames. That involved another urge to run to the lavatory and cry, although this time I was on the subway, and there was nowhere to go.

I was only six weeks pregnant when I had the abortion. The doctor told me it was just a bunch of cells, and it would have looked like a scrap of cotton wool. I know she's wrong, though. I know that in ten years' time they'll do scientific research and find out that even at four weeks, the scrap of cotton wool has a smiling face. I still long to know if it was a boy or a girl. The doctor said these things don't matter, but they do.

"I think I need some meatballs or something," I tell Harry. For some reason, I am suddenly absolutely ravenous.

He looks down at his coffee cup. Harry is a strict vegetarian. He has nut roast at Thanksgiving and tofu burgers at home.

"Sorry," I mutter.

And I get up, scraping my chair, and join the queue for chicken and turkey and meatballs and ham.

Harry became a vegetarian because he was always bullied at summer camp. For years, the animals in the fields around the camp were the only friendly faces he saw. Then one day he asked his mother where the meat on his plate came from, and when he found out it was from a cow, he pushed the plate away and said that he couldn't eat his friends—so he never has. And he's never had a girlfriend who's eaten his friends, either, until now. I feel guilty, I think, as I pick up the metal tongs and pile the meat onto my plate—but I also need food. After the abortion I didn't eat for a few days.

When I bring the plate loaded with turkey and meatballs back to the table, Harry turns away from me for a moment, then when he has recovered from the sight and smell of my plate, turns back and tells me that his friend who has been traveling in Thailand will be joining us.

"What friend who's been traveling in Thailand?"

"John. You know, my English friend John."

I shake my head. I don't know John at all. But when he arrives a few minutes later, and I look up and see him for the first time, I realize that he is strangely familiar.

"Not because I know him, of course," I tell my roommate, Karin, later. She is reading my *Harpers & Queen,* while I am reading her *New Yorker.*

"So why do you think he's so familiar then?" she asks, stirring her coffee.

"Because I fancy him."

Karin nods.

"More than you fancy Harry?"

"A lot more. In fact, there's no comparison."

"Is it because of getting pregnant?" she asks, putting the magazine down.

"No. It's because of nature. I thought Harry was the one, but he's not. It's John."

"And what's so special about John?" she asks.

"He shaves his head, he's lending me his copy of *Wild Swans,* he smells of sandalwood, he learned how to give Thai massages at Wat Po."

"Doesn't Harry massage you?" She gives a wry smile.

"And I want to have his baby," I hear myself telling my roommate. "I really, really want to have John's baby."

London, August 1997

John and I are having sex and it's not working, so he goes off to play with his Game Boy in the living room. Sitting up in bed, I light a cigarette and switch on the radio. It's someone talking about balsamic vinegar, so I switch it off again. I'm so tired I can't even be bothered adjusting the dial to find a new station.

When John gets bored with his Game Boy, he puts an Oasis CD on the stereo. He has eyebrows like the Oasis brothers too—joined in the middle. Increasingly, I find my-self staring at them and wishing I could pluck them out with my tweezers. It's like the blackheads on his back. I have fantasies about squeezing them out when he is asleep.

After Oasis has finished, I hear John trying to log onto the Internet, but there must be a busy signal, because he keeps smashing the mouse down on the table and swearing.

Then my mobile phone rings. It's Karin, calling from Australia. She married a banker from Sydney and they moved there a year ago.

"Hi, honey."

"Hello, darling."

"Have you heard the news?"

"What?"

"Oh shit."

"I'm in bed. It's really late. What time is it there? What news?"

Then John comes running into the bedroom, shouting something at me.

"Harry just sent me an e-mail. He says Princess Diana's dead."

"What?"

Karin is still on the other end of the phone.

"Karin, is she dead? John just said Harry said Diana's dead. Is it true?"

"Car crash," Karin cries. And then the first cigarette goes out, so I light another one.

"Dodi's dead as well," says John, standing in the doorway

with his boxer shorts on. "Harry sent me an e-mail. And it's on the BBC site. They're both dead."

His boxer shorts are blue, and they are from Ralph Lauren. The shorts are the only free thing I ever got from them.

"It's on the TV," Karin tells me after a long minute when she is crying, and I am smoking, and John is standing in the doorway. "Go and look—it's all over the TV. It's official."

And then she hangs up, and John sits down on the edge of the bed, and tells me everything that Harry's told him in the e-mail. The driver was drunk. They were speeding in a tunnel. The paparazzi were chasing them. There were no suspicious circumstances.

At the art college where I now work, some of the final-year students have been painting Princess Diana. Not Tony Blair. Not Cherie Blair. Not Bill Clinton. Always Diana. I feel as if I know her, and they do too, which is why they painted her. I suppose everybody in the world feels like that.

John tells me to look at Harry's e-mail so I do. And then I log onto the BBC site, and then switch on BBC radio. It's a habit I acquired in America. Rightly or wrongly, when in search of the truth, I turn to the British Broadcasting Corporation.

Then I start to cry, partly because I am so tired, and partly because of Camilla Parker-Bowles. It all seems so unfair for Diana, now that she is dead. But then, nothing in life is fair.

John has been seeing a lot of his old girlfriend from Thailand lately. She is older than me, and she is married with children. On her birthday, he bought her some earrings. For my birthday, he bought me a book he thought I might like—but I didn't. In the last few months, I have become Princess Diana in my imagination, and John's ex-girlfriend has become Camilla Parker-Bowles. I hate John's ex-girlfriend and on Diana's behalf, I also hate Camilla.

"They murdered Diana," I say quickly. It's something that has just popped into my head, and I know that I must say it.

John shakes his head. "Don't be silly."

"Because of the land mines. That's what it was. That's why they killed her."

"Go back to bed."

I cry and I cry, while John watches me. Then finally, he comes over and briefly rubs my shoulders. It's not a Thai-massage rub. He stopped doing that ages ago.

"It's not our problem," he says. "We never knew her. It's nothing to do with us. Come on. Come back to bed."

"You don't understand."

"Well then."

John leaves me alone after that, and returns to the Internet.

Later on, I make a cup of tea, and then I have another cigarette and think about Harry. I wonder what he's doing now. John seldom talks about him to me, partly because I think he is jealous of our old relationship, and partly because I only recently told him that Harry had got me pregnant. When John and I first got together in New York, I didn't think it was right to say anything. It's only now, since John and I have been trying for a baby and failing miserably, that I've felt I should confess about the abortion.

"So us not having a baby might be down to you, then," John said when I told him the truth.

"What do you mean, it might be down to me? There's no blame in this."

"Maybe it did something to your insides."

"Oh piss off, John, it did nothing to my insides, don't be so bloody stupid. Women terminate their pregnancies every day."

"Terminate, that's a new word."

Our fights are shorter these days, because we opt out earlier, and stop talking sooner. I almost think I preferred it when John and I stayed up all night, yelling and swearing and slamming doors. At least I felt as if I still knew him.

On Sunday evening we are eating dinner, still with the BBC news on, when it is finally John's turn to cry.

"It is awful, isn't it," I sympathize. "Just so unfair. So bloody unfair about Diana. Such a shock."

"Not her," he manages to say. "Us."

"What?"

"Us. It's the end, isn't it. It's just the end."

"What?"

"I don't want us to be together anymore. I don't want us to live together anymore. I can't do it."

New York, December 2004

I am on holiday in New York, and I have been invited to Thanksgiving dinner with some of Harry's vegetarian friends. I am by myself for the night—I'm here on a work trip, seeing some art dealers for the gallery where I now work—and he's taken pity on me.

"Tell me again what's in a nut roast?" I ask Harry as we head downtown in a cab.

"I can't believe you've lived in London for all these years and never found out."

"Look, I know what's in Body Shop banana conditioner, I just don't know about the nut-roast side of things."

I have just spent the afternoon shopping at a Ralph Lauren sale preview. I still get invitations to stuff like that, even ten years after I worked there.

"The only trouble is," I tell Harry, "I don't like the clothes anymore."

"Yeah, look at you," Harry says. "You dress like a woman who's forgotten what fashion is. You dress like—someone who works in an art gallery. Look at those clogs and socks!"

"Thanks very much. Clogs and socks are very cool things to wear in London at the moment."

"But hey," Harry interrupts, "if you want to take me to a Lauren sale preview next time, I won't say no."

Harry works for an advertising agency in Manhattan now, and he has developed expensive taste—at least, more expensive than the days of sneakers, corduroy jeans and MTV T-shirts.

Finally, we find his friends' place, and Harry tells the cab to pull up outside an apartment block that still has old 9/11 memorial posters ripped from the *New York Post* in the top windows. I don't know what makes me feel older now, looking at that, or remembering my breakup with John, and the day Princess Diana died.

"I'm surprised you weren't the one to ring me up and tell me about the World Trade Center," I tell Harry as we climb up the stairs outside and he rings the bell.

"What?"

"Well, you told me about Kurt Cobain, you told me about Princess Diana. I'm thinking, maybe you're the angel of death."

"And I'm thinking, you shouldn't put on a fake New York accent in an attempt to be funny." Harry shakes his head. "You sound like an Englishwoman who has watched too many Woody Allen films."

As we climb the stairs to his vegetarian friends' apartment, I see Harry has a gay-clubbing guide tucked into his jeans pocket. He may have picked it up out of interest, he may have picked it up for a friend, or it could have been planted there. All those ideas are wrong, though. I have visited Harry in New York twice in the last two years, and what began as an idea now seems suspiciously like a fact. Harry, my ex-boyfriend from ten years ago, is now probably gay. He burns ylang-ylang oil in a special metal burner, and he has a feng shui fountain in his bedroom and a good friend called Phil, whom he texts almost every day.

"What are you thinking?" Harry says as our hostess guides us into the apartment.

"Just wondering why there's a gay guide in your pocket," I say lightly.

"Oh that," Harry says. "Our agency did the design."

"Oh right."

"Why did you think there was a gay guide in my pocket?" he demands. Then he stares hard at our hostess, who is in a red cheongsam and has incredible breasts.

"She thinks I'm gay, Melanie," he complains to her. And she smiles with big, scarlet, glossy lips.

"Oh, I sleep with him regularly," Melanie counters. "He's not gay."

"All Englishwomen think straight New York guys are gay," someone else at the end of the table says—and everyone laughs, and I go hot and embarrassed.

I sit down next to Harry and his group of vegetarian friends, who are all delighted to have found each other during this season of animal slaughtering and turkey murdering. Outside, it looks like snow, and perhaps to encourage it, Melanie has a collection of snow domes lined up on the window ledge.

She opens some red wine, and the eight out of twelve of us who actually drink demolish the bottle in a few minutes, so a bottle of Grey Goose vodka is opened, and then Harry says he's brought some too, so he gets it out of his bag—along with some beluga caviar—and we have that in between courses, without anything real to eat, and soon someone puts Oasis on the stereo, and then we are all totally drunk.

"Oasis," I tell Harry in the kitchen when I come back from the loo and he meets me halfway by the sink. "It reminds me of John."

"Ah yes. Living with John in London. I remember that. The Oasis years."

"I sometimes wonder if John and I would still be together if I'd managed to get pregnant," I say. "And then I think, maybe it was a blessing that we didn't."

"I got you pregnant," Harry says, sounding almost proud, though once he was so ashamed of it. "We could have had a baby!" he shouts above the sound of Oasis, and I look at his eyes and see that he is far drunker than me.

He leans against the sink, swaying slightly, while I sip my vodka and stare out the window, wanting it to snow so that this filthy part of downtown can turn white and clean.

"I'm not the angel of death," he says. "I'm really not. I hated what you said about 9/11 just now. But I need to tell you something."

"What?"

"I heard from John." He sighs, and blinks hard at the ceiling.

"Go on, Harry. Just tell me."

"He's dying," he says. "I'm sorry, but he's dying."

"When did you hear?"

"After he went back to Thailand again. With his ex, that woman that you hate. She's looking after him. Her husband let her go to him. He has cancer."

I look at Harry for a moment and realize I have never seen him cry properly before, not even when I had the abortion. But now, tears are streaming down his face—almost as if he is crying all the Grey Goose vodka out of his system.

"Nobody else was going to tell you, so I volunteered," Harry says.

"Is he really truly dying?"

"He has a few months."

Oasis is taken off the stereo and replaced with Macy Gray.

"He's too young to die," I say, and light a cigarette.

"We're all too young to die, but we still die," Harry says—then he laughs at himself. "The older I get, the more bullshit I speak," he tells me.

"I want to go there," I hear myself say. "I want to go to Thailand to see him."

"You do?"

Then I think about it.

"Now I'm speaking bullshit. No, I don't. I hate what he did to me. I fell out of love with him and he made it worse by turning it into a war, and then he betrayed me with another woman. Sorry. There it is. That's the truth."

Harry nods, and takes a cigarette from me.

"You speak the truth, yea verily," he says in an idiotic upper-class English accent.

"American men who talk like something on the History Channel aren't funny, and they shouldn't do it," I tease him.

"Yeah, okay, sure, point taken," he replies.

Then Melanie appears in her red cheongsam, telling us we're being antisocial, so we follow her back into the dining room, and then I take Macy Gray off the stereo and put on Nirvana, and I kiss Harry, harder than I've ever kissed anyone in my life.

Twenty-something **Sarah Mlynowski** was born in Montreal. After receiving an honor's degree in English literature from McGill University, Sarah moved to Toronto to work for a romance publisher. Unfortunately, she never met Fabio. But she did write her best-selling first novel *Milkrun,* which has since been published in sixteen countries. Sarah is also the author of *Fishbowl, As Seen on TV* and *Monkey Business.* Her first teen novel, *Bras & Broomsticks,* will be available in February 2005. Currently a full-time writer, Sarah now lives in New York City.

If you'd like to say hello, visit her Web site at www.sarahmlynowski.com.

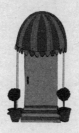

Know It All
by Sarah Mlynowski

My new roommate, Dee, claims she can see the future.

It's Thursday morning, and she's in the kitchen pouring herself a glass of my orange juice. "You should try to get on an earlier flight to California," she yells as though she's two stories up instead of a foot away from me.

"Why?" I'm crouched in front of the closet next to the kitchen, already late for work, debating what shoes to take with me on my trip. I think the six pairs I've laid out might be teetering on the edge of absurd. I'm only going for three days.

"There's going to be a blackout tonight," she says. She's wearing pajamas, her blond hair in pigtails, and my flip-flops. I lent them to her two weeks ago and she still hasn't given them back.

"Yeah? Did they say that on the news?" I can probably

get on an earlier flight if I have to. My mother is swimming in airline points. To cheer me up about the Brahm breakup, she offered me a business-class ticket to visit the world's most perfect—and sadly former—roommate, Janna, in California for the weekend. Janna, who would never borrow my flip-flops and not return them. Janna, who always made sure the bills were paid on time. Janna, who indulged me in my never-ending quest to find the city's cheapest Tropicana.

Dee shakes her head no and pours herself another glass. Does she think orange juice grows on trees? Dee's a friend of a friend of a friend who moved in three weeks ago. So far she seems normal. Washes her dishes. Changes the toilet-paper roll when she finishes it. Doesn't leave nail clippings on the living-room table. Doesn't look repulsed when I do. We should get along fine. If she gives me back my flip-flops.

"No," she says. "It wasn't on the news. I dreamed it."

"Very funny," I say and reluctantly eliminate one of my three pairs of gorgeous but impractical stilettos. I'll need something more comfortable for walking around Janna's apartment. Like my flip-flops.

"Didn't I tell you?" she asks. "I'm a little bit psychic."

"If you say so." I turn to her and smile, assuming she's joking. "Can you be a little bit psychic? Is that like being a little bit pregnant?"

"No, Shaun," she says, her lips pursed and serious. "I have premonitions."

My smile falters. I hope I haven't chosen a wacko for a roommate. "What kind of premonitions?"

She shrugs. "Random stuff. Usually about things people talk to me about. Like your flight. I dreamed about us being on the couch tonight reading by candlelight and watching a DVD on my laptop. You were complaining that you'd missed your plane. So I'm assuming there'll be a power outage."

Now I know why most people don't remember their dreams the next day—they're boring. "You dreamed about us reading and watching a movie? Dee, I think you need to get out more."

She laughs and heads to the bathroom. Flip-flop, flip-flop. I'm going to have to ask for those back. I know she'll think I'm a bitch, but they're mine. And they're going with me to California.

At a little after four o'clock, I hastily water the plants, zip up my coat and locate my keys under yesterday's mail. I'm lugging my still-stuffed-with-shoes suitcase (rescued flip-flops included) toward the front door, when the hall lights go out. Did a bulb just pop? A quick check reveals that the DVD player and microwave clocks are blank. No power. Damn. My flight departs in two hours, I'm late and I still need to flag a cab. I lock up, tow my ridiculously massive suitcase to the elevator and press the down button. Two minutes. Five minutes. Please, God, no.

After ten minutes, I force myself to accept the atrocious truth: the elevator works on electricity. There is no helpful little man standing above the shaft manually heaving the elevator up, saving me from having to take the stairs.

All twenty-eight flights of them.

Crap.

Since my bag weighs at least four hundred pounds, I can't actually lift it and must instead drag it down each individual stair, controlling the momentum by bumping it against my hip. One, bump; two, bump; three, bump… After counting ten I hit a landing. Then another ten. Twenty steps per floor. Twenty-eight floors.

Bump.

Of all the days for my building to lose power.

It's 4:30. By floor twenty my hip hurts. At nineteen my arms feel like rubber. At eighteen I contemplate using the city-size suitcase as a toboggan. Instead, I start to cry. I am definitely going to miss my flight. I was really looking forward to seeing Janna. To hearing about her new job. To talking about Brahm.

I force myself to stop sniveling when I see two guys on floor seventeen.

They don't offer to help. Apparently, along with my muscles, chivalry is dead.

Sixteen, bump…ten, bump…five, oh what the hell, slide and *whee!*

One.

I wheel myself into the lobby.

"Elevator's down," the doorman tells me. Thanks.

It's 4:52. I can still make it. It'll take me thirty minutes to get to the airport, leaving me just enough time to read *People* at the bookstore.

At Thirty-third and Second I frantically search for a cab.

And search. Until I realize the traffic lights aren't working. The entire street—no, the entire block—has no power.

Then like a patio umbrella in the middle of the desert, a taxi catches my eye. I wave the driver over.

He rolls down his window. "Where you going?"

"LaGuardia."

He laughs and drives away.

At 6:20 I lug my bag back to my building in defeat. I've missed my one and only chance at business class.

"The elevator isn't working," the doorman tells me. Thanks. Again. Leaving my bag with him, I curse myself for not living in a brownstone.

I find Dee, back from work, in the fetal position on the couch, reading by candlelight. "I told you so," she says. "The entire city is out. Subways, trains, airports… They say we'll be out at least till tomorrow."

Sweating profusely from my real-life StairMaster, I spread myself across the carpet like melted peanut butter on toast. I'd forgotten about her prediction. "How did you know?"

"I just did. And don't worry about the flight. Since all the airports are closed, your ticket will be reimbursed."

I roll my eyes. How gullible does she think I am? There were probably warnings of the blackout all week. They may have even been tacked to the bulletin board in the elevator, the board that I never read because I don't have a dog or want to buy a used futon. I grind my teeth in annoyance. "Let's talk about something else."

"Tell me about the guy whose picture you have up in your room. The guy with the messy hair."

"Brahm?" I asked, surprised at how open she is about her snooping.

"Yeah."

"He's my ex. We broke up last month."

"Why?"

Apparently, she's snoopy *and* pushy. "He wanted to move in when Janna left. I wasn't ready." I shrug as though it was no big deal. It isn't a big deal, really.

I remember the night we broke up. We were in my bed, and he was kissing my throat, telling me that since Janna was moving, we could use her room as an office or maybe a spare bedroom, why not, we'd been together for two years, he wanted to take the next step, he wanted to live with me, to cook with me, to clean with me. To shop for cheaper Tropicana with me.

I couldn't breathe properly, as if my room was bursting with hot post-shower steam. I loved him. Sure, I loved him. But was I in love with him? I felt a nagging in the back of my throat, like a vitamin you still feel two hours after you've swallowed it.

I loved his short, curly hair that stood up in opposing directions. I loved the way his eyes closed when he laughed. That he never shaved evenly—one sideburn was always an inch longer than the other. How he ate pickles with everything. Sandwiches, pizza, macaroni and cheese. I loved the way he wrapped my curls around his fingers when we watched TV.

I loved the way he talked about us. For my twenty-fifth birthday, we tried oysters for the first time. I couldn't believe that we were supposed to slurp them down without chewing. "That's how I feel when I'm with you," he said, grazing my hand across the table with his bitten fingernails. "Swallowed whole."

I wanted to feel swallowed whole, too, but I didn't. Not by Brahm. But I knew what he meant. I remembered losing myself entirely. And then remembered being told that the object of my devotion didn't feel the same. That I wasn't the one. I didn't get out of bed for two weeks, until Janna forced me into the shower, turning on the water and telling me that breaking up with me was the right thing to do if He didn't feel it.

"It must have been hard to let go," Dee says.

When I don't answer, she asks, "Want to watch a movie on my laptop? I have a six-hour battery and a DVD player."

"Sure. Let me think what I have." I rummage through my movies. *"Cocktail? The Firm? A Few Good Men?"* I'm hoping she's a Cruise fan.

"I love Tom," she says. "I lose myself in those eyes."

Me, too. They kind of swallow me whole.

The next morning, Dee pushes open the bathroom door when I'm brushing my teeth. Not that I have anything to do today. I'm not in California, and I can't even go to work because there's no power. "I had a dream last night, but you're not going to like it," she says. "It's about the guy we were talking about."

I spit a gob of toothpaste into the sink. "Tom Cruise?"

"No, your ex. Brahm. I dreamed that he was at a place called Jeremiah's."

"Jeremiah's? The corner store in the West Village near his apartment? How'd you know where he shops?"

"I told you, I dreamed it."

My back tingles, like hundreds of mosquitoes are feasting on my skin. "And?"

She sits on the closed toilet seat. "They were open even though they have no power. He walked in and bought a flashlight and a jar of pickles."

The man loves his pickles.

"And then the woman standing in front of him in line told him that with all those pickles he should probably stock up on some water. That's why she was there. For some H_2O."

"The woman? What woman?"

"The woman in line. She was wearing a camel V-neck. She had straight red hair and a million freckles. And bright green eyes."

What kind of a sicko is Dee? Would she make up a story like this just to upset me? I reapply my toothpaste and continue brushing. "And?"

She lifts her gaze to the ceiling as if she's watching a movie unfold. "They start talking about pickles. And where they were when the power went off. The guy behind the counter hands him his bag, and Brahm asks the redheaded woman if she wants to join him for a pickle-and-water picnic."

Maybe she really did dream this. I could have mentioned

his pickle obsession in my stair-induced stupor, and she conjured it up in her sleep. That's all it is. A dream, not a premonition. I spit again. "So what happens next? Do they get married? Am I invited to the wedding?"

She laughs. "They just met, Shaun. Don't be crazy. She says why not, and they walk to Washington Square Park and sit on a bench and eat their pickles. But they can't keep their eyes off each other. They have this instant connection, you know? Has that ever happened to you?"

What's wrong with this woman? "And then?" I can't resist asking. I want to know where her sadistic imagination will lead next.

"He asks her out for tonight. That's all I got. I heard the *chh* of your alarm buzzer through our toilet-paper-thin walls. I'm impressed that you have batteries in your alarm clock." And with that unusual praise, she laughs and disappears from the bathroom, closing the door behind her.

My new roommate is a freak, and I am dismissing her entire freakish dissertation from my mind. I will not give her, or her dream, or the supposed new love of Brahm's life any more thought.

I freak out at noon. What if Dee really is psychic?

I throw my novel on the floor and bang my head against the hard metal of my headboard. She's not psychic. Again, bang. There's no such thing as a third eye. Bang, bang. My roommate is a secretary for an investment bank. She is not Nostradamus.

Do I believe that Brahm is going to meet another woman

today? No. So what if Dee knew about the blackout? She probably read about it on some conspiracy Web site. She's not psychic.

I've had my cards read in the East Village. I spent fifteen bucks to have some woman with clawlike, blue-rhinestoned fingernails tell me that I will find love, money and that I will travel. Unfortunately, I'm still single, broke and I haven't left the tristate area in four years.

Enough. I'm putting the entire Brahm conversation out of my head.

At one I decide that I, too, need a flashlight. A flashlight from Jeremiah's. Who knows when the power will come back? I throw on my jacket and speed walk since the subways aren't working. When I push the door open to the store, I see no redheads. Ha.

Maybe I'll buy my flashlight and hang out. Brahm could easily come by today. When I spoke to him last night on the phone, he said he wasn't planning on doing anything. His office was closed because of the lack of power, and he wanted to bum around all day. In fact, he wanted us to hang out, but I'd told him I was busy. I didn't want him to get his hopes up.

I know I shouldn't be talking to him after the more-than-friends curfew of eleven o'clock. But I don't speak to him every night. Just last night, and the night before, and the night…oh, crap. Maybe it *is* every night. We don't have marathon conversations, though. Twenty, thirty minutes. One hour, tops. It's not my fault. He calls me. And we were friends for three years before we started dating, so we can't just *not* talk. And I like having someone to speak to before I fall asleep. I need an end-of-day phone call to signify bedtime, otherwise I lie in bed all night listening to the cacophony of honking and car alarms that sound like a five-year-old kicking a piano.

He said he wants to go for dinner this week. I told him I don't know if that's a good idea.

I don't want him to think I've changed my mind.

I buy one of those super-heavy, I-could-find-my-way-out-of-a-forest-in-the-dark-in-the-middle-of-a-rainstorm flashlights, but continue to wander around the store.

I don't want him to get his hopes up, but I don't want him to meet someone else, either. Pretending to browse, I keep my eyes peeled for Brahm. By the time I've combed every aisle at least twice, I'm relaxed. And feeling stupid for showing up. I'm cramming my bagged flashlight into my oversize purse, when I hear a woman's voice say, "I'll take six jugs of water, please."

Standing at the counter is a redhead in a camel blouse.

My body starts shivering, like the store's temperature just dropped thirty degrees. I don't believe it. How did Dee know? Did she set this up? Is it Dee in a wig?

I peer closely at Ms. Redhead, about to ask if she's a secret friend of my new roommate's, when through the window I see the familiar curly, messy hair. The familiar misshaven face of Brahm.

I leap into action, sprinting out the door before he has the chance to open it. He's wearing his black T-shirt with the lightning bolt on it, the one I once told him is my favorite, the one he now wears to death. A smile lights up his face as soon as he sees me.

"Hi," I say, trying to suppress the shock I feel by keeping my face blank and bleached of expression.

"Shaun," he says, smiling. "What are you doing here?"

"Buying a flashlight."

The redhead pays for her water.

"How's your day?" I ask, glancing at her out of the corner of my eye. I draw in a breath.

"Not bad. Do you want to hang out in the park for a bit?"

The redhead leaves and I exhale.

Shouldn't lead him on, shouldn't lead him on. "I can't, I have to get home."

His face falls. I wave goodbye. As I walk back to my apartment, a weird feeling comes over me, like I've been transported into the twilight zone.

Maybe this never even happened. Can I pretend this never happened?

Like the time I ran out of toilet paper and had to use a hand towel, this never happened.

I'm not sure if Dee is psychic, if she set this up, if I just ruined Brahm's life, but I do know one thing. I will try to never think of the redhead again.

A week later, when the power has been restored, and the chance of me finding a free weekend to reschedule my trip to California is pretty much nil, Dee once again barges into my bathroom before work. This time I'm on the toilet, and I'm too tired to yell at her to leave. I was on the phone with

Brahm until 3:00 a.m., talking about work, the weather, TV. And how much he misses me. And why I don't feel the same way he does.

"I can't explain it," I told him. Funny, I can tell him my feelings when he's not beside me. I feel safe with him on the other end of the phone line. Warm. "I don't know why I'm not in love with you. I wish I was, but I can't force it."

"Maybe it'll happen," he said. "We're so good together."

Now in the bathroom standing in front of me, Dee's wearing her glasses on her head like a hair band. "Can I help you?" I ask.

"I had another dream about your ex."

I groan. Maybe her glasses are her third eye. "Brahm? You sure?"

"Brahm. The guy with the curly hair."

"And?"

"It was about him and the redhead again."

I feel queasy, like I'm on a sailboat in choppy waters. "What happens?"

"He's on the six train, and she's rushing down the stairs on Thirty-third to make the subway. Brahm spots her running toward the car and, throwing his suitcase between the sliding doors before they close, he helps her inside. They share the same pole and start talking. They feel that connection again. He asks her out."

"He asks her out? On the subway?" No way. Impossible. He wouldn't ask out a random woman on the train. Would he?

She shrugs. "That was my dream. What I don't understand is why they didn't already meet at Jeremiah's."

I pay special attention to the toilet paper. "Guess you were
wrong." I haven't mentioned my Jeremiah's intervention, on
the off chance that I screwed up the fate of the universe and
will be held personally responsible.

She looks thoroughly perplexed. "Guess so." She exits the
bathroom, leaving me alone to think.

Is she full of it? Is she for real? What do I do? Will I miss
him if he's dating someone else? Will I be able to sleep at
night when he no longer calls? Do I let them meet?

I don't know, I don't know, I don't know. Yes, no and no.

Because Brahm leaves the office at six-thirty, he gets on
the subway at 6:38. Therefore the redhead will attempt to
embark at 6:42. I calculate a margin of error of ten minutes, which means I should be looking for her at 6:32. But
what if he leaves early today? Maybe that's why he's never
met her before. But now their eyes will lock around the pole
and they'll fall in love.

I must stop them from meeting.

At a quarter to five I leave work early to lurk outside of
the Thirty-third and Park station. By half past five I'm bored
out of my mind, thanking my lucky stars that it's August and
not the middle of freezing-cold January.

At 6:34 I spot the redhead from Jeremiah's. She's wearing black slacks, a red blouse and red sling backs. I admire
her shoes before jumping out from behind my cover bo-
dega. "Excuse me," I ask, stepping directly in her path.

She has a wide, round face, with eyes the color of the inside of a cucumber. "Yes?"

Um… "Do you know what time it is?"

"Sure," she says and looks at her watch. "Six thirty-five."

"Thanks." That was way too quick. She'll still make the train. "And can you tell me how to get to Central Park?"

"Sure." She leans in close and gives me directions.

Two minutes later, I thank her and let her disappear down into the subway. I wait a few seconds and follow in her footsteps. I peek over the turnstile, and although the platform is relatively empty, the redhead is waiting by a bench.

Hurray! She missed Brahm's train. That's it. This must surely be the end of this redhead and Brahm. Mission accomplished. I've altered the fate of the universe. I glance over my shoulder nervously, refusing to feel guilty as I make my way home.

Mmm. Bacon.

On Saturday the aroma of crisping meat wakes me up. Funny, I would have pegged Dee as a vegetarian. Being in touch with the earth and all that stuff. What do I know? Maybe being a psychic is more like being a witch. Maybe she needs to drink the blood of sheep and eat cow intestines.

I stretch and stagger into the kitchen.

"Want some breakfast?" she offers.

"Sounds divine," I reply, putting my anti-Dee thoughts aside in honor of this splendid meal.

She scoops two eggs out of the pan and slides them onto a plate. Then she makes a smiley face by adding a curved slice of bacon as she asks, "Can you explain something to me?"

I see that she's already halfway through a glass of my Tropicana, but I don't even mind, since my meal smells so delicious. "Sure."

"Why is it that I had another dream last night about Brahm and the redhead?"

Again? It's enough already. And how should I know why she dreams what she dreams? "What happened?" I try to keep my voice steady, as though none of it matters. I still haven't told her about my interventions, afraid she'll tell me I'm breaking some kind of intergalactic law.

"I dreamed that they're at the Astor Place Barnes & Noble and both reach for the last copy of the new Grisham novel."

"And?"

"They compare Grisham's literary work with his legal thrillers, and she asks him to join her for coffee."

"She asks him out?" Getting aggressive, is she?

"What I'm wondering is why I keep dreaming that they're meeting for the first time. They should have already met twice by now."

I shrug. "Maybe you're not as psychic as you think you are."

She looks confused and cracks two more eggs into the frying pan. "No, that can't be. Have you spoken to Brahm recently? Do you know if they've met?"

I stuff my mouth with bacon so I can't be expected to answer.

"Wait a sec," she says, mouth widening as if she's about to yawn. "Did you do something?"

"Do something?"

"Yeah. Like prevent them from meeting somehow?"

I chew extra slowly. Swallow. Fake chew. Fake swallow.

"Well, would there be consequences if I did?" I don't understand how this works. "What would have happened if I had gotten on an earlier flight to California? Would I have made it there?"

"Hello? Yeah. That's why I told you to take an earlier flight."

Something seems amiss here. Why else would she have that dream if not to warn me? "Are you saying it's okay to mess with the future?"

"I've seen it done before. I dreamed that my sister missed my father's birthday, so I reminded her and she called him. I don't know. Maybe if there was some cosmic reason that she was supposed to forget his birthday, she would have forgotten it anyway. I don't know. But nothing happened."

I breathe a sigh of relief. At least I haven't botched the fate of the world. Unless the redhead and Brahm's future offspring would have found a cure for cancer, or invented a flying chair or something. I take another deep breath and confess in a rush, "I've been stopping their meetings before they could happen."

"You have?" She calmly turns over the eggs. "Why? Didn't you break up with him?"

"Yeah, but the idea of him kissing someone else makes my skin crawl. I can't sit idly by and let them meet. I just can't."

She nods. "Fair enough. I understand. I've been there. So are you going to try to stop them from meeting today?"

"Yes. Any chance you could tell from the sun what time it was?"

"Nope."

I sigh. "I guess I'll stalk the bookstore."

I arrive at Barnes & Noble a half hour later. After two chai teas and a scone, I spot Ms. Redhead browsing in the romance section on the second floor, and I make a mad—but hopefully subtle—dash over there.

"Hey," she says. "Didn't you ask me for directions yesterday?"

Damn, she recognizes me. She's going to think I'm a psycho stalker. I think I *am* a psycho stalker. "Thanks for that."

"No problem. That is so weird that you're here. The universe must be trying to tell us something."

I lower my gaze and pick up a book.

"Are you visiting New York?" she asks.

"Me? No."

"Really? And you needed directions to Central Park?"

Damn. "Oh. Um…I have no sense of direction." Change subject, change subject! "Do you read a lot of romances?"

"Yeah. It's my favorite genre. I like happy endings."

"Don't we all."

"I'm heading to the café for a cup of coffee. Want to join me? I'm Simone, by the way."

Simone. Apparently Simone would have asked *anyone* to join her for coffee today. "Sure. I'm Shaun."

In the café once again, I order another chai and she orders a cappuccino. Even though I want to hate her, I like her. She laughs at my jokes. Asks me about my job. Asks me what books I like. She just moved from Boston to New York because she got a job with a Manhattan publisher. Her new place is in the Village.

Twenty minutes later I spot Brahm at the magazine rack. He doesn't see me. Tucked under his arm is the new Grisham novel. He hurries down the stairs.

"I have to get going," I tell Simone when our drinks are drained. "But we should do this again sometime."

She smiles. "Sure. Here's my new business card. And here's my cell," she adds, scribbling a number on the back. "Call me next time you're going to the bookstore and maybe we'll meet up."

"Operation Stop Brahm and Simone, take four," Dee says two mornings later, pounding on my door.

"Not again," I whine.

"They're meeting tonight at the Union Square movie theater. He and a friend sit next to her and her co-worker, and they start chatting."

"On a Monday night?" Who goes to a movie on Monday night, and how does it happen that both of them decide to see the same one? What type of absurd coincidence is that?

The very thought makes me feel sick. Especially since I had sex with him last night. Okay, I know I shouldn't have. But we were on the phone until two, and he said he missed me and wanted to see me, and I thought, Why not? I told him he could come over if he wanted to, and to wear the lightning bolt shirt, and ten minutes later I was in my red-feather outfit and he was kissing me. And it felt so nice and safe. I can't let him meet someone new, I just can't. "Dee, I don't understand, why do they keep meeting?"

"I don't know."

"What do you mean you don't know?" I shout. "What kind of psychic are you? Eventually it'll stop, right? They can't keep bumping into each other indefinitely, can they?"

"I don't know."

I need to put an end to this right now. I search in my purse for her business card and call her. "Hey, Simone. It's Shaun. Your bookstore buddy? Any chance you want to catch a book signing tonight?"

"Sure," she says. "Another editor just left me a message about doing something tonight. I think she wanted to see a movie, but a book signing sounds great."

It's 8:00 a.m. Thursday morning.

Dee is pounding at my door.

She enters, and I pull the pillow over my head. "Go away," I moan.

"He gets out of a cab tonight at eleven on Houston and Broadway. She gets into it."

I call him at ten and tell him I'll meet him for a drink. By eleven I'm drunk and under his satin sheets. He plays with my curls and tells me he loves me. I pretend I'm asleep.

On Friday morning Dee wakes me up at six. "Starbucks. Forty-second and Third. Forty minutes. He spills coffee on her shirt. Go."

★ ★ ★

Ten hours later she calls me at my office.

"I wasn't feeling well today, and left work to take a nap. They're meeting tonight in line at the Au Bon Pain on Mercer and Eighth Streets. He's standing in front of her. They both buy chocolate chip muffins. She drops hers on the floor. He offers her half of his."

I leave work and block him before he even crosses the street. He puts his arm around my shoulders and we window-shop. I spot an adorable pair of flip-flops and while Brahm waits outside, I buy them for Dee. Why not? She'll love them.

Saturday morning, 7:00 a.m.

Flip-flop! Flip-flop! Dee stomps from her room to mine and whips open my door. "I can't take it anymore! I can't stand dreaming about Brahm and the redhead continuously. It's driving me crazy."

I jump out of bed. "Where are they?"

"Shaun," she says carefully. "You have to let go."

There's no time for her dillydallying. I'm already half dressed. "Tell me where they are."

She sighs. Loudly. "They're sitting at a table on the patio of French Roast in the West Village."

"How are they sitting together if they don't even know each other yet? How is that possible?" What is going on? Will this ever end?

"Shaun," Dee says. "I really don't think you should intervene this time."

"If you didn't want me to intervene, why did you wake me? If you didn't want me to stop it, you shouldn't have told me."

She shakes her head. "I'm not making your choices for you."

The phone next to my bed rings and I turn my back to her and snatch it up. "Hello?"

"It's me," Brahm says. "Have you eaten? Want to go for brunch?"

"Sure," I say slowly, trying to process this phone call. "Where do you want to go?"

"How about French Roast?"

Huh? "Sure. Thirty minutes?"

Thirty minutes later, panicked that I'm late, and exhausted from the run, from the week, from these damn interventions, I approach French Roast and see the back of Brahm's curly-haired head. He's sitting on the terrace, his face tilted toward the sun. Every few seconds he looks down and eagerly scans the street, searching for me.

He's freshly shaven, uneven and lopsided, wearing the lightning bolt shirt.

And suddenly I remember that I was once a girl who wore my hair up every day for a year because He, the boyfriend before Brahm, remarked in passing that he thought my neck was sexy.

Brahm opens his eyes again and searches.

I have a splinter in my throat. My heart pounds faster, louder, until I can feel it in my neck and fingers.

I have to let him go. I want him to be with someone else. Someone who feels swallowed whole. Who feels he's the one.

My heart breaks and I flip open my cell. I dial. Slowly.

I know someday I'll feel it again, too. But until then?

Maybe Dee and I'll take a vacation. I'll trade in my business-class ticket for two economy seats to California. Or maybe Vegas. Bet Dee kicks ass at the tables.

She answers on the first ring.

"Simone?" I ask. "What are you doing for brunch? There's someone I'd like you to meet."

Isabel Wolff was born in Warwickshire and studied English at Cambridge and is the author of five best-selling romantic comedies—*The Trials of Tiffany Trott, Making Minty Malone, Out of the Blue, Rescuing Rose* and *Behaving Badly,* all of which have been published world-wide. She lives in Notting Hill with her partner and their baby daughter. In her spare time Isabel enjoys playing table football, making cakes and catching buses. If you want to know more about Isabel and her books, please visit her Web site at www.IsabelWolff.com.

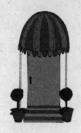

In Agony
by Isabel Wolff

"Problems, problems," Jane muttered as she opened her mailbag on Monday. "Problems, problems," she repeated testily. "As though I don't have enough of my own." The thirty or so envelopes seemed almost to vibrate with indignation, resentment and rage. There were brown ones and white ones, airmail and Basildon Bond. There were typed ones and handwritten ones, some strewn with smiley faces and hearts. Jane's practiced eye had already identified from the writing the likely dilemmas within. Here were the large, childish loops of repression, and the backward slope of the chronically depressed. There, the stabbings and scorings of schizophrenia and the cramped hand of the introvert. Jane fancied she could hear them, like childish voices, whining and pleading for help.

"Dear Jane," she read, "I have a problem… Dear Jane,

I just can't sleep… Dear Jane, I'm so terribly lonely… Dear Jane, I feel so bad." Dear Jane, she thought to herself bitterly. Dear Jane. Dear, dear, *dear!* "Oh dear," she repeated irritably as she turned on her computer. "Off we go again."

For Jane was neither an enthusiastic, nor even sympathetic, agony aunt. She had always regarded the *Post*'s problem page with something close to contempt. "But here I am—in agony," she muttered. She longed for some anesthetic to ease the pain. But "Ask Jane" was undeniably popular. More importantly, it paid the bills. Because for two years Gavin hadn't earned a cent, having given up his job in the City to write. He'd been "troubleshooter" at Debit Suisse. "But I'm the real troubleshooter now," thought Jane. And it sometimes amused her to think that Gavin's literary career was subsidized by the codependent, the abandoned and the bald.

Jane had been a journalist for ten years; but her spell as an agony aunt had never featured on the imagined trajectory of her career. She had visualized a seamless progression from the diary, to the news desk, to signed interviews, to glamorous features (with photo byline) and thence to some highly visible—and frequently controversial—column in some respected broadsheet. Her readers would gasp at her erudition. No subject would elude her. She would pontificate on Britain's entry to the Euro, on drugs and welfare and defense. Her trenchant opinions would be regurgitated at lively dinner parties in Islington and Notting Hill. She would be invited to appear on *Newsnight,* on *Today* and *Question Time.* Instead, she found herself dealing with premature ejaculation, nasty neighbors, infidelity, impotence and debt. This unexpected professional detour had happened entirely by chance.

Two and a half years previously, Jane had been doing a reporting shift on the news desk of the Sunday *Post.* As she put the finishing touches to what she thought was a rather good profile of Cherie Blair, she noticed a sudden commotion. People were running. Doors were slamming. An atmosphere of tension and panic prevailed. Enid Smugg, the *Post's* ancient but hugely popular agony aunt, had gone facedown in the trifle at lunch. Before Enid's stiffening body had even been stretchered out of the building, Jane had been deputed to complete her page. Keen, above all, to appear willing, she had gritted her teeth and agreed; and, despite her lack of experience, or even natural sympathy, she'd acquitted herself pretty well.

Too well, she now realized bitterly, because she'd been stuck in the job ever since. Still, seventy grand was good money, she reminded herself, and God knows they needed the cash. Their flat in Regent's Park was gorgeous, but the mortgage on it was vast. But Jane adored her husband, Gavin—"Gorgeous Gav"—and she believed that his boat would come in. Moreover, she was secretly quite happy to be the breadwinner—it placed Gavin firmly in her debt. And she especially liked the fact that he no longer went to work. Jane had visited Gavin's office a few times and had been disconcerted and demoralized by the sight of so many sweet-faced, lithe-limbed blondes. For Jane was a plain Jane—tall, big-boned and rather flat-faced, and she knew she'd married out of her league. She quite liked having her handsome husband safely at home, out of harm's—and temptation's—way.

Above all she luxuriated in the knowledge that it was her professional sacrifice that enabled him to write. He'd probably dedicate his book to her, she mused contentedly. When it was published. Which it would be, quite soon. The phone would ring one day and it would be an editor from Harper-Collins or Faber, begging Gavin to let them publish his intergalactic thriller *Star-Quake!* Jane had to admit that Gav's books weren't quite her thing. But then she'd never really been a sci-fi fan. Gavin was an avid amateur astronomer and aimed to become the new Arthur C. Clarke. Jane had a sudden, happy vision of them attending the royal premiere of *Star-Quake!* in Leicester Square. There they were, standing next to Nicholas Cage and Michelle Pfeiffer in the lineup to meet Prince Charles.

Gavin had not yet allowed Jane to see his manuscript. But a few nights before, when he'd left for his astronomy evening class, she'd gone into his study and sneaked a look. She'd found the story a little hard to follow, with its huge floating aliens and exploding supernovas and fur-clad talking snakes. But still, it was genre fiction, Jane reasoned, and there was a huge market for that. In any case, she supported Gavin unquestioningly because she adored him. She always had. That's why she was prepared to be "in agony" as she jokingly put it—so that Gav could fulfill his dream.

At least—and thank God for this—none of her friends knew that "Ask Jane" was her. For she had resolutely refused to have either her surname or photo on the page. *"Got a problem? Ask Jane,"* it announced above a photo of a disembodied—and clearly female—ear. Jane had assumed, when she first started doing the agony column, that her stewardship of it would be short-lived. She'd imagined that before long some celebrity would be hired to take over, or some famously humiliated political wife. For a while there'd been talk of Trisha from daytime telly, and even Carol Vorderman. But weeks had gone by, then months, and here Jane still was, two years on. But not for much longer, she thought happily, because soon Gavin's writing career would take off. "You're my rock, Jane," he'd say with a smile, which made tears prick the back of her eyes. "You're my asteroid—no, my shooting star." Well, she certainly shot from the hip. Or rather, from the lip. But that's why people wrote to her. They wanted firm, robust advice.

She turned back to the day's bundle of letters with a weary, regretful sigh. Christ, it was tedious—and it wasn't as though any of the problems were *new.* She had long since covered every conceivable dilemma—low libido, domestic violence, bad breath, bereavement and debt. Pregnancy (both wanted and unwanted), nasty neighbors and thinning hair. She'd helped Divorcing of Dagenham, Paranoid of Petersham and Borderline Bulimic of Bath.

"Who have we got today?" she muttered. "Phobic of Finchley? Suicidal of Solihull? Jealous of Jupiter would make a nice change," she added sardonically, "or maybe Miserable of Mars." Jane never felt guilty about her lack of sympathy for her readers. If these people wanted lovely, kind, "mumsy" Clare Rayner, then they could damn well write to her instead. But "kind" simply wasn't Jane's style. Her advice was uncompromisingly tough. She prided herself on being as sharp and to the point as an assassin's blade. Oh yes, Jane liked to tell it straight. First off was Sandra from Suffolk. Not getting on well with her husband's mum.

"Dear Sandra," Jane typed. "It's a *great* pity you spoke to your mother-in-law like that. Let's face it, calling her a 'twisted old battleaxe' is *not* going to make relations more cordial! May I respectfully suggest that you try and *think* a little before you open your big trap. In the meantime I enclose my leaflet on tact." Jane reread her letter, sealed the envelope, tossed it in her out-tray, then turned to the next.

Oh God—another fatso with low self-esteem. "Dear Terry," she wrote. "I know you'd like me to tell you that looks don't matter, and that some nubile blonde is going to fall in love with your 'great personality.' But the fact is, poppet, that no self-respecting woman is going to be seen dead with a guy weighing eighteen stone. Here's the Weight Watchers number for your area, so ring it right now and lose the lard." On further consideration, she decided the letter might be a little harsh. So she scribbled, "Do let me know how you get on," at the bottom to soften it a bit. Not that anyone ever did let her know. They never got back to her. Her replies went out into the void, like meteorites hurtling through space. In the two years she'd been "in agony" she'd never heard from anyone again. Occasionally, she would wonder why, but she had long since concluded that the brilliance of her advice obviated the need for further help. Now she earmarked the four letters she would feature on this week's page—money trouble, transvestitism, booze and menopause—then turned to the final letter in the pile.

"Oh God, Betrayed of Barnes," she said irritably. "You poor thing—boo hoo hoo!" "Dear Jane, I don't know what to do," she read. "I've been married for seven years and love my wife dearly but fear she has started to stray. She is far more attractive than I am and I often feel insecure." At this, Jane felt a sudden pang of recognition, which she did her best to suppress. "I have no hard evidence," the writer went on, "but I believe she's seeing a colleague at her TV company, because she talks about him a lot. It's 'Ronnie this' and 'Ronnie that,' so I assume it must be him. What's more, she's been dressing particularly well lately, with an attractive new hairdo, and once or twice I've detected alien aftershave on her clothes. I have never been possessive," the man continued. "I've always encouraged my wife to see her friends, attend evening classes and go to the gym, but I'm now so anxious that I feel ill. Please, please advise me, Jane. Yours in desperation, Alan."

"Well Alan," Jane wrote back, "it seems to me you've got three options. You can a) stick your head in the sand and hope the problem will go away. But the problem with having your head in the sand, sweetie, is that you leave your backside dangerously exposed. Or you can b) confront her. But if you do, you'd better prepare yourself to hear something you're not going to like. Or you can c) have her followed. Go to a private detective—just look one up in the Yellow Pages—and get a Dick Tracy on the job. At least that way you'll know for sure. So bite the bullet, Alan, and best of luck."

Jane finished the letter with a sense of satisfaction. She'd given him the best advice she could. She wondered what the upshot would be, but knew that she'd never get to know. So she was rather surprised, a fortnight later, to hear from Alan again. "Dear Jane," he wrote. "Thank you for the excellent advice you gave me recently. I had my wife followed, as you suggested, with surprising results. It turned out that her colleague, 'Ronnie,' was in fact a woman—Ronnie is short for Veronica apparently." Well then, you're a lucky bunny, Alan, thought Jane as she raised her coffee cup to her lips. "However," she read on, "my suspicions about my wife were sadly proved right—in an unexpected way. The detective's dossier revealed that she *has* been having an affair with a man who attends the same evening class. It appears they share a passion for amateur astronomy. He's a married man, very attractive, a former banker who's trying to write. I'm devastated, as you can imagine. But what I need to know *now* is, should I get in touch with this man's wife?"

Lauren Henderson was born in London, where she worked as a journalist before moving to Tuscany to start writing books. She now lives in Manhattan. She has written seven books in her Sam Jones mystery series: *Dead White Female, Too Many Blondes, Black Rubber Dress, Freeze My Margarita, Strawberry Tattoo, Chained!* and *Pretty Boy,* the last five published in the U.S. by Crown. The Sam novels have been optioned for a movie deal and translated into fifteen languages. She has also written two romantic comedies, *My Lurid Past* and *Don't Even Think About It,* published in the U.S. by Pocket. With Stella Duffy, she has edited an anthology of girls-behaving-badly crime stories, *Tart Noir,* and their Web site is www.tartcity.com.

Dating the Enemy
by Lauren Henderson

We treat the people we want to love like adversaries.

"You can't trust what people say anymore," says my friend David.

"Everyone knows now what people want to hear. We all know exactly how to show the socially acceptable sides of ourselves. Don't listen to what they say. Watch what they do. They can't disguise that."

David gave me that advice when I first moved to New York. I thought he sounded as paranoid as a character from a horror film telling the others how to spot the aliens. But he was right. We're fighting for our emotional lives. Guides to dating rules might as well be called Lao-tzu's *Art of War*. As soon as you let down your guard they knife you. Then you crawl back to your friends to have your wounds licked while they analyze where you went wrong and what was going through your attacker's head, with the finely honed skills of thirty-somethings who have already paid extortionate amounts to have their sensitive psyches probed by Upper East Side analysts.

We dress in gray and black and khaki. Combat trousers, big sweaters, bags strapped across our chests so that our hands are free to defend ourselves. The bare minimum of makeup. Big ugly rubber-soled shoes, in which we can run away from trouble. Our one sign of frivolity is the occasional bright, lace-trimmed, thermal vest. And pretty underwear, seen, alas, mostly by ourselves. We are urban survivors, striding across concrete pavements, ducking and weaving to avoid being elbowed by passing strangers who think we're in their path, dodging cycle deliverymen riding the wrong way down one-way streets, navigating through subway systems and a network of late-night bars where we drink too many martinis and smoke too many cigarettes to forget the last person who looked as if they could be the one and turned out to be a liar on a quick break from their ex.

We spend a fortune on cabs.

Case study one: Paola goes out for a drink with friends and bumps into a guy she nearly had a fling with at a work conference a few months ago. They fooled around but she didn't actually sleep with him because they're on the same work network. He's younger than she is and lower down the pecking order—she was nervous of the gossip. By not actually having sex with him she could keep her options open.

All good excuses. Actually she was scared.

So now here he is again, keen, handsome, attentive and making it clear that he still wants to sleep with her. A sure thing. And, from the fooling around, she assumes that the sex will be excellent. But she's out with a couple of people from work, and they know him. No way is she going to let down her guard, show that she wants to take him home, with the danger that it won't work out and that word will get around: it might make her vulnerable. What if he only wants her for sex? If they were both going in the same direction at the end of the night they could share a cab; but they aren't. So she lets it go. He asks her to ring him. She says she will. She won't. It's too close to home. Think of the risks.

We are perpetually sensitized to possibility. Phrases of cheap music run through our heads; we're always at the stage where they're meaningful. Even the most banal lyrics seem directly applicable to our current tortured situation.

"If only you were here tonight
I know that we could make it right…"

We would die rather than confess to liking the singers; our images demand that we listen to the latest hip bootleg remix, not trashy sentimental pop.

Case study two: Laura's the only one of our fighting unit in a relationship. She loves Skip and he loves her. He keeps asking her to marry him. They met four years ago and spent the first few months fucking each other's brains out. Laura ate like a horse and lost five pounds. After a year they decided to move in together. Both of them were ecstatic. The first night they spent in their new apartment, Skip rolled over with his back to her and said that he was really tired. That was it. They've hardly had sex since.

She tried to talk to him about it but every time he had a different excuse. He was stressed at work, he'd overdone it at the gym, now that they were living together they were going to have to get used to not having sex every single night. Gradually the excuses faded away, to be replaced by what turned out to be a manifesto. Why did sex matter that much anyway? Surely what mattered was how much they loved each other. Most people had much less sex than they boasted about, after all. They were just another normal couple. Laura shouldn't get so worked up about this. Hadn't she heard the story about the jar full of coins?

And every so often he would have sex with her, when he sensed that the strain of celibacy was becoming unbearable. The night before last had been one of those times.

"Pity fuck," says Phil.

"Relationship-maintenance fuck," I correct.

"Well, no. The trouble is," Laura says helplessly, "is that it was *good*. You know what I mean? It wasn't a let's-get-this-over-with-so-she-can't-complain-for-another-few-months fuck. It was like the old times. That's the thing. Nothing's changed. And that just makes it worse. I mean, he can still do it like that, so why doesn't he?"

"Would you have preferred it to be perfunctory and loveless?" David inquires.

"'You're going through the motions but you don't really care,'" Paola sings, a snippet of an old song that's just been covered and remixed within an inch of its life and is enjoying a brief heyday in the charts, the original singer long forgotten.

"No, he did care, he does care," Laura says miserably. "And yeah, I would much rather the sex was crap. At least I could say, okay, that side of things is over, and deal with it. But when it's that good, it's like he's keeping me on a string. Doling out something from time to time just so I keep from starving completely."

"You do have that I-had-good-sex-recently glow," David observes.

"Yeah, what's your problem, bitch?" I say jokingly. "You had great sex the night before last! That's probably more recent than anyone round this table!"

Laura shoots me a foul look. But so does everyone else.

"What's the jar-full-of-coins thing?" Phil asks.

Three of us start to speak at once. David makes it through.

"That if you put a coin in a jar for each time you have sex the first year in a marriage, and take one out every time you have sex after that, the jar'll still have coins in it when you die."

"Whoa," Phil says. "That's why I'm never getting married."

This is a complete bluff, a moment of machismo. Phil would love more than anything to get married. We all know this so well that no one bothers to call him on it.

"Look," Paola says to Laura, her voice sober. Clearly she has decided to be the voice of reason. "It'll never get much better. You've got two choices—leave him or have affairs. I think you should have affairs. Bet he never asks questions. Shit, he'll probably be grateful."

"Well-concealed commitment issues," says David, grave as a doctor diagnosing a fatal disease. "That's a tough one."

"Maybe he's depressed," says Phil. "That's the first thing to make a guy lose his woody. The trouble is, even the new antidepressants don't exactly up your libido."

We all look at Phil.

"Yeah," he says. "But you know, the thing is, I don't care! I'm so happy on my Prozac right now I don't care if I ever get laid again!"

We all edge back in the booth like vampires who have just spotted a clove of garlic in the middle of the table.

"We'll do that one later," Paola decides. "Right now we're still on Laura."

"I'm scared of rocking the boat," Laura says. "The rest of the time it's so perfect. And maybe if we get married it'll get better."

We all laugh sardonically. Laura has talked about this problem enough times that we are allowed to find this amusing.

"What makes you think that?" David looks weary. We have all had this conversation with her, over and over again. "If moving in together fucked up the sex, then marriage'll be ten times worse."

"But it's so perfect in every other way," Laura repeats hopelessly. "I mean, I don't have to tell you guys that."

We all know and love Skip. He's funny, sweet and dealt very well with the trial-by-fire of meeting Laura's friends. He has a good job that he enjoys and is good-looking without being so unnecessarily handsome that other women hit on him all the time or are automatically hostile to his girl-friend. He's easygoing, not a slob, and obviously adores Laura. Your ideal man. As a gay best friend.

"What happens if I do leave him?" Laura is so scared by the thought she can barely get the words out. "Back on the street again, out there in dating hell…" She shivers. "No offense, you guys…"

We shrug to show that none has been taken.

"You all know what I went through before I met Skip. I honestly don't think I can do that again. My God, I'll be single for the rest of my life."

Laura doesn't actually say it; she knows we'd shoot her down. But we can see her thinking it. Better a stable relationship with a guy who loves her, the social certainties of being in a couple, the end to loneliness, than our nocturnal, bar-crawling existence, our latest reports from the war front.

I can't blame her.

"Is he getting it anywhere else?" asks Phil. Prozac has not managed to suppress his cynicism.

This is the first time anyone has put this question to Laura. She looks shell-shocked.

We don't know how to advise Laura, or anyone with long-term relationship problems. No one does, apart from our shrinks. Long-term relationships require patience, compromise and faith, and we are familiar with none of the above. Indeed, we see them all as signs of weakness.

"I hung on, hoping she'd change," one of us will say feebly, and the others will expel their breath in tight hisses from clenched teeth, like the last puffs of a milk frother making cappuccino. In our world, you never hang on. You explain that the person's behavior is unacceptable, that they have breached your tolerance limit, that you value yourself too much to put up with their latest sin of omission or commission, and you move on, head held high. Your friends applaud: you have done the right thing.

We are terrified of being like our parents, either trapped in unhappy marriages or undergoing bloody, prolonged divorces. We all remember what those felt like, our limbs strapped to four horses all running in different directions. Even now, we are barely managing to put the pieces together again, with the help of the aforementioned expensive therapists. No way are any of us getting into that kind of mess ourselves. Our parents' pathetic excuses for the misery we went through are still vivid to us. The lesson we have learned is never put up with anything. Any signs of trouble and we're out of there.

We are all desperate to be in love. But we are more desperate to hide it. So for pride's sake, we pretend, to ourselves and others, that it's all about sex instead.

★ ★ ★

I'm waiting for Ivan to call. It's been a week now and my stomach is processing food faster than I can eat it. I'm chain-smoking and ringing my friends constantly to discuss what might have gone wrong on the date that would mean he wouldn't want to see me again.

"Go to bed with someone else," says David. "It's perfect. You distract yourself and then, when he does call, you can be really cool."

"What, just go and pick some guy up in the bar on the corner?" I say sarcastically.

"You must know someone… What about that guy you were seeing a couple of months ago?"

"Seamus?"

"He was really into you, wasn't he?"

"Yeah," I say smugly. "Took him ages to stop calling."

"And the sex was good, wasn't it?"

"Great," I confirm. "It was the conversation that was the problem."

"Well, that's perfect!" David says enthusiastically. "Call him up right now and tell him to come over because you need to get laid. If a woman I'd been seeing gave me a call like that I'd be ecstatic. Even if I was busy, or dating someone else, I'd be ecstatic."

"Wouldn't you think I was a slut?" I ask.

David is my, and many other women's, Official Man. We touch base with him to see what men are really thinking. The trouble is that he tells us.

"No way. I'd be hugely flattered and I wouldn't be able to stop thinking about you. So ring him."

"Oh, David," I whine, "I can't. He's only just stopped calling. It would be cruel. It would give him false hope."

The mere thought of seeing Seamus again—reading that happiness in his eyes, his pleasure at seeing me—makes me feel horribly guilty.

"Bullshit. Just be straight with him. Tell him you don't want to date him but the sex was fabulous and you want to get laid."

"You'd never do something like that yourself," I say. "It's all very well advising other people to do it."

Silence. My phone beeps.

"David, I have another call, hold on—"

I switch over. It's Paola. I tell her I'll call back.

"Was it Ivan?" David says.

"No," I say.

We observe a moment's silence, as if in mourning.

"Anyway, I feel really bad about the way I treated Seamus," I say.

I do feel bad. But also, shameful though it is to admit it, I am cheered up just a little by the knowledge that, while I am pining for Ivan, someone else is doing the same for me. "Here I am complaining about Ivan not ringing, just disappearing like this—"

"You don't know that," says David, automatically reassuring. "He might just be busy at work. You know, girl time is very different from boy time."

"—and that's exactly what I did to Seamus."

"You haven't had sex with Ivan yet."

"Well, that makes what I did to Seamus even worse. I never returned his calls. I was a real bitch. And now I'm whining about someone doing that to me. I don't deserve Ivan to ring me back."

"Hey." David's voice sharpens. "It's all tactics. Remember that. You didn't promise Seamus anything, did you?"

It's a rhetorical question: he knows the answer already.

"So there's no guilt," he continues. "You didn't break any promises."

"I could at least have told him what was going on."

David sounds weary now.

"Forget the conscience," he says. "That isn't how it works. You know that."

Our pockets are full of matchboxes from bars we can't even remember, hangouts we have been swept along to at three in the morning by groups of people we don't know that well. It's not so much that we think if we stay out till dawn we might finally stumble across The One, bleary-eyed and blinking, like us, in the daylight; no, we want to postpone the moment of going home alone to our single-bedroom apartments until we're too drunk or tired, or both, to be anything but grateful that there are no witnesses waiting up to see the state in which we stagger through the front door, throwing our keys clumsily at the hall table and missing.

We are in our thirties. We all earn plenty of money and

have only ourselves to spend it on. We are very spoilt. We know we're spoilt, but it doesn't make us feel any better.

Paola's on a radical diet. She's decided that she needs to lose ten pounds. Paola probably does need to lose ten pounds, but we're worried about her reasons—she's frantic to get a steady boyfriend—and her methods, which are frighteningly drastic. All she's eaten for the last three weeks are meal-substitute bars and the occasional piece of fruit. And she's taken up circuit training.

"Her body is just not up to this," Laura says. "I mean, think of the shock to the system!"

"Not as much of a shock as it would be if she gave up drinking," I say.

We exchange a glance. This is the trouble. The one vice Paola is allowing herself is alcohol. She's drinking as much as ever, only now with much less in her stomach to soak it up. As if to compensate for the deprivation through which she's putting herself, she eats her meal bar and then comes out with us to consume the same amount of cocktails that she did when she was still packing away heaped platefuls of comfort food. Every night we have to practically mop her up off the floor and pour her into a cab.

The reason Paola doesn't have a boyfriend is that she gets off with men practically as soon as she meets them. She hasn't been on a first date in the last couple of years that didn't end, at least, with a tongue-sandwich fumble in the back of a cab. Mostly, this city being a brutal arena in which women who give away too much too soon are seen as weak, the men never call her again. But sometimes they do. In which case she decides that they must be desperate. Why would they want a fat girl otherwise?

Paola isn't fat by any standards but the near-anorexic ones of this city. One would think that the legions of men who keep asking her out would eventually convince her that she's attractive, but it doesn't seem to work that way. Instead, the way she behaves toward them creates a self-fulfilling prophecy.

"She blames everything on her weight because it's easier that way," Laura says.

I agree. "But if she loses it, what's her excuse going to be?"

"That's the problem," Laura says darkly. "I'm sure that's why she's getting so drunk."

"Fear of not having anything to hide behind."

"Exactly."

"Oh, fuck," I say selfishly. I have enough to deal with right now without the prospect of a hundred-and-twenty-pound Paola in deep existential crisis.

Case study three: Ivan seemed perfect. A friend of a friend, highly recommended. Attentive, funny, sweet, caring, good job, nice apartment. Someone older than me, stable, a rock in high seas. For every question I ask about him he asks ten about me. It's wonderful. He rings me regularly. We're making plans for the next few weeks. Then nothing. Two weeks later, I finally get a phone call telling me that he's hooked up with an ex-girlfriend; they'd had problems that they've now resolved. And—the clincher—she's madly in love with him.

"He's trying to set up a competition between the two of you," says David.

"What's this madly-in-love thing?" says Laura. "What are you supposed to say—I love you more? You've only known him a few weeks!"

"You should have said—'What are you really telling me?'" says my therapist. "Think more about your own emotions and less about his."

"What's his emotional history?" says Paola. "Has he been married? Lived with anyone? For how long? What do you mean, you didn't ask him? You've always got to find that out! If a guy's hitting forty and he's never been married or lived with anyone, he has serious issues to resolve."

I realize that I am very, very tired. I go to bed instead of hitting the bars with my posse and I sleep for twelve hours straight. I don't feel that much better in the morning but at least I don't have a hangover. Maybe this is a new start.

Yesterday I was walking down Fifth Avenue, listening to my iPod, when a wash of peace flooded through me. I felt invisible, or at least transparent. I wanted to open my arms wide and stand there, letting people walk through me as if I were a ghost. It was wonderful. Does that mean I don't care anymore? That would be such a relief.

"Typical of you to have a Zen breakthrough on the middle of Fifth Avenue," Laura says.

"I know!" I say. "And I wasn't even outside Gucci!"

"What does your shrink think about it?" she says.

"I haven't told her yet," I admit. "I'm keeping it to myself."

And as I say this, I realize how good it feels. Maybe I shouldn't even have told Laura. David, Laura, Paola, Phil—we're each other's safety net, and everyone outside is the enemy. And now I wonder how much it's actually helping. Perhaps I should start keeping more things to myself. I don't know if it would help, but it might be worth trying.

Something has to change, after all. Maybe I'll start with this.

Megan McCafferty is the author of the comic com-ing-of-age novel *Sloppy Firsts* and its sequel, *Second Helpings*. She also edited the short story anthology *Sixteen: Stories About That Sweet and Bitter Birthday* (Three Rivers Press, 2004). A former magazine writer and editor, she lives with her husband and young son in Princeton, New Jersey, where she is currently at work on the third book in the Jessica Darling series. Find out more at www.meganmccafferty.com.

From This Moment
by Megan McCafferty

I'm lost and late for my wedding.

"Where in the holy hell are you?" barks Tino from my cell phone.

"Somewhere on Route 37…"

"East or west?"

East? West? Why not go ahead and ask for longitude and latitude? I take a guess.

"West?"

"Just keep going, then," he says. "We can't start until you get here."

"I know."

"If this relationship is going to work, we need to discuss your time-mismanagement issues."

"I know."

"Remember, Cleo," he says before hanging up, "this could be the biggest day of *your* life."

"I know."

But it isn't. Tino's not my groom and I'm never the bride. I'm the lead singer for Diamondz!, "New Jersey's most exciting, high-energy and elegant dance band." And every weekend, I get paid to be no small part of the biggest day of someone else's life. I'm the image the brides and grooms are buying when they hire us for receptions, making me the most important person outside the wedding party, which is funny because I'm the only one who seems to be aware that this job is *so* in need of a saltine.

When I took the gig, I convinced myself that I'd be doing a lot of songs by Lionel Ritchie, Air Supply and Journey. "Hello," "The One That You Love," "Open Arms"— stuff so painful that it's kind of fun in a karaoke way. But most of my cheesy, easy-listening favorites are sung by men. So the bulk of my repertoire consists of Cher, Celine and Shania, with a few disco classics and old-fart standards thrown in. Velveeta: *like* real cheese, but not. The most challenging thing about the vocals is trying not to yawn.

My cell rings again. Tino, and I'm ignoring it this time. Screaming at me won't get me to the Holiday Inn any faster.

Tino Perillo is the business manager/band leader/keyboard player for Diamondz! He looks like Danny DeVito's brother—that is, if Danny got all the height and hair—but he's a 35-year industry veteran and has seen some crazy stuff. "People die, screw, take a dump—all on the dance floor!"

he loves saying. The story he always tells is about the time a bride's huge, sprayed hairdo caught fire, just like you see on *America's Funniest Home Videos.* He put out the flames by dumping a bowl of fruit cocktail on her head. The bride threatened to sue, even after Tino offered to pick the still-sizzling maraschino cherries out of the charred remains of her David's Bridal tulle headband. Nothing so thrilling has happened in the two months I've been with the band, though I have seen more than one Golden Girl throw out her hip trying to get down, get funky to The Electric Slide.

Tino's son Junior plays bass and sings all the male leads. His smooth vocals are outdone only by his pickup lines and he never leaves a reception without a bombed bridesmaid's phone number. It helps that he, unlike his father, has a full head of hair and is over five feet tall. Our percussionist, Freddy "Flash" Reynolds, has toured the Atlantic City circuit with Tom Jones and Neil Sedaka and he loves to shoot his mouth off about what pros they are. The oldest member of the band, Richard Butts, plays a dozen instruments, which, in his mind, makes him a Jersey version of Prince—only fat and white. He believes he's destined to go platinum with the solo project he's been working on for seventeen years in his basement recording studio. He's also a middle school band teacher, only like, the *worst* job for someone with his name. Vondra Brown is our one-woman horn section, and the only way she and I could have less in common is if she had a penis. Need a visual? Think a pre-stomach-stapled Al Roker in a lady's tux and mascara.

Then there's Johnny Stevens, the lead guitar player, who

does have a penis, and knows how to use it. We've been fucking long enough to be a *thing,* if not an official couple. Our relationship, if you can call it that, does not run any deeper than my diaphragm, and that's fine. In fact, the only explanation for this arrangement is that it's practically a job requirement for female singers to sleep with one of the other members of the band. It's a big whatever, whatever, whatever. I'm thirty and single. The only annoying thing about it is the thirty part, and that's only because it means I'm too old to audition for *American Idol.*

Another piercing *riiiiiiiiiiiiing.* It's my mother. Before I pick up, I make a mental note to rig the phone to play a song. Maybe…? I can't think of anything that hasn't been schmaltzed by Tino.

"Hey, Viv," I say. "I'm lost."

"Vivian," she corrects. "And tell me something I don't know."

"Is the Holiday Inn after IHOP?" I ask, zooming past the pancake house.

"Yes," she replies. "Who are my future clients today?"

"Not a clue," I said. "They booked before I was in the band."

"Give them my business card."

"Okay, Viv,"

"Vivian."

"Okay, Vivian."

She smooches a goodbye kiss into the phone.

Viv should be happy that I didn't call her The Terminator, my private nickname that describes both what she does and how she does it. My mother is one of the state's top divorce lawyers, and if she's taught me anything, it's that marriage is a doomed institution. This is her professional and personal opinion, a lucrative one at that. She and my dad split right before she started law school because he had the nerve to stay a penniless saxophone player after they wed, even though my mother thought it was bohemian and romantic before.

"I should have known better," she says, as she always says when she talks about my father.

But most couples don't know better, and so Tino has made a sport out of predicting whether the newlywed couple of the evening will make it five years. He then follows up on their fifth anniversary to see if they're still together. Google makes this so much easier than it used to be, and nine times out of ten he discovers his prediction is right.

My cell. Tino. I shut it off.

According to Tino, breakups within the band are more devastating than divorce. He's been with Diamondz! longer than any of his three ex-wives, and despite my chronic lateness, Tino says I'm a keeper because I'm the first chick singer who isn't certifiably insane. This goes a long way. Before me was Vernique, who had a problem with numbers— at the DellaPietro/Sanchez wedding, she sang all the way through the first chorus of "We Are Family" (#46 in the Diamondz! songbook) before Tino tapped her on the shoulder and told her that the rest of the band was playing "Respect" (#64). Before Vernique was Ms. Danielle, who hurled whatever was within reach—water bottles, floral centerpieces, mike stands—at any poor fool who made the

mistake of addressing her without the formal title. Before
Ms. Danielle was Coco, who everyone called Coo-Coo because of the inconveniences of her purpurachromatopho-
bia: fear of the color purple.

I don't have such hang-ups. And I've also been very good
for business because I'm a major improvement imagewise.
I've seen videos of the singers before me, who all lived by
the motto of height (hair), bright (makeup) and tight
(clothes). But the closest I'll get to a compliment is that I'm
"nondescript."

"That's good," Tino booms. "We want them to remember the songs, not you."

While stopped at a light in front of Fuddruckers, I check
out my reflection because I won't have time to freshen up
at the hotel. I'm tastefully made up with red—but not too
red—lips and enough mascara and liner to make my blue
eyes pop. My hair is molded into a chignon that is always
too chic for the room, in a believable-but-bottled-blond
shade my mother hates.

"L.A. has literally gone to your head," was all she said
when she saw it during her first and last trip out West. Viv
was born—and will forever be—a no-nonsense brunette.
She's always reminded me of Linda Lavin, if Alice wore Ar-
mani and charged $350 an hour.

"Never Say Goodbye" comes on the radio. It was one of
my favorites in high school, so it boosts my spirits and
makes me feel less stressed about not knowing where I am.
I want to program it into my cell so I can shout-sing the
lyrics—*TOOGEEHHTHAHH!   FOHEHHVAHH!*—

whenever I want. But Johnny holds a grudge against Bon Jovi because—as he'll tell anyone within two seconds of a "Howya doin'?"—they booted him out of the band in 1983 because he was prettier than Jon. He really is, too. Even though Johnny and I don't have a real connection, I can't help but feel that singing along with Bon Jovi is a betrayal. In the end, I switch stations because a wailing interpretation of any anthem by New Jersey's second favorite rock band would put too much of a strain on my voice before a gig. The job may be a joke, but there's no reason to be un-professional about it.

I'm dying for a cigarette but it's another vice that's bad for my voice and besides, The Terminator would kill me if I lit up in her Lexus. I hit the dashboard clock until the real time vanishes and 12:00 a.m. 12:00 a.m. 12:00 a.m. flashes in my face. I still don't know where I am, so I might as well keep the time a mystery, too. I grew up around here, so I guess I *should* know the particulars of Route 37, a three-lane, stop-and-go stretch of highway flanked by fast-food franchises, furniture outlets and car dealerships. The road is so blah that it's just begging to be forgotten. And naviga-tion isn't one of my strengths, one of many reasons I left L.A.

Viv says this: "If a game-show host offered my daughter a million dollars to name the street that runs parallel to her home for the first eighteen years of her life—and the past six months—the laws of probability decree that she'd have as good a shot at guessing correctly as a chimpanzee on a laptop has of producing *The Da Vinci Code* or whichever book a monkey could be expected to produce at random when given enough time for endless possibilities. And if asked how she could possibly *not* know the name of that street—for the record, Loon Lake Boulevard—a street down which I have driven her, or she has driven herself, more times than the amount of hypothetical money offered for this knowledge, my daughter would undoubtedly shrug and say, 'Whatever, whatever, whatever.'"

This is a direct quote, I swear. I've got a gift for memorizing lines, a talent I haven't had an opportunity to use lately. I only have to hear a scene once and I can commit it to memory, and I've heard this particular monologue many, many times. Viv is always going on about how I have a "frightening lack of direction" and she doesn't just mean my problems with getting from point A to point B in a car.

"You have a frightening lack of direction," she said, as she always says when I deliver bad news. In this particular case, I had just told her that my apartment had burned down, I was broke and I needed a place to live.

"Everything happens for a reason," my dad said, when I gave him the same news. He always says that, too, because he, like me, doesn't get riled up about setbacks. But then, as my mother pointed out, he could afford to be so Zen about it because he knew I wouldn't be moving in with *him* in his one-bedroom Sonny Crockett condo in Miami.

I can still remember my mother's face the day I returned to my childhood home, one of those boxy seventies-era bi-levels in a neighborhood that bores you with its bi-level, split-level, bi-level, split-level ordinariness. Not even Botox could hide her concern—a wrinkle for every year of *my* life dented her forehead. I set down the canvas Trader Joe's bag containing my wallet, toothbrush and diaphragm (my only earthly possessions that survived the apartment fire because they were with me, out on a one-night stand that would have otherwise been forgettable if it hadn't possibly saved my life) and tried to erase the lines by convincing her that this arrangement, like everything, is only temporary. I've refused to make my move official by notifying the post office or friends from my former West Coast life. That would be admitting that this short-term housing arrangement has already lasted longer than I thought it would. Besides, anyone who needs me will find me somehow. I don't think about those who won't.

And living with my mother in The House That Hate Built is just a pit stop between where I used to be and where I'll end up. This not-really-here attitude is fitting, because our house is in never-ending transition. Rather than buy a state-of-the-art McMansion in a wealthier part of the state, Viv invests all her money into staying put. She pours thousands and thousands of dollars into one remodeling/redecorating project after another, often pricier versions of Vern's makeovers on *Trading Spaces*. She wouldn't listen when I questioned her decision to pay someone to cover her fireplace with rusty bottlecaps. According to her, anyone who has slept on a couch dragged in off the street wasn't qualified to have an opinion on interior design.

"All I'm saying is that most things look better on TV," I said. "Which is why I've always thought it would be the perfect medium for me."

"I think *employment* would be the perfect medium for you," The Terminator fired back.

When I first returned home, Viv tried to persuade me to go back to college for a degree in music education. But I'm not into the idea of directing the local middle school's production of *Godspell*. And besides, you can't teach talent, which is why I never regretted leaving college. If anything, I wish I had taken the money spent on my first and only year enrolled in Montclair State's theater program and used it for cosmetic surgery. If I had gotten the fat sucked out of my ass, turned my A cups into Cs and had the tiny bump removed from the bridge of my nose, could I have gotten that part on *Beverly Hills, 90210* as Trini, the troubled runaway-turned-pop-star?

But I'm too scared to go under the knife now. In L.A., the land of plastic surgery cautionary tales, I heard about this girl who wanted to remove some of her butt luggage and the doctor screwed up and she ended up totally deformed, like Jaws himself had taken a huge bite out of the fatty flesh on her upper thigh. They never show outcomes like that on *Extreme Makeover.* But what if I'd gotten plastic surgery before I'd heard about that? What if I had gotten the part and made out with Jason Priestley with such tongue-bathing enthusiasm that my guest stint turned into a recurring role that somehow convinced a casting director to give me the Academy Award–winning part in a controversial independent film? What if *I* were Hilary Swank? Of course, my new boobs would've ruled out *Boys Don't Cry,* but I'm sure something else would have come up. But I'll never know.

I zip past the Pineville Multiplex Cinemas, and will myself not to think about the blockbusters that might have been. Unlike all of my neurotic friends in the business, I don't see the point in talk, talk, talking about the past. It's a no-brainer that my way is the happier way, even if my refusal to hash out my history makes it impossible for me to practice method acting. To be honest, "The Method" isn't all that crucial when the role in question is say, Wilma Flintstone in Six Flags *Yabba Dabba Doo Revue*.

But I'm okay with this. My favorite show is *Inside the Actor's Studio* because, despite my current job, I consider myself to be an actress who sings, not vice versa. Julia and Nicole and Renée all talk about how they were about to give up on stardom, but then their big break arrived and now they are all better artists as a result of the struggle. Right now must be my low point. I'm just waiting for my turning point. The moment I'll refer to when I'm interviewed by James Lipton, and he asks when I knew that I'd make good on the HOLLYWOOD HERE I COME!!!! boast immortalized under my high school yearbook picture.

Actually, arriving in Hollywood wasn't the hard part. The hard part was Arriving with a capital A.

"Where are all the shows about failed singers and actresses?" my mother asked during a recent viewing of *Inside*. "When they talk about the factors that lead to their decision to give up. Grow up. Get a job. Get married."

"You want me to get married?" I asked, shocked.

"No, dear," she said with a sigh. "But even that would be better than this, if only because it meant that you'd made a decision about something. *Anything*."

What she didn't know is that I *had* made a decision. A decision to be hopeful about this job, despite the cheese. The Holiday Inn is more than a few exits on the turnpike short of Hollywood, and I may not even make it there this afternoon, but Diamondz! showcases my talent for hundreds of wedding guests every weekend. It was closer to my dream than waitressing at Nacho Mama's or any of the other Mexican joints that had employed me over the past decade in L.A. All it would take is *one* well-connected person to hear my voice and make me a star. I read a *People* profile about international pop sensation Anasomethingorother, who got her start as a singer in a wedding band. I had never heard of her before, none of her hits were in the Diamondz! songbook, but I took *People*'s word for it. She made it. Why not me?

Hallelujah! I see a star on the horizon, and it's perched atop the familiar kelly-green sign for the hotel. As I pull into the parking lot, I look up and read its soothing white script: Relax, It's The Holiday Inn. So I do.

I stride right up to the main entrance and burst through the electronic doors. According to the clock behind the check-in desk, I'm expected on stage in two minutes to sing the bride and groom's first dance. This is plenty of time. I don't need to get there so early that some bridezilla can get all up in my face asking me if I'm *sure* I know how to sing this song, that song, whatever, whatever, whatever. Wedding bands are neck in neck with tribute bands in terms of lack of respect. Like, we're repeatedly reminded to use the back entrance located by the Dumpsters that reek of piss and moldy potato peelings—a rule I ignore on principle. Nobody's furiously picking out the green M&Ms to make *us* happy. We're lucky if we get a few soggy deli sandwiches thrown our way.

I strut across the worn floral carpet, past stragglers still noshing on cocktail hour spinach puffs and mozzarella sticks. I enter the Crystal Room, take the stage and step in front of the mike with just enough time for the band to shoot dirty looks and Johnny to pinch my ass. Normally, I think this is kind of sweet. But right now, it makes me want to put yellow police tape around the whole disaster area so he'll just stay away. It's as if I already know we're never going to sleep together again.

"What's the special song?" I ask, meaning the couple's first dance. I'm not afraid of Tino anymore because I'm here now and all is forgiven.

"The Shania," Tino replies knowingly, rolling his eyes.

The Shania is as tired as the lifts in Tino's patent leather shoes. So many couples have chosen it as their special song that it's anything but. Still, I think it's better than couples who pick a quirky song on purpose, to prove just how non-conforming they are, despite the big white dress and the garter toss and all the other traditional wedding stuff that they'll tell you their parents forced them to include at the risk of disappointing Aunt Edna. Tino says that nine times out of ten, that "quirky" song is "Margaritaville."

I size up the crowd of about a hundred and fifty or so, just to get an idea of the evening ahead. Most of the women, young and old, are cheaply overdressed in sequined designer knockoffs that they think are classy. The men are in synthetic-blend sports jackets and too-skinny ties. I see cowboy boots. It's a typical South Jersey hootenanny and I will be singing a lot of unchallenging crossover country songs.

I'm up there with a smile shellacked to my face, *whootwhooting* and clapping along with the band as they play Buster Poindexter's "Hot! Hot! Hot!" for what Tino has declared "the most smokin' bridal party of 2004!" Then Tino puts on his *yowza, yowza* announcer voice for the grand entrance of the bride and groom.

"Annnnd noooooow, put your hands together to welcome, for the very first time, Mr. and Mrs. Ronald Schlomann!"

As the room explodes with applause, I think to myself, *Ronald Schlomann?*

Schlomo?

And before I can even shake off what a surreal coincidence that would be, *my* high school boyfriend comes running through the doors like a football player taking the field for the biggest game of the season. He's still built like a linebacker, though a little softer, puffier than he used to be. Same kinky-curly hair like a blond Berber carpet. Same red-flushed cheeks. Same squinty, jokey eyes. Same Schlomo.

I'm sweating from my chignon down and shivering from my stilettos up. The storm fronts clash and crash, creating a raging, category five hurricane in my belly because it's definitely him. See, this isn't just some guy. Schlomo was *the* guy for me in high school. He was my first kiss, my first feel-up-under-the-bra, my first making-love, my first fuck.

This is so bizarre that all I can do is remember the first

time we did it. Schlomo stood in front of me, erection in hand, wearing nothing but a shit-eating grin, a condom and…tube socks. I guess he was too excited to get completely undressed. Or maybe his feet were as cold as mine are right now. I don't know. The fact that I did not laugh him right out of my bedroom is a testimonial to just how much I loved him.

And I have never loved anyone since.

I haven't spoken to him since our freshman year of college, when I found out from a friend who was at Rutgers with Schlomo that he had cheated on me with the cheerleader at the top of the pyramid. (Her?!?!?!) I stopped thinking about him shortly after. I haven't let myself think about him since. Out of sight, out of mind. Out of mind, out of memory. Out of memory, out of misery. It helped that I left for L.A. shortly after.

His bride has a goofy, gummy smile that takes up too much of her face. Her dress weighs more than she does. It's even got an abundance of ass plumage, which to me, is just a huge insult because it's like, *Oh gee whiz, my butt is so tiny that I have to adorn it with a gigantic bedazzled bow just so people notice it.* I'm considering crashing into Flash's drum kit in outrage, but I don't. Tiny ass aside, Schlomo's bride is simply not attractive enough for such theatrics.

I'm gripping the mike stand like it's a scrawny little neck, locking eyes with Mrs. Schlomann, Schlomo's mom. She adored me so much in high school that she insisted I call her Wendy, which is not her name, but I did anyway. Her real name is actually Susan, and I never found out what was up with Wendy. But as someone who chose a dozen stage names before settling on Cleo Coltrane, I'm not one to judge.

Wendy is wearing a magenta, satinesque gown and her hair is done up in an Aqua Net tower. She looks like one of the lucky passengers who gets all gussied up to sit at Captain Steubing's table on *The Love Boat*. She will regret her fashion decisions when she gets the proofs back from the photographers, and the weird thing is that I still feel friendly enough to tell her this. That's how chummy we were, Wendy and me, about as tight as a mom would be with the girl who was regularly jerking off her son—and then more—in the back seat of the Honda she drove to work every day.

And right next to her, propped up by the stick jammed firmly up his butt, is Mr. Schlomann, who never told me to call him Cy, but I did anyway, which was one of the reasons he didn't like me. Another reason he didn't like me is that he knew I was jerking off his son in the back seat of his wife's Honda, and I have a feeling that was a whole lot more action than Wendy was giving him. Schlomo's parents were worse off together than my parents were apart and I can't imagine things have improved since then.

This is what's going through my mind. What *isn't* going through my mind is the reality of what's about to happen next.

"Annnnd nooooow, to kick off this celebration, the bride and groom would like to share their first dance as husband and wife!"

Their first dance. I'm supposed to sing. For them. Now. In the middle of all this reminiscing, I'd forgotten why I was there. The Shania begins as it has in countless weddings before, with Flash's soft rock drum strokes, and Tino's gentle keyboard chords.

I catch a glimpse of myself in one of the mirrors on the wall, me in all black and her in all white. Here's this bride, swaying on the dance floor like Frankenstein with a taffeta fetish, who has been dreaming about this day since she threw a weddingpalooza for her Barbie and Ken dolls, and here I am, the woman who her husband will always remember for being his first *everything*. Schlomo will look up at me when my voice, the voice of his high school sweetheart, rings out at his own wedding reception, reminding him of all the wonderful times we had together, and he will surely regret every decision that has led him to this fate. Schlomo will shoot me a wink, the way he always did after all my high school shows when the lights were up and the audience was on its feet and I, the star, was taking my solo bow. It was his way of saying, *Plays are gay but I'm proud of you.*

And then, as if he's reading my innermost thoughts, Schlomo takes his eyes off the bride and gazes up at the stage, at me. I expect a delicious flash of horror, regret, surprise like, *Holy shit! The love of my life is at my wedding!*

But his eyes go right through me. It's the kind of blankness that's reserved for a total stranger, for someone he won't even extend the courtesy of fake politeness.

He has no idea who I am.

This song doesn't have much of a lead-in before the vocals, so it's already clear to everyone—the band, the bride and groom, the guests—that something is terribly wrong. The ballroom has gotten eerily silent, except for the *tsk-tsk-*

*tsk*ing of the snare drum, and the synthetic strings suspended in the air.

Tino taps me on the shoulder, and calmly whispers a command.

"Sing."

But I can't even breathe. This is a simple song, but there's no way I'll be able to squeeze enough oxygen out of my diaphragm to support the notes. A reservoir of flop-sweat is collecting in the gap between my real boobs and the fake ones built into the dress. My tongue tastes like one of the rusty bottle caps on my mother's fireplace. My blood is slamming through my veins to a techno beat, even though the song is a ballad.

"Sing," Tino says again, only this time it sounds more like, *Sing, you crazy bitch, or I'll make sure you never sing again!*

I've never had stage fright before. Well, once. But I wasn't onstage. It was at a party my parents threw when I was really little. I must have been just a baby because my father left when I was four and it was before that, but I still remember a haze of cigarette smoke and dark drinks in short glasses, and women and men alike dressed in foody hues that you just don't see anymore, not even in the ugliest bridesmaid dresses: salmon, avocado, tangerine.

And the soundtrack to these parties was always wordless, voiceless—just bluesy, boozy jazz performed by artists whose names I already knew by heart: Charlie Parker, Miles Davis and my father's favorite, John Coltrane. My father took the needle off the record player and asked me to sing along with him while he played "My Funny Valentine" on the saxophone. That was my dad's idea of a lullaby. I knew all the words because we sang it together before I went to bed, on the rare nights he was home, when he wasn't playing gigs on cruise ships and screwing one of the backup singers.

On this night, he wanted me to sing for his dinner guests. He was wearing a shiny paisley shirt, unbuttoned to reveal a chest tanned on the high seas. His mustache hugged his smiling lips, and his feathery hair glowed golden under the track lights. He hated popular music, but he looked just like a rock god posing for an album cover.

"She's our little star, isn't she, Viv?" he said.

"Stop encouraging her," my mother said, crossing her arms tighter than her wrap dress.

I believed *him*. But instead of singing, I cried and peed my pants. The audience shifted in the dining-room chairs and I was shooed away for the rest of the night. I don't remember why I couldn't sing, only that I couldn't. Maybe I didn't want this private thing between me and my dad to become a big show for his friends' entertainment.

Later, after my dad left for good, I sang quietly to myself under the covers, *stay, funny valentine, stay.* I quickly realized that reliving the pain didn't make me feel better about it.

"Give up. Grow up. Get a real job. Get married," my mother says.

"Everything happens for a reason," my dad says.

"This could be the biggest day of *your* life," Tino says.

Schlomo's eyes are still on me.

I never believed in the idea of being in the right place at the right time. Fate was simply being *some*place at *some*time.

But now, I suddenly understand that I've been moving in a very specific direction all these years, though I didn't know it. Start with any point in my life, and you'll see how every whatever, whatever, whatever has led to this. Like, if I hadn't been cut by *90210,* I wouldn't have needed a roommate in L.A. If my stoner roommate hadn't burned down our apartment after trying to make a hookah out of our fire extinguisher, then I wouldn't have moved back East. If I hadn't moved in with my mother, I wouldn't have seen the ad in the *Asbury Park Press:* FEMALE SINGER NEEDED, 18–25. And if I hadn't been female, and a singer who could still *pass* for twenty-five just as long as no one asked for any legal documents to prove it, I wouldn't have gotten the job after winning Tino over with a chest-thumping version of "My Heart Will Go On." And if I hadn't impressed Tino, I would've never sung with Diamondz! and never been hired for this wedding. If I hadn't done any of these things, I wouldn't be reunited, right now, with the only man I have ever loved.

Schlomo used to tell me that he would never throw my letters away.

"They'll be worth something someday," he said.

I wonder if he still has them. If, without knowing it, we've been holding on to the same dream all these years.

I turn to Tino and whisper, "Will they stay together?"

Tino jerks his head.

"No."

This is my turning point. Only it's not the kind you hear

described by Julia and Nicole and Renée. Not the kind I'll ever get to share on cable TV. It's the kind you hear from happily married couples, the ones you believe when you ask them how they knew and they tell you they just *knew*.

I find deep significance in their special song. So much, that it has become my song. Our song.

"From this moment," I sing, low and slow. *"Life has begun…"*

My voice goes out to Schlomo, and only him. His life also begins today, but not in the way he thinks it has. Mine is the performance of a lifetime, for a lifetime.

Louise Bagshawe is the author of many UK best-sellers, including *The Go-To Girl* (known as *Monday's Child* in the UK) and *The Devil You Know.*

What Goes Around...
by Louise Bagshawe

"I know it's hard to believe, but eventually you're going to get over it."

Emma McCloud looked at her husband and blinked. As if she were trying to take it in.

John McCloud looked nervously around Le Petit Coq, the fancy French restaurant he had booked them in to for dinner. He had ordered cheese soufflé, partly because he liked cheese, and partly because it took half an hour to prepare, and that way the waitress wouldn't bother them. Ordinarily, he didn't mind being bothered by the waitresses here—all of them long-legged, bottle-tanned and under twenty-five—but tonight, he needed some privacy. For Emma, he thought nobly, as much as for him.

"Say something," John said, his American accent low-pitched so that none of the neighboring tables could hear.

"And don't start with the crying, okay? That's Mary-Beth Astor at table four."

Emma turned round semiautomatically. Yes, she registered in a small part of her brain. John was right; there was Mary-Beth, the fourth wife of Richard Astor, the famous TV producer. Mary-Beth was twenty-two, with pneumatic tits, a fountain of scarlet hair and lips plumped up monthly with cow collagen. She had also had one of those Botox injections that paralyzed the muscles in your forehead that let you frown, thus giving her a permanently surprised air. She looked like an inflatable sex doll, with her round, lazy, open lips always lined a shade darker than her lipstick. She was sitting there with a friend, a brunette version of herself. Salads—doubtless *sans* dressing—were being delivered to their table. And, of course, John was anxious that they not upset Mary-Beth. He *cared* about the opinion of Mary-Beth.

Emma smothered a small giggle. Wildly inappropriate for the occasion, of course, but it just came out. What was a Surrey girl to do?

John scowled at her. He thought, *I hope she's not going to make a scene.* He hated that about her, the sentimentality, always clinging, always fussing about the children. She had fought him for so many years on the most trivial things, and sometimes the waterworks had come out. He thought of them as her nuclear weapon. What busy executive wanted to see his wife crying in public? Goddamn limey broad. Weren't they supposed to have a stiff upper lip? Just because he'd wanted to send Brad and Sophia overseas to boarding school instead of educating them here in the U.S. He was the one that paid the bills; he should have had the final say. But Emma was always making things difficult.

"What do you want me to say?" Emma asked softly. A waiter hovered to refill her glass, and to his annoyance, she didn't wave him away. A splash of chilled Pouilly Fuissé swirled into her glass, and his wife lifted it, sipping at the pale gold liquid like she was enjoying it. Like this was just a regular dinner. Man, he hoped she wasn't going to cope with this by getting publicly smashed.

Emma looked presentable tonight. She had always dressed well, he couldn't deny that; neat Chanel suits, pearls, kitten heels. Tonight she wore a rose-colored silk suit with the diamond studs he had given her last Christmas in her ears. Her hair was dark and neatly bobbed. She looked sophisticated and elegant, but hardly a babe. He knew that the trim body under that suit had stretch marks, and then there were the laugh lines around her mouth and eyes. All of his friends' wives—first wives, anyway—had popped off to see the dermatologist and then the plastic surgeon when those first appeared. But not Emma. She seemed unaccountably happy with herself; never went on a diet, and, unimaginable in L.A., was content to look her age. Of course, she had good skin and stayed out of the sun, but that, in his opinion, was no substitute for the surgeon's knife. Emma had good humor and good homemaking skills. Even before he had gotten on the Hollywood studio gravy train, before he had given up his foolish screenwriting dreams to become a studio executive, Emma had kept a great house. On a tiny budget, she had managed to cook delicious meals, to always have fresh flowers around the place, and to keep the kids happy without parking them in front of the TV all day long. And later, he was the only husband he knew who hadn't had to hire an interior decorator.

But Emma refused to adapt to her surroundings. That was her problem, he told himself righteously. Imagine not caring about going to premieres, not caring about wrinkles, and not caring about getting on in the Hollywood social scene. Emma had turned down countless opportunities to co-chair one of those all-important, $2,000 a plate charity balls. She said her "job" mattered to her too much to take time off. Her stupid little book company. As if she needed to work! It embarrassed him. He thought she did it deliberately. Just like that business with the children's schools.

It would be better for him and better for her to end it now. He had been cheating on her for years, anyway. Not that she'd ever suspected a thing. Now Shelby was pressuring him for a ring, and he thought it was the right thing. Sophia had left for college exactly one week ago. Society wouldn't demonize him; on the contrary, they'd see he'd stayed in his marriage for the sake of his children, and now they had both flown the nest, he was taking a little time to pursue his own happiness. They'd applaud him for waiting the way he applauded himself.

Twenty years of marriage. John couldn't say when it had gone wrong, exactly, when he'd started looking at other women, because when he was twenty-four and Emma was twenty-five, she had been his everything, working a night job to support him while he cranked out those screenplays that never sold. Ah, back then she had been so young and beautiful. Even Shelby was not so beautiful as Emma had been. But the years had stolen the elasticity from her skin, and the two children had left marks on her belly, and, besides, he'd gotten a high-paying job; and with that came more options. Men weren't made to be monogamous anyway. Thank heavens he'd eloped with her and married in Las Vegas. Nevada was not a community-property state, and she had signed no pre-nup. Even though his salary was astronomical, he liked to live above his means…to go first-class everywhere. This restaurant, French cuisine with outrageous prices, was just another example of that.

But hell. John McCloud stretched his legs under the table and stole a glance at the barmaid. She was new, fresh in from Texas, and his buddy Sam Goldfarb, in Business Affairs, swore that he'd had her last week, and that she was sensational. *And* that her tits were real. Mmm, McCloud thought, big Southern titties and a tiny little waist, and an obliging disposition towards powerful studio players. Not sure if he believed Sam had actually laid her, though, because Business Affairs wasn't glamorous enough. But he might have better luck. He could get her a part. He imagined a flat little butt. Maybe he'd try it, later.

After he had dissolved matters with Emma.

They had large credit debts, as a couple. Once his lawyers had gone through the paperwork, she'd be left with barely a quarter mill. Maybe even less. But after the divorce, with the joint debts paid off, he could earn more money. This time he'd keep straight. And she would get none of the future wealth he'd generate.

The main thing was to get her to sign the papers.

"How long has it been going on? And who is it?" she finally managed.

"Not long," he lied. "And it's Shelby Harris."

"Shelby." He could see Emma's mind working, trying to place her. "Shelby the yoga girl? The twenty-two-year-old?"

Shelby had instructed their daughter in yoga. He remembered that first sight of her out by the pool, in that outrageous thonged leotard over flesh-colored tights, all firm young blondeness and large silicone boobs.

"Yes. She's a very spiritual person."

"I'm sure she is," Emma said dryly, with that English accent of hers his friends thought was so smart-sounding. Well, she hadn't been that smart when it came to keeping him. "John, she's less than half your age."

"We have a mental connection. Look, I'm sorry to cause you this hurt. But I think it's better to be honest. Honest as to what I need. I'm at that kind of a place in my life right now."

"Did you realize it was our wedding anniversary?" she asked softly.

Damn. "Yes," he lied. "I thought it brought a period to this passage in our lives. Like closing the circle. With honesty, the way we started out."

Emma took a large, fortifying sip of her white wine. She wanted to make sure that John couldn't read her. A part of her brain that was detached, a bit like the part that informed you you were drunk when you were, wanted to videotape this moment and keep it before her forever. "Closing the circle!" She almost felt pity for him, but not quite. What a miserable little shit he was, and he didn't even seem to know it.

Shelby wasn't the first. She might not even have been the twenty-first. Emma had buried herself in her children and her job, and tried to forget all about the loser she was married to. And now, thank God, he wanted an "amicable" divorce. The head rush of relief she experienced was rather like being back in the seventies in the front row of a Who concert. Emma quickly made a plan to call Father Freddy, her local parish priest. She could get an annulment without any trouble; John had never meant any of their marriage vows. And then, there would be Paolo.

John was like all the other miserable, stressed-out, money-grubbing executives here; only interested in a rolling line of bimbos with nothing to say except "divorce settlement." He would wind up with four or five Mary-Beth clones, and divorce one after the other until he had nothing left. Young girls that would be out screwing the pool hand and spending his money on blow. She thought about Paolo, his dark eyes and intelligence and Italian appreciation of her still-firm but nicely rounded butt. Emma forced herself to look serious.

He fished hastily in his pocket. Better get her ink on his documents before she started to cry. Wedding anniversary. Who knew? What a nightmare. "These are some papers my lawyers drew up. I hope you'll sign, because I think it'll be better for the kids if we do this amicably."

"I totally agree," Emma said quietly.

"Okay. Good. So what I'm proposing is that we sell the house and stocks and pay off our balances, and split the rest, not that there's much, but we'd be debt-free."

"Fine with me," she said.

He couldn't believe his luck. "You know that this gives you an opportunity to start over. It could be the best thing that ever happened to you."

She was silent.

"Your future and my future will be split." Would she realize that she'd have no claims on his future earnings? He hoped not. He'd need it all. Shelby had picked out a four-carat flawless Tiffany diamond. "A fresh start for both of us, including financially. You have…your books, after all." He could pretend her little hobby, her independent press, meant something.

"So your company and mine would be separate…?"

"It's still a good deal, Emma. I'm being generous, because that's what you deserve," he said warmly. "You get half of what we have now, and yes, we separate our jobs out, which is only fair."

He pushed the papers across to her. "One copy is for you to keep. I signed both already. Please, Emma, for the children's sake, won't you do the civilized thing?"

She nodded and signed both, folded one up neatly and put it in her crocodile purse, then handed the other across to him.

The waitress sidled up to them with the wine list.

"We'll have champagne," Emma said.

"You're taking it pretty good. It's the best thing."

"I absolutely agree. I wasn't going to tell you tonight, but I've met someone, too. I was waiting for the children to go off to college before I told you. You've made it so much easier for me."

"You?"

Emma grinned at the stupefied look on his face.

"Yes, me. It's Paolo Forza," she said.

"Paolo?" he spluttered. The man they met at the Cannes

Film Festival? Paolo, the urbane, charming Italian count with the huge, ancient villa outside of Rome he'd envied so much? Emma would be a contessa.

"And it's excellent that we're splitting up our interests. I received an order to buy me out from St. Martin's Press in New York. I think I'm going to clear about eight million dollars."

The waitress appeared and filled their champagne flutes. He picked his up, but set it back down because his hand was trembling. Suddenly his wife looked so beautiful to him.

"I have to warn you though, John. I heard a rumor that you're on the outs at the studio. That they were going to fire you for expense-account fraud. Even something about a prosecution." She smiled reassuringly. "Of course my information might not be reliable, because the same person told me that you'd been sleeping with Shelby for years, and of course it hasn't been going on long. But perhaps you'd better check it out all the same."

Emma lifted her glass and toasted him.

"To fresh beginnings, my dear."

Lisa Jewell was born in 1968 in London where she still lives with her husband, Jascha, and baby daughter, Amelie. She has written four bestselling novels *(Ralph's Party, Thirtynothing, One-Hit Wonder* and *A Friend of the Family)* and is currently grinding her way painfully through the fifth. Visit her Web site at www.lisa-jewell.co.uk.

Rudy
by Lisa Jewell

Rudy brushes up the nap of his tan suede desert boots with an old toothbrush. He picks a bit of dried food off his gray T-shirt and checks the fly on his beige brushed-cotton combat trousers. Turning towards the mirror, he hooks his shiny conker-colored hair over his ears and pushes his fringe out of his face. His top lip curls itself up over his teeth to allow for a tooth inspection and he's ready to go.

He moves through his sparsely furnished flat, dominated by his collection of guitars, displayed on stands: two Fenders, a twelve-string, two acoustics and a bass. He pulls the door closed behind him and takes the narrow stairway that separates his hallway from the kebab shop upstairs. He has to walk sideways because his feet are too big for the steps. Mojo, his dog, follows closely behind, his claws tapping on the bare floorboards.

On the street outside, he puts his hand to his eyes, shielding them from the sunshine. He doesn't get any daylight in his flat and the sudden burst of light brings tears to his eyes. He doesn't own any sunglasses, because he always loses them.

Rudy is on his way to Parliament Hill. Even though it's a mile and a half away, he's going to walk. Rudy walks everywhere. He doesn't believe in cars, he hates London Transport and the thought of negotiating a spindly little push-bike through the ruthless streets of London makes him break out in a sweat. He'll get in a cab if someone else orders it and he'll accept a lift if someone offers it, but otherwise, Rudy walks.

Rudy is what you might call nonconformist. Rudy hasn't got a job. He busks on the Underground, he signs on, the state pays his rent. He hasn't got a girlfriend. He sleeps with a girl called Maria nearly every other night, but he won't call her his girlfriend. He doesn't watch the telly, he doesn't read the papers, he doesn't read books, he refuses to buy CDs. He's a vegetarian and he lives over a kebab shop. He breaks the rules. Even the shape of his body, the size of his feet, the length of his fingers are nonconformist.

He's tall, very tall, about six-foot-three, with thick, unruly hair that he keeps tucked behind his ears. It's thinning a bit on top, but unless he's sitting down or with someone taller than him (unlikely), that remains his secret. He has his father's Italian features—thick eyebrows, and expressive mouth and very, very long eyelashes. That's the first thing that most women ever say to him. "God, your eyelashes are *so* long."

Very embarrassing.

He keeps himself in fairly good condition, washes his hair every morning, shaves every day, buys himself clothes occasionally, nice clothes, tactile clothes, chunky hand-knitted jumpers, moleskin trousers, huge desert boots for his size elevens, a big cashmere overcoat. It's all secondhand of course—he couldn't afford to buy nice stuff like that *new.* But when you know which shops to go to, when you know exactly what you're looking for, it's amazing what you can pick up for next to nothing.

Rudy's thirty-three years old and he's never had to work in an office, answer a phone or write a memo. He's never experienced that moment of ultimate flatness when you open your payslip and find that your boss *hasn't* given you a surprise pay rise, that your tax code *hasn't* changed overnight and that the accounts department *hasn't* cocked up and given you too much money by mistake. He's never had to wake up before ten o'clock or stay late or go to an office party. He only wears ties for weddings and funerals and he gets his hair cut whenever he feels like it. He can take his dog to work and have his lunch whenever he wants and for as long as he likes. He doesn't have to be nice to anyone he doesn't like (except the police when they come to move him along every now and then) and he doesn't have to go on training courses or learn a company mission statement. He doesn't have to pretend to be ill if he wants to stay at home and watch television and he doesn't panic if someone in his department gets a better car than him. And best of all, better than anything else, he doesn't have to pay those thieving bastards at the IR a single penny of his hard-earned cash. In fact, the only thing he has in common with someone who works in an office is that if he wants to smoke a fag he has to go outside.

He lights a cigarette now, a slim white Craven A. He lights it with a lighter shaped like a pistol, which Maria gave him for his birthday, and smokes it as he walks.

The sun-baked August streets of Kentish Town are thronging with fantastic women in fantastic clothes: midriff tops, halternecks, hotpants and skimpy sundresses. They are patchworks of honey, gold and strawberry pink skin. Some are rake-thin, some are muscular, some are flabby and some are curvy. They are all absolutely beautiful. He could fall in love with every one of them.

Rudy can feel his libido rising as he walks.

In the park, Rudy picks up a reasonable looking stick— about a foot long with a good wide berth and no sharp bits—and tosses it skywards. It spirals across the horizon a few times before coming to a halt underneath a bouffant horse chestnut. Mojo is there almost before it's landed, skidding to a halt and having to retrace his steps a little. He locks his powerful jaws round the stick and brings it back to Rudy.

"Good boy…good boy." Rudy buries his fingers into the

warm ruff of thick hair under Mojo's chin and gives him a good tickle. He picks up the stick from where the dog left it at his feet and throws it again. He watches the huge animal gallop off into the distance for a while and then turns his gaze to the bench at the foot of the hill. Is she there? He tucks his hands into his pockets and starts the steep walk back down towards the bench. There is someone sitting there, hard to tell even if it's a man or a woman from this distance. His pace quickens. Mojo appears at his side and joins him as he walks purposefully downhill, his rubber-soled suede boots squeaking against the greasy tarmac path underfoot.

A shape emerges from the undefined blob sitting on the bench. It has bare shoulders and brown hair. Could be. Could be her. The hair is long—yes, it is definitely her—and is held back with a black plastic claw-type-thing—reminds Rudy of an eagle's foot. He loves that thing.

She turns briefly to watch a hyperactive Highland terrier tear past in pursuit of a pigeon. Her nose, in profile, is perfectly straight, like it's been hand-finished with a plane. Her mouth is turned up ever so slightly into a small smile and she's wearing that dress again. That dress that Rudy loves so much. It's a sort of crushed velvet and tie-dyed about ten different shades of claret and bottle green. It has very thin shoulder straps and, as witnessed on the one occasion that Rudy has seen her walking, a skirt of the perfect weight and shape to be easily inflated by the slightest gust of wind, revealing an extra inch or two of her lovely legs. There's no wind today, though. It's bright and still and excitingly warm, no clouds in the sky at all, save for a few smudges to the east that look like they've been left there by grubby-fingered children. Parliament Hill is as busy as you'd expect it to be on the warmest day of the year—there are people everywhere, stretched out on the grass, semiclothed and sunbathing.

Rudy approaches the bench and considers his next move. Where to sit? Right here at the furthest edge of the bench, away from her? Towards the middle, closer to her, but still leaving her "personal space" unencroached upon? Or should he just take his chances and plonk himself down there at her side? His breathing becomes hard and heavy as he tries to scrape together the nerve to sit down. In and out. In and out. In and out. Just do it, just do it, just… bloody…well…do…it. His breath by now is audible and the girl turns to meet his eye. She looks uncomfortable. Fuck. He lets his breath go, takes the other end of the bench and pulls a battered old paperback from the inside pocket of his jacket. Doesn't know what it is. Some old shit that Maria lent him a couple of years ago. "Oh, you'll love it. It's so funny and so observant about *men* and *life* and *relationships.* You must read it." So he'd just smiled and said thanks and tucked it into the bowels of his overcoat thinking, "How many years do I have to know you, Maria, before you'll understand that I don't like reading, I don't like books, I don't like words, I don't like other people's thoughts in my head—how many books are you going to lend me before you realize that I'm just not interested?" But then he'd noticed that it was written by the same guy who wrote the book that the girl in the Velvet Dress was reading. So last week he'd pulled the book out of his pocket and he'd started reading it. And it was quite funny, he supposed. About a man who runs a record shop in North London who's useless in relationships. It might have reminded him of himself if he had a job or if he ever actually had any relationships.

Rudy opens the book and then inexplicably clears his throat rather loudly, as if trying to attract someone's attention. The girl cocks her head a little in his direction and Rudy decides to turn the throat-clear into a full-on coughing fit. The girl turns away and immerses herself visibly deeper into the book on her lap. So, no sympathy, thinks Rudy. Hmm…interesting. Very interesting. Not even a flicker of concern. She's either a heartless bitch or she's just very shy. Rudy decides to go with the "very shy" option. It fits in better with his overall fantasy of her. If she turned out to be a heartless bitch, then he'd just have been wasting his time every Saturday morning for the past six weeks.

That was when she'd first appeared—six weeks ago—from nowhere and straight into his life, just like that. The first time he'd seen her he was walking so fast that all he could make out was a blur of crushed velvet and shiny hair. The second time, he'd passed her slowly enough to distinguish a perfect nose and a paperback novel. The third week, he'd approached her from behind and been enchanted by the plastic claw holding her hair back from her face, its talons digging brutally into the thickness of her hair. By the fourth week he'd got up the nerve to sit on the bench with her, but had stood up again after less than a minute and continued on his way. It was last week that he'd had the brainwave about the book. It gave him something to do while he sat here, something to quell the awkwardness and embarrassment of the situation.

The girl in the Velvet Dress looks away from her book very briefly and smiles ever so slightly at Mojo, who's eyeing her dolefully from where he's stretched out under the bench.

Rudy smiles to himself. Nothing warms Rudy to a stranger more quickly than a flattering remark or an affectionate attitude towards his dog. This girl on the bench, she'd given Mojo a nice look the first time she'd seen him, too, that same half-smile she'd used just now when the Highland terrier had run past her. She obviously likes dogs, which is good. Which is vital, in fact. I mean, Mojo is his best friend. Now, if she liked Muddy Waters and B. B. King and could play a bit of flamenco guitar as well, then she might just turn out to be his perfect woman.

Not that he'll ever find out. Of course not. He isn't going to *talk* to her or anything. He never does. Because the woman with the Velvet Dress and the Hair Claw isn't the first woman that Rudy has shared a bench with on Parliament Hill. Oh no. This year there's been the woman with the Blue Nail Polish and Jaunty Hat and before that the woman with the Pink Nose Stud and the Pigskin Rucksack and then the woman with the Raffia Bag and the Diamante Hair Grips, the one with the Dangly Earrings and the Snakeskin Shoes and the one with the Ethnic Ankle Bracelet and the Big Silver Rings. Rudy likes accessories. Not for himself, but on women. He loves them. Women can hide behind clothes, behind fashion, but it's through accessories that women give themselves away.

So—what does Rudy know about this stranger, about the girl in the Velvet Dress?

She's single, that's for sure. They all are, all these girls in the park. Of course they are. Why on earth would they be sitting alone in the park on a Saturday afternoon if they had someone to be with?

The velvet tells Rudy that she's sensuous, receptive to textures, likes a bit of luxury in her life. He imagines her to be the type of woman who might stop at a posh Belgian chocolate shop on her way home from work and ask for just one Champagne Truffle, gift-wrapped in a tiny little box. No wolfed down Mars Bars for this girl, no KitKat on the way to work, Twix bar in her office drawer or gobbled Cadbury's Wispa when she thought no one was looking. Just a brief moment of pure luxury.

He imagines her taking her chocolate home, all aquiver with excitement and then making herself a proper cup of tea, in a pot, with leaves.

He imagines her with a cat, a Persian, maybe, or a Rag-doll. Something with luxuriant fur. She probably buys him a piece of cod every now and then, or poaches a chicken breast for him, in milk.

The dress would have been a treat, too. Something she'd seen in a shop window, fallen in love with, saved up for for weeks. It would have been tissue-wrapped and handed to her in a shiny paper bag with rope handles. She still keeps the bag, in the back of her wardrobe. A souvenir of a perfect moment.

The girl in the Velvet Dress slips her finger between the next two pages of her book and chuckles almost imperceptibly under her breath at something she's just read. She turns the page over and sighs contentedly.

Rudy clears his throat again and eyes her surreptitiously. Were you watching, you might think that he's about to talk to her, that he's getting up the nerve. But you'd be wrong. Rudy doesn't need to talk to her, he doesn't need to get to know her—he already knows so much. He's never spoken to any of the women. That would just spoil everything. He prefers getting to know women without having to talk to them. That way he doesn't have to find out that they're thick, or bitchy, or boring, or silly, or shallow, or that they have a horrible accent or an ugly voice, or that they just really don't want to talk to him. At all. Better just not to try. Better just to sit there on the bench and breathe them in, work them out from the telltale clues they subconsciously leave all over the place. The body language, the jewelry, the book, the *accessories.* The way they react to Mojo, the way they react to him, the way they react to the weather and to things going on around them. Bitten nails or long nails, short hair or long hair, clean shoes or scruffy shoes—you could learn more about a person's levels of self-esteem looking at signs like that than you could in a whole year of psychotherapy. Probably.

But what about affection, you might ask, what about contact, what about *sex?* The thing is, you see, Rudy doesn't actually *need* any physical contact with his bench women. He has Maria for that sort of thing, the barmaid at the Lady Somerset. Naughty little Maria with her uplift bra and her thick lipstick and her tiny little buttocks and lethal hipbones that protrude like shark fins from either side of her abdomen. She's half his size all over, and at least ten years older than him. She's on for anything, any time. She isn't interested in chat or love or going out or anything. She just likes coming back to his flat after the pub closes and crawling all over his big long body for as long as he'll let her. She's great. But she's nowhere near his ideal woman. She's way too thin, for a start. But she gives him exactly what he needs and in a funny sort of way, he loves her for it.

The girl in the Velvet Dress looks at her watch (plain, leather strap, looks like she's had it for years), folds down the corner of her page, closes it and slips it in to her bag (drawstring-top leather duffel). She stands up, hitches the bag on to her shoulder and turns to leave.

And then something unbelievable happens. She stops,

turns around and looks at Rudy. She stares at him for what feels like at least ten minutes and then opens her lips, very slowly. Her cheeks start reddening and she begins twisting her hands together self-consciously.

She smiles. "Bye," she says. She sticks one hand up at him, stiffly, palm-first, and begins walking away.

"Yeah," mutters Rudy, sitting bolt upright, dropping his book at his feet and, a few seconds too late, "yeah—see you." She's already halfway into the distance. "See you."

He watches her amble down the hill, her hands in her pockets, her head downcast.

Jesus.

Jesus Christ.

What was that? What the fuck was that?

Rudy leans down to pick up his book, his head swimming. She spoke to him. The girl in the Velvet Dress spoke to him. She said, "Bye." What does it mean? What does she want?

He frowns and tucks the book back into his inside pocket. Why did she speak to him?

And then a terrible realization dawns upon him. She's been coming here on purpose just to see him! Every week, the same bench, the same time. It's obvious. She's…she's… stalking him. He's being stalked by a mad, obsessive, lonely, unloved, unhinged woman. Oh Jesus!

He stands up quickly and looks around him, making sure she's no longer in sight. She isn't.

"Come on, boy." He slaps his thigh and Mojo joins him as he begins to walk back down the hill.

Rudy needs a drink now. His hands are shaking slightly and a light film of sweat clings to his brow. His pace quickens as he hurries down the tarmac path, towards Highgate Road, towards the Lady Somerset, looking over his shoulder every now and then as he walks.

Since she was first published in 1995, **Marian Keyes** has become a publishing phenomenon. Her first six novels, *Watermelon, Lucy Sullivan Is Getting Married, Rachel's Holiday, Last Chance Saloon, Sushi for Beginners* and *Angels,* have become international bestsellers, published in twenty-nine languages and selling nine million copies. In 2004, her collection of nonfiction *Under the Duvet* and her seventh novel *The Other Side of the Story* have been major successes in the U.S.A.

Her work has come to the attention of Hollywood; *Rachel's Holiday* was optioned by Touchstone Pictures. *Lucy Sullivan Is Getting Married* has been made into a sixteen-part television series. *Watermelon* was a made-for-TV movie in 2003, and *Last Chance Saloon* has been filmed in French for a 2004 release.

More information about Marian is available at www.mariankeyes.com.

The Truth is Out There
by Marian Keyes

Los Angeles International Airport: teeming with passengers, arrivals, film stars, illegal immigrants, a dazed English girl called Ros and, of course, the odd alien or two freshly landed from another planet. Well, only one alien, actually. A small, yellow, transparent creature who liked to be called Bib. His name was actually Ozymandmandyprandialsink, but Bib was just much more *him,* he felt. Bib was in Los Angeles by accident—he'd stolen a craft and gone on a little joyride, only planning to go as far as planet Zephir. Or planet Kyton, at the most. But they'd been repairing the super-galaxy-freeway and diverting everyone and somehow he'd lost his way and ended up in this place.

Ros Little hadn't landed from another planet, she just felt like she had. The twelve-hour flight from Heathrow, the eight-hour time difference and the terrible row she'd had the night before she'd left all conspired to make her feel like she was having a psychotic episode. Her body was telling her it should be the middle of the night, her heart was telling her her life was over, but the brazen midafternoon Californian sun dazzled and scorched regardless.

As Ros dragged her suitcase through the crowds and the drenching humidity towards the taxi line, she was stopped in her tracks by a woman's shriek.

"It's an alien!" the helmet-haired, leisure-suited matron yelled, jabbing a finger at something only she could see. "Oh my Lord, look, just right there, it's a little yellow alien."

How very Californian, Ros thought wearily. Her first mad person and she wasn't even out of the airport yet. In other circumstances she'd have been thrilled.

Hastily Bib assumed invisibility. That was close! But he had to get out of here because he knew bits and pieces about planet Earth—he'd been forced to study it in "Primitive Cultures" class. On the rare occasions he'd bothered to go to school. Apparently, Los Angeles was alien-spotting central and the place would be overrun with X-Filers in a matter of minutes.

Looking around anxiously, he saw a small girl-type creature clambering into a taxi. Excellent. His getaway car. Just before Ros slammed the door he managed to slip in beside her unnoticed, and the taxi pulled away from the crowd of people gathered around the hysterical matron.

"But, Myrna, aliens ain't yellow, they're green, everyone knows that" was the last thing that Ros heard, as they skidded away from the curb.

With heartfelt relief, Ros collapsed on to the air-conditioned seat—then froze. She'd just got a proper look at her cabbie. She'd been too distracted by Myrna and her antics to notice that he was a six-foot-six, three-hundred-pound, shaven-headed man with an eight-inch scar down the back of his scalp.

It got worse. He spoke.

"I'm Tyrone," he volunteered.

You're scary, Ros thought, then nervously told him her name.

"This your first visit to L.A.?" Tyrone asked.

"Yes," Ros and Bib answered simultaneously, and Tyrone looked nervously over his shoulder. He could have sworn he'd heard a second voice, an unearthly cracked rasp. Clenching his hands on the wheel, he hoped to hell that he wasn't having an acid flashback. It had been so long since he'd had one, he'd thought he'd finally grown out of them.

When the cab finally negotiated its way out of LAX, Los Angeles looked so like, well, *itself* that Ros could hardly believe it was real—blue skies, palm trees, buildings undulating in the ninety-degree haze, blond women with unfeasibly large breasts. But as they passed by gun-shops, 24-hour hardware stores, adobe-style motels offering water beds and adult movies, and enough orthodontists to service the whole of England, Ros just couldn't get excited. "It's raining in London," she tried to cheer herself up, but nothing doing.

To show interest she pressed her nose against the glass. Bib didn't, but only because he didn't have a nose. He was enjoying himself immensely and thoroughly liked the look of this place. Especially those girl-type creatures with the yellow hair and the excess of frontage. Hubba *hubba.*

Tyrone whistled when he drew up outside Ros's hotel. "Class act," he said in admiration. "You loaded, right?"

"Wrong," Ros corrected, hastily. She'd been warned that Americans expected lots of tips. If Tyrone thought she was flush she'd have to tip accordingly. "My job's paying for this. If it was me, I'd probably be staying in one of those dreadful motels with the water beds."

"So, you cheap, huh?"

"Not cheap," Ros said huffily. "But I'm saving up. Or at least I was, until last night…"

For a moment terrible sadness hung in the air and both Bib and Tyrone looked at Ros with compassionate interest laced with a hungry curiosity. But she wasn't telling. She just bit her lip and hid her small pale face behind her curly brown hair.

Cute, Bib and Tyrone both realized in a flash of synchronicity. She's cute. Not enough happy vibes from her though, Tyrone felt. And she's not quite yellow-looking enough for my liking, Bib added. But she's *cute.* They nodded in unconscious but undeniable male bonding.

So cute, in fact, that Tyrone hefted her suitcase as far as the front desk and—unheard of, this—waved away a tip.

"Maaan," Tyrone said aloud as he lumbered back to the car. "What is *wrong* with you?"

After the glaring midafternoon heat, it took a moment in the cool shade of the lobby for Bib's vision to adjust enough to see that the hotel clerk who was checking Ros in was that Brad Pitt actor person.

What had gone wrong? Surely Brad Pitt had a very successful career in the Earth movies. Why had he downgraded himself to working in a hotel, nice as it seemed? And why wasn't Ros collapsed in a heap on the floor? Bib knew for a fact that Brad Pitt had that effect on girl-types. But just then Brad Pitt shoved his hair back off his face and Bib realized that the man wasn't quite Brad Pitt. He was *almost* Brad Pitt, but something was slightly wrong. Maybe his eyes were too close together or his cheekbones weren't quite high enough, but other than his skin having the correct degree of orangeness, something was off.

Before Bib had time to adjust to this, he saw another Earth movie star march up and disappear with Ros's suitcase. Tom Cruise, that was his name. And he really *was* Tom Cruise, Bib was certain of it. Short enough to be, Bib chortled to himself smugly. (Bib prided himself on his height, he went down very well with the females on his own planet, all two foot eight of him.)

The would-be Brad Pitt handed over keys to Ros and said, "We've toadally given you an ocean-front room, it's rilly, like, awesome." Invisible, but earnest, Bib smiled and nodded at Ros hopefully. This was bound to cheer her up. I mean, an ocean-front room that was rilly, like, awesome? What could be nicer?

But Ros could only nod miserably. And just as she turned away from the desk Bib watched her dig her nails into her palms and add casually, "Um, were there any messages for me?" While Brad Pitt scanned the computer screen, Bib realized that if he had breath he would have been holding it. Brad eventually looked up and with a blinding smile said, "No, *ma'am!*"

Bib wasn't too hot on reading people's minds—he'd been

"borrowing" spacecraft and taking them out for a bit of exercise during Psychic lessons—but the emotion coming off Ros was so acute that even he was able to tune in to it. The lack of phone calls was bad, he realized. It was very bad. Deeply subdued, Bib trotted after Ros to the lift, where someone who looked like Ben Affleck's older, uglier brother pressed the lift button for them.

Bib was very keen to get a look at their room and he was half impressed, half disappointed. It was very *tasteful,* he supposed the word was. He'd have liked a water bed and adult movies himself, but he had to say he was impressed with the enormous blond-and-white room. And the bathroom was good—blue and white and chrome. With interest he watched Ros do a furtive over-her-shoulder glance and quickly gather up the free shower cap, body lotion, shampoo, sewing kit, emery board, cotton buds and soap and shove them in her handbag. Somehow he got the impression that she wasn't what you might call a seasoned traveler.

A gentle knock on the door had her zipping her bag in a panic. "Come in," she called, and Tom Cruise, all smiles and cutesy charm was there with her case. He was so courteous and took such a long time to leave that Bib began to bristle possessively. *Back off, she's not interested,* he wanted to tell Tom. Who'd turned out not to be Tom at all. He only looked like Tom when he was doing the smile, which had faded the longer he'd fussed and fiddled in the room. At the exact moment that Bib realized why Tom was lingering, so did Ros. A frantic rummage in her bag and she'd found a dollar (and spilled the sewing kit on to the floor in the process). Tom looked at the note in his hand, then looked back at Ros. Funny, he didn't seem pleased and Bib cursed his own perpetual skintness. "Two?" Ros said nervously to Tom. "Three?" They eventually settled on five and instantly Tom's cheesy, mile-wide smile was back on track.

No sooner had Tom sloped off to extort money from someone else than the silence in the room was shattered. The phone! It was ringing! Ros closed her eyes and Bib knew she was thanking that thing they called God. As for himself he found he was levitating with relief. Ros flung herself and surfed the bed until she reached the phone. "Hello," she croaked, and Bib watched with a benign smile. He almost felt tearful. But anxiety manifested itself as he watched Ros's face—she didn't look pleased. In fact she looked bitterly disappointed.

"Oh, Lenny," she said. "It's you."

"Don't sound so happy!" Bib heard Lenny complain. "I set my clock for two in the morning to make sure my favorite employee has arrived safely on her first trip in her new position, and what do I get? 'Oh, Lenny, it's you'!"

"Sorry, Lenny," Ros said abjectly. "I was kind of hoping it might be Michael."

"Had another row, did you?" Lenny didn't sound very sympathetic. "Take my advice, Ros, and lose him. You're on the fast track to success here and he's holding you back and sapping your confidence. This is your first opportunity to really prove yourself—it could be the start of something great!"

"Could be the *end* of something great, you mean," Ros said, quietly.

"He's not the only bloke in the world," Lenny said cheerfully.

"He is to me."

"Please yourself, but remember, you're a professional now," Lenny warned. "You've three days in L.A. so put a smile on your face and knock 'em dead, kiddo."

Ros hung up and remained slumped on the bed. Bib watched in alarm as all the life—and there hadn't been much to begin with—drained out of her. For a full half hour she lay unmoving, while Bib hopped from pad to pad—all six of them—as he tried to think of something that would make her happy. Eventually she moved. He watched her pawing the bed with her hand, then she did a few, half-hearted, lying-down bounces. With great effort of will, Bib summoned his mind-reading skills. *Jumping on the bed.* Apparently she liked jumping on beds when she went to new places. She and Michael always did it. Well, in the absence of Michael, she'd just have to make do with a good-looking—even if he did say so himself—two-foot-eight, six-legged, custard-yellow life-form from planet Duch. *Come on,* he willed. *Up we get.* And took her hands, though she couldn't feel them. To Ros's astonishment, she found herself clambering to her feet. Then doing a few gentle knee-bends, then bouncing up and down a little, then flicking her feet behind her, then propelling herself ceiling-wards. All the while Bib nodded unseen encouragement. *Attagirl,* he thought, when she laughed. Cute laugh. Giggly, but not daft-sounding.

Ros wondered what she was doing. Her life was over, yet she was jumping on a bed. She was even enjoying herself, how weird was that?

Now you must eat something, Bib planted in her head. *I*

know how you humans need your regular fuel. Strikes me as a very inefficient way of surviving, but I don't make the rules.

"I couldn't," Ros sighed.

You must.

"Okay, then," she grumbled, and took a Snickers from the mini-bar.

I meant something a bit more nutritious than that, actually.

But Ros didn't answer. She was climbing, fully dressed, into bed and in a matter of seconds fell asleep, the half-eaten Snickers beside her on the pillow.

While Ros slept, Bib watched telly with the sound turned off and kept guard over her. He couldn't figure himself out—his time here was limited, they could find the spacecraft at any time so he should be out there cruising, checking out the females, having a good time at someplace called the Viper Room. Owned by one Johnny Depp, who modeled himself on Bib, no doubt about it. But instead he wanted to remain here with Ros.

She woke at 4:00 a.m., bolt upright from jet lag and heartbreak. He hated to see her pain, but this time he was powerless to help her. He managed to tune into her wavelength slightly, picking up bits and pieces. There had been a frenzied screaming match with the Michael person, the night before she'd left. Apparently, he hadn't wanted her to come on this trip. Selfish, he'd called her, that she cared more about her job than she did about him. And Ros had flung back that *he* was the selfish one, trying to make her choose between him and her job. By all accounts it had been the worst row they'd ever had and it showed every sign of being their last.

Human males, Bib sighed. Cavemen, that's what they were, with their fragile egos and sense of competition. Why couldn't they rejoice in the success of their females? As for Bib, he loved a strong, successful woman. It meant he didn't have to work and— Oy! What was Ros doing, trying to lift that heavy case on her own? She'll hurt herself!

Puffing and panting, Ros and Bib maneuvered her case on to the bed and when she opened it and started sifting through the clothes she'd brought, Bib realized just how distraught she must have been when she'd packed. Earth still had those quaint, old-fashioned things called seasons and, even though the temperature in L.A. was in the nineties, Ros had brought clothes appropriate for spring, autumn and winter, as well as summer. A furry hat—why on earth had she brought that? And four pairs of pajamas? For a three-day trip? And now what was she doing?

From a snarl of tights, Ros was tenderly retrieving a photograph. With her small hand she smoothed out the bends and wrinkles and gazed lovingly at it. Bib ambled over for a look—and recoiled in fright. He was never intimidated by other men but he had no choice but to admit that the bloke in the photo was very—and upsettingly—handsome. Not pristine perfect like the wanna-be Brads and Toms but rougher and sexier looking. He looked like the kind of bloke who owned a power screwdriver, who could put up shelves, who could stand around an open car-bonnet with six other men and say with authority, "No, mate, it's the alternator, I'm telling ya." This, Bib deduced with a nervous swallow, must be Michael.

He had dark, messy curly hair, an unshaven chin and his

attractiveness was in no way marred by the small chip from one of his front teeth. The photo had obviously been taken outdoors because a hank of curls had blown across his forehead and half into one of his eyes. Something about the angle of his head and the reluctance of his smile indicated that Michael had been turning away when Ros had clicked the shutter. *Real men don't pose for pictures,* his attitude said. Instantly Bib was mortified by his own eagerness to say "Cheese" at any given opportunity. But could he help it if he was astonishingly photogenic?

For a long, long time Ros stared at Michael's image. When she eventually, reluctantly put the photo down, Bib was appalled to see a single tear glide down her cheek. He rushed to comfort her, but fell back when he realized there was no need because she was getting ready to go to work. Her heart was breaking—he could *feel* it—but her sense of duty was still intact. His admiration for her grew even more.

Luckily, in amongst all the other stuff she'd brought, Ros had managed to pack a pale gray suit and by the time she was ready to leave for her 8:00 a.m. meeting she looked extremely convincing. Of course Bib realized she *felt* like a total fraud, certain she'd be denounced by the Los Angeles company as a charlatan the minute they clapped eyes on her, but apparently that was par for the course for people who'd recently been promoted. It would pass after a while.

Because of her lack of confidence, Bib decided he'd better go with her. So off they went in a taxi to Danger-Chem's headquarters at Wilshire Boulevard, where Ros was ushered into a conference room full of orange men with big, white teeth. They all squashed Ros's little hand in their huge, meaty, manicured ones and claimed to be, "trully, trully delighted," to meet her. Bib "trully, trully" resented the time they spent pawing her and managed to trip one of them. And not just any of them, but their *leader*—Bib knew he was the leader because he had the orangest face.

Then Bib perked up—a couple of girls had just arrived into the meeting! Initially, he'd thought they were aliens, too, although he couldn't quite place where they might be from. With the unnaturally elongated, skeletal limbs and eyes so wide-spaced that they were almost on the sides of their heads, they had the look of the females from planet Pfeiff. But when he tried speaking to them in that language (he only knew a couple of phrases—"Your place or mine?" and "If I said you had a beautiful body would you hold it against me?") they remained blankly unresponsive. One of them was called Tiffany and the other was called Shannen and they both had the yellow-haired, yellow-skinned look he usually found so attractive in a girl-type. Although, perhaps not as much as he once had.

The meeting went well and the orange men and yellow girls listened to Ros as she outlined a proposal to buy products from them. When they said the price she was offering was too low she was able to stop her voice from shaking and reel off prices from many of their competitors, all of them lower. Bib was bursting with pride.

When they stopped for lunch, Bib watched with interest as Tiffany used her fork to skate a purple-red leaf of radicchio around her plate. Sometimes she picked it up on her fork and let it hover in the general vicinity of her mouth, before putting it back down on her plate. She was *miming*, he realized. And that wasn't right. He switched his attention to Shannen. She was putting the radicchio on her fork and sometimes she was putting some into her mouth. He decided he preferred her. So when she said, "Gotta use the rest room," Bib was out of his seat in a flash after her.

He'd really have resented being called a Peeping Tom. An opportunist, he preferred to think of himself. An alien who knew how to make the most of life's chances. And being invisible.

But how strange. He'd followed Shannen into the cubicle and she seemed to be ill. No, no, wait—she was *making* herself ill. Sticking her fingers down her throat. Now she was brushing her teeth. Now she was renewing her lipstick. And she seemed happy! He'd always regarded himself as a man of the universe, but this was one of the strangest things he'd ever seen.

"I should be nominated for an Oscar," Ros thought, as she shook her last hand of the day. She'd given the performance of a lifetime around that conference table. But she tried to take pride that she *had* done it. Between jetlag and her lead-heavy unhappiness over Michael she was surprised she'd even managed to get dressed that morning, never mind discuss fixed costs and large order discounts.

However, when she got back to her hotel, she insisted on shattering her fragile good humor by asking a not-quite-right Ralph Fiennes if anyone had phoned for her. Ralph shook his head. "Are you sure?" she asked, wearing her desperation like a neon sign. But unfortunately, Ralph was very sure.

Trying to stick herself back together, Ros stumbled towards her room, where no force in the universe—not even one from Planet Duch—could have stopped her from ringing Michael.

"I'm sorry," she said, as soon as he picked up the phone. "Were you asleep?"

"No," Michael said, and Ros's weary spirits rallied with hope. If he was awake at two in the morning, he couldn't be too happy, now could he?

"I miss you," she said, so quietly she barely heard herself.

"Come home, then."

"I'll be back on Friday."

"No, come home now."

"I can't," she said gently. "I've got meetings."

"Meetings," he said bitterly. "You've changed."

As Ros tried to find the right words to fix things, she wondered why it was always an insult to tell someone that they'd changed.

"When I first met you," he accused, "you were straight up. Now look at you, with your flashy promotion."

He couldn't help it, Ros thought. Too much had changed too quickly. In just over eighteen months she'd worked her way up from answering phones, to being a supervisor, to assisting the production manager, to assisting the chairman, to becoming vice-production manager. None of it was her fault—she'd always thought she was as thick as two short planks. She'd been *happy* to think that. How was she to know that she had a natural grasp of figures and an innate sense of management? She had bloody Lenny to thank for "discovering" her, and she could have done without it. Everything had been fine—better than fine—with Michael until she'd started her career ascent.

"Why is my job such a problem?" she asked, for the umpteenth time.

"My job!" Michael said hotly. "My job, my job—you love saying it, don't you?"

"I don't! You have a job, too."

"Mending photocopiers isn't quite the same as being a vice-production-manager." Michael fell into tense silence.

"I can't do it," he finally said. "I can't be with a woman who earns more than me."

"But it'll be our money."

"What if we have kids? You expect me to be a stay-at-home house-husband sap? I won't do it, babes," he said, tightly. "I'm not that kind of bloke." She heard anger in his voice and terrible stubbornness.

But I'm good at my job, she thought, and felt a panicky desperation. She didn't want to give it up. But more than her job, she wanted Michael to accept her. Fully.

"Why can't you be proud of me?" She squeezed the words out.

"Because it's not right. And you want to come to your senses, you're no good on your own, you need me. Think about it!"

With that, he crashed the phone down. Instantly she picked it up to ring him back, then found herself slowly putting it back down. There was nothing to be gained by ringing him because he wasn't going to change his mind. They'd had so many fights, and he hadn't budged an inch. So what was the choice? She loved him. Since she'd met him three years ago, she'd been convinced he was The One and that her time in the wilderness was over. They'd planned to get married next year, they'd even set up a "Meringue Frock" account—how could she say goodbye to all that? The obvious thing was to give up her job. But that felt so wrong. Oughtn't Michael to love her as she was? Shouldn't he be proud of her talents and skills, instead of being threatened by them? And if she gave in now what would the rest of their lives together be like?

But if she didn't give in...? She'd be alone. All alone. How was she going to cope? Because Michael was right, she had very little confidence.

For some minutes she sat abjectly by the phone, turning a biro over and over, as she pondered the lonely existence that awaited her. All she could see ahead of her was a life where she jumped on hotel beds by herself. The bleakness almost overwhelmed her. *But just a minute,* she found herself thinking, her hand stopping its incessant rotation of the biro—she'd managed to get all the way from Hounslow to Los Angeles without Michael's help. *And* she'd managed to get a taxi to and from work. Had even held her own in a meeting.

To her great surprise she found that she didn't feel so bad. Obviously, she felt awful. Frightened, heartbroken, sick and lonely. But she didn't feel completely suicidal, and that came as something of a shock. She was so used to hearing Michael telling her that she was a disaster area without him that she hadn't questioned it lately...

How about that? She remained on the bed, and her gaze was drawn to the window. In all the trauma, she'd forgotten about her "toadally awesome" ocean view and it couldn't have been more beautiful—Santa Monica beach, the evening sun turning the sea into a silver-pink sheet, the sand rose-colored and powdery. Along the boardwalk, gorgeous Angelenos skated and cycled. A sleek couple whizzed by on a tandem, their no-doubt perfect baby in a yellow buggy attached to the back of the bike. He looked like a little emperor. Another tall, slender couple in-line skated by, both sunglassed and headphoned to the max. Hand in hand, they glided past gracefully, their movements a ballet of perfect synchronization.

"Fall," Bib wished fiercely. "Go on, trip. Skin your evenly tanned knees. Fall flat on your remodeled faces." He had hoped it might cheer Ros up. But, alas, it was not to be, and on the couple glided.

Ros watched them go, gripped by a bittersweet melancholy. And then to her astonishment, she found herself deciding that she was going to try to in-line skate herself. Why not? It was only six-thirty and there was a place right next to the hotel that rented out Rollerblades.

Hardly believing what she was doing she changed into leggings, ran from her room and in five minutes was strapping herself into a pair of blades. Tentatively, she pushed herself a short distance along the boardwalk. "Gosh, I'm quite good at this," she realized in amazement.

Bib held on to Ros's hand as she awkwardly skidded back and forth. It had been a huge struggle to convince her to get out here. And she was *hopeless.* If he hadn't been holding on to her hand, she'd be flat on her bum. Yet, her ungainly vulnerability made her even more endearing to him.

Bib had followed the evening's events with avid interest. He'd been appalled by Michael's macho attitude, the nerve of the bloke! He'd longed to snatch the phone from Ros and tell Michael in no uncertain terms how fabulous Ros was, how she'd terrified a roomful of powerful orange men. Then when Michael hung up on Ros, Bib used every ounce of will he could muster to stop Ros from ringing him back. He worked desperately hard at reminding Ros how wonderfully she'd coped since she'd arrived in this strange threatening city, even though it was so obvious, she should know it herself—

"Careful, careful!" he silently urged, squeezing his eyes shut in alarm, as Ros nearly went flying into a woman who was holding on to a small boy on a bike.

"Sorry," Ros gasped. "I'm just learning."

"S'okay," the little boy said. "Me, too. My name's Tod and that's my mom, Bethany. She's teaching me to ride my bike."

Bethany was in the unfortunate position of having to hold tightly on to the back of Tod's bike and run as fast as Tod cycled. Bib eyed Bethany with sympathetic understanding because he was in the unfortunate position of having to run as fast as Ros was skating. Which got faster and faster as her confidence grew.

"Wheeeeeh!" Ros shrieked as she sped a good four yards, before losing Bib and coming a cropper.

When she returned the skates to the rental office, her knees were bruised but her eyes were a-sparkle. "I had a lovely time," she laughingly announced. Then she sprinted joyously across the sand to the hotel, Bib puffing anxiously behind her, tangling himself in his six legs as he tried to keep up.

★ ★ ★

She woke in the middle of the night, the exhilaration and joy of the night before dissipated and gone. She felt cold, old, afraid, lonely. She wouldn't be able to cope without Michael, she didn't want a life without him.

But then she remembered the in-line skating. She wasn't normally adventurous, usually needing Michael with her before trying new things. Yet she'd done that all on her own and it was a comfort of sorts.

"I am a woman who in-line skates alone," she repeated to herself until she managed to get back to sleep.

Then she woke up, got dressed and went to work, vaguely aware that there was a new steadiness about her, a growing strength.

When she returned from her day's work, exhausted but proud from holding her own as they inched their way tortuously towards a deal, she bumped into Brad Pitt in the hotel lobby. From the look of things he was just knocking off work.

"Did you have a good day?" he inquired.

Ros nodded politely.

"So, what kind of business are you in?" Brad asked.

Ros considered. She always found this awkward. How exactly did you explain that you worked for a company that made portaloos? A very successful company that made portaloos, mind.

"We, um, take care of people," she said. Well, why shouldn't she be coy? Americans were the ones who called loos *rest rooms,* for goodness' sakes!

"D'ya take care of people on a movie set?" Brad never

missed an opportunity. The door to his career could open absolutely anywhere—there was the time he'd seen the director of *Buffy the Vampire Slayer* in his chiropractor's waiting room, or the occasion he'd crashed into the back of Aaron Spelling's Beemer—so he was always prepared.

"Actually, we have," Ros said with confidence.

Quick as a flash, Brad's lightbulb smile burst on to his face and he swooped closer. "Hey, I'm Bryce," he murmured. "Would you do me the honor of having a drink with me this evening?"

A good-looking man had invited her for a drink! What a shame that nothing would cheer her up ever again. Because if anything would do the trick, this would. But even as a refusal was forming in her mouth, Ros found herself pausing. Wouldn't it be better than sitting alone in her room waiting for the phone to ring?

"Okay," she said wanly.

Bryce looked surprised, women were usually delighted to spend time with him. Then he clicked his fingers. "Oh, I get it. You're English, right? You kinda got that Merchant-Ivory repressed thing going on. Love it! Meet me in the lobby at six-thirty." And smoothing his hair, he was gone.

In her room, Ros checked the phone, picked it up, trembled with the effort of not dialing Michael's number and frogmarched herself into the shower. America, the land of opportunity. She should at least try, after all Bryce really was gorgeous.

From the jumble of clothes thrown on the bed she managed to make herself presentable. A short—but not too short—black dress, a pair of high—but not too high—black sandals. But as she watched herself in the mirror, it was like seeing a stranger. Who was this single girl who was going out on a date with a man who wasn't Michael?

When the lift doors parted, Bryce was loitering in the lobby, sunbleached hair gleaming on to his golden forehead, white teeth exploding into a flashgun smile. Ros's spirits inched upwards. Maybe things weren't so bad. On the way to his car, she noticed Bryce patting his hair in the window as he passed by, then pretended she hadn't.

The bar was low-lit and quiet. "So as we can really, like, *talk*," Bryce said with a smile that promised good things, and the mercury level of Ros's mood began its upward climb again. As soon as they'd ordered their drinks, Bryce started the promised talk.

"…and then I got the part as the shop clerk in *Clueless*. They toadally cut it, right, but the director said I was great, really great. It was a truly great performance, I gave and gave until it hurt, but the goddamn editor was, like, toadally on my case…"

Ros nodded sympathetically.

"…of course, I should have got the Joseph Fiennes part in *Shakespeare in Love*. It was mine, they even toadally told my agent, but on-set politics, it's a toadal bitch, right?"

Ros nodded again. Despite Bryce's many tales of woe, his smile glittered and flashed. But as his litany of bad luck continued, Ros began to notice that he didn't ever make eye-contact with her. Yet the intimate smiles continued anyway. Eventually, wondering if he was coming on to some girl behind her, Ros looked over her shoulder. And saw a mirror. Ah, that explained everything. Bryce was flirting with his favorite person. Himself.

On and on he droned. Great performances he nearly gave. Evil directors, cruel editors, leading men who had it in for him because they were threatened by his talent and looks.

"Hey, I've done enough talking about me." He finally paused for breath. "What do *you* think of me?"

Ros could hardly speak for depression. With Bryce she felt more alone than she had on her own.

"Would you mind terribly if I left? Only I'm ever so sleepy. Must be jet lag."

"We've hardly been here thirty minutes," Bryce objected. "I'm just warming up."

To her dismay, Bryce offered to see her back to the hotel. And up to her room. At her bedroom door she realized he was about to try and kiss her. She braced herself—she didn't have the energy to resist him. He looked deep into her eyes and trailed a gentle finger along her cheek. Despite him being the world's most boring man, Ros couldn't help a leap of interest. After all, he was so handsome. Slowly Bryce lowered his perfect lips to hers, then paused.

"What are you doing?" Ros whispered.

"Close-up," Bryce whispered back. "A three second close-up of my face before the camera cuts to the clinch."

"Oh for goodness' sake!" Ros shoved the key in the lock, twirled into her room and slammed the door.

"Hey," Bryce was muffled but unbowed. "You ballsy English girls, toadally like a Judi Dench thing! Y'ever met her? I just thought with you both being English…"

"Go away," she said, her voice trembling from unshed tears. This was the worst that Ros had felt. Wretched. Absolutely wretched. Was this all she had to look forward to? Boring, self-obsessed narcissists?

Bib had been against the idea of a drink with Bryce from the word go. He just hated those men that thought they could fell women with one devastating smile. He'd tried to warn Ros that Bryce was nothing but a big egomaniac, but she wouldn't listen and—*now* what was going on? Someone was outside their room, pounding and demanding to be let in. It was a man's voice—perhaps it was Bryce back to try his luck again?

"Open the bloody door!" a voice ordered, and as Bib watched in astonishment, Ros moved like a sleepwalker and flung the door wide. A man stood there. A man that Bib recognized. But he wasn't any of the would-be film stars, he was…

"Michael!"

Though it killed him to do it, Bib had to admit that Michael was looking good. With his messy curly hair, rumpled denim shirt and intense male presence he made all the wanna-be Toms and Brads look prissy and preened.

"Can I come in?" Michael's voice was clipped.

"Yes." Ros looked like she was going to faint.

"What are you doing here?" she asked as Michael marched into the room.

"I wanted to kiss you," he announced, and with that he pulled Ros to his broad hard chest and kissed her with such lingering intimacy that Bib felt ill.

Finally he let Ros go and announced into her upturned face. "I've come to get this sorted, babes. You and me and this job lark."

"You flew here?" Ros asked, dazedly.

"Yeah. 'Course."

Hmm, Bib thought. Hasn't got much of a sense of humor, has he? Most normal people would have said something like, "No, I hopped on one leg, all six thousand miles of it."

"I can't believe it." Ros was a picture of wonder. "We're broke but you've traveled halfway around the world to save our relationship. This is the most romantic thing that's ever happened to me." And Bib had to admit that Michael did cut a very Heathcliffish figure as he strode about the room, looking moody and passionate.

Bad-tempered, actually, Bib concluded.

"You come home with me now," Michael urged. "You knock the job on the head, we get married and we live happy ever after! You and me are meant to be together. We were great until you got that promotion, it was only then that things went pear-shaped."

With his words, the joyous expression on Ros's face inched away and was replaced by an agony of confusion.

"Come on," Michael sounded impatient. "Get packing. I've got you a seat on my flight back."

But Ros looked paralyzed with indecision. She leaned against a wall and made no move and the atmosphere built and built until the room was thick with it. Bib was bathed in sweat. And he didn't even have perspiration glands.

Don't do it, he begged, desperately. *You don't have to. If he loved you he wouldn't ask you to make this choice.*

To his horror he watched Ros fetch her pajamas from under her pillow and slowly fold them.

"Where's your suitcase?" Michael asked. "I'll help you."

Ros pointed and then began scooping her toiletries off the dressing table and into a bag. Next, she opened the wardrobe and took out the couple of things that she'd hung up. It seemed to Bib that her movements were becoming faster and more sure, so in frantic panic, he summoned every ounce of energy and will that he possessed and zapped her with them.

You don't need this man, he told Ros. *You don't need any man who treats you like a possession with no mind or life of your own. You're beautiful, you're clever, you're sweet. You'll meet someone else, who accepts you for all that you are. In fact, if you're prepared to be open-minded and don't mind mixed-species relationships, I myself am happy to volunteer for the position…* He stopped himself. Now was not the time to be sidetracked.

"I'll fetch your stuff from the bathroom," Michael announced, already briskly en route.

Then Ros opened her mouth to speak and Bib prayed for her words to be the right ones.

"No," she said, and Bib reeled with relief.

"No," Ros repeated. "Leave it. I can't come tonight. I've got a meeting tomorrow."

"I know that, babes," Michael said tightly, as if he was struggling to keep his temper. "That's what I mean, I want you to come with me *now.*"

"Don't make me do this." Misery was stamped all over Ros's face.

"It's make-your-mind-up time." Michael's expression was hard. "Me or the job."

A long nerve-shredding pause followed, until Ros once again said, "No, Michael, I'm not leaving."

Michael's face twisted with bitter disbelief. "I didn't know you loved the job that much."

"I don't," Ros insisted. "This isn't about the job."

Michael looked scornful and Ros continued, "If you love someone, you allow them to change. If marriage is for life, I'm going to be a very different person in ten, twenty, thirty years' time. How're you going to cope with that, Mikey?"

"But I love you," he insisted.

"Not enough, you don't," she said, sadly.

For a moment he looked stunned, then flipped to anger. "You don't love me."

"Yes, I do. You've no idea how much." Her voice was quiet and firm. "But I am who I am."

"Since when?" Michael couldn't hide his surprise.

"I don't know." She also sounded surprised. "Since I came here, perhaps."

"Is this something to do with Lenny? Are you having it off with him?"

Ros's incredulous laugh said it all.

"So have I got this right?" Michael was sulky and resentful. "You're not coming home with me."

"I've a job to do," Ros said in a low voice. "I fly home tomorrow night."

"Don't expect me to be waiting for you, then."

And with the same macho swagger that, despite everything, Bib admired, Michael swung from the room. The door slammed behind him, silence hummed, and then— who could blame her, Bib thought sympathetically—Ros burst into tears.

* * *

No more Michael. The thought was almost unbearable. She lay on the bed and remembered how his hair felt, so rough, yet so surprisingly silky. She'd never feel it again. Imagine that, never, *ever* again. She could smell him now, as if he was actually in the room, the curious combination of sweetness and muskiness that was uniquely Michael's. She'd miss it so much. As she'd miss the verbal shorthand they had with each other, where they didn't have to finish sentences or even words because they knew each other so well. She'd have to find someone else to grow old with. It was all over, she was certain of it. There would be no more rows, no further attempts to change the other's mind.

They'd had so many angry, bitter fights, but what was in the air was the stillness of grief. The calmness when everything is lost. She'd moved beyond the turbulence of rage and fury into the still static waters of no return.

What would she do with the rest of her life, she asked herself. How was she going to fill in all the time between now and the time she died?

Rollerblades planted themselves in her head. Immediately she told herself not to be so ridiculous. How could she go in-line skating?

But why not? What else was she going to do until bedtime, and despite all the events of the evening it was only still eight-thirty. She pulled on her leggings even though they had a tear on one knee and ran across the sand. She was surprised to find how uplifted she was by whizzing back and forth at high speed on her skates. It had something to do with pride in what a good in-line skater she was—she really was excellent, considering this was only her second time doing it. Her sense of balance was especially wonderful.

The little boy, Tod, who had been there the previous night was there again, with his long-suffering mother Bethany. Bethany was red-faced and breathless from having to run and hold on to Tod while he cycled up and down the same six yards of boardwalk and Ros gave her a sympathetic smile.

Then Ros went back to her room and against all expectations managed to sleep. When morning came she woke up and went to work, where, with a deftness that left the Los Angeles company reeling in shock, negotiated a thirty percent discount when she'd only ever planned to ask for twenty. Blowing smoke from her imaginary gun, she gave them such firm handshakes that they all winced, then she swanned back to the hotel to pack. Successful mission or what?

Bib was in agony. What was he going to do? Was he going to go back to England with Ros, or home to his own planet? Though he'd grown very fond—too fond—of Ros, he had a feeling that somehow he just wasn't her type and that revealing himself, in all his glorious custard-yellowness, would be a very, very bad idea. It killed him not to be able to. In just over two days he'd fallen in love with her.

But would she be okay? She *thought* she was okay, but what would happen when he left her and there was no one to shore up her confidence? Would she go back to Michael? Because that wouldn't do. That wouldn't do *at all*.

He worried and fretted uncharacteristically. And the answer came to him on the evening of the last day. Ros had a couple of hours to kill before her night-flight, so instead of moping in her room, she ran to the boardwalk for one last in-line skating session. Bib didn't have anything to do with it—she decided all on her own. He'd have preferred a few quiet moments with her, actually, instead of trundling alongside her trying to keep up as she whizzed up and down, laughing with pleasure.

Bethany and Tod were there again. Time after time, Bethany ran behind the bike, holding tightly as Tod pedaled a few yards. Back and forth on the same strip of boardwalk they traveled, until, unexpectedly, Bethany let go and Tod careened away. When he realized that he was cycling alone, with no one to support him, he wobbled briefly, before righting himself. "I'm doing it on my own," he screamed with exhilaration. "Look, Mom, it's just me."

"It's all a question of confidence," Bethany smiled at Ros.

"I suppose it is," Ros agreed, as she freewheeled gracefully. Then crashed into a jogger.

As Bib helped her to her feet, he was undergoing a realization. *Of course,* he suddenly understood. He'd been Ros's training wheels, and without her knowing anything about it, he'd given her confidence—confidence to do her job in a strange city, confidence to break free from a bullying man. And just as Tod no longer needed his mother to hold his bike, Ros no longer needed Bib. She was doing it for real now, he could feel it. From her performance in her final meeting to deciding to go in-line skating without any prompting from Bib, there was a strength and a confidence about her that was wholly convincing.

He was happy for her. He really was. But, there was no getting away from the fact that the time had come for him to leave her. Bib wondered what the strange sensation in his chest was and it took a moment or two for him to realize that it was his heart breaking for the very first time.

LAX airport was aswarm with people, more than just the usual crowd of passengers.

"Alien-spotters," the check-in girl informed Ros. "Apparently a little yellow man was spotted here a few days ago."

"Aliens!" Ros thought, looking around scornfully at the overexcited and fervent crowd who were laden with Geiger counters and metal detectors. "Honestly! What are these people *like?*"

As Ros strapped herself in her airline seat, she had no idea that her plane was being watched intently by a yard-high, yellow life-form who was struggling to hold back tears. "Big boys don't cry," Bib admonished himself, as he watched Ros's plane taxi along the runway until it was almost out of sight. In the distance he watched it angle itself towards the sky, and suddenly become ludicrously light and airborne. He watched until it became a dot in the blueness, then traipsed back through the hordes of people keen to make his acquaintance to where he'd hidden his own craft. Time to go home.

Ros's plane landed on a breezy English summer's day, ferrying her back to her Michael-free life. As the whining engines wound down, she tried to swallow away the sweet, hard stone of sadness in her chest.

But, even as she felt the loss, she knew she was going to be fine. In the midst of the grief, at the eye of the storm, was the certainty that she was going to cope with this. She was alone and it was okay. And something else was with her—a firm conviction, an unshakeable faith in the fact that she wouldn't be alone for the rest of her life. It didn't make sense because she was now a single girl, but she had a strange warm sensation of being loved. She felt surrounded and carried by it. Empowered by it.

Gathering her bag and book, slipping on her shoes, she shuffled down the aisle towards the door. As she came down the plane's steps she inhaled the mild English day, so different from the thick hot Los Angeles air. Then she took a moment to stand on the runway and look around at the vast sky, curving over and dwarfing the airport, stretching away forever. And this she knew to be true—that somewhere out there was a man who would love her for what she was. She didn't know how or why she was so certain. But she was.

Before getting on the bus to take her to the terminal, she paused and did one last scan of the great blue yonder. Yes, no doubt about it, she could feel it in her gut. As surely as the sun will rise in the morning, he's out there. Somewhere…

Lynda Curnyn is a native New Yorker who hasn't migrated very far from her Brooklyn birthplace. She spent her adolescence on Long Island, but escaped to downtown Manhattan just as soon as she could. After getting a liberal arts degree from New College at Hofstra University, she went on to New York University for her master's degree in English literature. Now, after more than a decade of working in publishing, she has finally settled down to her dream of full-time writing. She is the author of the bestselling novel *Confessions of an Ex-Girlfriend*. Her next two novels, *Engaging Men* and *Bombshell*, tell the stories of two best friends as they conquer the amazing, inspiring and sometimes humbling world that is single life in New York City. When she's not writing, Lynda spends way too much time shopping for furniture. Say hello at www.lyndacurnyn.com.

Here We Are
by Lynda Curnyn

She wouldn't have even woken up if it hadn't been for the cat, meowing, meowing, meowing, making her wonder if she should ever have children. But she got up, of course. Went to the kitchen, of course. To retrieve the daily can. Was that all the cat had to look forward to nowadays? It didn't seem like enough.

It wasn't until Lauren felt the cool kitchen floor beneath her feet that she realized her fever had finally broken.

Four days she had been in the house; four days she had been alone. Four days and she'd barely spoken to a soul.

Except for her mother, who called to see whether Lauren was eating enough, drinking enough and once it was clear her daughter's health was not dire, whether she was dieting enough, dating enough. And her assistant, whom she had acquired along with her heady new art director title, and who called six times on the first day with claims of emergencies that required Lauren's attention. By day two, the phone had stopped ringing; by day three, Lauren was calling into the office herself, only to learn that everyone was managing fine without her. So fine, in fact, Lauren suspected the promotion she had fought for, the salary hike she had become slave to, would all be gone by the time she got back.

By day four, the thought was not unappealing.

The night before, when her fever spiked, mostly because she refused to give in to Tylenol, she succumbed to a feeling of hopelessness, listening to the wind press against the windows beside her bed, wondering how she had wound up, at thirty-four years old, alone in an oversize studio that swam around her with emptiness.

In the morning she realized it was because she had no furniture.

It wasn't that she hadn't thought about furniture. In fact, she thought about it every time one of her well-meaning friends dropped by, questioned her uncarpeted floor, her chairless desk, her tableless kitchen. People had expectations of art directors living in sleek, well-designed spaces. So many expectations, she stopped having people over. She couldn't take their questioning glances. Even now she felt the old arguments rear up inside. She had just moved in, she told them. Okay, six months ago. But she had been busy. She hadn't gotten a twenty-thousand-dollar-a-year pay hike for nothing. Then there had been bills to pay, an assistant to manage, a cat to feed, a mother to placate. A father to bury.

She left the kitchen, and not just because the cat had al-

ready wolfed down the daily can and was eyeing her with dissatisfaction. She needed to get out, needed to do something
about this furniture business and she needed to do it today.
It was Saturday, after all. The first one in a long time where
Lauren felt no pressing need to go into the office in the
name of some higher cause she could no longer remember.

Contemplating her clothing options, she headed for the
window, pushed back the curtains and sighed at the sight
that greeted her.

Sometime in the night the sky had opened up, blanket-
ing the world in snow.

Which only made her want to return to bed. And she
might have, if the thought of another day in bed didn't do
her in. Instead, she slumped on the desk, which was the only
other piece of furniture she owned, besides an end table she
had pulled from the wreckage of her parents' divorce. The
desk had been salvaged from the wreckage that was her father's life. He had sat at the desk for hours at a time, working, he had said. Working had required a pack of Camels, a
bottle of vodka and a wall to stare at.

Now as she studied the faded spot in the wood where
his arm once rested, the long burn where his ash had fallen,
she remembered the loneliness of the room where he had
spent his last days. She wasn't sure why she had taken the
desk. "I don't want anything," she had told her brothers
when it came time to clear out the house. But somehow
the sight of everything he owned, everything he had worked
for, piled out by the curb for collection had her hauling the
old thing home. She should have taken something else, but

she could no longer remember what else there was. All she could remember was the lonely room, anchored by the desk, bordered by a smoke-stained wall.

She blinked, her own wall going blurry before her, then jumped up, went to the window again, pressing her face against the cool glass to watch the few flakes that still whirled to the ground halfheartedly, as if to say, "No hurry now— the damage is done!" Somehow the sight of the world obliterated by whiteness made her life feel like a great big pile of nothing.

When the phone rang, she realized no one had called for days.

"Hello?" she said, trying not to sound as desperate as she felt.

"Hey, Lauren."

Jason, she realized with no small surprise. They'd met at a party of mutual friends, a wine tasting thrown by a former colleague. After one too many claims of "ripe fruit" and "smooth finish," she had headed to the kitchen in search of something to drink that didn't require a soliloquy after each sip. She had just fished a beer out of the back of the overcrowded refrigerator when he appeared in the doorway. "My soul mate," he said, startling her (she had, after all, just been contemplating calling an old boyfriend for booty). But as he went on to extol the virtues of the brew that apparently bonded them, she realized she was drinking his beer. He was a freelance writer he had told her. Poor, she had thought. Still, she gave him her number. He was attractive in the way she liked—lean, bookish with a bit of an edge, a stirring wistfulness in his eyes. She even went out with him a few times. But just as she felt that first wish, that first anxious clutch of hope, he announced he was going to New Zealand. "Sayonara," she had said, feigning indifference, believing she'd never hear from him again.

Now he was back. Not only back, but calling her.

And despite the fact that she was barely a girlfriend, she found herself whining like a wife. "I want to go out," she said. In one long burst, she told him about the flu she had suffered, the furniture she needed to buy. It occurred to her once she was done that she should have asked about his trip. But after a week alone, she was capable of such transgressions. Capable of anything really. Capable of going out in the snow after a bout of the flu. Capable of agreeing to meet him on the corner between their two apartments when he offered to shop with her. "You really want to come with me?" she asked. "I don't mind," he said. "I like the snow." She supposed she did, too.

So that was how she found herself, bundled three layers thick, bracing herself against a wind that was strangely absent, despite all the predictions she had heard. *It's coming,* she thought, walking faster.

She almost didn't recognize him at first. It was as if she had only seen glimpses of him until now, teeth glinting, eyes laughing over the top of a beer bottle, a plate of Peking duck. The coat she recognized, some kind of flannel wool she wasn't sure she liked (she might have even told him so). It must be the hat that made him look different, she thought once she stood before him, studying the black skullcap pulled over a lean face littered with stubble, green eyes studded with sleep. This was what Jason looked like on Saturday morning. Then she remembered this was the first time she had ever actually seen him on a Saturday morning. She hadn't slept with him yet, and that fact hung heavily in the air between them now.

"Don't kiss me," she said by way of greeting. "I mean, I might be contagious," she added, cringing at the realization that she sounded just like her mother, who shied away from such intimate greetings with claims of germs and fresh lipstick. Her mother, who had never remarried after the divorce and who spent her Saturdays clipping coupons for things she would never buy and filling up shopping carts for a family she no longer had to feed.

It's the beginning of the end, Lauren thought, relieved once they were walking side by side, if only because she no longer had to look at his bewildered features. That mouth. Those eyes. She should have slept with him while she had the chance. Before she blew it (because she always did).

"So how was your trip?" she said, remembering her earlier transgression.

While he talked about places she had never seen, much less considered, she remembered how on their first date, he told her his goal was to see fifty countries. "And then what?" she'd asked. "Sixty," he'd replied. It would never work, she had thought, imagining all those airplanes to board, the packing and unpacking, the arguments over whether to spend the day at this monument or that museum. All it made her want to do was stay home.

Even now, as he told her how he had hiked a mountain

with two friends and a guide, she wondered about him. She didn't see the point, really. Once you got to the top, all that was left was coming down again. The highest she'd ever been was the top of the Empire State Building, which had only made her gaze down with indifference.

"One of the guys got sick on the second peak," he said. Then he went on to explain that there was less oxygen at higher altitudes, how the body functions began to shut down, according to priority function: reproductive, digestive, immune. She found herself momentarily intrigued by the idea that there was a place in the world where her reproductive system was not a priority and she remembered why she liked him. He knew things. Things she had never considered.

By the time they reached their destination, Jason was holding her hand, and she began to feel hopeful, especially once they stood at the end of a long street lined with antique stores rumored to have everything she was looking for.

"Well," she said, looking up at him, "here we are."

"Here we are," he echoed, his gaze dropping to her mouth.

"Shall we?" she said.

"We shall," he said, a smile tugging at his mouth that sent her stumbling over a snow mound in a mad scramble to reach the first doorway.

The moment they entered the store, Lauren was glad she wasn't alone. Somehow the sight of all that gleaming furniture made her feel vulnerable. "Can I help you?" said the saleswoman, rousing herself from the wingback where she sat.

"I'm looking for an armoire," Lauren replied with satisfaction. She knew it was the piece she should start with. One of the magazines she had read said the armoire could "define the architecture of the room." And, she thought, remembering her bare walls and barren floor, what she needed most was definition.

"Any particular style?" the woman asked now, eyebrows raised.

It occurred to Lauren that she really had no idea. She turned to look at Jason and saw he had left her side to stare at a black-faced Buddha smiling before a small rock pond. How could he help her? He'd never even seen her apartment. And she had seen a bit too much of it. Since she felt silly saying, "Something pretty," she replied, "I'll know it when I see it."

"I'll show you what I have," the woman said in a tone that implied she couldn't care less whether what she had would satisfy. Then she strode through the tangle of tables and chairs and desks toward the back. Lauren followed, glancing up to see that Jason had abandoned the Buddha and was by her side once more.

Four armoires later, they practically fled from the store. Everything was too imposing and, Lauren discovered, too expensive. They were out on the street again in moments, blinking against the brightness of the day, buoyed by the possibility of more. At least she was anyway. But since Jason seemed complacent enough to carry on, carry on they did.

And on and on and on. There were so many stores. So many possibilities.

Too many possibilities.

There was the Victorian-era piece that was pretty enough, but too small to hold a TV. There was the walnut cabinet that could hold a TV, but was as bland as a cheap motel room. There was the wardrobe with the funky antique hinges that she could have remodeled to hold a TV, but then should she really have to do all that work? There was the Indonesian teak with the pretty carved doors, but she didn't think she was an Indonesian teak sort of girl.

By the fourth store, when she rejected a perfectly lovely French country cabinet for being too rustic, Jason said, "You can find something wrong with just about anything."

By the fifth store, she began to become suspicious of him. Really, what man likes to shop to such lengths? Even she didn't like to shop to such lengths. In fact, she would have put it all off to next week, only she knew next week there would be bills to pay, an assistant to manage, a cat to feed, a mother to placate and soon enough it would be six months later. Soon enough it would be a year. A year in which her friends drifted away while she doled out excuses why she couldn't have them over, couldn't even meet them in a café. She wouldn't have the time, with all she needed to do, all this furniture she needed to buy. She might not even have a boyfriend if the effects of this little expedition were any indication. Then she would be sitting at home, in bed of course because, really, there was no other place to sit.

Now as she studied Jason, who was eyeing a phonograph by the door with what looked like genuine interest, she wondered if he even fit in her life. Should she really be dating a man who seemed to have all day to look at furniture she would likely never buy and phonographs that would likely never utter a note? Should she be dating a man who had so much time to waste? Didn't he have anything better to do on a Saturday? Errands to run? Rocks to climb?

Then she remembered how he had boasted to her, that first night, of his easy schedule that allowed him to come and go when he wanted, travel whenever the whim took him. It occurred to her that maybe he didn't have a pressing need to do anything, and she shouldn't, at least according her mother, be dating a man with that kind of work ethic. Not at her age anyway.

By the seventh store, they had their first official fight. More a tiff really, but magnified in her mind, probably because they shouldn't be having fights yet, shouldn't even be shopping for furniture yet, not at this stage, not when they hadn't even had sex yet. Which was probably why she felt a flicker of irritation when he stopped before an Oriental cabinet she would never in a million years consider, and pronounced it perfect for her.

She looked at the cabinet, looked at him, curious what it was about this particular monstrosity that made him think it was so perfect for her. Then she remembered that three stores ago he had told her about the Oriental cabinet he had picked up for five hundred dollars. She wondered why men always assume women wanted what they had. A therapist she'd had once told Lauren that what she desired most was to have a penis. The therapist, of course, was a man, a man she stopped seeing shortly thereafter.

"Don't *you* have one just like this?" she said, with so much accusation in her tone that even she cringed.

Jason frowned. "Well, I wouldn't recommend something I wouldn't buy myself."

Perfectly logical, she thought, but since she was too far gone, since she had seen too much furniture, dated one too many men not to realize their relationship was doomed, been dumped one too many times not to know when to deal the first blow, she said, in a voice thick with sarcasm, "I think your furniture is getting in the way of this relationship."

"I think *your* furniture is getting in the way of this relationship," he said, eyes gleaming with irritation. "And you don't even own it yet!"

He was right, of course. Which was probably why Lauren bought him lunch at the first diner they came across. That and the fact that she was hungry, really hungry, for the first time in days. Now as she sat across from him, her stomach full, her heart lighter, he teased her about her furniture trials.

"It's not every day you buy an armoire," she said.

"Thank God," he replied, rolling his eyes.

"I guess I hope to have that armoire for the rest of my life." A pretty big commitment, she realized, wondering if she was ready to make it. If she would ever be.

"Well, at least you know what you don't want," he said, studying her face so intently she was forced to look away.

* * *

"Shall we call it a day?" Jason said once they were out on the street, faced with the decision of where to go next. Lauren felt startled by his words, and surprisingly sad. Not that she wanted to shop any longer. Gazing up at him, she realized what she wanted most was to be with him a little longer. And he wanted to go home.

Maybe he sensed her sudden sorrow. Clearly he had misinterpreted it, because before she knew what was happening, he had taken her hand and was leading her down the avenue. "One more place," he said when she tried to protest. "It's on the way home. I know you'll find something perfect there."

And though she doubted such a place existed, she allowed herself to be led.

It was only when they reached 14th Street, only as they passed the clusters of drugstores and discounters, that she began to wonder. And to worry. But before she had a chance to argue, she found herself standing beside him in front of the kind of store she hadn't even known existed in Manhattan. A large banner flapped from the front window, declaring it to be the "Largest Discounter Of Furniture In The World!"

She was having a hard time generating the same level of enthusiasm. "Here?"

"I bet you've never been here before."

He had her there, she realized, following him inside, though she wasn't sure if it was to escape the cold or because she had no better options.

Within moments, they were surrounded by displays of living rooms and dining rooms and bedrooms so many rows thick they blended together in one big sad heap. "I think my fever is back," she said.

"C'mon," he said, pulling her through a sea of couches and sofas and tables that managed to glow beneath the harsh fluorescent lights.

Finally he stopped, stepping into one of the living rooms, leaving her to stand on the periphery, staring at a powder blue couch, shapeless but inviting. She could see herself growing larger on that couch, thighs sprawling to accommodate the overstuffed pillows.

"Here's one," he said, drawing her attention away from her sprawling thighs.

She looked up to see him standing proudly beside some kind of cabinet that completed the suburban despair that couch conjured up. Gazing into his hopeful eyes, she tried to determine if he was kidding.

"It's oak," she said, realizing he wasn't.

"Oak is good wood," he said, running a hand over the door. "Solid. You'll have this for years."

Somehow the thought of staring at this cabinet, durable and colorless, for the rest of her life, depressed her. She looked at him once more, noticed his eyes seemed more faded beneath the aggressive light, his skullcap less hip and edgy and more sturdy and warm. She noticed for the first time the gray hairs that littered his stubbled jaw. A vision filled her mind of his face, eyes sunken, skin etched by time, and suddenly she knew with a certainty she could not possibly have what he would look like when he was very old.

She stepped closer, touching the door as if declaring some truce, and grabbed the first excuse that came to her. "It doesn't match the desk."

He frowned. "I thought you said you had no furniture."

"I do, I mean, that is, I have a...a desk," she said, thinking of the faded place in the wood, the long burn, and suddenly feeling foolish. Foolish for hanging on to a desk that she should have left out by the curb.

"Can I help you?"

Startled, she looked up to discover a salesman had stepped into the pre-fab living room where they stood, his gaze roaming back and forth between them, summing them up. And just as she was about to beg off the assistance he offered, she caught a glimpse of her and Jason in the mirror that lined the far wall, she misshapen in down, he warm and reliable in wool. We are a couple, a couple buying furniture together, she thought. At least to this man we are.

"She's looking for an entertainment center," Jason explained, breaking her spell.

"An armoire," she said. She didn't like the words *entertainment center.* Somehow they conjured visions of big-screen televisions surrounded by shouting barrel-chested men.

"Let me show you what we have," the salesman said, his stride hopeful as he led them through the store, though there was really nothing to hope for. She had given up the moment she had seen that banner waving in the wind. The powder blue couch.

Still, she followed, nodding complacently while the salesman extolled the virtues of this piece or that, until finally even he gave up, releasing them from his hospitable captivity, leaving them to wander on their own.

So they wandered, Lauren trailing behind Jason, her hands gliding listlessly over sofas she would never sit on, skirting tables where her friends would never gather, lost in thought. So lost, she nearly crashed into Jason when he stopped short before a blue vinyl recliner.

"Now this," he said, sitting down, "this is something worth having."

Oh dear, she thought, watching in horror as he pushed himself back into full recline. Then she nearly laughed at the sight of him, eyes closed in pleasure. With mock solemnity, she said, "Darling, this will never work. I could never live with a recliner like this." She'd meant the words as a joke, but the moment they were out of her mouth, she thought, *Could* I live with a recliner like this?

His eyes flicked open and he stared at her, that now-familiar smile playing about his mouth. "So now we're sharing a recliner, are we?"

She shrugged, then met his gaze. "You never know where that recliner might wind up. A girl has to think of these things." Then, embarrassed to admit she did think of these things, she stumbled further into the joke. "Maybe we can get you and your recliner your own room."

He frowned, his eyes ponderous and, surprisingly, sad. She thought of her father, sleeping on the couch during the months before her mother banished him from the house.

Shutting her eyes briefly against the memory, she stepped forward, closing the gap between them to kiss his furrowed brow, his flesh warm against her mouth.

They could have left the store then. They should have left the store then. Except Jason had taken a sudden interest in sofa beds. "I really need to move on from my futon," he said as he roamed restlessly from couch to couch, plopping down on one, reclining on another. She followed suit, not because she felt an urge for a couch—in fact she didn't feel an urge for anything anymore, which was probably why she sank onto a love seat across from Jason, who had already settled on the hideous matching couch, eyes shut.

She let out a sigh as she leaned back, felt a stir of old dissatisfaction. "Is this it?" she asked, gazing around her. "Is this all there is?"

He opened an eye to look at her. "Is this all what is?"

"This couch, that chair." She studied his relaxed form, the comfort he seemed to find everywhere. She almost resented him for it, wondering how he could be so happy with so little. A job he surfed through, endless countries to canvas. "Are you happy?" she asked.

He blinked at her. "Now?"

"I mean in general."

He shrugged. "Sure."

"With your job? Your trips?" She said this a bit thickly.

"Well, I wouldn't be doing them if I didn't enjoy them."

She thought about this for a moment, wondering if it could be that simple. Not for her, she realized. Even if they were giving away happiness, she'd probably put it in storage, she thought, thinking of all the months she'd lived without. She remembered her father's house, the lonely room on the top floor. Remembered the shock of seeing how he lived, the guilt of discovering too late. It disturbed her, that picture of her father, alone in a room ruined by his life. She hadn't seen him for months, hadn't known him for longer. Would it have mattered if she had come running every time he broke down? Would it have mattered if she'd cared a little more?

It was too hard. Too hard to care for others.

She looked at Jason. "Do you think some people were meant to be alone?"

"I think some people were meant to be." He smirked as he said this. She thought he was smirking anyway.

"I'm being serious."

"Well, I'm being funny."

She felt a smile tug at her mouth, but she fought it back. She hated that. Hated when people tried to make her smile when she didn't want to smile.

"I want to know what you think."

"I think," he said, his gaze roaming over her face, "you have a nice nose."

She touched her nose, as if she had forgotten it was on her face. "It's my father's nose but my mother will never admit it."

"Maybe it's your mother's nose but your father will never admit it."

"My father's dead," she said. It was the first time she had

said this aloud and now the words floated before her, between them, alarming her, embarrassing her. She waited for the expected apology when, really, it wasn't his fault. Though she sometimes suspected it was hers.

Instead, he said, "How long ago?"

"Three months."

She saw his eyes widen with understanding, felt understanding expand inside her. Three months. It wasn't such a long time ago, though she felt as if he had been gone for ages. As if he were never really there. She tried to remember him now, but all she could think of was that lonely room. A room, she realized now, that was as spare and lonely as her own.

"I'm sorry," he said finally.

I'm sorry, too, she thought, meeting his gaze, memorizing his face, before she got up and headed for the door.

They walked in silence on the way home, arms swaying in unison, only touching when the sidewalk narrowed, forcing them together until the shoveled path widened once more.

When her building came into view, Lauren felt herself go quiet inside. She said, "What I'll regret the most after we break up is that we never took a vacation together."

"So now we're breaking up, are we?"

"You know what I mean," she replied.

"I'm not sure I do," he said, taking her hand, turning her to face him now that they had reached her doorstep.

She looked up, seeking out her window as she did, before she finally turned to him, watching the flakes fall quickly against his face, and disappear just as fast.

"Well, here we are," she said.

"Yes, here we are," he echoed, his gaze roaming over her face. Then he smiled. "So do I finally get to see the infamous apartment?"

She thought of the barren room she had left behind, the pale walls and empty floors. Then she looked into his eyes, remembered the boy she had met at the party, the laughing eyes and wistful glance, the wish she had felt and just as quickly forgotten. And before she could think better of it, she opened the door and let them both inside.

Stella Duffy has written eight novels, the latest, *State of Happiness,* is published by Virago in the UK and Thomas Dunne Books in the U.S. and was long-listed for the 2004 Orange Prize. With Lauren Henderson she is the co-editor of *Tart Noir*, from which her story "Martha Grace" won the CWA Short Story Dagger Award of 2002. Stella has written more than twenty short stories and many feature articles for a variety of UK newspapers and magazines.

In addition to her writing work, Stella is an actor and improviser; she is a member of Improbable Theatre's acclaimed Lifegame company with whom she has worked throughout Britain, off-Broadway and at the National Theatre.

Stella was born in London and grew up in New Zealand. She now lives in London with her partner, the playwright Shelley Silas.

Siren Songs
by Stella Duffy

Ryan moved into the basement apartment with a heavy suitcase and a heavier heart. And the clasp on his suitcase was broken. And the clasp on his heart was broken, shattered, wide open, looted, empty. When Ryan moved into the basement apartment he was running away from a broken heart. A slow, loping run, limping run, with no home, job or car. Never a great idea for your beloved girlfriend to have an affair with your boss. The new apartment was cold, dark, dingy and not a little damp. It suited his mood, suited his budget, suited him. The bedroom had a small bed. Double certainly, but small double, semidouble. As if the bed itself knew what a mess Ryan and Theresa had made of things and kept its edges tight to remind him of where he had once been, the expansive stretch of past love. And where he was now.

Where Ryan was now was as bad as it had ever been.

There had been other breakups of course, Ryan was a grown man, he'd broken hearts, mended his own, broken again. But this one was different. He had loved Theresa, really-properly-always. Love with plans, love with photo albums full of future possibilities, love made concrete by announced desire. Loved her still. And she had loved him, too. But not enough. Just not enough. Not enough to wait while he worked too late, not enough to stay quiet when he shouted, open when he closed, faithful when he played first. Ryan had played first, but Theresa played better. Ryan lost. His fling was a one-night forget-me-quick, hers was his boss and a fast twist of lust into relationship-maybe into thank-you-goodbye. Goodbye Ryan, hello new life.

Ryan did not blame Theresa, he blamed himself and his past experiences and his present ex-boss and the too-grand future he had planned for her in the lovely big apartment with the lovely big rent. The plans and hoping and maybes and mistakes first tempted and then overtook them both. Ryan believed in the future and Theresa was swamped by it. Either one could have been left out in the cold, in this case it was Ryan. Cold in damp sheets and small apartment and no natural sunlight and tear-stained—yes, they were, he checked again, surprising himself—tear-stained pillows. Saltwater outlines on a faded lemon yellow that desperately needed the wash-and-fold his new street corner announced so proudly. And they'd get it, too, these depression-comfortable sheets—once Ryan could make it back up the basement steps into the world. From where he lay now a decade didn't seem too long to hide. He lost some weight, bought some takeaway food, felt sorry for himself and listened to late-night talk shows. He followed the pattern. Waited it out. Morning becomes misery, becomes night and then another day, almost a week and, eventually, even the saddest man needs a bath.

Ryan stumbled his bleary, too-much-sleep, too-little-rest, too-little-Theresa way through the narrow apartment. Touched grimy walls, glared at barred windows, crossed small rooms with inefficient lighting. But then he came to the bathroom. The Bathroom. A reason to take the place at his lowest, when the bathroom looked like a nice spot for razor blades and self-pity. Ryan checked out just two apartments before he moved into this one. The other was lighter and brighter but only had a shower, a power shower in a body-size cubicle. Good size, it would take even his boy-hulk bulk, but Ryan needed more. Needed to stretch into his pain, luxuriate in his sadness. And while heartbreak was pounding in his chest, Ryan's prime solace was the picture of himself in a bath of red, Theresa's constant tears washing his drained body. It was a tacky image to be sure, a nasty one, bitter and resentful and "you'll be sorry when I'm gone." Entirely childish, utterly juvenile, ludicrously self-pitying.

It worked for Ryan. He paid the deposit.

The glorious used-to-be-a-bedroom bathroom, highest window in the apartment, brightest room in the gloom. Bath with fat claw feet, hot and cold taps of shiniest chrome, towered over by an incongruously inappropriate gold shower attachment, smooth new enamel to hold his cold back and broad feet. A long, wide coffin of a bath, big enough for his big man's frame, deep enough to drown the grief. Maybe. Picture rail and intricate cornices and swirling whirl of center ceiling rose, peeling and pockmarked but still lovely, fading grand. Set high into the flaking plaster of the wall was a grille. An old-fashioned cast-iron grille; painted gold, picked out, perfect. The ex-owner had started to renovate the whole place, got as far as the bathroom plaster, the golden grille, and stopped. Dead. Heart attack while painting the ceiling. One corner remained saved from his endeavors, nicotine-stained from the bath-smoking incumbents of years gone by. Ryan liked it, the possibility of staining. Considered taking up smoking. And then decided death-by-cancer would take too long. And he couldn't count on Theresa to rush back to him in a flurry of Florence Nightingale pity. (Though pity would do. Love had been great, but right now, ordinary old pity would do just fine.)

The first time he managed to get out of bed, away from the takeaway cartons, the television, the radio, the box-set DVDs and a wailing Lou Reed on a self-solace sound track (Ryan was in mourning, he hadn't stopped being a boy), he ran himself a bath, poured a beer and poured his protesting body into the welcoming water. Ryan was still picturing stones in his pockets and blades on his wrists, heavy stones, long vertical cuts, slow expiration. He had loved her. So very much. But he'd known nothing and the truth had all been proved to him in the end. Love's not enough, he wasn't enough, siren songs only last as long as the mermaid keeps her hair. Theresa had her hair cut a week before she dumped him. He thought it was for her new job. Seven days later he knew it was for her new man. James was a good boss, but he did have this thing about small women in sharp suits with short haircuts. Theresa had been wearing suits for a couple of months, lost a little weight, tightened up her act, her arse. Ryan noticed the clothes, the body, he read the signs, he just didn't know they weren't for him. The hieroglyphs of Theresa, road maps to a new desire.

There he was, in the bath with blades on his mind, but the water was hot and his skin was beginning to crinkle and in the comfort of the beautiful room, the only beautiful room, he thought—for the first time that week, for the first time since—that he just might make it through. Through this night anyway. And of course, truthfully, he wasn't going to cut his wrists. Not really, not even slightly scratch in actress-poetess-girlie style. He was just picturing escape from heartbreak and the possibility of Theresa running her hands through his hair in the hospital, in the coffin. Just the possibility of her hands in his hair. Ryan likes his hair. Theresa loved it. Maybe he should cut it off and send it to her. She could make a rope of his hair and climb back to him. If she wanted to. She didn't want to. Theresa on his mind, in his hair. Theresa on his hands, time on his hands, nothing to do but think of her.

And then the singing started. Soft singing, girl-voice singing, slight held-under, under the breath, under the weather, under the water, coming from somewhere that was not this room but close. Coming through the steamy air, the curled damp hair, and into his waterlogged ears. Coming into him. At first Ryan thought it was from next door. Another dank basement on either side of his, one more out back across the thin courtyard, too. But it was three in the morning. And the left-hand basement was a copy shop and the right-hand one a chiropodist. No reason for middle-night singing in either of them. Across the court-yard then. Past the rubbish bins, over the stacked empty boxes, around the safety-conscious bars and through the dirty glass. But although the window was high and bright it was also closed. Shut tight against the nameless terrors that inhabited his broken break-in sleep without Theresa. And this voice was floating in, not muffled through walls or glass, but echoing almost, amplified. And gorgeous. So very gorgeous. Just notes initially and then the mutation into song, recognizable song. Peggy Lee's "Black Coffee." Slow-drip accompaniment from the now-cold hot tap. Gravelly Nico "Chelsea Girls," Ryan soft-soaping his straining arms. Water turning cold and dead-skin scummy to Minnie Rip-perton "Loving You." And finally, letting the plug out and the water drain away from his folds and crevices while a voice-cracking last-line Judy Garland saluted "Somewhere Over the Rainbow." Torch-song temptress singing out the lyrics of Ryan's broken heart.

Ryan dried his wrinkled skin and touched the steam-dripping walls of the bathroom. Reached up to the golden grille. The grille that ran the height of all four apartments this old house had become. The grille that was letting in the voice. The voice that woke him up.

Ryan went to bed. Slept soundly. Arose with his alarm clock. (Midday, no point in pushing too far too soon.) Ate breakfast. (Dry cereal. Sour milk.) Tidied the apartment. (Shifted boxes and bags, some of them actually into the rubbish bin.) And, with a cup of coffee in hand, made a place for himself on the low wall opposite his building. He waited three hours. Buses passed him and trucks passed him, policemen talking into radios at their shoulders passed him. Schoolchildren passed him shouting and screaming at each other, entirely oblivious to Ryan's presence, his twenty years on their thirteen making him both invisible and blind. Deaf, too. An old man passed him. Stopped, turned, wanted to chat. The weather—warm for this time of year, the streets—dirty, noisy, not like they used to be, young women—always the same. Ryan did not want to converse, did not want to be distracted from his purpose. So he nodded and smiled. Agreed to the warmth, shrugged off the noise, and couldn't help but agree about the women. The conversation took fifteen minutes, at most. In that time Ryan looked at the man maybe twice. But the man didn't think him rude. He thought him normal. The man was old after all. Didn't get many full-face chats anymore. Nannies passed with squawling babies in buggies. Dog walkers passed, pulled on by the lure of another thin city tree, the perfect lamppost. And one cat, strolling in the sunshine, glanced up at the sitting man and walked off smirking. Tail high in the air, intimate knowledge of Ryan's futile quest plain and simple. And laughable. Ryan knew it was laughable. But still, at least he was laughing.

At six in the evening, as the sun was starting to go down behind the building opposite, with a red-orange glint battering his eyes, a woman rounded the corner. She was

young. Very young he thought. Too young to be living
alone, surely? Scrabbling for keys in the bottom of her bag
she walked right past him, turned abruptly, looked left and
then right, crossed the road and walked up the steps to the
door that led into the thin shared hallway and then the dark
staircase to all three of the apartments above his. On her back
she carried a backpack. In her backpack she carried a sleeping baby. The girl didn't look as if she sang lullabies. Not
often. And he'd heard no crying baby through the grille. He
watched the lights go on in the front room of the top-floor
apartment, her blinds fall down the window, crossed her off
his list. Shame. Too young, too mothering. Nice legs though.

He waited until midnight. It was time for dinner, sup-
per, hot chocolate, bed. No one else came. The young
mother turned off her lights. The other apartments stayed
empty and dark. He was cold, late-spring day turned into
crisp still-winter night. The woman in the top apartment
needed to be careful of her window boxes. This hint of frost
wouldn't do her geraniums any good. He could tell her that,
when he found her, if he found her, if she sang the songs.
He crossed the road and let himself into the hallway. Looked
at the nondescript names on their postboxes. Wondered
which and who and went downstairs to the darker dark.

Ryan turned on every light in the apartment and ran a
long bath, made a fat sandwich of almost-stale bread and
definitely stale cheese (cleaning was one thing, proper shopping was definitely a distant second on the getting-better
list) and lowered his chilled body into deep water, sandwich
hand careful to stay dry. And just when he'd finished the first

mouthful, a door upstairs opened and closed. Then footsteps, more muffled. Another door. A third. He waited. Swallowed silently, chewed without noise, saliva working slowly on the wheat-dairy paste, teeth soft on his tongue. And then, again the water was cold, the food done, his arms just lifting water-heavy body from the bath, he heard it again. Singing through the grille, slow voice through the steam. Billie Holiday tonight. A roaring Aretha Franklin. And surprise finale theme tune to *The Brady Bunch*. Sweet voice nudged harsh voice twisted slow and smooth into comedy turn. He leaped even farther then. Wet hand reaching to the grille, stronger determination to find her. Bed, and alarm set for 6:00 a.m. Maybe she worked late, left early. He would, too. Theresa was there, in his bed, in his head. But she wasn't hurting just now. Or not so much anyway. He must remember to buy some bread.

For a full week Ryan follows the same pattern. Gets up early, runs to the closest shop, buys three sandwiches, takes up his post opposite the house. The young mother comes and goes. Smiles at him at first and then gives up when he doesn't smile back, when his gaze is too concentrated past her, on the steps, on the windows, up and down the street. The old man passes every morning and every afternoon. Each time a new weather platitude, a new women truism. Ryan thinks he should be writing these down. The old man is clearly an expert in the ways of women, in the pain of women, the agony of women-and-men. Ryan changes his daily shifts by two hours each time. In twelve days he will have covered all the hours, twice. There are two other occupants of the house. One of them is the singer. He will find her. Theresa is fading. Still there, still scarring, but fading anyway. There is something else to think about, something else to listen to. It does help. Just as they always say so. Just as the old man says so. She left him a message yesterday morning, Theresa. And he only played it back five times. It was just a message, some boxes he'd left behind, when he planned to pick them up. She had nothing more to say to him. Even Ryan, even now, knew it didn't need playing more than five times.

And in the night, when he hasn't yet found the other two, caught the other two, followed their path from the door to hallway to specificity of individual window, while all he still knows for sure is the young, young mother, at night Ryan listens to the songs. Every night a new repertoire. Deborah Harry, Liza Minnelli, Patti Smith, Sophie Tucker, Nina Simone. A parade of lovelies echoing down the grille and into his steamy bathroom, through the mist to his eyes and ears, nose and mouth, breathing them in with the taste of his own wet skin, soapsuds body, music soothing the savage beast in his broken breast. Ryan is really very clean. His mother would be proud. (She never much liked Theresa.)

The following Sunday, his eyes switching from one end of his street to the other, the old man just passed ("Never trust a pretty woman in high heels, either she'll trip up or you will"), about to start on his cinnamon bagel, he sees the door open on the other side of the street. The door to his maybe. A woman comes out. Middle aged, middle dressed, middle face between smile and scowl until she checks out the sky—it is sunny, she turns to smile. She is dressed to run. Locks the door behind her. (She has a key! She is one of them!) Makes a few cursory stretches, jogs down the steps, up again, down, stretch and away to the west end of the street. Ryan notes the time. Twenty minutes later she is back. Red-faced, puffing hard, she is not running fast now, did not start off fast, either, a slight lean to the left, lazy— or unaware—technique, bad shoes maybe, she stops at the steps. Sits, catches her breath. She takes off her shoes, re- moves a stone from one, replaces the sticky insole in the other. Runs fingers through her hair, red fingers, red face, faded red hair. She is his mother's age maybe. Ryan has a young mother, but she is his mother's age all the same. He is both disappointed and comforted. If she is the singer, then they are lullabies. Not the young mother lullabies to the wailing baby, but this older woman's lullabies to him. And they work. He is soothed. Would sleep in the bath but for the cooling water. She wipes sweat from her forehead. She is not beautiful, or particularly strong. She does not look like the singer of the songs. He watches her go inside and some minutes later follows. In the hallway, before descending the dark stairs to the basement (a lightbulb to replace, time to do it now, time and inclination) he catches the scent of her in the air. Woman older than him and more parental than him and sweatier than him and under all that a touch of the perfume she must have worn yesterday, last night. A stroke of the perfume she will wear again, proud to have been out and sweating, pleased with her slow progress toward firm-

ness from age, flushed through with the pumping blood.
Ryan scents all this in the hallway. And is happy to think of
something not himself. Not Theresa. Brand new.

Then the songs change again. Britney and Whitney and
Christine and Lavigne and other song lines he doesn't know
the name of but knows what they look like, what they all
look like, MTV ladies of the night, little bodies and lithe
bodies with low pants or high skirts and bare midriffs, flash-
ing splashing breasts beneath wide mouths with good smiles.
They are up-tempo these songs and they don't soothe him
anymore, but they do excite him, awaken him a little, remind him of what else and possibility and—when they rail
and rant and proclaim and damn (mostly men, mostly boys,
mostly life)—Ryan is reminded he is not the only one. The
identification with sixteen-year-old girls may be a little unusual, but he is not the only one. He is glad to be joined in
his suffering-into-ordinary. Glad to have companionship in
his ordinary-back-to-life. And, given the choice, he feels
happier shouting along with the Lolitas than looking on
with the old men. Ryan has never done letch very well.
Naked and wet, he is all too aware of his own vulnerability.

Ryan decides the third woman must be her. The She.
The Singer. The One. Of course, either of the other two
might be the singer, but he just can't see it. Not the young
mother, tired as she seems to be from the baby and the college books she carries in and out every day. He knows they
are college books. He has stopped and asked her. Helped
her with them once, when the baby was screaming and she
couldn't find her keys, and then another time, too, when

it was raining, summer rain, hot rain, and she needed to get the baby and her shopping and her books all inside at once. She asked him then if he was always going to sit on the low wall opposite the house. If he didn't get bored. And Ryan wondered before he answered, what it must look like, him there, every day. How to answer her question without sounding insane. Or frightening. He told her that it was dark in the basement flat. He wanted to be outdoors. And she nodded, agreed. She used the fire escape herself quite often. Not that it was very safe. Not that she'd ever let the baby out there. But she needed to see the light sometimes, have it fall direct on her skin. And then she went upstairs. Grateful for his help with the books and the baby. And he smiled, realizing he'd told her the truth.

It couldn't be the older woman, either, his singer. Not that she didn't have a good voice. He'd heard her as she ran. She was getting better at running, faster, a cleaner stride. After the first few times listening to her own panting, she decided music would be easier and played tapes to keep herself going. Show tunes mostly. He heard her coming round the corner. Of course she had the slightly out-of-tune twist that comes from only hearing the sound in your ears and not your own voice as well, even then though, he knew she could sing. But she was a high, very soft, sweet soprano. Quite breathy. Perfectly nice but not strong. And the siren who sang down into his bath time did so with a low growl, a full-throated roar, a fierce, passionate woman's voice. This older lady was sweet, but she wasn't the one. She nodded at him now, as she had started to do when she got back to the house, wiped her brow, loosed the pull of her shoelaces. He heard the click of her tape recorder and the *42nd Street* tap-skip-hum as she made her way up the steps.

Ryan nearly missed Carmella the first time. He'd almost given up waiting. Was worried about what it looked like to be sitting there day after day. Was worried that the old man thought he was a fixture, that Ryan himself was a fixture like the old man. Was worried he needed to get a job. The redundancy package that left him without Theresa and without an apartment only left him with three months of feeling sorry for himself as well. And he'd wallowed through the first and now sat through another. He needed her to be the one. And, just as he was thinking now might be the right time to get up from the wall and walk to the shop and buy a newspaper, look for a job, there she was. Tall and slim and gorgeous. She'd been singing it last night, "Girl from Ipanema" in her swinging gait. Walking slowly down the stairs from her apartment, out of the gloom of the hallway to the glass of the front door. She stopped to check her mailbox. Long perfect nails, each one pretty pink. And Ryan knew this was her, she, the one, his singing angel. He started to get up from the wall, he didn't know what he would say but he knew he had to say it, must make a move, he'd lost Theresa, this wouldn't, couldn't happen again. She opened the door, he had his foot on the bottom step, she pulled the door back, he was looking up, she down, brown eyes met blue eyes, she smiled, he smiled, he started up, she started down. And kept coming, she fell on the second of five steps. Ryan decided it was meant to be. She fell into his arms, they tumbled to the pavement, arms and legs, hands and feet. When he sat up she was leaning against him, his right hand holding her left shoe. She smiled again.

"How kind. If you wouldn't mind?"

And he knelt to replace the shoe and knew with startling clarity that this time, this one, this vision…was a man. A beautiful, tall, delicious, perfect, angelic…man. Ryan replaced the size-ten shoe and looked up.

"You may stand. If you wish."

He did. Both.

"I'm Carmella. I live on the second floor. I'm a singer."

"Yes."

"I have to go. I'm sorry. I have a show."

"Yes."

"Thank you so much."

She walked away. Ryan called after her, "No. Thank you." Except that he didn't. When he opened his mouth there was no sound. She had stolen his sounds. And then Ryan laughed and gave in. Maybe the dream woman was not waiting for him on the other side of the grille. Maybe she wasn't really there. But she has woken him anyway.

That night Ryan lies in the bath and waits for his siren. She comes through the mist, singing of dreams and awakening. Of perfect men and wonderful women. The next day, waiting by the doorstep at the appropriate time for the appropriate woman, Ryan asks each one of them out. He asks the young woman to breakfast—on the way to the nursery, via the park, then quick to college.

"Thanks, I'm really busy, but…yeah. Okay. Thanks. Anyway."

The older woman agrees to lunch. An hour—and then another half—grabbed from the office, damn them, why not, why shouldn't she, after all?

"I'm never late back. Who'd have thought? Late back? Me!"

And then with Carmella to dinner. In her high heels and short skirt and no need to catch when they fall.

The young mother is delighted and charmed and astonished to be treated as anything other than Jessie's mum. The older woman is delighted and charmed and astonished to be treated to anything by a younger man of Ryan's age. And Carmella who is Colin is delighted and charmed and astonished to be treated generously by such an obviously good-looking, obviously straight man. (And it's such a long time since Ryan thought of himself as good-looking that he too is astonished, charmed, delighted.)

There is eating and drinking. They are nice, good to do. There is music and singing. Of course there is singing. Time passes. Because it does. Ryan feels better. Because he can. Life goes on. It cannot go back. The baby grows, the young woman takes on another year at college. The older woman enters a six-kilometer fun run. It takes her ninety-eight minutes to complete the course and Ryan waits for her at the finish line. Carmella gets another gig, a better show, learns a whole new repertoire. And buys a new wig, lovely shoes. Ryan gets a job, one he thinks he might like, where the office is high above the street and floor-to-ceiling windows let in the light missing from his home. He begins to date again: good dates and inappropriate dates and wildly misjudged dates. And then the right one comes along when he isn't even looking, when he has a paper to be worked on this minute, before lunch, right now. Passes his desk. Stops for a chat. Stays for coffee. Ryan has met another woman. Carmella sings into the night. A right woman, a good woman. Carmella sings clean through the morning. And Ryan tries harder and the new woman tries harder and it works. Carmella tries out her opera routine, segues into slow ballad, then fast rock, hint of lullaby calm. Ryan and the new woman are giving it a chance. For now, for as long as it can, for as long as they will. As is the way of these things.

And, in the basement apartment with the deep claw-foot bath and the sound of possibility echoing down the golden grille, Ryan and his new love, Chantal, bathe happily ever after. More or less.

Anna Maxted is a freelance writer and the author of the international bestsellers *Behaving Like Adults, Getting Over It* and *Running in Heels.* Her latest novel, *Being Committed,* will be published this fall by ReganBooks. She lives in London with her husband, novelist Phil Robinson, their son and two cats.

The Marrying Kind
by Anna Maxted

For a short time, Michelle was a hippie. This aberration occurred during college. She wore gypsy skirts, skim-read left-wing newspapers and ate a lot of vegetarian food. Suddenly, it wasn't enough for her to be merely "in love." This limp inferior emotion had to be upgraded to "loved up." A reference to ecstasy, which I found affected and irritating. Worse, she was suddenly *kooky.* "Oh! I'm so ditsy!" was the message, even though her sharp eyes, black as currants, assessed you. She proclaimed the wonders of alternative health.

I have to tell you, Michelle couldn't fool me. I'm no expert, but the deal on hippies is that they're *caring.* The entire point of them is that they boo war, they don't overspend on shoes, and they would eat dirt rather than use a Flash Wipe in their kitchen. A Flash Wipe (a disposable cloth infused with a powerful bouquet of poisonous chemicals, to clean household surfaces, and sold, I'm ashamed to say, in packs of fifty) is just typical of this selfish, convenience, fast-food age. And Michelle *loved* Flash Wipes. So much more hygienic than an old germ-ridden rag.

Happily, the pose ended the minute she returned from college to her friends in North West London.

"Michelle!" said Helen. "Where are your…clothes?" Boom, that was it. Helen Bradshaw—less a *fashionista* than a fashion-missed-her, despite working for a women's magazine—criticizing *her* sense of style. It was important to Michelle to feel superior to Helen. It was how their friendship had survived. Embracing the New Age philosophy (peace, love, whales, er, couscous) was another excuse for Michelle to look down on Helen. Helen was a capitalist (her pay at *Girltime* was dreadful, her crime was she wanted to earn more), and she blew what little cash she had on six-inch heels instead of worthy causes, such as dolphins. But it was impossible, Michelle realized, to look down on someone when they were attired normally and you were wearing dungarees. Jesus, thought Michelle, I look like a freakin' baby.

I can't tell you what a relief it was for Michelle to revert to type. (Intensive grooming, fake leopard-skin tops, big shiny car, Jackie Collins novels, spending money, money, money on little old *moi*). But it's only fair to explain why the ill-starred foray into floor cushions and plates of beans had occurred at all.

Men.

All Michelle had ever wanted, from the time she was a

little girl, was to get married. Oh, I know. So very uncool. But true.

And, at college, even though it was 1991, it was considered—I do loathe this phrase—*right on* to be a hippie. (I think the only alternative was to be a young Margaret Thatcher, and Michelle wasn't interested in posh boys. She knew she wasn't their type. They'd only waste her time. Meanwhile, she noted that both Aaron Levitt and Jonathan Kaplan had stopped shaving and said "basically" a lot.)

The hippie pose worked at first.

Men gazed at her while she talked. They seemed *interested*. Though if in her as a person or as a body she wasn't sure. Occasionally, it turned out, neither.

The man with whom Michelle professed herself to be "loved up" was an astrologer named Josh. He had long shiny black hair (Michelle had a suspicion he washed it in lashings of hot water and luxury shampoo every other day, but this was denied) and asked Michelle her birth date. She told him and he whispered, "Now I can find out all about you. It's like you've given me the key to your house."

Michelle didn't believe in all that shit, but found it pleasing that Josh *wanted* to find out all about her. Hence, the loved-up nonsense. Sadly, the day after they kissed, they met for lunch, and Michelle said to Josh, "So, what have you been doing this morning?" Forty minutes later, he finished telling her. Then he sat back, sighed and asked, "Hmm. And what *else* have I been doing?" The louse didn't even try to put his hand up her skirt.

Michelle left college as she began it, single, and without a degree.

I'm sure you're judging her. Because, despite the fact that any sane person would prefer to live a life rich in love and affection—as opposed to one poor and starved of it— if a woman professes a desire to marry, she is regarded as somehow weak and pathetic. At least, she is in Britain. (Strangely, if you live with a "partner," that's okay.) Why, only last week I found myself at a table with three authors, all of us cozily discussing our children. It emerged that they all lived with their "partners."

"Marriage!" scoffed one. "I don't understand why anyone *does* that anymore!"

Another author thought to check, belatedly, if *I* was married. I imparted the bad news. And Big Mouth—too stupid to understand that marriage is not a wretched constant, but as good or bad as those within it—looked at me as if *I'd* made the faux pas.

Huf. So for obvious reasons, I'm a little touchy about people judging Michelle for wanting to marry.

You have to understand that from the second that she was born, and her mother murmured, "My beautiful princess," Michelle was expected to marry. In her parents' circles, it was what people did. And they were happy. If they *must,* they had affairs, but had them discreetly. That way, no one got hurt. At least, not in public. Living together—note, these are the opinions of Mr. and Mrs. Goldblatt, not me, whatever works for you, *I* say—living together was a nonsense, a nothing, there was no point to it. You lived with a man if you were a cheap girl and he was just using you for sex. (Here, I beg the feeble excuse, "It's their generation.")

I'm aware, there are other options. They are:

One. Gayness. Fab as it is, homosexuality never occurred to Michelle, and thank goodness because life's tough enough without having to come out to your parents when they're Lewis and Maureen Goldblatt.

Two. Singledom. Michelle was forced to endure single-dom in short bursts and she didn't love it. She had no plans to embrace it long term. She wanted a man to embrace, thanks.

You won't be surprised to hear that once Michelle stopped eating pulses and got a manicure, her wish was soon granted. She met Sammy. If I were being snide, I wouldn't *totally* define Sammy as a man. I happen to be quite close to Michelle's friend Helen Bradshaw, and I know that poor Helen spent a lifetime in dog years listening to Michelle whine about Sammy. Privately, Helen described Sammy as a "namby-pamby bore." If that sounds harsh, I promise you that Michelle described him in public as far worse. That boy wouldn't cut his hair without permission from Mummy. They ate at Mummy's on Friday nights where she decently refrained from cutting up her son's food for him. No girlfriend needs an opponent like *that*.

And yet. Michelle dated Sammy for over five years. Admittedly, dating Sammy had compensations for Michelle. She could do whatever the hell she liked. Her parents approved. Everyone presumed it would "end in marriage." (A dubious phrase if ever there was.) Also, Michelle liked to be the main attraction. She always made an entrance at parties, nails asparkle, cheeks red with blush, hair coiffed and teased till it *pouffed* just so, Diamante black top hugging her food-deprived figure, beaming, gleaming, husking, "Hello *sweetheart!*" to people whose names she didn't know.

Sammy would arrive a second or two later, dragging his feet, hands deep in his pockets, eyes half-closed, meekly resigned to his inferior status.

He followed her everywhere, and yet he was barely there. He even spoke as if it didn't matter. His voice was quiet and nasal. I'd call it a drawl except "drawl" is too go-getting for Sammy. I'd prefer to say, "He talked very slowly." Truth was, Sammy didn't *have* to go-get. He'd already got. His father was known in certain circles as The Big Bagel. Not because he was round and doughy with a hole where his heart should be—why do we always assume the sinister?—but because he was a sizable part of the New York bagel business. And as he said at least three times a year, he planned on handing his entire bagel empire to Sammy.

In this, The Big Bagel might have been rash, but he wasn't stupid. He invited Sammy to come to New York, to learn about the business. There would be no trouble obtaining a green card. Anyone would have leaped at the chance. Sammy barely budged off the sofa. That boy certainly preferred to watch life from the side of the pool rather than jump in. He would have happily stayed in his ugly house in Temple Fortune (an indifferent London suburb) watching as much reality television as he could cram in between bed and work (telesales), letting a wife and a family come to *him,* allowing the world to rough and tumble and grow around him until he reached an untenable age and quietly left it.

However, Michelle was present—overseeing a new cleaner—when The Big Bagel rang, and overheard the conversation. To be honest, she *heard* the conversation, as she had picked up the phone in the bedroom. (Sammy probably thought the click was wax in his ear.)

"Oh my God, we're GOING TO NEW YORK!" she screamed, and threw her arms around him.

Sammy, used to taking the path of least resistance, let Michelle book the tickets on his credit card. Possibly, they had sex that night. Michelle—I trust you'll be discreet—wasn't mad on sex. She disliked men grabbing at her hair. Eleven lovers and (until Sammy, who'd been taught not to grab) not one exception. Also, she hated sweating off her makeup. She had this nasty sensation of the chemicals seeping into her pores, of bouncing up and down with a face like a melting clown. She always worked out in the gym bare-faced. But in the bedroom, there was scant regard for health or hygiene.

Michelle had a ball in New York. She loved the place, she loved the people. They weren't afraid to speak up. They had *energy.* There was so much to do and the shopping was glorious! Unlike in stodgy whey-faced London, no one in New York called you "boring" for going to the gym. Jesus, you could work out in a freakin' shop window, that was how progressive they were! And the food! So much choice in what not to eat!

Sammy, I apologize, loathed New York. He hated change. He had a horror of exploration. He didn't like speaking to people he hadn't known for at least a year. In London, people didn't expect him to speak because his girlfriend spoke for him. In London, people were *used* to Sammy. They didn't care that he had a dead-end job, it made them feel better about their own meandering career paths. They knew who his father was, they appreciated that Sammy never talked about him—in London we're strange like that, we don't like to be graphically reminded that our friends are richer than us, or will be.

Well. The good people of New York were agog at Sammy. The guy had, like, *nothing* to say for himself! His father was The BB, he didn't give a damn! What the hell was his problem? Didn't he *want* to succeed? It was all there, laid out for him! Ah, but Michelle! Michelle was *so great!* What a fun girl! Why was she wasting her time with him?

Sammy stuck it out on the Upper East Side for just over two years. Then he fled back home to Mummy, who could at last stop sulking. Truth was, Sammy would always feel he was a disappointment to his father—he wasn't brainy, he wasn't sporty, he wasn't a businessman. And perhaps his father knew that he would always be a disappointment to Sammy for having divorced Sammy's mother. Michelle could hardly reside in The Big Bagel's rent-free apartment without Sammy, so, furious and miserable, she followed him home. And then, shock, horror, she dumped him.

Incredible!

I was delighted for her. But from the way her family re-acted, you'd have thought she'd turned down the king of England. I'll pause here to say what a pity that was. For Michelle, now twenty-six (talk about ancient), had not wanted to dump Sammy. She had wanted very much to marry him. Not because she loved him, alas. But because her little clique of friends—not Helen, but Helen was different—were all engaged, or just married. Worse, her younger sister, aged twenty-three, lived in a big white house in Pinner, and she and her husband (a doctor) were expecting their *first freakin' baby*.

Being single made her look like a loser. She knew they all talked about her, pitied her. She was desperate to be part of the pack again, to discuss conservatory furniture, What My Husband Bought Me, child-friendly areas with good schools—despite that Michelle couldn't think of much worse than being tied to a small person. When they went to Pizza Express for their girls' nights out, Michelle ordered a salad. All the rest tore into Four Cheese This and Pepperoni That—getting grease on their wedding rings—because, it seemed to Michelle, they were loved unconditionally and no longer had to worry about growing grossly obese and having to be rolled downstairs.

(It didn't occur to Michelle that even if her married friends weren't loved unconditionally, their husbands would think twice about divorce, as they were sensible men who did not wish to live in wretched penury for the rest of their days.)

So. For Michelle it was a brave decision. It would have been nice, therefore, if her parents had appreciated this and supported her. One would like to assume they wanted their eldest daughter to be happy. And yet, they made their disapproval unpleasantly plain. Now. To a reasonable soul, the explanation Michelle provided was unassailable. ("Sammy bores me rigid—I can't stand to be in the same room as him, and if he kisses me in that gross, slobbery way of his, I get this, like, *lurch* of revulsion.")

Really. Who could argue with that? You'd have to be some kind of debating champion.

Lewis and Maureen excelled at bridge, which I hardly feel qualifies. And yet, they saw fit to object. They even dragged Jemma (she of the white house and doctor husband) into the fray. The poor girl—not for her the pregnant bloom—she had hemorrhoids and looked like a beach ball. It was hardly fair to force her to "talk sense" into Michelle. The sisters had never been close, the final insult was that Jemma's normally minuscule bosom had temporarily out-swelled Michelle's. There was a feeble attempt to persuade Michelle that the lurch of revulsion might actually be a lurch of excitement. Then Jemma drove home in the Freelander in tears.

So Lewis and Maureen went on the offensive. (Very offensive.) A lot of piffle about being sensible. Good prospects. A nice boy. At your age. Settling down. Look at your sister. Too choosy. On the property ladder. Get a reputation. Other things to consider besides *romance*. Too late. Grandchildren. Even Roberta and Leon's daughter. Did well for herself. People keep asking. *People keep asking!!* Pardon, but I insist on drawing your attention to that one. Of all the cheek! Call themselves parents?! So what if people keep asking? Let them ask! Not that it's any of their goddamn business!

Forgive me. I just find it insufferable that Lewis and Maureen were less bothered about Michelle's *life* than the prying opinions of their neighbors. Why, if this wasn't a free country, they'd have bullied her up the aisle to spend the rest of her days with a man who repulsed her, just so that when Mrs. Lily Frosh up the road inquired after their daughter, they'd be able to provide an answer that *they* felt didn't imply failure on their part, that wouldn't have her tutting and shaking her head and whispering to Irene Frankel in synagogue, who would then pass it on up the row to Nina Koffler (the poor rabbi, he might as well have read the sermon to himself) until the whole congregation was aflame with the shocking news that the Goldblatts' eldest girl *still* couldn't find a nice Jewish boy, and what *would* become of her…?

Ha. She met Marcus.

So as you know, I sighed just then but it didn't translate to the page. The reason is…well. I have to confess. Michelle and Marcus figured in a previous tale I wrote about Helen, and I'm afraid I wasn't too kind to Michelle. She appeared to be that spiteful, infuriating friend—most women have at least *one*—who a girl hangs on to for no decipherable reason other than masochism. Helen's father died and Michelle didn't call or come to the funeral. When she finally deigned to ring, it was to invite Helen to her birthday "boogie." When Helen confronted her about her silence/absence, Michelle told her, frostily, that "women in my family don't attend funerals." As Helen rightly observed, this would cause a problem when one of them snuffed it.

Nor did Michelle distinguish herself throughout the rest of Helen's tale. Indeed, from Helen's viewpoint, it seemed

318 *Anna Maxted*

that the prime reason Michelle got together with Marcus was to spite *Helen*. Oh boy, is that a bad reason to get together with any man. (Helen's nine-year crush on Marcus, her landlord and flatmate, had recently ended in an excruciatingly awful one-night stand, the consequence of which was mutual loathing.) Helen—who in her defence *was* in the clutch of grief, even if she didn't realize it—was pretty scathing about Michelle from start to finish. At the time, I endorsed every word.

But, gosh. I guess that back then I didn't *know* the details of Michelle's background and upbringing. (A shocking admission from an author, please keep that information from my publisher.) Now that I do, I feel I understand her better, I even *like* her. Feel a little sorry for her. Oh, but she'd hate that. A fine attribute in a person, don't you think? A self-pity in others is so life sapping, you have to invent a million lies to tell them and it draws the energy out of you like an all-day wedding. Michelle had pride. I think the whinging about Sammy owed a lot to the fact that Michelle liked to talk about herself.

Ah, well. Back to Marcus. What can I tell you? He was different from Sammy. Certainly, he was more suited to Michelle. Which was good. Marcus was a fitness instructor, ambitious, fit, good body. (His penis was kinda small, so he was lucky that Michelle was no *Sex and the City* Samantha. Michelle was more concerned with the size of his wallet.) Not, I hasten to add, that Michelle was a money-grubber. The last thing I want to do is to reinforce a racist stereotype. For one thing, my mother would kill me. My old colleagues on the *Jewish Chronicle* wouldn't be too impressed, either.

No. Michelle was unpretentious and she didn't see the moral good in pointless struggle. Let's not forget, she'd been schlepping Sammy around for the greater part of a decade, and his idea of a good time was a takeaway eaten on a sofa in front of *Jay and Silent Bob.* But she wanted to be treated nice. She liked luxury, and who doesn't? And it wasn't as if she didn't plan to work herself. She had taken a course and hoped to set up as a freelance beautician. It was a pleasure to find Marcus, who took care of his appearance, liked to be seen at the finest restaurants (he was yet to be caught *eating* in one) and whose disposable income was at her disposal.

Thus far, they were perfect for each other. I have to admit that Michelle did enjoy needling Helen. Let's put it down to Michelle's own insecurity. Remember, her parents were not the sort we all hanker after—proud and loving no matter what a beast you are. You can imagine that when she was little, they whipped away their approval whenever she was willful, i.e., disagreed with them. It must have shaken her confidence.

And if your self-opinion is a little wobbly, you're more inclined to care what other people think. Michelle needed Helen to be jealous of her "catch," and thus reinforce her hope that Marcus was a man worth pinching. (Not that Helen had any real claim, bar having trod in that muddy puddle before Michelle put her foot in it, so to speak.)

Michelle was happy. She enjoyed showing off Marcus to all her married Pinner friends, whose own men were already developing paunches—watching football instead of playing it, eating *two* pepperoni pizzas where their wives confined themselves to merely one—and they admired his triangular torso, despite themselves. (Then they sped home and blew up in a rage at their husbands for eating chocolate. A sweet tooth, it was so…*unmanly,* and when was the last time you ran on a treadmill?) By a quirk of fate, Marcus was Jewish, so at last her parents gave Michelle some peace, and Rabbi Markovitch was finally able to make himself heard in synagogue.

And how did Marcus feel about our lovely Michelle? Good news. He was smitten. This for Marcus was unusual because he tended to wander from woman to woman rather like a dog wanders from tree to tree. An exciting new scent would catch his attention and he'd amble off. *Sorry!*

Marcus got away with this impudent habit because as well as being pleasing on the eye, he wasn't a man who had problems talking. He was witty, acid, and he loved to gossip, particularly about the celebrity clients at his health club. Marcus gave a fine impression of a man who was, as they say, *in the loop.* And in this cynical, media-savvy age, where we no longer believe what we avidly read in the papers, a lot of women found it thrilling to have a boyfriend who literally touched the stars. At first. Eventually, they tired of going out with a big girlie gossip who had the conversational habits of a fishwife. So, Marcus's fickle nature suited both parties.

As for Marcus, he surprised himself at how much he let her get away with. But he was in love. Michelle made him feel *fabulous.* She never made disparaging remarks about his private parts—unlike some women. She never tired of discussing famous people. Secretly, Michelle found his loquaciousness an acquired taste (she was accustomed to autocracy in dialogue), but she adjusted. Then discovered its advantages. As a woman whose dreams were frequently populated by variations on Ben Stiller, Liza Minnelli, Kate Moss and Rob Lowe (nothing kinky, all they ever did was have intimate chats with the dreamer), Michelle was in her element with Marcus.

She was devastated, *devastated,* I tell you, when J. Lo and Ben "postponed" their wedding. "But," she wailed to Marcus, "they were really in love!" Helen's spoilsport friend Tina tried to tell her it was a publicity ploy with tax breaks but Michelle wouldn't hear of it.

Every Hollywood split, Michelle felt in her heart. She was surprised and a little disappointed in Harrison Ford when he left his wife after all those years to shack up with Ally McBeal. She still bore a grudge against Jennifer Aniston (Brad and Gwyneth were so good together, why couldn't he see that?). Demi and Bruce, the breakup—*shattering* (but she was holding out for a reconciliation, their relationship was so cordial now), and she'd never *quite* warmed to Cruise & Cruz. The Tom and Nicole arrangement had been so cozy. She couldn't imagine either one asking for a divorce. Did Tom stamp into the bedroom and shout it, "I wanna DIVOOOORRRCE!" or was it a subdued announcement, sitting down, over coffee. "Look. I think we should…"?

Marcus understood that these people were the landscape

of Michelle's emotional life, that she was easily as close to
them as to her blood relatives. Closer, probably. And that was
fine by him, because he was pretty pally with them, too. It
gave them a warm feeling to see in their precious *Hello!*
magazine that Steven had invited Gwyneth to his son's bar
mitzvah. Bet Jennifer wasn't on the guest list. Their conversations regarding the stars, their choices, their highs and
lows, were interminable. Marcus swore that Meg would
never get over Russell's marriage to that Danielle girl and
Michelle agreed. "*Oh!* like, totally, I mean, who *is* she, a freakin' *nobody*…." When Michelle prompted Marcus to ask her
to marry him, he accepted. Michelle was beautiful, she ate
small portions (some women ate like pigs), she was proud
of him, his career, she admired his dress sense, she wasn't sex-
ually voracious (so uncouth in a girl). She *was* messy—Marcus was insanely neat—but that was rectified by a cleaner,
and she was awed at his instinct for what made a home *home*.
His Poggenpohl was dear to him, I'm not being rude here,
it's a *super* exclusive kitchen range, pricey, but so worth it
(I'm quoting Marcus as, alas, my own kitchen is cheapy-
cheap from a horrid store).

Once the monster diamond ring was secured from Tiffany, and Marcus had recovered from the shock, they held
an engagement party—with a modest gift list, at Harrods.
Certain people, I'm sad to say, speculated on how long the
alliance would last. Laid bets, even. (All the while heartily
tucking into the smoked-salmon bagels and fish balls, paid
for, of course, by Michelle's suddenly fond parents.) It's
human nature to bitch about marriage—fair enough, as it

is human nature to bitch about most things—but one or two acquaintances seemed to have a vested interest in its failure.

They murmured amongst themselves, bagel crumbs at the sides of their mouths, that Michelle was, mmm, quite self-obsessed. And so was Marcus. Michelle was, you know, a tad selfish. And so was Marcus. Michelle wasn't what you call, ahem, a great intellectual. Nor was Marcus. Michelle could be so catty. And so could Marcus. Think he'd cheated on her yet? It made you wonder what was missing in these so-called friends' own petty lives to make them so keen for misery to afflict the lives of Michelle and Marcus.

I get confused with the use of irony, but I'm almost certain it was ironic that the only people present at the wedding (besides the bride and groom) who didn't entertain thoughts of imminent disaster, infidelity, divorce and divorce settlements were Lewis and Maureen Goldblatt. Now that their eldest girl was striding up the aisle in an elegant cream princess dress, wearing a tiara encrusted with seed pearls, toward a handsome man who looked only a little scared to see her, they felt that all was right in the world, and always would be.

This, as anyone with half a brain knows, is a highly dangerous assumption. Life can be, as the poets tell us, a right bastard. There is no guarantee of happiness, however special you feel you are. Fate has fickle fingers (whatever the hell that means). Even if you've had more bad luck than other people, and feel you've done your share of suffering, who knows, maybe destiny has it in for you, and is about to heap yet more agony upon your shoulders. God does *not* give you as much as you can carry, often he gives you a great deal more, which is why at least half of us are clinically depressed and on Prozac.

If you're in any way superstitious, the Goldblatts' open satisfaction at the marriage of their eldest daughter was a harbinger of doom.

Not to mention that neither Marcus nor Michelle were prototypes of loveliness, and so one rather feels that they *deserve* to fall flat on their faces.

In addition, what could be more unfashionable than to claim a happy union for this most bourgeois of couples? What could be more unlikely? Marriage, as we're all told till we're sick of hearing it, is a difficult, complex state, often impossible to negotiate, strewn as it is with trip wires and potholes and suspicious dinner receipts in back pockets. What hope for two middling-intelligent, medium-unpleasant people such as Michelle and Marcus?

Well, here's the thing. Fate is not in charge here. *I* am. And I approve of marriage. It's often romantic, optimistic, a beautiful gesture. Also, call me soppy, *I* believe that there's someone for everyone. Marcus is not *my* cup of tea, as we say here, in ye olde Englande. But he was Michelle's. As for Michelle, plainly, she's a pain in the behind. I wouldn't choose her as *my* wife. But Marcus did, and discovered to his surprise that he'd made the right decision. Perhaps it was a fluke. Because really, to assign those two a happy ending is wrong and unfair—there are so many far sweeter, more deserving candidates out there, currently enduring woe after woe.

I confess. At first, I was fully convinced that Marcus would betray Michelle with a client, or that Michelle would embark on a steamy e-mail affair. I was all set to conclude on a note of despair and a stern moral warning. What can I say? I found, like they found, people grow on you.

Adèle Lang is the author of the *New York Times* best-seller *Confessions of a Sociopathic Social Climber*. She is also coauthor of *How to Spot a Bastard by His Star Sign* and *I'm Not a Feminist But…*

Her hobbies are reading, writing and winding up men.

Don't You Know Who I *Am*?
by Adèle Lang

Tape 001 (unedited version): Transcribed 31/1/04

I am attempting the very tricky task of speaking into this Dictaphone for the benefit of my ghostwriter while slumped face forward over one of the many toilet bowls I now own and wondering why the view down there remains the same whether you're disgustingly rich and famous or not… It doesn't seem fair really… I mean, I drink a much better quality of alcohol these days, and the toilet's a genuine antique and you'd think that at those prices the lid would be non-stick.

[long pause]

So, anyway. Where was I? Oh, yes, that's right. Ta-da! I'm still here! Still kneeling over the toilet bowl trying to avoid throwing up all over this Dictaphone which, *by the way*, I really resent having to lug around for twelve whole bleeding hours. It's a total invasion of privacy, if you ask me. But, this is what I've got to do apparently, if I want to *[adopts posh voice]* "tell the world my story…" What gets me is how book publishers expect you to do all their work for them, like you're some sort of skivvy or something. *And* I'm going to have to flush this toilet live on air which I know isn't very ladylike but I don't have any option, now, do I? Since *no one's* actually shown me how to switch this sodding tape off—

[tape stops suddenly]

Oops! Still trying to get the hang of all the different buttons round here… Oh, right. There it is… *[sound of toilet flushing]*. I mean, call me a stupid tart like the rest of my critics seem to do these days, but aren't I meant to be "DALLAS—THE WORLD'S MOST BONKABLE BABE"? As the tabloids so flatteringly put it before they turned on me like a flock of baying wolves and started getting really derogatory… My mum says I should ignore them because they're just jealous because they all want to shag me but know that they can't. Not anymore. Not now that their publicity-hungry wives have found out and sold their pathetic lies to anyone who'll listen. Well! See if I care.

[tape stops]

[rustling of newspaper] You know, even *if,* say, I really was a fame-hungry home-wrecking bitch, I *am* only human and

personal comments on the amount of Botox I've been doing recently really, really hurt…*[starts sobbing]*.

[tape stops]

Sorry. Got a bit carried away back there. Like, I might *seem* older than my years but, like my publicist keeps telling me, deep down I'm really just as vulnerable as the next nineteen-year-old girl. A moment ago I was going to look in the mirror above this toilet just to check that I really *am* still nineteen years old despite what it says on my passport. But the mirror above the toilet is broken…*[nervous giggle]*…You know, it always surprises me what damage a house-brick can do when you hit a mirror really, really hard with it after you've just found out you only got to number two in the pop charts.

[long pause]

Ow!…Ow! Fucking ow, ow, ow!

[tape stops]

I am now having to stand upright over the toilet while still talking into this Dictaphone and using my one free hand to wipe all the blood off my knees, which I think must have come from the bits of mirror on the floor. And so now guess what? Both my feet are bleeding, too! And I can't find any toilet roll to mop it up 'cos I don't know where it's kept, and I know I'm meant to be a really down-to-earth sort of star who does her own grocery shopping and stuff, but this is fucking ridiculous…

JUANITA!!!! GET YOUR BUTT IN HERE…*NOW!*

[long pause]

That was me shouting loudly just then. Not because I'm a prima donna or anything, but because Juanita comes from another country and her English is really crap… Hear, listen.

Juanita, honey! Come and speak into Dallas baby's new Dictaphone!

[female voice of Latin descent] "*Sí, señorita.*"

See what I mean? I *so* love people with accents. Me, I always wanted to be French when I was little…like Audrey Hepburn in *Dr. Zhivago*. 'Course, I also wanted to be as beautiful as her too but, believe it or not, I was actually a complete *moose* as a child until I got my tits done.

[tape stops]

To be honest with you though, I'm never really at my best first thing in the evening. Even when I *haven't* just found out I've been beaten to the number-one spot in the charts by a sodding glove puppet… I was woken up an hour ago by *that* particular answering-machine message from my record company who—and I hope they are *listening* to this—are threatening to drop me just because I refuse to record my next album until the producers provide me with my own oxygen tent, flotation tank and repaint all the studio walls white.

So, of course, Juanita then had to rush to my bedside and give me a vitamin jab before I could even *think* about rac-

ing to this toilet and throw up the dregs of last night's secret Malibu & Coke binge.

[nervous giggle]

I say "secret" because, if the press hear what I've been
drinking, I'll never hear the end of it. I'm meant to be on
my third attempt on the wagon and if my publicist finds
out that I've just fallen off, the bitch will rat on me again…
Then I'll probably be packed off to that poxy detox-farm-
to-the-stars, the one which, if you ask me, turns previously
interesting people into complete and utter morons. Call
me a snob—which I'm not, I'm working-class and very
proud of it, my dad's been unemployed for *years*—but the
stench of a bunch of stars with night sweats was enough
to make me vom the last time I was there. So guess who
then also got diagnosed with bulimia nervosa as well as borderline alcoholism? Even *though*—and I can promise you
this, hand on heart—I never so much as *touch* food if I can
help it.

[tape stops]

You know, it's really strange talking into a Dictaphone all
by yourself. I half expect my publicist to leap out from nowhere and press the Pause button because I've just said
something that could totally wreck my career. Not that I've
got anything to be ashamed of anymore…not now I've become a born-again Christian-Buddhist-Scientologist.

And, anyway, I'm sure whoever's editing this tape for the
Girls' Night In book will take out anything that makes me
look stupid. Which is another thing that really pisses me off,

by the way. Why is it that just because I'm blond—and not even a *natural* one at that—the press automatically calls me a bimbo? You don't win Rear of the Year three times in a row *and* go on to host your own show on cable if you're as thick as pig shit, believe you me.

[tape stops]

[sound of echoing footsteps] I am now walking down one of the corridors of my house—there's twelve of them, you know. Juanita's running me a nice hot bath because apparently I'm a water sign and water signs are always at one with water.

[tape stops]

Testing, testing. One, two, three.

[tape stops]

Good. I'm still here then. You know, it never ceases to amaze me about how when, the minute you take electrical appliances into the bath with you, the things always slip out of your hands and into the water. I've lost loads of Nokias, Palm Pilots and iBook laptops that way.

I know that might sound pathetic…owning so many expensive phones and stuff…but it's not. I need them to make human contact because being a famous celebrity can cut you off from reality if you let it. I mean, me, I've *definitely* become a bit of a recluse. In fact, I can count on one hand how many times I've left my house this week… Once for my swimsuit calendar. Once for my cameo role in a soap. Once for my new pop video. Once for my keep-fit one. Once for the launch of my new fashion label, and my new Web site, and my new cookbook. I think that's it. Oh, and once for the guest appearance I made at that awful nightclub.

[long pause]

Between you and me, lip-synching to songs is so sodding difficult I think it would actually be easier to *sing* the fucking things. But like my publicist said to me afterward, if gay men want to hear live music they should go to a live-music venue, not to one of *my* gigs. Anyway, even when I did try for some street cred and sing something out loud that night, half the punters' ears started bleeding, which I thought was a bit insensitive considering everyone knows I'm a vegetarian.

[long pause]

Anyway, to cut a long story short because I think I'm meant to be recording a short one, I'm going to show up all the other authors involved in the *Girls' Night In* book by appearing more caring and cleverer than them. I mean, let's be honest here. They're not nearly as famous or as attractive as me and so don't have half as much to live up to. So what me and my publicist thought was that I should actually attend a glittering event hosted by the book's charity. Normally I don't have time to do things like this because—and I'm sure the charity will sympathize with me here—I'm way too busy trying to get maximum press coverage myself.

[tape stops]

You can't see the gorgeous dress I've just changed into for my big night out…and neither can I! It's completely see-through! It's got long sleeves, a high neck and a full-length skirt so it's actually really elegant… *[sound of doorbell ringing]*… Hang on a sec, I think someone might be at the door.

[tape stops]

[whispers] My minders have just turned up and I'm a bit pissed off to be honest. I wanted black ones so I could look ghetto-fabulous, but the security agency I use say they have a strict equal-opportunities policy and—by the looks of it—an even stricter immigration one. My two certainly aren't going to fade into the background at night.

[male voice] "Hey, Jeannie, how's it goin'?"

That's the ginger. Clearly from Essex. And if he thinks we're going to bond over our humble roots or the fact that he knows my real name, he's got another thing coming. As a famous celebrity, I'm very wary of people who think that just because you both went to the same high school and visited the same mates in prison, you've automatically got something in common.

The skinhead's said nothing yet, though he did give me a salute, which was quite sweet, I thought.

[tape stops]

[sound of clinking bottles] Hiya. It's me again. I've just told my bodyguards to help themselves to the nonalcoholic sports drinks from my cocktail cabinet. They won't find any though. I never drink the stuff unless I'm being paid to. But still, I guess at least for now they're just shuffling bottles

rather than breaking them over the heads of a fan like the last ones did when I went to the opening of that up-itself art gallery. I was mortified, let me tell you, seeing as the cretins used the full bottle of champers I'd nicked from a drinks tray on my way out from the venue. I mean, how was I to know it was part of a sodding exhibit?

Anyway, as you can probably tell, I'm not particularly crazy about having minders watching my every move. Unfortunately, as a famous celebrity you can't be too careful these days and I do have at least *one* stalker that I know about. In fact, he's sitting out there across the road from my house right as I speak. He just lolls on a blanket all day and night, and it's really starting to give me the creeps.

My bodyguards reckon he might be a homeless person, but they can't fool me. Everyone *knows* that homeless people can't afford to live in *my* neck of the woods.

[tape stops]

[sound of phone being slammed down] I have just finished ringing round all my most recent ex-lovers because, unless I want to look like a sad cow who can't keep hold of a man like most of my other famous female friends, I need an escort for tonight. My exes reckon they're otherwise engaged—some have even got married—and haven't I read about them in the gossip columns recently? As if! I only ever read my own press clippings. And, even then, I still have to get Juanita to do it for me because, like most highly artistic types, I've suffered from severe dyslexia ever since I left school with no qualifications.

But I'm determined to keep up appearances tonight because my great mate Peru is bound to be there with Bobbie who dropped me the minute he realized that I wasn't going to do him any favors in the Sexiest Man Alive Under 30 magazine phone polls—not when they're being voted by spiteful and bitter nine-year-old schoolgirls. Peru's in a soap at the moment and plays a right slut…which is a good thing, really, since she's not that great an actor.

My other close friend in the business, Tibet, will no doubt be draped around the one great love of my life, Wozza "Two-Fists" Wanker. He's a footballer, I think, but I reckon his game must have started to suffer since he met Tibet. The way she's always all over him, you'd think she'd never had a man before if you hadn't read the *National Enquirer.*

'Course, I could try calling Bill, the old and ugly multi-millionaire who'll buy you a Porsche if you refuse to sleep with him first, but I'm really not that desperate anymore. Not now I can afford to buy my own.

[tape stops]

[sound of man loudly protesting] Juanita has just invited my stalker into my flat because he's got to get washed and scrubbed up for tonight. He's under strict instructions not to use my customized liquid soap and shower gel that I got sent for free from some greedy, grasping shop that clearly wants a personal plug from me and won't be getting one. It's not that I'm a bitch. It's just that I really can't cope with people who beg.

[tape stops]

* * *

[loud woofing in background] I'm in the back seat of my limo with my minders, my stalker and my stalker's dog, which I brought along because my archrival, Tennessee, is bound to show up with her stupid mutt as she's such a bloody show-off. Mine's not as small and white and fluffy though, which is why I'm going to switch off this tape—we're pulling up outside now and I can't do as many drugs as I've just done *and* hold this Dictaphone *and* keep a fully grown German shepherd tied to a piece of string under control, too.

  [tape stops]

[sound of sirens] On a stretcher. In an ambulance. Dying. Sorry…
  [tape stops]

Surpri-ise! It's me! I am still in the ambulance but feeling a lot better. The medic's just plunged a needle into my chest which perked me up no end! And he seemed quite perky too since I'm currently a 38DD!

Anyway, you'll never guess what happened at the charity do… I was walking down the red carpet with my entourage in tow, following behind some foreign dignitary from some third world country or another. And he obviously thought all the clapping and cheering was for him, so I quickened my step and caught up with him just to let him know it wasn't.

Then, just as I'd arrived at his side, all of a sudden I felt incredibly unwell, which I did think at first might have been to do with the small amount of recreational drugs I'd earlier consumed. But, just as I was about to pass out, shots rang out from the crowds behind the cordons and I suddenly realized that my bodyguards weren't doing their jobs properly and I must've been hit by yet another crazed fan! *That's* what was making me feel so dizzy and sick.

[tape stops]

Hiya. I'm at the hospital now. You'll be pleased to hear that I am making a full and rapid recovery, though, apparently, the foreign dignitary caught a bit of shrapnel and is still in intensive care. But what do you expect when your job is to represent the peace process in a war-torn country by hanging on to the coattails of a famous celebrity? I'm certainly no scholar myself but I'd dare bet that if I was in his position, I'd be more than grateful to lose half my lower intestines if it meant saving the life of a cultural icon.

Anyway, I've just spent a pleasant three hours in casualty signing autographs for all the medical staff and now I've got an interview! With MI6! I think they must be a regional radio station because I certainly haven't heard of them before.

[tape stops]

[muffled voice] I am currently being wheeled out of the hospital's main entrance under the cover of a blanket to avoid the paparazzi. Despite all this, I am in an utterly filthy mood.

[muffled shout] No comment! Fuck off and stop following me around!

[muffled whisper] MI6—who are spies by the way—informed me that it was the foreign dignitary who someone was trying to take out, not me. The fact that I collapsed at exactly the same time he was shot was pure coincidence. Like, don't these terrorists know anything? I mean, I've never been to whatdiyamacallit and I'm sure things are really, really bad there, what with the civil war and refugee camps and stuff. But still, trying to knock off a guy who's up for some crappy old peace prize when you could've killed a famous celebrity is a bit beyond belief.

[tape stops]

[sound of a male snoring in background] Hiya. Me again. I am back at home now, being consoled by my boyfriend who I met just a short time ago. We're very good friends, and I'm not going to say anything more at this stage. It's early days and I don't want to do what my best friend, Cairo—the supermodel, really sweet but a bit thick—does. I am not going to start banging on about how madly in love I am and then look like a complete loser when he dumps me in the morning... *[phone rings in background]*... Hang on a sec...

[long pause followed by lots of yelling]

That was my publicist. She's been fielding calls all night from journalists snidely inquiring after the state of my health. They still seem convinced that I'm suffering from nervous exhaustion even though I thought it would've been perfectly obvious to anyone that I collapsed from the shock of witnessing an assassination attempt. And the bastards also wanted permission to confirm the identity of my new "mystery man" who was seen entering my house through the tradesman's entrance. Naturally, I didn't want them to find out so soon, because my new boyfriend's not quite as successful as me and he might find all the press jibes a bit demeaning as I haven't officially appointed him my chief choreographer yet.

Still, I guess having my reputation unfairly ripped to shreds yet again will guarantee me more ticket sales at the box office…*[nervous giggle]*… Yes, I know, I know. I've been a bit coy about that one. It's just that I'm feeling very shy about the whole thing. It's my first attempt at writing, producing, directing and starring in a multimillion-dollar movie…what was that, babes?

[long pause]

My new boyfriend says that even if my movie bombs, at least the charity I'm representing for this book will get heaps of free publicity for all those *[adopts Scottish accent]* poor wee kiddies… Look, I don't want to go on like one of those whinging, whining celebrities who all need a good kicking as far as I'm concerned. But, if the thought of helping underprivileged children at the expense of my own career is meant to make me feel grateful, then Bozo here obviously hasn't got what it takes to handle a sensitive famous celebrity like me. And that means—and it really guts me to say this—I'm going to have to boot him and his Alsatian back out on to the streets.

Honestly! The pressures of fame. I am just hoping that whoever's ghostwriting this sodding story is ever so good at their job.

[tape ends]

Jennifer Weiner was born in Louisiana, grew up in Connecticut and now lives in Philadelphia with her husband, her daughter, and her small anxious rat terrier. She is the author of the *New York Times* bestselling novels *Good in Bed* (which is currently in development as a series for HBO) and *In Her Shoes* (which has been turned into a feature film starring Cameron Diaz, Toni Collette and Shirley MacLaine). Her third novel, *Little Earthquakes,* will be published in September 2004. She is currently at work on her fourth novel, a sequel to *Good in Bed.* You can find out way more than you ever wanted to know about Jen—and read her Weblog—at www.jenniferweiner.com.

Good Men
by Jennifer Weiner

It was three o'clock in the morning when Bruce Guberman and another half dozen liquored-up bachelors piled into the all-night World of Bagels and hatched the plan to kidnap the rat terrier known as Nifkin.

There had been twelve of them when the bachelor party had started, a lifetime ago, in the rented back room of a bar in Hoboken. First they shot pool, then they'd played poker with laundry quarters and subway tokens, sitting on folding chairs around a collapsible card table. Poker had seemed like a good idea when Tom, the best man, broke out the cards, only he'd insisted that the winner of each hand do a shot of tequila, which meant that by the fifth hand there was a lot of inadvertent bluffing going on.

Things only got worse after midnight when Tom and Chris presented Neil, the groom, with his wedding gift, which turned out to be three-quarter ounces of marijuana wrapped, as Chris described it, in a festive matrimonial Baggie. Tom liked the sound of that so much he repeated it over and over as the first bowl was packed and the pipe went around: Festive Matrimonial Baggie!

At one in the morning the stripper arrived—dressed, for some reason, like Snow White. She had on a blue dress with a full skirt, and her lips were painted bright red. Bruce blinked at her, trying to make sense of the costume—did she have a day job at Six Flags or something like that? Her black hair was glossy under the bar's smoke-ringed lights. It might have been a wig. Bruce was never sure of those things. He'd see Cannie, his girlfriend, on a Friday night and she'd twirl for him, grinning. "Don't I look different?" she'd ask. The question would throw him into a panic. What had changed? Had she lost weight, or bought a new lipstick, or gotten her hair highlighted? Was she wearing a new sweater or new shoes? Sometimes she'd take pity on him and tell him—"He cut three inches, so don't tell me you can't tell!" Sometimes she'd get sad and quiet. "You never even see me," she would say when he'd pressed her to tell him what was wrong. "I see you," he'd insist. "I just don't always see your hair!" In truth, the one thing he'd noticed without prompting was when she'd gotten her hair permed, and that was only because of the smell.

The stripper set up a boom box that blared some kind of generic disco with X-rated lyrics—*put your back into it, put your ass into it*. In a few minutes she'd wriggled free of her costume and was gyrating against Neil as if she was riding a mechanical merry-go-round—up, down, up, down, staring at him with a fixed, rigid smile, as Tom upended a bottle of tequila over the soon-to-be-bridegroom's head.

"I'm the eighth dwarf!" Tom hollered. "Horny!"

"There is no dwarf named Horny," said Chris, who was standing on a chair with his flannel shirt wrapped, turban style, around his head. "There's, let's see...Sleepy, Happy, Grumpy...Doc...Sleepy..."

"Dopey!" Tom yelled, flipping his long hair out of his eyes and motioning for the pipe. "There's a dwarf named Dopey! How sweet is that?"

The stripper clamped Neil's chin between her fingers and gave him a long kiss, turning her head this way and that, as if she was trying to shake water out of her ears. The pipe went around again, and Bruce inhaled deeply, thinking that maybe if he caught up with his friends the stripper's costume would start making sense. "Bashful," Chris said. He sucked in the smoke, held his breath, turned pink and exhaled, coughing. "Happy...Doc..." The stripper disappeared into the bathroom, then returned in street clothes and demanded payment in a thick Long Island accent. Bruce, who'd somehow wound up the most sober of the bunch, hustled up twenty bucks apiece from the six remaining members of the bachelor party, and handed it over. The stripper tucked the money into her purse, wished Neil good luck and headed for the door. She had her keys in her hand, and Bruce noticed that her key chain held a heavy plastic square with a baby's picture inside. The little girl was, perhaps, two years old. She wore a frilly white dress and a sequined headband wrapped around her mostly hairless head. The stripper caught him staring and smiled at him with more animation than she'd shown to Neil during the course of three songs and a simulated blow job.

"My daughter," she said. "Isn't she a cutie?"

And Bruce had smiled and nodded his assent, not want-ing to contemplate a world where women dressed up as Snow White, shucked off their clothes for a hundred and fifty bucks, and then headed home to their children.

"You got any kids?" she asked.

Bruce shook his head. "No kids," he said. She reached up and patted his cheek.

"You'll have 'em someday," she predicted. "You'll meet someone nice."

He wanted to tell her that he already had met someone nice. He wanted to tell her, to tell someone, about him and Cannie, and the talk they'd had that Saturday night, the talk that had begun with her bringing him a glass of wine and sitting beside him on the couch, close to him but not touch-ing, and asking "Bruce, where are we going with this? I need to know where we're going."

But the stripper was already shouldering her bag and turning to go. Neil was in the corner with Tom and Chris, smoking a cigar and swaying slowly back and forth, like a man trying to dance underwater. He had a beatific smile on his face and tequila soaking his hair. "I love you, man!" he called. His glasses were askew, practically hanging from his nose, and Bruce thought that he looked exactly the way he had when they'd met, in sixth-grade science class, two shy, smart boys who'd banded together in self-defense. Time to go, he thought, and went to find a pay phone.

The cabs came fifteen minutes later, and there was an-other bar, and another one after that, and lots of tequila on the way. Bruce remembered that during one of the rides,

Tom had tried to convince the cabdriver that Walt Disney was a stoner—"because how else do you explain a dwarf named Dopey?" At the final bar, they'd encountered a table full of women who all had penis-shaped swizzle sticks in their margaritas.

"We're at a bachelorette party," one of them explained, sucking on her swizzle stick as the woman in the center—the bride, Bruce assumed—squealed over the edible underpants she'd just unwrapped. "Pineapple!" she shrieked. Tom and Chris bought the bachelorettes drinks, and Tom asked if they'd had a stripper, and when they said no he stood on their table and had actually worked his pants down over his hips, proclaiming himself, once more, to be the eighth dwarf Horny, when the bouncer grabbed him around the waist, hoisted him over his shoulder and hustled all of them out the door.

So here they were in the all-night bagel place: Neil, who was getting married in the morning, and Tom, the best man, who'd been his college roommate, and Chris and Bruce, plus some guy Bruce didn't know who was passed out at the table with his head pillowed on his forearms.

Bruce nudged him. "Hey man," he said. "Are you all right?"

The guy looked up, bleary-eyed. "Order me a western omelette," he instructed. "I'm resting." His head fell back to the table with an audible *thunk*.

They ordered. Neil pulled a handful of napkins from the dispenser and started to clean his glasses. Tom shivered, as if realizing for the first time that his plaid shirt was still back at the bar with the bachelorettes. "Damn," he said, and gulped coffee. Chris grabbed for his mug.

"Cut that out," he snarled. "We didn't toast!"

Tom lifted his coffee. "To Neil," he began. "Neil…I love you like a brother, and…and…"

"Hold up," said Chris. He extricated his flask from his front pocket and unsteadily dumped whiskey into everyone's cup. He helped Tom raise his arm again. "To the last best night of your life," he said.

Tom looked confused. "Last night?" he repeated. "He's not gonna die. He's just getting married."

"Last best night," said Chris. "I meant, that this is the last really good time he'll have." He thought that over. "The last best night he'll have when he's single." He looked at Neil. "Right?"

"I guess," Neil said. "It's been pretty wild."

"Tell me how you knew," said Tom suddenly. He planted his elbows on the table and stared at Neil with his bloodshot eyes.

"How I knew what?"

"That you wanted to get married."

Bruce leaned forward, waiting for the answer.

Neil placed his glasses carefully back onto his face. "Because I'm in love," he said.

"Love," Tom said, and burped. "How do you know you'll still love her in three years, or five years?"

Neil shrugged. "I don't, I guess," he said. "I just know what I feel now, and I hope…I mean, we get along."

"They get along," Tom repeated.

"That's important," said Chris. "That's, like…a basis."

Tom shook his head. "But how can you know? I mean, you find someone, she turns you on, you get along, you spend some time, and before long…" He set two fingers on the bar and made a humming noise as he slid them forward. "It's like this!"

Chris was puzzled. "Love is like your fingers?"

Tom sighed. "Love is like an escalator. Or one of those people movers at the airport. You start going out with someone, and it's like this unstoppable thing. You go out, you move in, you decide, why not, because she's still looking good, and you're getting it every night, and then you're married, and then it's five years later, and she's not looking so good anymore, because maybe she nags you or maybe she's fat or maybe you just want your freedom back." He paused, swallowing coffee. "Maybe you want to be able to look at a girl on the sidewalk and think, *Yeah, maybe, it could happen, you could get her number and it could happen, it could work…*"

"Tom," Chris said, "that isn't happening now."

"You're missing my point! My point is that it could! My point is that any single woman in here, in this, this…where are we?"

Neil consulted his place mat. "World of Bagels."

"Any woman in World of Bagels could be the perfect match for Neil. Any woman in here could be his soul mate. And he'll never know, because that road is gone." Tom pulled something from his pocket and began gesturing with it. "'Two roads diverged in a yellow wood,' and you took this one, and you'll never know about the other road." Bruce squinted and realized that he was pointing with a penis-shaped swizzle stick. "You'll never get to know…" He cast his gaze around the bar. A pair of heavyset men sat at the counter, asses overflowing their stools, and a waitress old enough to be any of their mothers was squirting the counter with Windex.

"Tom," Chris said, "that is grim."

"It's the truth," Tom said. "I should know."

"Why? Did you get married when I wasn't looking?"

Tom shook his head. "But my parents were," he said. "I saw how it was for them. They got married when they were both twenty-one, had me, had my sister, Melissa, and it was like they ran out of things to talk about by the time I was six. They were just two people. Any two people who'd wound up in the same house, sitting across from each other at the same table every night."

"Did your parents get divorced?" Bruce asked.

"Whose didn't?" Tom answered. Bruce's didn't, but he knew better than to interrupt. "My father cheated on her for years. Told her the most stupid lies. Told her he'd be working late, and she believed him. Fucking working late."

"Did they have fights?"

Tom shook his head. "Not really. He just wasn't around. There was no one there for her to fight with. The worst thing that he did was to start smoking again. This was right before he left, when I was like thirteen and Missy was ten. He'd take his cigarettes onto the deck and light up right under Missy's bedroom window. And you remember how crazy they make you about cigarettes in school…how they tell you, like, one puff and it's instant death, and they show you those pictures of lungs?"

The guys at the table, except for the one who'd passed out, nodded. They remembered the pictures of the lungs.

"So he'd be out there, and he'd light up, and the smell of

the smoke would wake her up. And she'd lean out her window and ask him to stop. 'Daddy, don't.' All that shit. And he wouldn't. He'd just smoke and smoke, and get in his car and leave. Missy thought it was her fault. When he'd go away. She told me that a long time afterward. That she was the one who made him leave. Because she told him not to smoke."

The table sat silent, except for the faint snore of the passed-out guy.

"Where's your sister now?" Bruce asked.

"Missy? She lives in the city," Tom said. "She finished college, but she never got a real job. She just does temp stuff. She's mixed up, I guess." He paused, swallowed spiked coffee. "I think she never got over him going. Not really. She never stopped believing that it was her fault, and now…" His voice trailed off. "It's not so good with her."

Neil took his glasses off and started polishing them again, and Chris was stacking up packets of Equal and Sweet'n Low, building a tiny pyramid on top of his place mat. Bruce thought that they all knew girls like that, girls in trouble, girls who believed whatever misery inhabited the world was somehow their fault. They'd sat across from them in high-school history and watched them fill their notebooks with stars and hearts and scrolling letters, entwining their first name with the last name of the class president or the quarterback, without writing down a single word of what the teacher said; or they'd seen them in bars, laughing too loudly and drinking too much and leaving with the first guy who'd whisper the word *beautiful*.

Chris lifted his orange-juice glass. "To Tom," he said, "the best man."

Tom waved the toast off grumpily. But Chris persisted.

"And to me, and Bruce, and Steven." The passed-out guy, Bruce figured. "Good men."

Neil liked that. "Mediocre men," he said. "Marginal men." When the food came, everyone was laughing.

Neil pushed back his plate and looked around the table. "So who's next?" he asked.

"Next? Not me, man," said Chris. "I can't even get a girl to stay around for, like, a week." This was sort of a lie, because Chris was usually the one who did the dumping. Girls fell in love with him after two drinks in a bar, but Chris got panicky if they started calling too often.

"Tom? Nah, don't even answer," Neil said hastily.

"The thing is, I'd like to," said Tom. "I guess I still believe in it. Like, maybe when I'm forty-five, and I won't want to do it all the time. Then it won't matter, if she doesn't want to, either."

"Why don't you just find a girl who wants to do it all the time now?" asked Bruce.

Tom shook his head. "No girl wants to do it all the time. That girl does not exist."

"Or she doesn't want to do it with you," said Neil. Tom shoved him. Neil wobbled, then righted himself.

"Seriously, you want to wait until you're forty-five to have kids?"

"That's what my dad did. I mean, the second time," Tom said. "After he finally left, he was on his own for a while, then he married this aerobics teacher. And she's pregnant now."

"You're gonna be a big brother!" said Chris.

"Yeah," said Tom sourly. "Lucky me."

"Bruce?"

Bruce looked at his plate, feeling guilty about the unremarkableness of his own life. His parents had just celebrated their thirtieth anniversary. He guessed that they were happy, although he'd never really thought about it much. There were no affairs—at least, none that he knew of—and no big fights about money, or about how they'd raise him and his sister. His parents still held hands when they walked on the beach; his father still kissed his mother first thing when he came home from work. And they were in agreement on most major issues he could think of: religion (Jewish, semiobservant), politics (Democrat, although his mother seemed to care more than his dad) and their regard for his continuing status as a graduate student (dim—he always changed the subject when the question of his as-yet-unwritten dissertation came out so after three years his parents had simply quit asking).

And things with Cannie were getting critical. He knew that soon he'd have to decide to either move ahead with her or move on.

Cannie was a perfectly respectable prospect. He'd met her at a party Neil had dragged him to. "There's someone there I want you to meet," he had told Bruce. "A friend of Elizabeth's." Bruce learned later that Cannie'd gotten so nervous she'd drunk two more beers than her typical three-beer limit before Bruce and Neil even showed up. By the time he shook her hand her face was flushed, and wisps of hair were coming loose from her ponytail to curl around her cheeks, and she had a crowd of people gathered around her while she did a wicked rendition of what she'd later told him was her performance-art piece: Woman with Arm in Sling Attempting to Eat Crab Claw.

It had been loud that night, and hot and crowded, and for the few minutes they'd spoken, Cannie had to lean against him to make herself heard over the loud music. He remembered how her lips had grazed his cheek as she told him the most mundane facts—where she'd gone to school, what she did for a living. And he remembered how she'd laughed at his attempts at jokes, leaning her head back, resting her hand lightly against his arm or his chest.

The truth was that Cannie was the funny one. She could do dead-on impressions of his friends and his parents, and she delighted him with her turns of phrases, her sharp eye, the names she gave his things. "Oh!" she'd said the first time she saw him coming out of the shower. "It's your reclusive-billionaire bathrobe!" And when she'd visited him at the shore and had been babbling about some problem at the newspaper where she worked, and he'd put his hand playfully over her mouth, telling her there was only one thing he expected her to open that weekend, and she'd looked at him, her eyes sparkling. "What's that?" she'd asked, her voice muffled and her mouth warm against his palm. "My wallet?"

She was funny and smart and pretty, but she never seemed to believe him when he told her so, and she was constantly despairing about something—her hips, her butt, the weight she swore she needed to lose. Still, he loved her—or at least he was pretty sure that he did. At least this was what he told her when they made love, and when they said goodbye on the telephone at night.

But it hadn't been easy. For one thing, they lived forty-five minutes apart, which meant that one of them had to drive every time they wanted to see each other. And Cannie, he was quick to admit, was more ambitious than he was. She'd started as an intern at the *Philadelphia Examiner* and had worked her way up to the position of reporter, one of the youngest ones there. Meanwhile, he'd been out of college for five years and was still puttering around with his dissertation, unable to commit to an adviser or a topic, unable to get his head around the question of what he'd be—of who he'd be—once graduate school was over and he was tossed out into the real world.

They had fights. She thought his apartment was filthy to the point of being a health hazard, so they spent most of their time at her place, where he was forever knocking things over or breaking them—glass candleholders, baskets of potpourri, her waffle iron, her closet door. She thought he had no ambition. He worried that she didn't know how to relax, that she viewed life as one long race and viewed herself as a failure if she didn't finish first. And she could be moody, and would get into black, sullen funks where he couldn't make her laugh or smile or say anything but, "I'm a terrible person." Depression ran in her family. She'd warned him of that the first time he'd kissed her. "You should be careful," she whispered. "My whole family's insane. Clinically insane." He told her that he wasn't afraid. "My sister's on Prozac," she said, pressing her cheek against his neck. "My grandmother's had shock treatments." He kissed her again, and she made a noise like a little bird, and he thought as he held her that this could be serious, that this was a girl he could love for the rest of his life.

He and Cannie were both Jewish, both with jobs, steady incomes…so it was time, right? But when she had looked up at him, curled on the couch with her eyes wide, tracing the tip of one finger around the edge of her wineglass, asking, "Bruce, where are we going with this?," he'd opened his mouth and found that he had no idea what to say.

"Fine," she'd said. "You're not sure. It's no big deal. I can wait." When she lifted her gaze to meet his, he'd been worried that she'd be crying, but she wasn't. She didn't seem sad. Just determined. "I can wait," she'd said, "but I can't wait forever."

"So?" asked Neil. "Are you and Cannie next in line?"

"Maybe," Bruce said.

"Maybe?" asked Tom.

"Yeah, what's with maybe?" asked Neil.

Bruce said the first thing he could think of. "I can't stand her dog," he blurted. Cannie had a tiny little yappy dog, a terrier mix she'd gotten secondhand. The dog's name was Nifkin, even though she'd told him she'd wanted to call him Armageddon—after the Smiths song, she explained. "The chorus goes, 'Armageddon, come Armageddon, come Armageddon, come,'" she'd told Bruce. "I always knew that if I had a dog I'd want to call him that, so I could stand in the park and yell, 'Come, Armageddon!'" Bruce hated the Smiths, hated cutesy animal names, and thought that any dog under twenty pounds was more of a decorative cushion than a pet, but thought better of saying so.

"Nifkin?" asked Chris. "What's so bad about Nifkin?"

"Ah, you know," said Bruce. "He's got that yappy little bark, and he sheds, and he hates me."

"How come?"

"'Cause he gets to sleep with Cannie when I'm not around, but he has to sleep on his dog bed when I am. And when I'm at her place and she's not around he just sits on the couch and glares at me. It's scary." Which it was. Plus, Cannie was always kissing the dog, always petting him, holding him on her lap and talking to him in a tender lisping baby talk that Bruce could barely decipher. And Cannie knew he hated Nifkin, which didn't improve the situation. Once, in a teasing mood, she said that if a genie came out of a bottle, Bruce would wish for her dog to be turned into a sack of weed. And Bruce, in a teasing mood, said, "You bet I would." Ever since then Cannie held his remark against him. She would bring it up in fights. "You look at my dog and I see murder in your heart!" she'd say, cradling the trembling terrier against her body. Sort of teasing, but sort of not. Like when she talked about the way their children would look, or how many bridesmaids she wanted, or which suburb they'd live in after they'd been married for seven years and it was time for their children to start school.

Tom drained his coffee and set the mug down on the table with a slam. "The dog," he said, "must be eliminated."

"Huh?"

"Bruce," he said, "I'm doing this for your future. I'm doing it for the future of the *species*. No dog, no problem. The dog has got to go."

And so there they were, in Neil's car, heading south on the Jersey Turnpike to Philadelphia. Bruce sat shotgun and sipped tequila—not enough to incapacitate him completely but enough to convince him that the Liberation of Nifkin was, in fact, a good idea. Tom and Chris were in the back seat, and the drunk guy was draped over both of their laps, head tilted sideways—"So if he pukes," Chris explained, "he'll be guaranteed an unobstructed windpipe."

"Hey," Neil said anxiously, "try to get his head out the window if he starts. I've got to take this car to the airport after the wedding."

"A lot of rock stars choke on vomit," said Chris, and then he fell asleep with his head against the window and his hair blowing in the wind.

Having a plan had sobered them up. Now, with the spring air rushing through the open windows, and the miles slipping by, Bruce felt alive, almost electric, with purpose. They couldn't change the world that night, they couldn't rescue Missy, they couldn't solve the riddle of how to know when you were ready for marriage and the larger riddle of how to make it work, but the problem of a ten-pound terrier with a bad attitude and a stupid name—this they could solve.

They were going to sneak into Cannie's apartment, and Bruce was going to lure Nifkin into the living room with the remains of Steve's western omelette. Tom and Chris would throw Chris's coat over the dog, scoop him up and smuggle him into the car. Then they could drive him to Penwood State Park and set him free.

"He'll be out in the wild," Tom said. "Where he belongs."

Bruce thought there'd probably never been a dog that belonged in the wild less than cosseted, pampered, spoiled-rotten Nifkin, who dined on hamburgers and scrambled eggs and slept on an embroidered monogrammed pillow when he wasn't in bed with his mistress, but he didn't say so. He took another burning gulp of tequila. He'd almost gotten himself to the point where he believed the plan could work: dog eliminated, Cannie's bed empty, Bruce close on hand to dispense sympathy, and no pesky questions about how Nifkin had managed to unlock the apartment door and make his way to the sidewalk outside.

"It'll be great," said Chris, who'd woken up at the tollbooth.

"It'll be beautiful," said Tom.

"But what if he comes back?" Neil asked. "Like…like Lassie or something. Don't you hear about that sometimes? Those dogs who go across the whole country to find the house they used to live in?"

There was silence. Bruce thought about Nifkin. He had a heart-shaped identification pendant on his rhinestone-trimmed collar, and on snowy days Cannie had been known to dress him in miniature Gore-Tex boots and a sweater she'd knitted herself. He didn't think Nifkin was the type of dog to cross the country in search of his mistress. He thought Nifkin was the type of dog who wouldn't cross a snowy street without his boots on.

"Don't worry," Tom said finally. "He won't want to come back. He'll probably be happier out there…with the squirrels and all." He stared out the window dreamily. "Dogs love squirrels."

"Okay," said Bruce. He could almost picture it—Nifkin being adopted by a band of skunks, hopping across streams, chasing birds. Running free.

Neil killed the headlights as they pulled onto Cannie's street, and killed the engine as they approached her apartment building, so that the car glided over the pavement like a shark in black water.

"Go, men," Neil whispered. "And remember—you're doing this for love."

Then Bruce's key was in the door and he was in Cannie's living room. He opened the box with the omelette inside and set it on the floor. "Nifkin," he whispered. "Hey, Nifkin!"

But there was nothing.

"You guys wait here," he said. Chris and Tom nodded. Bruce bent, pulling off his shoes and then his socks. He eased over the floor toward Cannie's bedroom, whispering the dog's name. Still nothing.

He opened her bedroom door. He saw a pink dress hanging from the closet—her bridesmaid's dress. He could see her sleeping, a lump curled on her side underneath the blankets. And beside her, a much smaller lump. Nifkin.

In slow motion, he reached down and eased back the covers. The dog didn't stir. Neither did Cannie. He slipped his hands under the terrier's body. But instead of stiffening and thrashing, the way he usually would, instead of trying to bite him, Nifkin merely opened his eyes and stared.

Cannie rolled into the space the dog had occupied. She turned on her side, sighed, then was silent. Bruce and the dog stared at each other, Bruce dangling the dog, one hand cupped under his midsection, and the dog looking at him without even blinking. He thought about his parents, holding hands on the beach. He thought about graduate school, and how maybe it wouldn't be as bad he'd imagined to just finish up, get his degree, go on and do something—anything—with his life. He thought about Neil, half-asleep in the driver's seat, getting ready to say "I do."

"Marry me?" he whispered. The words hung in the air. The dog kept staring at him. Cannie wriggled, muttering something, sighing against the pillow as she dreamed.

"Marry me," he said again. The dog yawned, then closed its eyes.

Bruce set Nifkin back down beside his girlfriend and pulled the covers over them both. He kissed Cannie on the cheek. "I love you," he whispered into her ear. His breath ruffled her hair, and he saw her face, mouth slightly open and cheeks flushed with sleep. He closed his eyes and leaned against the wall, feeling the weight of everything he'd drunk and smoked settling against him. He was suddenly more tired than he'd ever been in his life. But he didn't lie down. He didn't move. He stood there, in the dark, with his eyes closed, waiting for his answer.

Jenny Colgan is married and lives in London.

Dougie, Spoons and the Aquarium Solarium
by Jenny Colgan

Doug's toes popped into life like little exclamation marks hanging over the end of the bed, and he rubbed his sticky eyes and tried not to catch the gunk in his stubble. He let out a groan as last night crept back into his head. How had it ended again? Not well. He spooled it through his mind. Okay. He met a pretty girl in a nightclub, they'd danced, grinning foolishly at each other because it was too loud to talk, they'd come back here, they'd drunk whisky, they'd skirted the whole snogging issue by talking drivel about his record collection for hours, then he'd finally managed to snog her. That much he was sure of. More than snogged her? He turned his head, and his face crinkled at an open condom packet. Huh. He had definitely more than snogged her. So *why* the sense of utter foreboding?

She—Chloë, that was her name—was a dental assistant,

which sounded revolting to him, but he'd liked her, definitely liked her—absolutely—wasn't sweetly asleep and facing him on the pillow… Just in case he'd gone blind, he stuck out his hand and patted all around the bed and under the mattress. Nope. She was a thin girl, but not Flat Stanley.

Tentatively he sat up and stared round his twelve-by-twelve room. The cupboard was a possibility, but an unlikely one. It struck him what was wrong. She was gone, but her clothes were strewn all over the floor. Therefore, unless she was flapping along a mile away in an enormously long shirt and clown shoes, it meant that, well, it had happened again…

"CHLOË?" he shouted, hoping vainly that he might be able to do this without having to get out of bed and touch the icy floor. This didn't feel like summer at all, as per bloody Doncaster usual.

"CHLOË?" There was no response. Sighing, he pulled the duvet round himself and landed heavily on the floor, then performed a speedy duvet-to-dressing-gown maneuver which didn't involve exposing his entire naked body to the elements at any one time. He opened the door, but couldn't see her on the landing.

Sighing again, he picked up her bra and used it as a glove puppet.

"CHLOË! 'E 'ees 'olding me 'ostage! Save me! Save me!"

"I'm out here, you twat." The voice sounded hostile.

Doug went out to the landing, but it still seemed empty.

"Ah—good one."

"Up *here.*"

Chloë, entirely nude, was crouched and trembling on top of the old wardrobe that stood in the hall filled with shit he hadn't got round to throwing out yet. Doug stared at her.

"Hello again. Ehm, is this a sexual thing, or are you just a really fanatical duster?"

"Is it gone?" growled Chloë.

"Would you like some breakfast? I'll make you breakfast-in-wardrobe if you like."

"IS IT GONE?"

"Not exactly," said Doug, taking Fluffy out of his dressing-gown pocket.

Chloë screamed her head off.

"You know," said Doug patiently, "he's only a very baby python."

Chloë continued to scream. Doug considered the situation.

"I don't suppose there's any point asking you for your phone number, is there?"

"Eek! Eek! Eek!"

Doug left the house for work eating a slice of toast and giving bits to Fluffy.

"Why can't we meet a nice girl, eh, Fluff? I mean, we're nice guys, aren't we?"

He turned into the road.

"Hmm. I hope she doesn't want to use the bathroom. I forgot to mention we had your dad staying for the weekend."

From inside the house came the sound of glass breaking.

"Eek! Eek! Eek!"

★ ★ ★

Doug and his fat friend Spoons had set up the Aquarium Solarium with the money Spoons got when his dad was hiding it from his dodgy road-haulage business. The solarium had been Spoons's idea: "People can come in, get all their reptile needs and a suntan at the same time—and it rhymes! Brilliant, eh?"

Doug took care of the reptile end, and didn't quite share Spoons's vision. He personally wouldn't mind lying down completely naked and defenseless amidst lots of writhing dangerous things, but lots of people, apparently, did. The solarium wasn't going too well at all, although it did mean Spoons got to be bright orange at all times. This didn't help his pulling tactics though, as being fat, snaky and bright orange isn't actually that much more attractive than, say, just being fat and snaky. Doug, being tallish, and ruggedish, was a bit of a looker for a herpetologist, and supplied much of Spoons's fantasy requirements.

"Tops?" asked Spoons avidly.

"Yes," said Doug.

"Fingers?"

"Yup."

"You did it?"

"Yes, yes, yes."

"And you're miserable?"

"Spoons, I'm a sensitive guy, okay? Maybe I'm just looking for that little bit more."

"What, like up the bum?"

"I just don't understand it. Every time I meet a nice girl she goes screaming in the opposite direction."

"Yeh, that happens to me, too."

"*After* she's met Fluffy. But I'm just…I just need to meet a girl who shares my interests, you know what I mean."

"If I met a girl who shared my interests," reflected Spoons gloomily, "we'd just wank all the time. I'd never see her."

Suddenly, outside the shop, loud yells were heard and there came the sound of a car crashing. The shop bell tinkled. Spoons and Doug looked at each other and raised their eyebrows.

Into the shop strode a dramatically beautiful woman, all shiny black hair and slashed red lipstick. She was wearing a long, expensive and unnecessarily fiddly coat, which looked designer. However, none of these things screamed attention to themselves *quite* as much as the eight-foot boa constrictor draped round her neck like a—ahem—boa.

"What a beauty!" said Doug and Spoons both at once.

"Thank you," said the woman, flushing.

"We meant the boa," said Spoons.

"I know," said the woman.

Spoons nudged Douglas unnecessarily hard.

"Get off with her!" he whispered loudly.

"Can I help you, madam?" said Doug, gulping.

"It's Jumbo," she said. "We're new in town. I've come to buy him everything he needs—no expense spared. Also, do you know of where I can get a fake suntan around here?"

Doug and Spoons's eyes grew as round as a cross-section of the rare Australian ring snake.

* * *

Her name was Maia, and she had been brought up in Indonesia. She took to the Fluffster immediately, coiling him round her little fingers like a rope trick. The Fluffster, however, didn't take to Jumbo AT ALL and scuttled back to the safety of Doug's inner pocket after realizing he was—at this age at least—being pretty comprehensively out-snaked.

Maia was a primary school teacher, but had had to leave her last school after an incident she didn't seem to want to talk about too much; although now, six to eight weeks on, there were still definite signs of distension in Jumbo's belly.

Doug was in love.

"Would you, ahem…"

Maia had wandered out of the solarium covered only in a very slinky towel and Jumbo, which reminded Doug all too pleasantly of Nastassja Kinski. Spoons was gulping and quietly trying to stop hyperventilating in the background.

"Yes?" she purred.

Doug sighed. Asking girls out wasn't normally one of his problems. It was usually about the six-hour mark that his troubles started…but this one had him floored.

"I mean, if you're new in town…"

It occurred to him for a second that Doncaster probably didn't have a great deal to offer somebody this exotic. Maia, however, smiled widely.

"Oh, could you show me around? Do you know any good chip shops?"

Behind him, Spoons made a high-pitched whining sound.

★ ★ ★

Doug wandered up on time to Harry Ramsden's. Jumbo appeared to have a long piece of leather string coming out of his mouth attached to another woman's hand. She looked a bit shellshocked, and Maia appeared to be giving her two hundred pounds.

"Just two," she said to the shocked waiter as they swept into the restaurant. "Jumbo's already eaten."

Maia launched ahead, just as Doug noticed Chloë getting up to leave with a clutch of squealing girlfriends. She raised her eyebrows at him.

"Playing with the big boys now, I see."

He stopped.

"Look, Chloë, I'm sorry about the other night…"

"Oh, don't worry about it at all. I'm clearly just not slimy enough for you."

"Snakes aren't slime— Oh, forget it. And I am sorry." He'd forgotten how pretty she was. She looked like a dancer, even just pulling her coat on.

"Well, if I ever start up a tarantula collection, I'll ring you."

"Douglas! Our table's ready!"

Chloë smiled and walked out of the restaurant, giving him an extremely wide berth.

"Spoons, please, just stop panting like a dog. You're steaming up the cases."

"I just… Oh, *please* tell me. *Please.*"

"There's nothing to tell. We talked a lot about snakes and the shop. Entirely, in fact, about snakes and the shop.

She's thinking about opening up a branch in Melton Mowbray."

"That's brilliant! Global entrepreneurs, definitely. Er… were you feeling her up whilst you were doing it?"

"*No.* To be honest, I wouldn't have felt entirely secure *vis-à-vis* Jumbo and my right hand."

"What—you mean you didn't score?"

"Nope."

Spoons slumped.

"Fuck! Dougie, *I* could have taken her out and managed that."

"I'm just…I mean, she's everything I've ever wanted— she's bright, she's beautiful, she loves members of the reptile family…"

"She tans…"

"She tans…"

"And the problem is, exactly?"

The bell tinkled. Maia stalked in looking like a Bond girl in a tight red leather jacket, Jumbo practically caressing her left breast. She looked breathtaking.

"Darling, which football team do you support?"

"Ehm, Newcastle. Why?"

"I thought so…" Maia drew a team strip and two tickets out of her bag. "And here—I bought an extra sock and cut the foot off so that Fluffy can wear a strip, too."

Doug reached out his hand and held Spoons up before he fainted.

"Where's the office? I'll go and put it there for you,

and you can try it on when you're not scooping out gecko poo."

"Ehm, uhm, it's through the back…"

She sashayed off and vanished.

"If I were you I'd take one of those little garter snakes over there and use it as a WEDDING RING," predicted Spoons.

"I would, too," said Mr. Nebbington, who came in every day to stare at the animals in a vaguely disconcerting way for hours on end.

Fluffy popped out of Doug's pocket. He was obviously just looking around—but it looked weirdly like he was shaking his head, that was all.

"What's she doing in the office?" asked Spoons, fifteen minutes later. "Maybe she stripped naked and is rolling herself in butter and Smarties," he added thoughtfully.

"Hmm," said Doug, and went through to have a look. Maia and Jumbo were hunched over what looked like a huge pile of files. He cleared his throat, and she straightened up guiltily.

"What are you doing?"

"Ehm…actually, I was looking for a catalogue. I, ehm, want to buy Jumbo a little cowboy hat."

"Are you sure that's wise?"

She shrugged. "Well, he ate the beret."

Doug looked back at the papers. "I'm not sure…"

"No, definitely not— Ooh, look! My shoelace is untied!"

Before Doug had a moment to think, she stretched fully over from the waist, bending away from him. Her skirt hitched up and up...

Doug shook his head. His life didn't usually feel much like a porn film. He had, in fact, not quite believed that women actually ever behaved like this. But the fact was, unless she was wearing a very bizarrely patterned pair of knickers, Maia didn't have any pants on. He wondered briefly if she'd possibly just forgotten, but his reliable trouser snake rather thought otherwise.

She turned her head up to him coquettishly from somewhere near the floor.

"Will I get to see you tonight?"

"Uh-huh-huh huh, ehm, ra*ther*!"

He watched a part of her beginning with "b" sashay out the door. And, sadly, it wasn't her brain.

The problem, thought Doug to himself as he put on his tie, was...could this maybe be perhaps just a little *too* perfect? It was like ordering a pizza and getting a five-course banquet delivered to your door, made up of all your favorite foods—say, in Doug's case, five different types of pizza. He wasn't quite sure what he'd done to deserve it.

"So did you think up the solarium idea all by yourself?"

"No, that was Spoons. He thought it would be good 'cause it rhymed."

"Wow. How did he raise the internal necessary backing

capital…er, I mean, you know, the cash to buy the shop and stuff?"

They were sitting in the Café Flo. The management had found them a whole private section, which seemed amazing. Well, he assumed it was the management. Certainly the room had got up and walked out en masse.

"Wouldn't you rather talk about something else?" said Doug. "Like—I don't know… What's your favorite film?"

"Anaconda," she said firmly. "Waiter, has your kitchen got rats?"

"Of *course* not, madame!"

"Shame. Anyway, back to Spoons…"

Still, she seemed keen enough to come back to his flat. And she was wearing a spray-on dress, which on another woman might have looked a bit tarty, but on Maia looked— well, high-class expensive-hotel tarty.

Doug grinned at his trusty wardrobe as he made coffee. He didn't think they'd be needing that tonight.

Sure enough, when he returned, Maia stood in his bedroom, completely naked, except for the omnipresent Jumbo. Doug nearly dropped the coffee. He wished Spoons were here—not joining in, just to see it for one second and then have to go home again. She was magnificent.

"Do you know what really turns me on?" she purred.

"I would guess that would be snakes," said Doug.

"No!" She caught hold of his tie and pulled him slowly towards her. He felt unbelievably turned on, even with the knowledge that, if he so wished, Jumbo could bite off his head like a cocktail cherry.

"Money."

"Money? I thought you were a primary school teacher."

"I want you to talk money to me, Dougie. It really turns me on."

"Ehm, God, I don't know…florin?"

She pulled him closer and kissed him hard on the lips, till he thought the top of his head was going to explode.

"Tell me…tell me how much money the shop makes."

"What? I don't underst—Jesus!"

She was on her knees and had unbuttoned his trousers.

"Tell me, Dougie…"

"Oh God, don't stop that."

"I will if you don't—"

"Three thousand a week give or take…oooh."

"Yes, yes…"

Doug had his eyes tightly shut now. His mind was being blown, amongst other things.

"And how much of that do you pay in VAT?"

"What!? No, no, *please* don't stop."

"How much do you pay in VAT?"

"Oh…my…God."

"How MUCH?"

"Nothing. NOTHING! NOTHING! Ahhhhhh…"

"A *honey* trap?" said Spoons, eating a honey doughnut at the same time and seemingly unable to distinguish between the two.

"I think you're going to get nicked. I'm really sorry, Spoons."

"It's my dad's fault. Those bloody lorries." He sighed. "Undercover. Who would have thought the Inland Revenue would be so *thorough?*"

"I know. She took us in, right enough."

"I mean, where the hell did they find a woman who loved snakes and suntans and chips and Newcastle United and who would fancy you as well? Must have taken them *ages.*"

"No, Spoons, you see…"

The door swung open, tinging loudly. Maia and Jumbo stood there with four menacing-looking men in pinstriped suits with briefcases strapped to their wrists.

"It's all through the back," she announced. "Take it down."

She faced the boys.

"No hard feelings. It's just business."

They stared at her.

"So, I mean…where did you get Jumbo?" asked Doug.

"His real name's Mambo. He's professionally undercover, too. Oh and there's…"

She nudged Jumbo/Mambo, and the snake lifted its huge flat head. There was a clicking, whirring noise.

"…a miniature camera implanted in his head. Painless, I assure you. But extremely useful."

Doug shook his head in disbelief.

"Well, for what it's worth, you really convinced us you loved that snake."

"Thank you," she said. "Just doing my job. Really, when

I'm not working, they make me want to vomit, scream, run away and burst into tears."

Spoons, who hadn't been listening, nudged Doug hard.

"Doug…does this mean you're not going out with her anymore?"

Doug clasped him on the shoulder.

"Yes, Spoons. Yes, it does."

"Ehm…can I go out with her then?"

"Spoons, she's going to put you in prison."

"Yeah, but when I come out, maybe?"

"Spoons, she's not really who she says she is."

"I don't care," said Spoons miserably.

"We'll talk about it," said Maia crisply. "Perhaps over forms 11a-95c. See how cooperative we both can be."

Spoons was beaming as she led him off into the un-marked vehicle.

"Hello, snaky man." Chloë was walking down the street carrying two bags of shopping with her hair in lit-tle bunches and her summer sandals on. Doug felt his heart lurch.

"Hello there. Ehm…you know, I'm not really involved in that line of work these days."

"Oh really?" she said, putting the shopping bags down.

"No, I kind of…gave it up. I think in future I'm going to stick to the more rectangular animals."

She nodded. "What, like bears and stuff?"

"Bears, maybe…anything with right-angles. Giraffes, stuff like that."

"Huh."

They looked at each other for a bit.

"So do you…?"

"Well, maybe…"

They both spoke at once, then smiled foolishly at each other.

"Yeah, all right," said Chloë.

Later, walking away, Doug patted his pocket.

"Don't worry, Fluffster. I'm sure she'll come round sooner or later…"

In 1995, **Chris Manby** met a New York psychic who told her she would write seven novels. She has just finished her eighth. Which means she probably won't marry that millionaire either!

Raised in Gloucestershire, England, Chris now lives between London and Los Angeles. She enjoys reading in-flight magazines, and she hopes that continually crossing time zones is an effective anti-aging strategy. Her latest novel, *Getting Personal,* is published by Red Dress Ink.

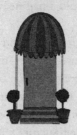

Acting Strangely
by Chris Manby

"Peter," said Linzi. "What on earth are you doing?"

"I am having a nice cup of tea," he said. "It's still a little bit too hot to drink."

"Peter, you are blowing into the empty air between your two cupped hands," said Linzi.

Peter took a sip of that empty air and sighed with pleasure. Peter was studying "The Method."

"You could make me a real cup of tea," he suggested hopefully.

"Can't boil any water," she reminded him. "The stove still isn't working."

Neither was the central heating. Which is why Linzi was wearing a woolen ski cap as she prepared for her big date.

"Nice look," Peter commented when he saw the little black dress/yellow bobble hat combo. "Very *Sex and the City*."

Linzi's teeth chattered as she tried to apply some lip gloss.

Harder than you would imagine while wearing woolen mittens.

"Why couldn't we have chosen Hollywood over Broadway?" Linzi often mused as her first stinking New York summer with no air conditioning became a stinking New York winter with no heat. Linzi and Peter had made the move to New York from London together. They'd done everything together since they met ten years earlier at a youth theater group in the North of England. Now Linzi wanted to design sets for the theater. Peter was an actor with three radio commercials under his belt.

At that moment, however, they were an illegally employed personal assistant and an equally work-permit-challenged hotel porter. Peter, at least, got accommodation with his job. Linzi sublet an apartment the size of Carrie Bradshaw's shoe cupboard. Which was a big part of Thomas Malvern the Third's attraction for Linzi, thought Peter. Thomas Malvern the Third had an apartment the size of a Nike shoe *factory.* And it overlooked Central Park.

"Where's he taking you tonight?" Peter asked in his best portrayal of "disinterested."

"Chi-Chi. That new restaurant in the Village," Linzi replied.

"What? The one with the supermodel chef? And a longer waiting list than the British National Health Service?"

"That's the one," said Linzi.

"How did he get a reservation?"

"Thomas Malvern the Third can get a reservation *anywhere.*"

Linzi had taken off her hat now and was horrified to discover that her newly washed hair had dried in a terribly pe-

culiar configuration beneath it. "Bugger," she said as she
tried to tease it back into shape. Any shape but the one it
had taken. "Why did this have to happen tonight?"

After a few moments' struggle, she threw her hairbrush
onto the unmade bed and threw herself down after it.

"He's going to dump me!!!!" she wailed.

"Because of your hair?" asked Peter, as she pummeled her
fists into the pillow. "Linzi, darling, is everything all right?"

Everything was not all right. Linzi had been seeing
Thomas Malvern the Third for almost three months now.
And at first it had been wonderful. Phone calls, flowers,
evenings in the city's hottest restaurants, *weekends in the
Hamptons.* Thomas Malvern wooed her like a true prince
charming his princess. But then she capitulated, if you know
what I mean. And now the thrice-daily phone calls were
flowing firmly in the wrong direction. Linzi couldn't remember the last time she had seen Thomas Malvern the
Third's caller ID brighten the screen of her cell phone.

"He is going off me," she predicted gloomily.

Peter didn't know what to say.

"How on earth could I have expected him to stay interested in me anyway," she continued with a rasping sniff.
"Every time we go out he is surrounded by New York society girls with their perfect highlights and their perfect
makeup and their perfect bloody manicures." She said this
last while chewing off a hangnail. "I'm an English girl. I can't
do *groomed.*"

"Linzi." Peter put on his best reassuring voice. "You are
every bit as lovely as the local girls."

"He never calls me anymore."

"Perhaps he's just been busy."

Linzi scowled at her friend, as always seemed to be the result when he tried to say the sort of thing he thought a girl would say under the circumstances.

"Okay. So maybe he is going off you a little…"

That didn't work, either.

"Peeee-teeerrrrr!" Linzi wailed. "Be nice to me."

"You're seeing him tonight," Peter reasoned. "All isn't lost yet. Just try to be especially charming."

"That won't work anymore," Linzi said sadly. "I just can't compete."

"You daft cow," said Peter. "You're wonderful. You're marvelous…"

"Don't start singing," Linzi warned him.

"But you make a man want to sing! If only you could see yourself through my eyes."

Linzi sat suddenly upright. "That's it!" she said. "Peter, you're a genius. I need to make him jealous. I need to make him see me through a new admirer's eyes."

At seven-thirty, Linzi teetered into Chi-Chi with as much confidence as she could muster. In the beginning, Thomas Malvern the Third would never have asked Linzi to meet him *at* the restaurant. His car would have been summoned to carry her there. How funny it had been to see his big black limousine swing into the tatty street where she lived. Embarrassing almost. But Linzi had quickly got over the embarrassment. And now she missed it. She missed that car. The last time Thomas Malvern's limo had picked her up was on the evening she finally slept with him. She caught the subway home the next morning.

Now he let her make her own way to the restaurant where he had already been installed for half an hour with a society blonde called Paris. Paris got up and kissed Thomas goodbye when his official date arrived, but Linzi recognized a challenge in the other girl's eyes. A challenge the other girl thought she had already won.

"Good evening, my darling," said Thomas Malvern the Third.

Linzi suddenly wondered whether he called her "darling" so he wouldn't ever say the wrong name.

"You look beautiful this evening." He always said that, too.

Linzi caught a glimpse of her hair, which never did quite go right, in the mirror behind the bar. She touched it instinctively and almost drew her beau's attention to the way it made her look as though she had bumped her head on a low beam. But then she remembered Peter's parting words. "Act 'as if,' my angel," he told her. "Even if you feel like something the cat dragged in, you must act as though you're the most desirable woman in the world. Other people take their cues from the image we project to them. We're going to wrestle back control of this relationship from Thomas Malvern Third Class."

"Thank you," said Linzi out loud, accepting the compliment as though she felt she deserved it.

But half an hour later, Peter's pep talk was a fast-fading memory and Linzi felt herself wilting for lack of attention again. Thomas leaned back in his chair and surveyed the busy restaurant. Every few moments he would spot someone he knew. An eyebrow would be raised, greetings exchanged, someone would stop by the table to shake hands. Thomas didn't introduce his date to anyone, convincing Linzi even further that he was in the process of phasing her out of his life.

Peter, dear old Peter, had promised he would help her. But how? What could he really do except be there to pull her together again when the inevitable happened, just as he had done a hundred times before when Linzi's latest Mr. Right turned out to be Mr. Not Right Now, Er, In Fact Not Ever; I've Been Seeing Someone Else... Linzi contemplated the long nights that doubtless lay ahead, recounting the end of her romance with Thomas Malvern the Third until it started to sound like a fairy tale and then listening to Peter tell her that the man was mad, she was a goddess and Third Rate Tom was definitely gay if he couldn't see that...

Thomas grimaced momentarily at a spasm of indigestion. Was Peter back at his hotel sticking pins in a wax effigy, perhaps? Thomas let out a discreet belch over his shoulder and turned back toward Linzi with a smile she had seen him use on overattentive waiters. A smile of imminent dismissal.

"Linzi," he began. "I think we need to—"

Don't say it, don't say it, Linzi squeaked inside. *Don't say we need to talk. That could only mean one thing.* And so soon. She closed her eyes. But before Thomas could finish his sentence, they were interrupted.

"Thomas! Thomas Malvern, you old dog!"

Oh no, thought Linzi. *Not another one of his awful friends.*

The young man was racing across the restaurant toward them. He practically vaulted over an empty chair en route.

"Hey! Thomas!" He slapped Thomas hard on the back. "It's been *forever*. I don't think I've seen you since Minty Ferguson's party in Great Neck."

Thomas Malvern narrowed his eyes as the stranger pumped his hand.

"Of course, you were a lot slimmer in those days!" the interloper guffawed. "Mind if I join you?" He already had. He'd pinched a chair from an empty table and swung it around so that he sat leaning over the back of the chair like a cowboy.

"Eddy's been telling me all about that business idea of yours," the stranger continued in a whisper. "Have to say I'm impressed. Might be tempted to throw a little money your way myself."

Thomas Malvern the Third's face softened.

"Oh yes, Eddy's told me all about what's going on with Thomas Malvern the Third, but I have to say, he kept this quiet!" Linzi pursed her lips disapprovingly as the man gestured toward her with his thumb. "Hubba hubba. Where did you pick up this little pearl?"

"This is Linzi," said Thomas.

"Harvey Yardley Johnson Junior," said the stranger with a smile. And a wink through the plain glass lens of his specs.

Linzi's mouth dropped open.

It was Peter. This Great Gatsby reject was not Thomas Malvern's friend but her own!

"Malvern," said "Harvey" in his perfect Ivy League accent. "You are a lucky dog. The luckiest dog in this town. If I had a girl like this one I would not be able to sleep at night until I had made her Mrs. Y.J.J. I would not be able to eat. I would not be able to *blink* for fear someone might steal her away from me while my eyes were closed…"

Overdone, thought Linzi. But the speech was over, thank goodness. Peter/Harvey got to his feet and bid them both adieu with a courtly bow. Just one last touch. As he walked away, he looked back over his shoulder toward Linzi. Longingly. And "accidentally" caught Thomas Malvern's eye.

Oh, Peter, thought Linzi, as she managed a little smile. At least we'll have this to laugh about.

"What was it you wanted to say?" Linzi ventured when Peter was safely out of sight—having greeted half the restaurant like old friends as he went.

"What?" said Thomas, still watching the door.

"You said that you thought we should…"

His brow wrinkled low over his eyes. "Can't remember," he said presently.

And so Linzi made it to the entrées with her title as Thomas Malvern the Third's girlfriend still intact.

"Linzi?"

The next interruption arrived at almost the same time as the seared tuna.

"Linzi Douglas? Is that really you?"

Linzi turned to face the man who was addressing her. He didn't do her the courtesy of taking off his dark glasses.

"Well, fancy seeing you here in Manhattan! How's the theater treating you?"

"Very well," said Linzi.

"You know," the man addressed Thomas Malvern the Third. "This girl here really is one of the leading lights in

British theater design. The West End simply hasn't been the same without her."

"And how are you, er…" Linzi stuttered.

"Quentin," Peter introduced himself. He held out his hand to Thomas. "Quentin Featherstonehaugh. I gave Linzi here her first job straight out of college. Of course, it wasn't long before she eclipsed me." Quentin's queeny cut-glass English tone instantly commanded respect. As did the talcum powder currently greying his hair. "She's the Drusilla Edmonton of her generation," he added.

Who on earth was Drusilla Edmonton?

Thomas Malvern the Third nodded as though he knew.

"London's loss is most definitely Broadway's gain. Linzi," Peter/Quentin continued. "I hate to bring it up here, but I don't know when I'll see you again. I wonder, when was the last time you spoke to poor Peter?" The real Peter turned his back on Thomas and lowered his voice so that it seemed at once discreet and yet remained perfectly audible to the entire restaurant. Amazing stagecraft.

"You will have heard about his visit to hospital?" Peter nodded meaningfully. "Now, I'm not saying that you should feel in any way responsible for what happened—goodness knows there are enough other young men in London who are in love with you who haven't ended up in rehab—but I really think Peter might benefit from a letter. Perhaps if you spell it out to him that there really was never anything between you, it might kick-start his recovery. I fear he's waiting for you to change your mind. Not even the threat that he might be cut out of his multimillion-pound inheritance and lose his title if he persists with such silliness seems to affect him."

"That's terrible," breathed Linzi.

"Please write to him at once."

Peter/Quentin turned back toward Thomas Malvern the Third with a smile.

"I'm so sorry to have interrupted your evening. Linzi, do call me." He handed her a card and exited stage left. Linzi examined the card under cover of the tablecloth. It was, in fact, an old London Underground ticket onto which Peter had scribbled, "Spinach in your teeth, my dear."

Linzi immediately closed her lips over her smile. But Thomas didn't seem to have noticed. When Linzi looked up Thomas was looking at her intently. And with intent. It was a look she hadn't seen since the Capitulation.

"I think I remembered what I was going to say," he told her.

Linzi's stomach lurched.

"I was going to say we should go somewhere fun this weekend."

And so Linzi found herself ordering a pudding. Two spoons. Very romantic. In fact, so romantic, that they only used one. Thomas Malvern the Third was just opening his mouth for some ice cream like a baby bird, when the fracas began.

"Let me in!" someone shouted.

The sound of scuffling from the restaurant lobby. The maître d' and two bouncers were struggling to keep the shouting someone out.

"Raaaaaar-arrrrggggghhhh!"

They failed.

"Where is she?" shouted a very wild-looking guy from the top of the stairs that led from the lobby into the huge, tranquil dining room. "Where is she?????!!!!"

"Sir," the maître d' tried to reason with the interloper. "Perhaps you'd like a nice cup of chamomile tea while we try to find your friend."

"I don't want tea!!! Just tell me where she is!"

The mad young man raked his hands through his disheveled black hair. His voluminous shirt was unbuttoned to the waist (revealing a rather impressive torso, thought several of the ladies *and* gentlemen present). He wore tight black jeans tucked into well-worn riding boots. The effect was not unlike a modern-day Heathcliff. Hearts fluttered as almost every woman in the room hoped she was the *she* he was searching for. Only Linzi failed to take any notice, intent as she was on feeding Thomas. She held out another spoonful of Chi-Chi's speciality cardamom gelato. But before it reached her lover's mouth, the spoon and its contents were sent flying through the air.

"There you are," the mad man spat at her. "And who the hell is this?" He turned on Thomas Malvern the Third.

"I'm Thomas Malvern the Third," said Thomas. "Who the hell are you?"

"My name, as this young woman knows only too well, is Peter St. John McKenzie. Which would have been her name, too. Had she not left me standing at the altar of St. Paul's!"

A gasp went up around the restaurant.

"Yes, Linzi Douglas, I imagine I'm the last man yc thought you would see in Manhattan tonight. You th you'd got away with it, didn't you? You thought you could just leave England and your trail of devastation behind you…"

Linzi was open-mouthed.

"You thought you could break my heart and forget about the consequences."

Peter's expression was twisted. Horrible. Terrible. The entire restaurant was still and silent as he delivered his tortured speech.

"Do you know what this woman did to me?" Peter grabbed Thomas Malvern by the necktie and roared into his face. "Do you know how she left me to *die*? She crushed me. She *castrated* me. She chewed me up and spat me out."

"Peter," said Linzi. "That's enough."

Peter ignored her.

"I'm going to put you out of your misery," Peter whispered to Thomas Malvern. "You won't have to go through what I went through. You won't become a shadow of a man. This is the best way, Thomas. It really is the best way."

Peter reached for something tucked into the top of his boot. Something small but solid-looking and covered with a handkerchief. He held it against Thomas Malvern's temple.

"Ohmigod, ohmigod, ohmigod!"

"He's got a gun!" someone shouted.

Thomas Malvern the Third started to pee his pants.

"Peter!" Linzi shrieked. "Peter, don't do this!"

"It's for the best, Linzi," Peter cried passionately. "First ⟨…⟩ en me. I can't live without you a moment longer. ⟨…⟩"

⟨…⟩!" Linzi threw herself upon him, knocking him out

of the way. For a moment the room seemed to move in slow motion as Peter fell with Linzi on top of him and the gun sailed up into the air.

"Loooooooook oooouuuuutttt!!!!" someone shouted.

Everybody waited for the bang.

It wasn't much of a bang.

A carrot landing on carpet doesn't make that big a noise.

"What the…?"

Peter was laughing as he stood up. The restaurant staff, including the chef who had provided the vegetable of assault, applauded from the top of the stairs.

"I thank you!" said Peter as he took a well-deserved bow.

The entire restaurant gave him a standing ovation.

Only Thomas and Linzi remained unimpressed. And wet, in Thomas's case.

"You *know* this man?" Thomas asked.

"Of course she does," Peter interrupted. "We were going to be married. She jilted me at the…"

"The performance is *over*, Peter," Linzi fumed. "Will you kindly please stop with the acting?"

"You'll be hearing from my lawyer," said Thomas Malvern the Third to Peter. And to Linzi. It seemed the fun weekend was off.

Linzi took the subway back to her tiny apartment. Nothing she could say would persuade Thomas Malvern the Third to let her anywhere near his limo again. She left Peter in the restaurant, lapping up the adoration from a whole new set of fans, strutting about like he'd just won a standing ovatic for his rendition of Hamlet rather than ruining her lov

Peter didn't seem to care that his acting had had the exact reverse effect she had hoped for. It was like the time while they were still at school, when he had disguised his handwriting in a Valentine's card and refused to admit he sent it as a joke when Linzi's boyfriend subsequently dumped her for playing around. Or the time he had ruined a wonderful dinner party by telling Linzi's prospective beau—a strict vegan—that the vegetable risotto she'd cooked wasn't a patch on the 100% beef burger Peter and Linzi had shared for lunch. Or the time he told another beau—a refined classical musician—that her favorite party trick was to burp the national anthem. Or the time he…

Suddenly it seemed that Peter loomed large in every break-up Linzi had ever had. Why hadn't she noticed?

There was a knock at the door.

"Who is it?" she muttered through the gap.

"It's Thomas Malvern."

Linzi flung the door wide.

It was Peter.

"Good impression, eh?"

Linzi just scowled.

"Still cold in there?" Peter observed when he saw the hat she put on to keep her warm while she took off her makeup. "You should try 'The Method.' I just have to pretend I feel warm and, hey presto, I—"

"I think your acting techniques have done quite enough one night."

him in anyway.

pretty good," Peter reminisced. "Don't you

think? It's a funny thing, this method acting. One minute I'm me, Peter McKenzie, the next I really am Quentin Featherstonehaugh, the bitchy old theater queen, or Harvey Yardley Johnson Junior, the trust-fund layabout, or Peter St. John McKenzie, the man with the broken heart…"

Peter fixed Linzi with a particularly intense stare.

"God, he *loved* you," Peter said.

Linzi turned from her makeup mirror to shake her head at her impossibly charismatic friend. She had broken her record for being annoyed with him by a whole two hours but she knew she wasn't going to last much longer.

"You were very, very good," Linzi conceded.

"It's all about drawing on your own experiences," he told her. "Sense memory, it's called. To pretend I was in love with you, all I had to do was remember a time when I was in love with you…"

Had she heard him right?

"When was that?" Linzi asked him.

"Ongoing," said Peter. "From the minute I first saw you at the Little Northern Lights Theatre Group. From the first time you gave me a Chinese burn."

"You had just put chewing gum in my hair…"

Peter walked toward her and stood terribly close. Close enough to kiss her. And then she saw the softness in his eyes and realized that was why she had always forgiven him.

"What am I supposed to do now?" she asked as a smile spread across her face.

Peter let his lips lightly brush her neck.

"Oh, I don't know," he told her. "Act naturally?"